PASSION

An Anthology of World's Great Short Stories

EDITED BY SANTOSH KUMAR

CYBERWIT.NET
2003

PASSION

An Anthology of World's Great Short Stories

PUBLISHERS' NOTE

We aim to:

- Promote Poetry for Peace and Friendship
- Revive interest in Poetry in the era of scientific progress
- Publish different trends of contemporary creative writing world-wide
- Offer the most spectacular poems and short stories by the authors across the world
- Publish Poetry and Short story Anthologies featuring writers from USA, UK, Ireland, Romania, Germany, Netherlands, Australia, Italy, Canada, Argentina, Spain, France, Portugal, Japan, India and many others.
- Publish outstanding creative artists in our International Journal *Taj Mahal Review* devoted to Literature and Peace
- Promote original contemporary Creative Writing by so many voices and so many cultures

COUNT ON CYBERWIT

Where different nations meet at a single Place. Join us for the greatest gathering of Creative Artists, to create a better world to breathe in. Only creative artists can create a world of Peace, Love, Beauty and Freedom. Our books are meticulously edited by dedicated editors.

Published by

Radha Agrawal for Cyberwit.net,
4/2B, L.I.G. Govindpur Colony,
Allahabad-211004 (U.P.) India
Tel: 91-532-2541153
E-mail: cyberwit@rediffmail.com

ISBN 81-901366-4-X

First Printing

Typeset by Vaishnavi Processors & Printers 220/71-C/1, Kamla Nagar, Stanley Road, Allahabad-211 002

Printed in India at Astha Associates, D. N. Marg, Allahabad

I prefer commencing with the consideration of an effect. Keeping originality always in view-for he is false to himself who ventures to dispense with so obvious and so easily obtainable a source of interest-I say to myself, in the first place,' Of the innumerable effects or impressions of which the heart, the intellect, or (more generally) the soul is susceptible, what tone shall I, on the present occasion, select?' Having chosen a novel first, and secondly, a vivid effect, I consider whether it can be best wrought by incident or tone-whether by ordinary incidents and peculiar tone, or the converse, or by peculiarity both of incident and tone-afterwards looking about me (or rather within) for such combinations of event or tone as shall best aid me in the construction of the effect. ...That an American should confine himself to American themes, or even prefer them, is rather a political than a literary idea. A foreign theme is, in a strictly literary sense, to be preferred. After all, the world at large is the only legitimate stage for the authorial histrio.

Edgar Allan Poe (1809-49), ***Essays and Reviews***

PREFACE

No doubt, the short story has an advantage over novel in the fact that the novelist can indulge in a lot of lengthy, at times unnecessary speculations; he is free to provide a detailed psychological analysis of the character, as James Joyce or Virginia Woolf do in their novels. But the short story has to be brief. There is no scope for intolerable length and verbosity. The writer of short stories may concentrate on the peculiar aspect of the character, as Bret Harte does in 'Tennessee's Partner' or 'Miggles', or Stevenson in 'Markheim'; or create a distinctive atmosphere as Poe does in 'Eleonora' and 'The Pit and the Pendulum'.

A short story should be precise. That is why in the 20th century it became very popular genre. In the fast world of Information Technology, we lack sufficient leisure to peruse Richardson's novel *Clarissa*, or *The History of a Young Lady* (1747-48) in 8 volumes. "In an epic or a novel the unity of effect can never be maintained"(Poe). The short stories chosen for *Passion* reveal a rich variety of treatment. Most of the stories are from USA. The reason is perhaps the fast pace of life there. The predominant tone of the American stories is an intellectual integrity, and an impressive capacity to narrate precisely what the author wants to narrate. The honesty of these short stories in portraying various incidents and characters till climax is complete.

The very beginnings of the short story may be traced back to *Beowulf* written in the eighth century. The story of Beowulf narrates his adventures and exploits, who finally died of the dragon's fiery breath. Chaucer was one of the greatest short story-tellers. *The Canterbury Tales* depicts the life of the Middle Ages; Tale of Melibeus and the Parson's Tale, the romance of the knight and other tales contribute to the action. In *The Canterbury Tales* we find a vivid portrayal of the life and manners of the 14th century England. Both *Beouwulf* and *The Canterbury Tales* used verse as a medium to narrate the story. Chaucer may well be described as England's first story-teller. He has the power to narrate a story with psychological insight, humor, irony and convincing dialogue. Malory's *Morte D' Arthur* (1470) and Lyly's *Eupheus* show the Elizabethan interest in prose fiction. Robert Greene's (1558-1592) prose romances are obstructed by digression, and the narrative skill is hampered. Thomas Deloney's *The Gentle Craft*, a collection of stories about the shoemaker, is perhaps the best prose fiction during the Elizabethan era.

The twentieth century saw the full blossoming of the genre. Rudyard Kipling, H.G. Wells, R.L. Stevenson, A.C. Doyle, G. K. Chesterton, Arnold Bennett, E. M. Forster, D.H. Lawrence, Katherine Mansfield, Somerset Maugham- and several other short story writers revealed the scope and power of the modern short story.

Short Story in America really began with Washington Irving (1783-1859), whose

The Sketch Book (1819) showed "the heart of a poet" and "the gravest sweetest humor". Hawthorne (1804-1864), Edgar Allan Poe (1809-1849), Faulkner (1897-1962), Bret Harte (1836-1902), Edith Wharton (1862-1937), John Updike (b. 1932), Frank Norris (1870-1902), O'Connor (1915-64), Bernard Malamud (1914-86), Ring Wilmer Lardner (1885-1933), Sarah Orne Jewett (1849-1909), Hemingway (1899-1961) are some of the great exponents of the genre.

It may be remembered that in 1830 America didn't have the immortal writings of Poe, Emerson, Hawthorne, Longfellow, Whitman, or Melville; American writers around this period 'may truly be said to live more in England than in their own country'. And the English authors were their models.

The Short stories in *Passion* leave an impression that the American short-story writers are unique and excellent. Some of these authors reveal solitude and sorrow in their short stories, reminding us of Richard Yates' (1926-1992) collection *Eleven Kinds of Loneliness* (1962). They have very well blended 'the native tradition with Continental sources', and are quite successful in reviving 'the almost lost art' of short-story writing. Many American stories included in the *Passion* reveal the darkness, 'the house of tragedy', the soul in conflict with itself, the famous American tradition, which we notice in the works of Hawthorne and Faulkner. Some important themes of the stories in *Passion* are human isolation, alienation, love and hate, man-woman relationship, family conflict, the individual's struggle against the contemporary social order, spiritual quest. The short stories selected for *Passion* portray the most salient elements of consciousness. They exhibit a tight logic of development; they are created out of the author's response to contemporary events. The intensity of *Passion* is beyond question, due to genuine emotional depth, the freshness and directness of the presentation of situations. The social range and scope of these stories seems to be the greatest achievement of the authors.

Passion is marked by precise observation and characterization. The stories are incomparable in richness and variety, and they show a liberation of talent, a liberation influenced by American writers like T. S. Eliot and Pound. In plotting their stories, the authors reveal originality of style visible in immortal passages:

> After she had passed, he watched her reflection in the fifteen by twenty-four pane of glass that separated his world from the rest. He couldn't take his eyes off those legs. The calves were sinewy and rested on delicate ankles. The juxtaposition would seem unsightly on any other woman; one that more than ordinarily attracted him. The red dress did nothing to soften them, only accentuating the fullness of her thighs.
>
> (Julie Failla Earhart, 'Apple Blossoms, Old Money And Sex')

> "Daddy?" Tammy's small voice wasn't even noticed in the hum of big-people voices. "Daddy? Where's my Daddy?"
>
> Moving toward the big box, Tammy's lips trembled with each step. She couldn't find Daddy. No one noticed as she made her tiny way to the front of the room. She reached the pretty box and still no Daddy.
>
> (Danielle Ackley-McPhail, 'A Portrait of Black Velvet')

... Know what she said, Doc? She said, real soft and easy, Earl, listen to me! When I had my surgery, they took everything out. I hadn't felt a thing down there for 15 years. I said, but you were so, so... She said, that was just for you, Earl. And you're still just the man I need. Now ain't she something, Doc? Ain't she really something?"

(John R. Guthrie, 'Sex')

I ponder my hand in yours, even if only for a moment and the moment is fleeting. My feelings for you are deep; my love for you as abounding as life. I desire you, and want for your touch. Just as the oceans waves yearn to bathe the beach with their unending constancy of caress, I will adorn you with affection, until you sparkle as brightly as Christmas tree icicles against the evening fireplace firelight.

(Stephen R. Foster, 'The Hearts Hidden Poem', *Island Of Life*)

Impassioned love among older people, unlike in their younger counterparts, is not usually followed by that starry-eyed awe that seems to obliterate all reality except that which gravitates about the loved one. Both Harry and Sue were well honed by reality, and respected each other's strong sense of separateness.

(Joseph Aprile, 'The Final Days of Harry Stegman')

I faced the briers. The fire was a gigantic monster. It was hotter, stronger and larger as it continued to feed on new sources of fuel. The fierce blaze was drawing air toward it making its own draft and becoming uncontrollable, growing ever stronger like a storm. Flames ran through dry leaves, bushes roared like fiery furnaces, and trees became torches to heaven. The smell of smoke filled the air. I stepped back a few paces, ran toward the briers and threw the skull as far as I could over them back into the cemetery.

(Travis Black, 'Rest In Peace')

In the contemporary American short stories and fiction, we very rarely find the political theme. What seems to inspire the short-story writers intensely in *Passion* is private destiny of the people. John Updike asserts that the life of a nation is reflected, or distorted, by private people and their minute concerns.

Allahabad
July 1, 2003

SANTOSH KUMAR

CONTENTS

ANKIRAH 11
Adrian Cadar

THE STORY OF SHAMUS KELLY 15
Alex Kachmar

FADED MEMORIES 18
Alexxa Abi-Jaoude

IT'S JUST THE MAILMAN 21
Andrew Longworth

DENNIS' BOX 29
Angie Hulme

JESSICA 32
Annalee Johnson

THE GIRL 39
Brian Vincent Wemyss

MUSIC NON-STOP 41
Candice Maryanne Borg

SPIRIT OF LOVE 46
Carl E. Vance

THE ATTACK 52
Casey Ponciano

CAPTURED FREEDOM- PART ONE 57
Cassandra Marie Carlson

MONDAY 22ND JULY 59
Ceirion James Rees

DOUBTVILLE TO FAITH HAVEN 61
Clyde Mcdade

HER 63
Crystal Timbeross

MIRACLE FROM BEYOND 64
Dallas Cathcart

A PORTRAIT OF BLACK VELVET 67
Danielle Ackley-McPhail

THE PROPHET 69
Darius Gabriel Bugarin

GRANITE RIDGE 71
David Ferrier

INCIDENT AT THE UGANDA MUSEUM 73
David Tumusiime

WHO WAS FIRST: EGG OR HEN? 76
Denise-Annette Langner-Urso

CHILD'S PLAY 78
Denise Cassino

RAIN 82
Donald Edward Kidd

OUR RAISON D'ECRIRE 87
Duncan Reeves

A MAN ONCE A MACHINE 90
Dylan Skriloff

LIFE IN THE SUN 92
Erma Hernandez

MOUSETRAP MADNESS 96
Floriana Hall

DOMINATION 98
Honor Alisha De'Mandoren

SAYING GOODBYE TO UNCLE RICKY 104
Ian Stuart

THE TRAIN RIDE 110
Inessa Cutler

ME TOO... 116
Irving Bronsky

AN ICK FILES CHRISTMAS 126
Jeanne Owens

BLADES OF TERROR 130
JirQUEST

TWO ULTRA-SHORT STORIES 132
John R. Guthrie

THE FINAL DAYS OF HARRY STEGMAN 134
Joseph Aprile

HOW NOT TO DOCK A BOAT 140
Joy Bennett

APPLE BLOSSOMS, OLD MONEY AND SEX 141
Julie Failla Earhart

A CURIOUS WORLD 143
Kathryn Gabrielle

BREATHING 146
Kathryn Lynn Wilson

LET'S GO FLY A KITE 152
Katy Picard

STRANDED IN A SUPER 8 MOTEL: TWO DAYS IN IOWA 154
Kenneth F. Pearson

THE DEBTORS 157
Kenneth Ormsbee

THE LAST NORMALITY 160
Kevin Patrick Necessary

TARGET PRACTICE 164
Kirby Wright

MISS LAVINIA'S PORTRAIT 171
Laura Mae Oldham-Brownell

ALONE AND LOST 173
LeRoy Doran

THE JUST DREAMING PHASE 177
Lori D. Laird

I AM THE STORY I TELL MYSELF I AM 181
Mary Barr

THE MAGICAL PUBLISHING PEN 183
Mike Strictzer

TEARS 193
Moataz H. Emam

IN THE OLDEN DAYS 195
Mona Dash

DRIFTING AWAY 198
Nancy Latshaw

FRAGMENTS OF LOVE 199
Pat Phillips West

FLY ME AWAY, BILL 202
Peter Eric Williams

SUICIDAL DREAMS 204
Paul Steven

ALONE 206
Rachel Caris Thompson

THE BLUE PLASTIC BAG 209
Rani Drew

REAL 213
Rebecca

BUBBLES AND SEEDS 217
Rebecca Chen

ANIMATING THE MANNEQUINS 220
Rebecca Holder

THE GREAT SARS MASK GIVEAWAY 222
Robert M. Wilson

GOD HAS HEARD THY PRAYERS 224
Santosh Kumar

LONGING FOR LATTE 228
Sara M. Al Shami

THE DREAM 231
Sherri Emily Avery

ISLAND OF LIFE 234
Stephen R. Foster

A RAINY DAY 239
Sudheesh V Nair

LOVE IS LIKE 241
Thomas K. Hyland Jr.

HOW HAS THE WORLD TREATED YOU 244
Tom Dwyer

MY DREAM OF MY CELTIC LOVER 247
Tony James Lawless

REST IN PEACE 249
Travis Black

THE GOLDEN BOOT 257
Verne Morse

SUPER PATRIOTS 259
Voyat Sergey

AHMEDA 261
W. S. Mayo

THE HOUSE 263
Yvo Maron Jouvenaar

AUTHOR INDEX 265

ANKIRAH

Adrian Cadar

The deafening noise of a spaceship that flew almost touching the ground made the young Brennalyan startle. Rather mechanically than instinctively, due to the imminent danger, he jumped off the bed with a warrior-like movement which didn't fit him at all, grabbed the weapon at hand near the bed and rushed to the door of the shelter. His two sisters had been woken up too.

"What happened Tassyan? Who was it?" a gently voice was heard coming from the back of the shelter.

"Nothing happened, stay calm. It might have been one of the damned Accanian ships. But they didn't see us, the ship passed away", answered the young man in a low voice returning to bed.

He put aside his weapon, a generator of power fields being able to destroy everything around one mile and wrapped himself in a dusty tattered blanket. He hated that weapon. That sort of weapon had been used to kill his both parents two weeks before. While he and his sisters were in the old city looking for some food among the ruins left by the interplanetary war, a spaceship similar to the one that woken him, landed near their shelter. Two Accanians, each carrying a weapon like Tassyan's in their hands, got off. One of them entered the shelter where his mother was, he aimed at her without saying a word and a moment later, the person Tassyan loved the most was only dust. His father who had been one mile away trying to mend an old propelling capsule when the Accanian ship landed, ran to the shelter terrified of what might happen. He saw the other Accanian outside checking his weapon. Taking advantage of his lack of attention, the Brennalyan took out his little laser gun and shot at him. The portly Accanian dropped dead making a horrifying roar. On entering the shelter, he heard a fizzing sound and a second later the Brennalyan's body disintegrated into reddish grains of dust.

The Accanians were known as reward hunters and their planet, Accania, was light years away from little Brennalya. Those dreadful warriors killed at will in cold blood everything that moved. They were more than one hundred kilos weight. They had flat heads, dark hair and cunning, small strangely red eyes. Their hands having four, long, stumpy fingers were able to crush without difficulty any living thing on Brennalya. They rarely came on the lonely planet where Tassyan lived, because they could find nothing there.

Brennalya had been almost completely destroyed after the interplanetary war. Only about one hundred Brennalyans had survived because, when the explosion had erased every living creature on the planet, they had been at an official meeting in order to appease the interplanetary conflict on Meros, an interplanetary Center of Command situated at two light years from Brennalya.

Tassyan together with his two sisters, Kassyra and Metuah lived in a shelter which, when Brennalya was destroyed two years before, was in fact a blockhouse where war armament was stored. Only a room of one hundred square meters left of it after the destructive explosion. There were three improvised beds and a shining metal table used as a night table. A piece of an old mirror hanging on the left wall of the shelter was used by Kassyra and Metuah to dress up in the morning every two weeks when they would go to look for food in the old city situated at four hours' walk. There they chanced to meet one or two lonely natives who themselves were looking for cans of food they hoped to find among the ruins left by the explosion.

Brennalyans were so friendly that only by smiling they could become friends for life not only with each other but also with other species. They were not tall, few men were 1,80 meters. They always smiled and their eyes were so serene that only creatures with cold blood like Accanians could kill such kind beings. The clear complexion of their soft skin gave them a special aura. They had no hair but it didn't alter at all their pleasant presence.

One hour after the ship's flying over their shelter, Tassyan could hardly get off his bed rubbing his eyes.

"Metuah, Kassyra, get up! said he to his sisters. It's late and we must go to the city today."

Five minutes later they were both in front of the piece of mirror. Metuah was wiping the dust that was everywhere in the shelter, from her face while Kassyra stood still smiling and thinking elsewhere.

"Hurry up! Come!" said Tassyan apostrophizing her.

The young women immediately came to her senses and began wiping the dust from her face too with a soft piece of the blanket she used to cover herself during night. That moment they heard a deafening thunder clap not far from them. The two sisters stepped back frightened. Tassyan grabbed his weapon and rushed to the door.

"Stay here! Stand still!" He ordered them, though his tone betrayed kindness and love. A thick trail of smoke was rolling to the sky in the distance.

" Maybe one of those damned Accanian ships has crushed, said Tassyan to the girls who were paralysed with fear. I think that no one is still alive as it looks. Stay here! I will go there to see if I can find something useful among the pieces of the ship", he raised his voice to be heard as he was distancing himself from the shelter.

Hardly had he walked two hundred meters when Tassyan fell as if he had been mown down by somebody. He leaned in his elbows and pointed his weapon to the direction of the smoke. Less than a hundred feet ahead, an unknown being as running for its life. The frightened being that hadn't noticed Tassyan had the presence of mind to throw itself to then ground as soon as it saw him. The young man had already aimed and was ready to shoot. The being was getting closer and closer and Tassyan noticed that it had the sublime features of a woman. She was scared to death. Tassyan dropped his weapon and remained on the ground. He thought that he had nothing to be scared of, that the woman was not a danger either for himself or for his sisters. The young man raised a bit when the woman was a few steps away and she being so terrified fell on him. Tassyan caught her in his strong arms and they were now face to face. He was so amazed at what he saw. He was unable to keep his eyes off her. He was so dazzled by her beauty that his heart started beating so fast as if he was the one who had been running for his life five minutes before. Her golden hair touched her shoulders and the light spread by Kahr, the star that made life possible on Bennalya, seemed to caress it. Those dark frightened eyes betrayed an immense joy when they met Brennalyan's kind look. She tried to wipe the dust from her face but she realized she couldn't because she was immobilized to the ground. After a few moments of delight, Tassyan finally came to his senses, raised gently, gave her his hand and helped her up shaking himself off dust.

He could hardly believe his eyes. He had only heard of Lethyas from his parents, he had never seen one and now he had a Lethyas in front of him. He knew that those sublime and innocent beings were hunted by the Accanians for their ability to get into other beings' minds and to know exactly what they think. Lethyas had stopped communicating through words long ago, the only means of communication was telepathy. It was absolutely normal and natural considering their abilities.

No sooner had Tassyan shaken himself off dust than they heard a strong fizzing sound a few steps away. He threw himself to the ground pulling the Lethyas down. Tassyan looked ahead. In the distance the thick smoke continued to split the sky in two. An Accanian was preparing to download another field of power at them. The young man grabbed the weapon, aimed and shot. That damned strong fizzing sound heard again. A second later the Accanian disintegrated into grains of dust. Having forgotten she couldn't understand his words, he said to that wonderful woman standing next to him:

"That bastard! He almost killed us!"

But she knew exactly what he thought.

They raised, full of dust. She ripped a piece of cloth from her clothes and wiped the young man's face, smiling at him. He watched her as if he were charmed. "What's your name beautiful Lethyas?" he asked her in a low voice stammering. She burst into laughter and that made her more beautiful and more innocent. Tassyan was bewildered. He didn't know for a few seconds why she was laughing. Then he remembered that the beautiful Lethyas couldn't understand his words. That made him laugh too. They were standing looking at each other forgetting that the Accanian could have them killed a few moments before. Tassyan realized that words were useless because that wonderful being standing in front of him understood him without the help of words. He remembered that she knew every thought of his. Long afterwards did they stop laughing. They were face to face watching each other while he was holding her hand and it seemed that nobody and nothing could ever break them up. They heard a strange noise above. They looked up. A ship was flying slowly towards them. Tassyan quickly grabbed his weapon out she stopped him taking it and throwing it away, He didn't realize what was happening but the expression on her face assured him that there was no danger. She looked him straight in the eye holding more tightly his hand. The ship stopped about twenty meters above them. A door opened and the two were shrouded in a blue light. The young Brennalyan understood immediately that the ship had come after her. He had to let her go but his hands were holding hers more tightly. A tear trickled gently on her cheek. She slipped her hand off his took out a medallion and put it in the young Brennalyan's hand. She gave him a kiss on his cheek and the blue light disappeared. The ship took off and vanished as if by magic. Half an hour later, the young Brennalyan was still there looking up, thinking of that wonderful being.

"Tassyan, Tassyan!" he heard in the distance Kassyra's kind voice.

The young man woken from his dream. He could hardly believe what had happened. It might have been only a dream. That couldn't have been real. What had a Lethyas had to do with Brennalya? He had surely dreamt. Of course it must have been a dream...He looked ahead and saw Kassyra coming. That moment something slipped off his left hand. He bent and found a golden medallion. He wiped it carefully of dust and read loud, his voice betraying strong emotions: Ankirah...

THE STORY OF SHAMUS KELLY

Alex Kachmar

"When I turn 29, I'm gonna put a bullet through my head."

And that's how I meet Shamus Kelly.

I stroll into Klapper's Pub with my buddy Sam Brown and we sit down at the back corner table next to Karl Gruber the German and Michelle his girl (should be my girl). Klapper's has become a second home for me since I moved to Boston and I know most of the people here. Walter from Jersey is here and so is my fellow writer friend Pete Mora the converted Muslim poet and beautiful French-Canuck Susan Blanc who I haven't seen in a few weeks—she had mono—and we sit and talk and order pitchers of on-draft Kronenberg. Klapper's has everything on draft, over 112 drafts, and what they don't have on draft they have in bottles, perhaps the greatest selection of beer in the world. The choice of music when I walk in is Violent Femme's "Confessions", a great song, and I get to hear that disturbingly beautiful piercing voice of Gordon Gano, the direct descendent of Lou Reed, I dig it. I dig all the music they play and why I'm using the phrase "dig" I don't know but I like it, I dig the sound of it, it's from before my time but from a great time (the 1950s). I was born too late like ol' Miniver Cheevy and perhaps I use their language to keep them alive in desolation with me, but I do dig it all, the loud yet melodic noise of the California hardcore scene of the 80s, Bad Religion and the Dead Kennedys and Circle Jerks, and the pure raw sound of Charles Thompson aka. Black Francis aka. Frank Black, leader of the Pixies, timeless cool music that you feel flowing through your balls—I dig it all.

And then they play this beautiful yet obscure B-side track of my favorite musician Beck, "Brother" is its name and it's a beautifully sad song with incoherent and irrelevant lyrics but it doesn't matter, it's Beck, I dig it, and Gruber the German just finished the beer so I go to the bar to order another pitcher of Kronenberg and there sitting on the corner stool is this odd-looking creature with a full beard and shaggy uncombed blond locks, and his eyes are hidden behind a pair of dark shades. He's no taller than 5'6", I can see this despite the fact that he's sitting, but he's burly and plump, a good two-hundred pounds. He's smoking a hand-rolled cigarette and when I walk up to the bar and stand next to him, he exhales a series of doughnuts, takes off his glasses and looks at me—his black eyes are confident and venerable, not in the least bit occupied with despair or gloom, yet this odd-looking man stares at me with those black eyes of his and in a soft but assertive voice, he makes that oddly prophetic statement: "When I turn 29, I'm gonna put a bullet in my head."

* * *

Desolation is desolation and it's the same whether you're alive or dead, I learn this from Shamus, he goes on to tell me an abridged version of his life story—-he's a sad man with deep black eyes and he's a writer, only a writer can be this insane. He grew up in South Boston in a large Irish family of seven, four brothers, and by the time he was sixteen, he was done with school and worked full-time on the docks—-and every night he would come home to his small dirty apartment and he would lock the door and turn off the phone and read for hours, everything from Dostoyevsky and Tolstoy to Chaucer and Clemens and Hemingway, all the geniuses of literature, and all he dreamt about was becoming a writer. And so he began to write during his free time. On weekends he would never leave the apartment other than to buy groceries and he stopped talking to his family and his friends for that would have only distracted him, and after a few years of undergoing a treacherous schedule consisting only of manual labor, reading, and writing, exactly two weeks after his twenty-second birthday, he was done with his first novel, his only novel, a four-hundred page manuscript full of "truth and beauty" that contains all the secrets and meanings of life, and the only conclusion it comes to is that there is no meaning or substance to life, it's just an aura of desolation, an irrelevant occurrence of time and time itself might not even exist and therefore life is not even worthy of being called an irrelevant occurrence of time. And the day after he finished this novel, he quit his job and moved to a small village two-hundred miles west of Mexico City where he hibernated for a year, he just slept and ate and cleared his mind, it took him that long and he hasn't read a book since nor has he written a single word, and he never will again.

He prayed a lot in Mexico, in his opinion that was the only thing worth doing, and though he grew up an Irish Catholic, he never believed until Mexico—-his family was too busy for religion, they worked seventy-hour weeks and sometimes more and when Sunday came around, all they wanted to do was rest. But in Mexico it didn't matter what day it was, Sunday Monday Tuesday it was all the same, and at the center of his small Mexican village on top of a steep grassy hill was a tiny wooden church with no doors or walls, just four stilts supporting a pyramid-shaped roof with a crucifix at its tip, and in the back left corner was series of candles, each row slightly elevated above the previous, and next to the candles in the back middle of the church was a beautiful golden and magenta altar made by one of God's angelic Mexican artists [Orozco perhaps], and everyday no matter Sunday, Wednesday, or Friday, the people of the village would come to the church, all of them at different times, the Mexicans, the Aztecs, the Aztec-Mexicans, men, women, children, babies, and they would kneel in front of the candles and cross themselves and pray and they would leave a peso in the drop box, and then they would walk to the altar and kiss the golden visage of Jesus and the next day they would do the same. They were sad people with poor sad eyes, both the Mexicans and the Indians, and the saddest one of all was an old, tiny mestizo woman of ninety-years age who wore a black shawl and a faded white dress and she had wrinkled brown eyes and walked barefoot and something was not right in her life, something wasn't right in all their lives, and they prayed everyday at that sad church and even the dank dusty wind that blew through the church was sad; but it was a beautiful sadness. Shamus realized that if life is but a mere irrelevant occurrence of time (or it might not even be that), then one must hope and believe that there is something else somewhere, perhaps above or below on in the ocean or space, something far greater and more powerful and supreme to human existence where there is truth and beauty and meaning and peace. And so the Mexicans prayed and Shamus joined his village mates everyday at that sad church and he prayed too. And now he will spend the next year of his life traveling throughout the world hoping to find all the poor praying Mexicans, just to see them and know they exist. He figured he would start in the city where he was born and eventually would end up in his sad Mexican village where he will die in peace. He tells me this over a beer.

Shamus finishes his beer and leaves a tip at the bar, then walks out of Klapper's like the odd-looking ghost that he is, an irrelevant occurrence of existence, and years later I find out that Shamus did put a bullet in his head the day he turned 29 in his sad Mexican village.

FADED MEMORIES

Alexxa Abi-Jaoude

It's funny how one's memory becomes so selective with time. Why are some details so vivid in my memory, while others are merely a blur? I can remember what I was wearing; faded blue jeans, a red wool sweater and black loafers. I can still smell the distinctive aroma's filling my apartment; popcorn, coffee and strawberry scented candles. I can even tell you the score of the New York and Detroit game, 89-94. I also remember that the clothes in the dryer were white. I can't, however, remember what day it was, or what time it was when I left. To be honest with you, I don't even remember exactly what he said to me. Slamming my apartment door, starting my car and driving for three hours are also not very clear to me. It is only when I touch the back of my head and feel the tender scar, do I even remember the accident. And unless I see the hospital records, I usually can't tell you much about the doctors and nurses who tended to me.

But the flowers, now those I remember. Red, white, yellows? every colour of the rainbow. Roses and tulips and carnations, the room was flowing with bouquets of all sorts. I remember how every time I woke up, I could look around my room and find a new arrangement. The fragrance of the flowers managed to mask the sickly hospital smell. At times, when the drugs were at full strength, I would forget about the wires, the monitors, and grave faces of the doctors and make believe that I was an enchanted princess. The flowers, gifts from my subjects and the doctors were my servants.

He was my prince. Every sweet word uttered from his mouth is etched in my memory like stone. Waking to him stroking my face and seeing his eyes glisten with tears, showed me how much he cared. Seeing his drawn face and blood shot eyes, I knew, he would prove to my family the same thing. My prince was constantly by my side. Protecting me was what he always claimed he wanted to do, I suppose this is what he was trying to accomplish.

When trying to remember my hospital stay, I can seldom recall a conversation with my parents or sister. The accident was before they completely stopped associating with me, so I wonder why they wouldn't have come to visit. I once asked him about it and he took my hand and simply said, "Those who love you, came to visit you and those who don't, you shouldn't waste your time thinking about." I didn't try to argue. That usually just causes unwanted problems. Why bother trying to change the mind of a person who cannot be changed? So, instead I decided not to bring them up anymore. Deep down I know they love me. We just can't see eye to eye on certain matters anymore.

I would still like to know why they didn't come see me. Or why Julie and Anne, my best friends, were absent too. It's at times like this that I take great comfort in my unreliable memory. Maybe, like the way I can't remember the colour of the car that hit me, I can't remember any of their visits.

I can vaguely remember a visit from my life long friend, Kathy. I remember her sitting down and looking as though she were in a rush. As she asked me how I felt, she kept looking behind her shoulder at the door. I wonder what she had to do that day. It must have been pretty important; because when we used to talk she would always pay full attention to me. I remember Kathy kissing me on my forehead and leaving quickly after he came into the room and told her that he wanted some time alone with me. He likes having me to himself.

About a year ago, I found a stack of cards from my family and some friends in his toolbox while I was looking for a hammer. There were two from each Julie and Anne. After I found the cards, I felt better. I wonder why he didn't give them to me. I guess he forgot about them. He doesn't have the greatest memory either. I know now that they at least cared a little. It would have been pretty sad if none of my family or friends had even sent a card. The hospital is not really in the best location, so maybe it was the traffic that kept them away.

When I found the cards, I thought about calling those who had sent them. When he wasn't home one night, I even searched for my phone book. I couldn't find it. I seem to misplace a lot of stuff now. I wasn't always so disorganized. Before I moved in with him, I could find everything in my apartment. It must be the additional space. When I didn't find the phone book, I decided that I might call my parents. I didn't though, because I wasn't really sure what to say. I couldn't bring up the cards, because that was too far in the past. They probably thought I received them while I was at the hospital, so I thought it would be better to let them think that that was true. He would be arriving soon anyway.

I still haven't called anyone who gave me the cards. At times I feel compelled to ask him about them. I tried once to ask him about who actually called, or sent anything to me. He got pretty upset, and so I dropped it. I think he thought that I felt as though he did not do enough. Of course I assured him that I fully appreciated all he did for me. He told me that if I really meant that, then I would stop asking about others during my stay at the hospital.

My family stopped calling me just a few weeks after I was released from the hospital. I guess I can't blame them. Him and I are usually too busy to talk to them anyways. We don't use the phone much anymore. When it does ring, sometimes it sounds so foreign to me that I forget what the sound represents. That's just another way my memory tends to fails me. I forget simple details that at one time had significance.

Julie and Anne haven't called in years. I hope they aren't mad that I didn't call and thank them for the cards. I'm sure they'd understand if I told them the circumstances, but something always keeps me from calling. Maybe it's better this way.

Every once in a while I remember something new. Like recently I remembered something else about Kathy's visit. I remembered her coming in with a small box. She placed it on my nightstand, but when I woke up it was gone. At first I was sure that the box was real, but then I started to doubt my memory again. Now I think I could have confused some facts, because I remember him giving me the gold cross I wear around my neck that same day. It was in a small box just like the one I thought was in Kathy's hand.

I love that cross. I feel safer when I wear it. To me, it symbolizes all the good that he possesses. It reminds me of how much he cares for me. The cross shows me how much I need him. What would my life be without him? I don't speak to my family, and I hardly have any friends. He is all that to me. He often reminds me of that. He is my family. He is my friend. He is my prince.

IT'S JUST THE MAILMAN

Andrew Longworth

Lance Huffmeister sat on his flea ridden mattress, the morning sun deluging the sparse premises of his tent with neither a knock or a warning, and it took all the strength he was able to muster to apply the hook to the two canvas flaps he held accountable for welcoming the unwanted intruder. Somewhere outside a girl was bawling with the force of a bursting dam, her voice mitigated and finally rendered silent the moment she realized that the credulity of her parents bore no reliability that morning, if indeed they were even awake. Lance shook his head in the darkness. Too many people were crying wolf these days.

Suddenly a stir rustling on the mattress next to his. The equanimity of his partner veritably palpable, Lance resisted the intrinsic urge to step outside and leave the flaps open just to evoke an objection, anything from that lame excuse of what could have passed for a man in any other civil society. But indolence again prevailed, leaving him to endeavor with his mouth what his feet could no longer induce.

"You hear that, Colin?" he said. "I think that was a girl crying."

"I didn't hear it," Colin replied through the fragments of a yawn. "Go back to sleep."

"Poor thing," Lance persisted. "I think she may be looking for her mom. What do you think, Col?"

"Turn off the freakin' television," said Colin, rolling back into a prone position.

"Christ, Col," said Lance, "the next thing you'll tell me is the gas you just released was a deflated balloon. I say we help the girl."

The answer to his suggestion was a long mock snore that pervaded the tent and further aggravated Lance's headache. How funny was the notion that not only had the times changed but how they had changed. Just how he could have possibly conjured up a headache of that magnitude without the assistance of a single drop of liquor was as perplexing as his roommate (in this case tentmate since the day they had been served the eviction notice) sleeping all day. What had the ancient Greeks coined as a hero? An individual with the choice of two paths, both leading to catastrophe? It clearly had his name written all over it. Given the choice between spending the entire day in darkness with a slug too lazy to breathe these days and venturing out on his quest for something edible, he chose the latter, albeit with a heart heavier than the feet that he sometimes swore had foregone conventional creation and had obstinately decided to mold themselves out of cement.

Brushing the dust off his pants he hadn't washed in weeks, Lance felt vindicated in his belief that here, in this prototypical shantytown, with its tents and shacks with corrugated tin roofs, people cared as much about fashion statements as the dirt they slept on. Unlike here, the people in the apartment complex they had recently vacated would glare at you rapaciously, like a piranha waiting for the first drop of blood to invoke their feeding frenzy, with minor slips like a spot on your shirt or a hole in your pants sufficient to qualify for the whispering voices in the halls and the elevator. By comparison, the squatters here were herbivores. Worse yet, in his mind they had already been devoured and were now ready to claim the lowest rung in the food chain that placed you a rank below the insects. The upside to this newly acquired status was that the predators would now leave you alone, unless they stepped into you amidst a flurry of cusses leveled at the crap adorning the soles of their shoes. Bearing this in mind, Lance smiled as he passed the last of the metal shacks at the edge of Shantytown, his destination the huge dumpster behind the two star hotel Splendid, which offered a laminated menu compared to the occasional trashcan around here, carrying everything from soiled diapers to rotting food only the flies considered useful for their survival. Nonchalantly passing the wall dividing the civilized world from the supposed human rejects, Lance stopped and looked for people, maybe hotel guests or the concierge, before making his move.

Finding nobody, he slipped through the crack in the wall and quickly advanced to the dumpster that conveniently screened him from any potential guests who may have decided to enjoy the vista on their balconies, however sordid a picture it presented. He had to work quickly now. Combing through the dumpster's contents, he cheerfully snapped his fingers upon finding, in short order, two impeccably preserved half loaves of baguette, two miniature plastic containers of butter and jelly, and one shiny red apple that bore neither a bruise nor a dent. And that's why people starve in the world, he thought, filling the items into an old brown bag that had just harbored an empty bottle of Cutty Sark he now removed and tossed back into the dumpster. People.

They just didn't get it. What Lance never saw was the hand grabbing his cuff and violently throwing him to the ground like a sack of Sunday's trash. He dropped the paper bag on the ground, where it now lay between him and the guard he now recognized as Drew, a guy he had already had his sweet run-ins with, none of them pleasant. Lance rubbed his head after it had involuntarily met the concrete and now saw from the corner of his eye a couple on one of the hotel balconies, cheering on the guard to inflict further damage on the bum intent on stealing their waste. "What gives, Drew?" Lance meekly protested. "This ain't Fort Knox. You're acting like I was going after your family in there."

"And I told you," said Drew, "that you have no business being on the premises here, several fucking times. You're lucky I don't have your sorry ass just taken in. Now hit the road, Shitbird."

"You know what I'm looking for," Lance replied, slowly rising to his feet. "You know I never set a foot in that goddamn hotel. What's wrong with a bunch of trash feeding the homeless?"

"Nothing," said Drew, "except that I lose my job if I let people like you so much as look at this place. You knew the rules. You got caught. Happens to the best of us. And oh, we got cameras too."

"Fuck you," said Lance, picking up the brown bag.

"You were looking for trash just the same."

"Nope," Lance retorted, "I was looking at it."

"Didn't know you had a mirror with you on duty," said Lance and headed for the front exit of the premises.

"Dumb ass," said Drew, pointing with his stick to the wall. "That's where you came from. That's where you leave. We're gonna have the whole freakin' hotel check out if they see you leaving out front."

"Whatever," said Lance and waved to the couple on the balcony before heading for the crack in the wall.

The bag stays here," Drew ordered.

"I don't think so," said Lance and made a run for the wall with the guard in hot pursuit. He barely managed to slip through the crack when he felt the club connect with his arm, sending waves of brute pain shooting up his shoulder. He clutched the brown paper bag and rubbed his sore arm. What a price to pay for eating breakfast. Inflation sure had taken on absurd proportions these days.

Only after he had almost reached the tent did he notice that the bottom of the bag had fallen out owing to the sticky wet residue of the whisky bottle, taking with it everything but the apple. Shit. For a moment he considered returning to the dumpster to have Drew arrest him and have him thrown into jail, where at least he could treat himself to food without having to loiter for it. But then he imagined warding off prison inmates, possible rapists and crack addicts drawing a bead on his ass, and grimaced at the prospect of defending himself with one good arm. He shook his head and stuffed the paper bag into the nearest trashcan, keeping the apple for himself, rubbing it off his shirt before taking a bite out of it, making sure to finish it off before re-entering the tent. Inside, it smelled like weed. "Fucking pot head," Lance murmured, opening the flaps. "Plenty of vitamins and nutrients. Hell, you smoke enough of that and that pudding between your ears might convince you that you'll never have to go hungry again. Where did you get it from, anyway?"

"It's just a roach," Colin replied, taking a deep drag. "Want some?"

"Keep it," said Lance, "put it on your freakin' toast, for all I care."

"Not a bad idea," Colin replied, "what's wrong with your arm? Looks you were playing tennis out there, and you were the fuckin' ball."

A short glance at his arm re-enforced what Lance already knew, and he gently ran his fingertips over the bruise, now the size and color off an eggplant, although not even remotely as edible. Visiting the doctor was out of the question. With no address or identification handy, he could just as easily have passed for a dying fly having just crept out from underneath the swatter and begging for help. But then he realized that crap didn't speak. It only smelled.

"I'll get by," Lance replied, "it can't be a fracture, that's for sure. I'll just have my healthcare plan take care of it."

"You ain't got none," said Colin, stuffing out the roach.

"Sure I do," said Lance. "It's called time, and I've got plenty of it. And I never paid a premium for it in my life."

Their conversation was interrupted by a scuffle outside, and Lance heard the rancid voices of two Hispanics accompanying each shove and swing with a reference to their mothers, the supposed tainted sexual preference of each of the men, and animalistic grunts that could have just as easily been issued from a pigsty, which was not too far removed from the truth. A crowd of people gathered around the fray, with one part cheering on José, the other encouraging Pedro to land the knockout punch.

"What's the big deal?" asked Colin. "Are they in this for the workout?"

"Nah," Lance replied, shaking his head. "I think Jose stole Pedro's space, from the look of things."

"Barbarians," Colin quipped. "Have them fight it out in court. I'm sure the judge will settle this to everybody's liking."

Wheeling from a blow landed to the midsection, José picked a bottle off the ground and flung it at Pedro's head, missing by inches. Stunned by the iniquitous tactics employed by his nemesis, Pedro charged with full force, knocking José flat on his back. A couple more jabs to the face, and the fight was over, leaving José's nose bleeding in the dirt and quickly attracting the flies laying their claims to the spoils at the expense of the loser. People roared their approval over the spectacle as Pedro shook the dirt off his faded jeans. He drew blood from a cut on his lip he was nursing and spat out a tooth that he then picked up and complacently stuffed into his back pocket, to be retrieved and gloated over on demand.

Losers buried their knocked out teeth, praying for time to lend its generosity in quickly dissolving the unsolicited souvenir, while the winners would do anything from carrying it around like a rabbit's foot to encasing it and rewarding it with a permanent place on the pallet, the crate, or whatever item would serve as a trophy case. Somewhere in the heavily polluted grounds of Shantytown lay buried two of Lance's teeth, he remembered, and he knew that the odds were greater that the tooth fairy had replaced each of them with a dollar bill than the chance of him ever digging them out again. Some corpses were best left buried.

"Packs quite a punch, doesn't he?" said Colin, whose feet probably still hadn't touched the ground yet that day.

"Yeah," said Lance, "and what did the moron win? Absolutely nothing. A spot closer to the sewer entrance. That'll put him on Time's cover."

"Time to get up," said Colin, still lying flat on his back. "Time to live off other people's money for another day."

"Get me some white bread," said Lance. "And some butter would be nice."

"Sure thing," Colin chuckled and finally rose to his feet, knocking his head against the top tent-pole that somehow remained in place. "You head-butt the donors out there like that," Lance muttered, "and you won't get the saliva dribbling from their kissers."

"Morning blues," Colin replied, rubbing his head.

"Yeah," said Lance. "At fucking two o'clock in the afternoon. Wish I were that lucky."

"Later, man," said Colin and disappeared behind the entry flaps.

Lance sighed meekly in the dark, wishing now he had taken a drag from the roach to ease the pain, and likened the thump thump thump emanating from his arm to a kettle-drum that nauseatingly drowned out the rest of the chamber orchestra within his body steadfastly trying to pump blood into his brain that stubbornly insisted he was hurting. There was no other option but to take the pain, eat it, knowing it was quite probable that it would be the only thing he would eat all day. At least he had already eaten an apple, reminding himself cynically how people loved that apple-a-day proverb, but the real reason it did manage to keep the doctor away, he thought, was that his goddamn bills were too high.

The pounding in his arm gradually wearing thin in the dark, Lance got up to find dinner. Not having to scavenge for money to pay the rent was one thing, convenient indeed, but leaving the body's demands unfulfilled and denying it the nutritional visitors it needed would eventually condemn it to an excruciating solitary death, he knew. There was still Lincoln Park on Ash and Waverland Avenue, an enticing prospect for picnickers on such a hot day, although he hoped that they had kept the dogs at home since it wasn't a rarity for Rex and Rover to pester human beings that smelled like they did. With eight garbage cans that he had counted there on his last visit, Lincoln Park was easily considered the trusted source for food, not just in the minds of the armies of ants faithfully pillaging the dumps.

His hunch was correct, as blankets strewn throughout the grounds carried dozens of families, some enjoying the remnants of their lunch, others idly frolicking in the sun like tourists on the beach, the trashcans at a safe distance and rarely monitored. Loiterers like him combing through the waste were no anomaly, another one of the reasons picnickers kept the cans at bay besides the putrid smell of their contents. Lance counted three dogs, each one of them pre-occupied with the seemingly arduous task of chasing a Frisbee or a stick, only to have their owners watch them repeat the cycle the moment the dogs had retrieved it and deferentially laid it back at their feet. Good deal. Now if only the little kids could nap for a while, hence sparing him the embarrassment of overhearing questions pertaining to why people fished food out of the trash, then he could collect the food and then quickly get the hell out of Dodge without any regrets.

From his position at the edge of the park, he discovered three of the cans to be overloaded, with several paper plates and cups, which for whatever reason didn't make it into the cylindrical containers, scattered about only inches from the bases. Predictably, the two cans at both ends of the park were nearly empty, save for a newspaper or a Styrofoam cup containing cold coffee already gathering mildew. He made his way to the middle, ignoring the picnickers' distrustful glances that shifted from his morbid figure to where they believed to have stored their purses and wallets. A paper bag, virtually unused, lay at the top of one of the heaps, and Lance, eager not to duplicate the error he had committed that morning, turned it upside down and shook it to rid it of any contents. Finding none, he went about his business, bagging half a bag of chips, two sandwiches missing but a couple of bites, and a container of milk at least half full. Collecting loot like this was rarely this easy, although the process was not completed without a further reminder of how people perceived him, as if their glances at his arrival were not already a firm indication of it.

"Daddy," a little girl spoke up, tugging at her father's sleeve. "Who is that man?"

"Don't worry about him, Dear," came the answer from her dad. "That's just the trash collector."

"Daddy, what's a trash collector?"

"People who collect trash, Dearest."

"Why do they collect trash?" the girl persisted. "It's dirty."

"So are they," said her father, his voice as patronizing as a schoolmaster's. "So are they. They collect it so you and Mommy and I can stay clean."

"Uh-huh," the girl replied nodding, her focus undeterred by what her father had just said.

"Stop staring at the man," said her father, jerking his daughter's shoulder around.

Lance bypassed the other two cans stuffed to the brims, uneager about receiving more choice remarks from bored children. Adding to that, the dogs were tiring, their hanging tongues vacillating like defect pendulums requiring repair, a lucid sign that he would be their next likely target the moment they replenished their batteries. Clearly, he had not earned his stripes in the business yet, unlike those hardcore veterans on Broadway who could absorb abuse as easily as a crash test dummy, their shaggy beards and ratty hair complimenting their filthy clothes, only one hint that people were perfectly capable of dropping below the level of resignation.

His pace torpid and deliberate, Lance headed home, ignoring his own desires to flop into the grass and cool off in the shade and maybe enjoy the weekend that had now been perpetuated for months without a Monday in sight. On his way back to the tent he inadvertently tripped over a can of beans lying in his path, sending the owner of the food, a black fellow, people just referred to as Jake, into spasms of fury that could not have been reciprocated by a pitbull.

"You will pay for that," he vowed. "Man, will you ever."

"Ease up, man," said Lance, already wondering what payment the guy had in mind. "I'll pick them up for you."

"Piss off," Jake replied. "Ain't no such thing as beans with dirt as a fucking sidedish."

"Sorry about that," said Lance. "And I mean that."

"We'll fix you up," was Jake's terse reply before he disappeared into his shanty. Inside the tent, Colin was spreading butter onto a fresh slice of white bread Lance instantly recognized as his favorite brand.

"You devil," said Lance, "what gives? Where did you find the gun to rob people?"

"In my mouth," Colin replied. "Called a tongue. And no gun could ever puke out worse lies than mine. Today my wife happened to kick the bucket."

Before Lance could reveal his relatively meager findings the earth was shook by a long sonic boom that rattled tent-poles and metal panels alike.

"What the hell was that?" Lance snapped.

"Nothing, man," replied Colin, continuing to apply the spread to his bread. "It's just the mailman."

"Shit," Lance replied, "A mailman carrying plastic explosives strapped to his back, more like."

"You worry too much," said Colin.

The word that traveled throughout Shantytown was that a miniature gas tank used for cooking had exploded into the man's face, nearly decapitating him and blinding his roommate. The claim to fill the shanty that had belonged to both men was hotly disputed, resulting in several more scuffles involving four families in all. From inside the tent, Lance watched the spilled beans still lying in the dirt, now garnering massive armies of ants nibbling away at the prized possession for their queen. Lance shook his head, watching another two prospective tenants exchange blows over the rights to the vacated unit. Kind of made you want to work for a living again.

Later that night while lying in bed, Lance felt something excruciatingly hot tugging at his senses, at first mistaking it for the pain in his arm that had not entirely subsided yet. When the heat spread to his legs and feet, he panicked.

"Colin," he said, "wake up."

"What is it?"

"Do you feel anything?"

"Yeah," Colin replied, "kinda hot in here."

Lance turned on the flashlight and scanned the tent. He found an amber circle glowing at one side of the tent, quickly spreading and gnawing through the canvas.

"Get up, Col," Lance barked. "The tent is on fire."

"Go to sleep, man," Colin muttered. "Nothing's on fire."

Lance sat on his bed and sighed. Then, suppressing a curse underneath his breath, he slowly rose to find water.

Author Notes:

This story deals with lethargy that seems to be abundant in society these days, with a major portion of time spent just to search for the bare necessities. Both Colin and Lance exemplify this nonchalance...

DENNIS' BOX

Angie Hulme

Dennis opened the door to tell whoever was knocking to go away.

'Damn hotel maids…' he muttered an threw open the door, ready to point to the 'Do Not Disturb' on the handle. There was no-one there…just a small box wrapped in shiny black paper with a white bow. Dennis picked it up, it just about fit in one hand, kicked the door shut as he went back to his bed. He slipped off the bow and tore off the paper. The box was square, chilly to his touch, and of no colour he could describe. Made of some sort of metal or plastic…he couldn't tell that either. Stuck to the top, folded into a wedge, was a piece of white paper. Dennis took it, wondering vaguely what it was stuck with, and opened it. It was written in an old-fashioned, close, perfect Copperplate.

Dennis,

I am a friend in need of your help. Please take care of this Box for me until I return, which I will do as soon as I can. When we meet I shall explain. But for now I beg you to keep it safe, and never ever open it! This last I entreat you not to disregard! The Box MUST NEVER BE OPENED! Or you may destroy everything! You will be handsomely rewarded upon my return.

Yours, P.

Dennis frowned and examined the box closer He saw no discernible way to

open it. Re-reading the note he paced the room. Handsomely rewarded for looking after a small box? He sure could use the money, life had been a bitch lately. Losing first his job, then his girlfriend, then his home…yes, he was sure he could use the money. But the warning made him uneasy…so forceful, adamant… threatening?

A polite request coupled with a reward would have been plenty! What was in the box that could 'destroy everything', it didn't even seem to have lid! Trying to force it out of his mind, failing, he showered. Then, tucking the box safely into his zippered coat pocket, he headed down to the Hotel bar for some company (alcohol, the back of his mind whispered) before bedtime.

By the time the morning came via his alarm and a thrashing headache Dennis had forgotten the box. Forgotten telling the barman and the some other guy all about it. Forgotten being carried to bed. But it flooded back as he dry-swallowed some pills and made him reel. Rushing to his coat he felt in the pockets. The box was still there.

And this morning, it seemed he could faintly make out a thin line about an inch from the top... He held it to the light and looked closely through the fog in his eyes.

There it was! A line! But...not just a line...one that signified, so Dennis automatically calculated, a lid! Hesitating only for a moment, recalling a warning – a promise of riches – Dennis slowly eased up the lid... Darkness rushed out and hit him square in the mind with such sudden force that he fell back, and passed out. But not before his terrified mind saw total, vivid blackness. Not before his petrified ears heard the crashing and grinding...and the evil laugh... When he awoke, he shot to his feet. He could see...but faintly...and what he could see was (nothing) darkness. Long, dark everlasting black. A slight breeze seemed to come form behind him and a small sigh echoed between his ears. He whipped round, expecting more darkness (nothingness) but there was light. Blinding, penetrating, dizzying, fantastic light! And it was shaped...like a woman. 'Dennis' a silvery voice spoke in his head. 'Dennis.' He sensed a underlying pain in her voice so crystal sharp that he stepped backwards.

'I-I'm sorry...' he began, afraid.

'I know...' came the silver-sigh. 'You were curious...not yourself...you didn't mean to. The same reasons I spoke when I opened my box.'

'Who...your...(?)'

'My name is Pandora. A long, long eternity ago, when there were many Gods and the world was blissful, I was given a box. A box just like yours. And I opened it.

'Pandora...? You...you...the ills...'

'Yes. I set free all the ill's of the World. In one moment when I lost control..'

'...H-Hope...(?)'

'Yes, I set free Hope last of all. But it was too late. I was then doomed to carry this...' she was suddenly holding the box Dennis had opened, now shut once more. 'Doomed to carry it until someone could take care of it for me, and not open it. I chose you. I promised you the one thing I knew you needed. That thing...the World will do anything for.'

'I...'

'No, Dennis.' The silver tinged black for a second, then returned. 'You opened the box. I am not here to judge. Please, listen.' Dennis opened his mouth, then closed it and nodded dumbly. 'You released Darkness, that which lies buried beneath the soul, that…which nothing can withstand. True Evil. Nothingness. You must open the box one more time.'

He shook his head sharply, trying to turn and run, finding himself paralysed so he could not. 'Please, listen. To every Darkness there is equal Light. You must re-open the box and release the Light.' Dennis whimpered and held out his trembling hands. 'Dennis, you must know what the Darkness did! Pure Nothing, It…destroys all…you must prepare for what you will see…' Dennis snarled and snatched the box.

'I'll see soon enough, and Light will fix it.'

Pandora faded slowly away 'No Dennis…' whispered the silver. 'Once Darkness has been released, it takes more than Light t…' Dennis snorted and looked blindly at the box in his hands. 'I destroyed the world, now I'm going to save it.' Slowly…he slid…open…the lid…and passed out.

Waking up he saw Light through his eyelids, and didn't need to remember. He stood, eyes closed, ready to see the new world. He opened his eyes…and saw…Grey.

JESSICA

Annalee Johnson

"I just don't understand Jessica," he sighed. When does he ever? He's only a Psychiatrist after all. "Well, Dr. Slater," I said, "I'm just a classic case of good girl gone bad."

"Yes, but I don't understand why!" He said exasperated.

'Fine,' I thought, 'I'll throw him a bone.'

"You really want to know?" I asked, "I'll tell you why. You see it all started with this guy, Sam."

Sam and I had known each other since we were little. We were the best of friends. When High School came around, we started dating. Everyone thought of us as the perfect couple. I was the happiest girl in the world. I had the greatest boyfriend a girl could wish for, good grades in school, and a fantastic relationship with my parents. Then she came. Her name was Amber Nicka. She was the Bad Girl, the one all the guys wanted to tame. As soon as she arrived, she set her eye on Sam. I should've known he'd succumb to her wiles sooner-or-later, but I was my usual trusting self. Thus, 2 weeks after she'd appeared, I found them going at it behind the school. You can imagine my shock and dismay. I refused to become cold to Sam, though. So, after we 'official' broke-up, he and I remained close friends. He confided that he and Amber would do drugs and drink weekends away together. 'Mostly drugs' he said, 'but the hint of alcohol made the high all that much better.' I warned him to be careful, but tried to be supportive.

One night, though, the two of them went too far. So far, that it landed Sam in the hospital, unconscious. Amber's parents confiscated her and left Sam all alone in the hospital, what with his parents out of the country and unreachable. As soon as I heard, though, I took the car and raced over. I stayed there for two days straight, not even bothering with school. Through those days, I was always waiting for him to open his eyes and see me and recognize the girl he truly loved. However, on the third day, Amber came by.

"Sorry I took so long." She said to me, "I didn't want to ditch school these past few days. I'll take over, you go ahead and take a break."

So I left and got some coffee. I came back and walked into the doorway just as

Sam's eyes opened.

"Amber?" He asked.

"Yeah, it's me," she said, "I've been here all along."

"I'm glad." He said.

I left them. I heard through the grapevine that Sam had been shocked that I'd never visited him, once he'd woken. Apparently no one believed that I had been at the hospital the entire I had been out of school, they all just assumed I was sick. Eventually, he called.

"Hey, Jess," he said. "How've you been?"

"Doesn't matter," I said. "How are you?"

"I'm getting better," he said. "I wanted to let you know that Amber and I are going to rehab together."

"I'm happy for you," I said.

Soon after, he left I became very sullen. I got into fight and fight with my friends and family. It finally got to the point where I simply gave up on caring.

"Which led to this," I said to Dr. Slater.

"I'm terribly sorry, Jessica," he said.

"Yeah," I said, "Everyone always is."

"But that was High school. You're out of college now, with a blossoming career. Why haven't you moved on yet?" He asked.

"Old trends die hard?" I grinned and looked at my watch, "I've got to go."

"Jessica," he said, as I stood, "I don't believe anymore sessions will do you any good if that's all you're willing to tell me."

"It's been nice chatting with you, Doc," I said.

Yeah, like I was ever going to tell him everything else. Too many hurts for me to cry about in front of a stranger. Especially one who may know part of the cause personally. Like Jack. God, Jack, you're utterly unforgettable.

Soon after Amber and Sam left, I changed quite drastically apparently.

My once long brown hair became short, black, and blue. In fact I pretty much turned into a walking, black-clad depression. All my old friends abandoned me in my obvious hour of need, and what used to be verbal fights quickly became physical. I still managed, somehow, to do well in my classes and with my teachers, though. Some part of myself would not give up on the grades that I'd worked so hard to achieve.

When Sam came back three months later, it was with out Amber, but with Jack

Palpton. Jack was his peer therapist, a part of the recovery program. Amber was still at the center and would remain for at least another three months. As soon as Sam got home he called me.

"Hey, Jess," he exclaimed, "guess what!"

"You're home," I stated, unenthused.

"Yeah," he said, "look, can I talk with you in person?"

"Where?" I asked simply.

"In the park. There's someone I'd like you to meet." He said.

"Great," I said and hung up.

I recognized Sam immediately. He was at our old hiding place among a grove of trees. I recognized him, but my heart didn't leap at the sight. He and Jack sat, talking animatedly. I approached and Sam did a double take at my appearance, and ended up staring at me slack jawed.

"What do you want?" I asked tersely.

"I wanted to introduce you to Jack Palpton, my peer therapist, he's part of my rehab program. He's here to monitor all that I do so that I don't mess up again."

"Nice to meet you Jessica," Jack said, "Sam has been telling me what a positive influence you've been to him."

I snorted.

"Fat lot of good I did," I said, "Nice to meet you Jack, but if that's all, I have to get going."

"Actually no," Jack said, "I'd like to ask you to help in Sam's recovery."

"I'll think about it," I said, and left.

About a week later Sam and Jack came back to school, for our senior year. Everyone was very huggy and supportive. I sat in class and waited. All the teachers sat him in the usual seat, next to me, to try to keep things normal.

One day, in a free period, while Jack was off getting some water, Sam decided to talk.

"You've changed, Jess," he said.

"No shit," I replied.

"Why?" He asked pleadingly.

"WHY?!" I nearly screamed, "WHY?! YOU want to you know WHY?!"

Just then Jack came back in and I shut my mouth. Sam tried again to talk but I stood and walked over to a window. Jack followed.

"I understand you used to be nice," he said coldly.

I glared out the window, refusing to let myself care what he might think of me. He sighed.

"I'm sorry," he apologized, "that was uncalled for. I need help from someone who knew Sam. Someone who can tell him how much he damaged his life and those around him."

I looked up at him. I met his eyes, perhaps the biggest mistake I ever did. As soon as I met the depths of his green eyes, I almost melted. Just as quickly as it happened, I looked away and felt his hand on my shoulder. I shook it off, though my body and heart tried fiercely to rebel.

"I'll write a letter," I begrudged.

"Thank you," he said, and left me.

For the rest of the period, I wrote a three page long letter to Sam. I handed it to Jack on my way out.

After that, Jack would often catch me alone and just quietly sit down next to me and start a conversation. Mostly I gave him brief and concise answers, but enough well thought-out and passionate ones that he kept coming back. I learned about his past, and what he hoped for his future. I knew I was falling for him, and hard, and I knew that I was a project in his eyes, another Sam. Yet, for some reason, I couldn't pull myself away.

The first time Jack and Sam saw me fight, they were both shocked. I hadn't been in a fight since Sam had come back, but I didn't start it this time. This girl just decided that I was a delectable challenge. So this girl only landed two punches on me before I had her on the ground, both arms twisted back, and my knee in the small of her back. She begged mercy and I let up. She had no mark of the fight. I, however, sported a black eye and a cut above my eyebrow. After it was over Sam went back to his populars and Jack came over to me. I sat propped against a tree my sleeve to my head.

"That wasn't a fair fight," he said.

"You're telling me," I sighed, "wearing rings is dirty fighting."

"I meant," he said, rummaging through his back-pack, "that you were obviously more skilled than your opponent, but you never once attacked, merely defended and disabled."

I shrugged. He pulled out a First-Aid kit, and I winced.

"Put your arm down," he said, and went to work on cleaning and bandaging the cut.

"There," he said, wiping off his hands, "good as new."

"Thanks," I said.

"No problem," he said, "just make me a promise."

"Depends," I said.

"Try not to get into anymore fights," he asked, and walked back to Sam.

A few days before school was to end for us seniors, Jack and I were having our usual conversation. He'd let Sam wander out of his sight as a reward for being good, so we were all alone, everyone else wandering around in a more interesting area.

"You know," he said, "I'm going to leave soon."

"Why?" I asked.

"This is my senior year, too," he smiled. "I have to get home and see my family before I leave for college."

"Stupid college," I pouted.

He laughed, and very unexpectedly, took my face into his hands and kissed me. It was heaven on Earth. He was the first guy I'd kissed since Sam, and you could tell he had experience.

"I'm sorry," he said.

"Why?!" I asked, and kissed him again.

"Stop," he panted, "I can't do this. I can't trust you enough."

"What do you mean?" I asked.

"I mean," he said, avoiding my eyes, "that your attitude is so haywire, I don't know which is the real you. And I need to know, I feel so lost otherwise."

I looked at him solemnly then stood up and left him there. When I got into my car, I looked back and saw him with his head in his hands, and he looked to be shivering, even though it was 90 degrees. I looked away, and drove home. Once again, the grapevine fed me info. Jack would be leaving the day after us senior were to be released upon the world. The night before he was to leave, I called him at Sam's.

"Hey, Jack," I said.

"Hi, Jess," he replied.

"Look," I said, " I know you're leaving tomorrow and all, but do you think we might be able to talk before then, in person?"

"Sure, when and where?" he asked.

"The park," I said, " where we first were introduced. When does your flight leave?"

"5 p.m." he said.

"How about 2 p.m. then?" I said after some quick calculations.

"Sounds good, bye then." He said.

"Bye," I said.

The next day I arrived early at the park, and something completely unexpected occurred.

"Hello, Jessica," I heard a voice say.

"Amber?!" I spun to face her.

She was as radiant as ever. There was however, I spark in her eye. A glint I should have recognized as anger as soon as I saw her, but I was too preoccupied.

"Surprised?" she asked.

"Yeah," I said, "I am."

"Well so was I," she hissed, "when Sam dumped me. He said he didn't feel our relationship was as 'real' as he first thought."

"I'm sorry," I said, " but how does this relate to me?"

"You're the 'real' reason," she glared at me, "You're the whore no one knows, the little slut who plays with all those around her, the…"

I don't know what it was. Maybe that she was calling me all that I hated, but I swung at her. Hit her right in the jaw. A warning punch mind you. No real damage to her. However, it landed me in more trouble than anything else I've ever done.

"Jessica?" I heard a voice gasp.

I spun and saw Jack standing there gaping at me. Amber saw the opportunity and tackled me. As the wind was knocked out of me, I saw Jack's jaw set and watched him turn and walk away. A fierce fight broke out between us two desperate women. When I finally managed to get home around 4 p.m., I had a ripped T-shirt, a fresh black eye, a sprained ankle and wrist, and a bruised windpipe. I called Sam's got Jack's flight info and set off before my parents could utter a sound.

As soon as I was in the airport, I ran to the terminal. Jack and Sam stood talking with their backs to me, by the entrance ramp.

"I though I'd reached her," Jack sighed.

"She'd just that way now, Jack." Sam patted his back.

"Last call for boarding." Called the flight attendant.

Jack started forward.

"Wait," I managed, through my bruised windpipe.

"What the hell happ…" Jack gasped.

"Let me talk," I wheezed.

He nodded.

"I came to say I'm sorry. Sorry you didn't know me before. Sorry that I couldn't help you with Sam. Sorry I didn't become what you wanted of me. Sorry that Amber caught me off guard."

Sam gasped at the mention of Amber.

"But I am also not sorry that I've fallen in love with you. Yes, I know, this is the first you've heard of it, but better late than never. The only reason I tell you now is not just to relieve myself of it though, it is so that you will not become what I am. I want you to know that I will love you no matter what you do, smart or stupid. You just need to know I love you."

Then I turned and began leaving, or rather limping.

"Wait," he said.

In that instance, I had this overpowering hope, that maybe life would turn out for the better. Maybe this would be my fairy-tale ending. I turned to him.

"Thank you," he said, "I'll never forget."

I smiled, and he smiled, and we both turned and walked away. Sam caught up to me within a matter of seconds, and even though I hadn't talked to him since the letter, he offered to be my human crutch. We became the friends again in that instance.

Sam and Jack shared constant correspondence and, though I never asked, Sam always told me what Jack was up to and that he had asked about me and such. Time flew by once Sam and I became friends again. He and I continued on into college together, there he met his true love, Elisabeth. She was a great woman, we became fast and great friends. They had a beautiful wedding, I was maid-of-honor. And what an honor it was. In the toast at the reception, I declared Elisabeth my honorary sister. Jack was invited. I caught a glimpse of him at the ceremony, but he didn't stay for the reception afterwards.

Jack is now a renowned Psychiatrist. Gee, who would have guessed. I keep track of him through the school he is currently working at and through all the articles, he writes. And Dr. Slater wondered why I wouldn't tell him more. It's not just the pain, it that fact that he may know part of my pain personally.

I always wished for a fairy-tale like life. You know, with how everything fits together perfectly, but this is life. This is my life. This is reality. Life is but an instance. An instance too precious to waste. I learned that the hard way.

THE GIRL

Brian Vincent Wemyss

Sarah was the sweetest girl Jason had ever met. Her eyes were dark blue, as he often notices as he takes her orders down. He always saw in her eyes a warm and wonderful person. She must be a very nice girl, he often thought to himself.

She would often take her place in the corner of the cafeteria, at the table where there was only space for two. It overlooked the duck pond, and Jason always found her looking at the pond, when not busy reading the newspaper or having a bite off her tuna sandwich. Jason admired her, as she looked so calm and radiant, and that persona which she exudes never seemed to change.

Jason works at the cafeteria, and would never miss the exact moment when Sarah would come in, order her coffee, decaf, grab something to bite, and head straight for her usual seat.

Everything she did seemed to captivate him, and he could never take his eyes off her unknowingly. Jason used to wonder to himself, where does she live, where is she coming from, where is she going to, and how long would she be here. The nametag which she wore everyday did not seem to help aid his curiosity.

One morning, Jason could not get up from bed. He was suffering from the biggest headache he had ever felt. He groaned, and he whined but he could not get up from bed. I must get to work, or I'll miss the girl, he thought to himself. For Jason, there was no better motivation to get to work than the thought of seeing the girl.

Slowly, he pulled himself up, dragged his feet across the room, and managed to get to the bathroom. He gave himself a good face wash, and got dressed hurriedly. He looked at his watch, 9.30. "She'll be in any minute, gotta hurry".

Quickly, he got on his motorbike, and rode as fast as he could, avoiding the pit holes that littered the road, as he did every morning. Only this time, it was much intense.

Jason was focused on getting to the cafe in time, and he did not notice when all of a sudden someone crossed the road right in front of him. He panicked, and slammed on the brakes, but not before going head on with the person he wanted to avoid. The impact sent the both of them flying through the air.

Jason landed a long distance away from his bike, and he could see through the corner of his eye, the person whom he collided into. He noticed the long hair, and the high heels, newspaper strewn all over the place. Then it momentarily dawned on him. It was the girl! "I collided with the girl, how could I". As he said this, he could not feel his body, and he felt like the whole world was crumbling on him. Jason slowly shut his eyes, and lay down, helpless, and hopeless.

Soon crowds began to gather, and they tried to help both victims. Then they saw something. In her hands, they found a card, and upon closer inspection, it read 'HAPPY 21st BIRTHDAY'.

MUSIC NON-STOP
Candice Maryanne Borg

No matter where he went, there was noise. Inside the woman with the striking blue eyes was drying her long blonde hair behind the wooden door. Outside was the hum of silence, which would soon become a roar as the men started their machines. But inside his head was the music, a thousand songs played on an imaginary record player, all his own, waiting to be born into the world through his biro.

The woman with the eyes came out of the fly-screened door. She was still in her nightclothes, and her hair was everywhere, electrified by the hairdryer. She paused on the landing and sucked in the air- while it was still free of petrol and only laced with the scent of manure. Her eyes danced over the sparse land and finally rested on her husband. She lifted her nightdress and placed her bare feet on the freshly cut grass and walked to him.

"You got up early this morning, " She stated as she took his body closer to her own. "Anything the matter?"

"Look at your hair," he ran his fingers through and her locks slowly began to relax.

"Don't answer my question then, Jack."

"Sorry- no, nothing is wrong. Just trying to find some piece and quiet."

The woman nodded her head, and once again looked out onto the property, and slowly closed her eyes and breathed in heavily. As she opened them, cries rang out.

"Is a mother's work ever finished" she began to walk away, but Jack held her. Kissing her lightly, he then shook his head and went to the source of the wails.

Amber began to make breakfast as Jack calmed Kate down. She supported Jack in every way, and new the talents he harbored. She knew that if they could get off the farm and into the city he would be understood- his music would be understood. But they had nothing apart from the farm- their cattle barely milking anymore and their hens hardly laying. It was through sheer luck they had even gotten the farm, otherwise they might have been living in a small, dingy apartment in the middle of nowhere. At least here their daughter was able to run freely, in mostly fresh air.

As the eggs fried, the machines started their roar in neighboring fields. Jack would soon be out there, contributing to the daily hacking, chopping and shredding. Amber switched on the small black and white TV, just in time for the news.

"A fierce fire has ripped through Sydney's water-side theme-park, Luna Park, claiming seven lives..." the reporter read in her monotone voice. Amber proceeded to flick the channel to something brighter, happier- something to reflect the sun outside.

Kate struggled as Jack tried to lay her back down to sleep. She could here the TV and her mother downstairs, "Mamma! Mamma!" Kate pointed out the door. "How about I sing you a song, Katie?" Jack hummed a tune and Kate focused on him for a second, and then again yelled for her mother. "Ok then, I give up!" He held his arms to his daughter and she scrambled forwards.

The vibration through the seat went unnoticed as Jack started up the plough and drove off into the fields. He had become accustomed, or as he so blatantly put it, numb, to his surroundings that he went about his work in a robotic manner, putting his real passion out of his mind. He wasn't dumb, he knew he could never be taken seriously- who had ever heard of a born farmer turned musician? He had a family, and that came with the responsibility of putting food on their table and clothes on their back. And everyone knows, music isn't the most stable profession.

Sweat dripped off him like water from a tap. It was June, but Northern NSW didn't seem to follow the seasonal rules. He turned off the machine and took out his water. Wiping the sweat from his brow, Jack peeled himself off the leather seat of the plough and looked back towards the house. From his position the cracking and faded paint wasn't as noticeable and broken shutters didn't seem to dangle so far off his old house. This wasn't how everything was supposed to have turned out. He had promised Amber a good life- he had never said that she would be wearing last years' clothes and storing Kate's baby things just incase another child was conceived. He wanted better for his girls, his beautiful roses. He had lived this life already and wanted better.

"Dinner's ready, Honey," Amber said quietly. She hadn't seen Jack since he came out of the field- he had withdrawn into their room and Amber had decided against disturbing him. She walked closer, just incase he hadn't heard. "Jack?" She put her hand on his thick shoulder. "I'll be there soon, Amb..." He said equally as quiet. She didn't push, and walked out. She had seen what he was doing and it made her smile. He was writing his music again.

They had married only months before Kate was born. Amber had loved his sense of humor- and his artistic nature that shone through his eyes. He wrote a song for her, and had promised her the world on the day he proposed. Jack had wanted to play her song at their wedding but Amber said no, and told him that she would hear it in nó time- when he achieved his dream and was discovered.

Only months after their wedding he stopped writing his music. He had also put the guitar away in the tool shed. To see him back at his desk, with his guitar beside him- tuned- made her so happy. She hoped she would soon be able hear her song. It seemed he had once again started to believe in himself. But she also wondered what had happened to make him sit back at his desk.

"I want try again, Amber," Jack said suddenly while they were cleaning up. "I really do. This isn't what I had planned for us..." He drifted off, shaking his head lightly. He looked about them, though their house was filled with love, it made him sick to the stomach thinking that Kate would grow up to be nothing, like he was. "I know you saw what I was doing this afternoon- I wanted to surprise you. I'm going to try harder, Amber. I promise."

"Jack- "she started, but she couldn't find the words. She wanted to talk sense, but she was so happy to hear the words, she couldn't bring herself to. Maybe sense wasn't needed this time. She nodded and smiled wide.

"You've waited long enough for that song. And I know we are living off the smell of an oily rag, but I've worked it out- we can manage. The only thing is- we don't have enough money for you and Katie to come too... I would love for her to be able to see the lights of the city but we can't..."

"I know, and someone has to be here... when did you want to leave?"

"Soon."

Jack revved the engine of his truck. He looked out his window to see Amber holding Kate's hands- helping her to walk. She still wasn't too steady, but it made Jack smile all the same.

"She's getting there," Jack said as Amber holstered her up to her hip.

"She sure is," Amber looked at her daughter and pushed her nose lightly. Kate laughed lightly. "When will you be home?"

"Soon," he promised. "Love you." He shifted the car into gear and took off. Gravel sprayed as the car turned on their unsealed driveway.

As he passed the gates, he sucked in the air heavily, deeply. This will work, he thought, and turned the corner.

Walking down Oxford Street, Jack finally felt like he belonged. Here, amongst all the freaks, geeks and low-life's of the inner city he felt he didn't stand out as much, even though he was still in his overalls. He scuffed his feet along the dirty sidewalk, his guitar in hand, his optimism shattered. He had been in the city two weeks now, and had written to Amber countless times about how well everything was going, when, in reality, he knew it wasn't. He looked about him, and wondered if any of the other freaks on this busy street were silently screaming too. "The fifth audition this week, Jack," he said to himself as he shook his head. "You are the biggest freak of them all!"

Jack had never wanted something so badly in his life. He wanted to be able to go home to his wife and tell her she was able to throw everything she owned away, to tell her she needn't have to worry about Kate's doctors bills, to tell her she'd never ride another tractor in her life. But he knew that wasn't going to happen, he had realized that after the first interview, but he kept trying for Amber and his little Katie's sake. He heard the voices of the men and women who had played to, sung to, as he walked along the crowded street.

"Your talent isn't what we want."

"Your songs are emotionless, body-less, and absent of meaning."

"The type of music you have chosen to write, well, it just doesn't work for you."

Sitting at the bus stop, words flooded into his head. He shut his eyes and tried to push them away, he didn't want to write anymore. He saw the bus driving towards him and stood up. He looked up and down the long street- he wouldn't see this place again. The squeal of the buses tires scattered the words in his head.

"Where to, buddy?" The driver asked cheerfully.

"Coodgee, thanks."

"Four- twenty, buddy," the driver looked closely at Jack. "You look like you got the world on your shoulders there, buddy," said the driver as he took Jacks money. Jack just smiled as the driver gave him his changed. Jack looked up the bus aisle looking for an empty seat away from people. He spotted one and began to amble along the aisle towards it when the driver called out to him.

"Hey, buddy, is that your guitar there?"

Jack turned to him, and looking out the window said, "No, not mine," and turned and kept walking.

At his hotel, Jack walked into the room's bathroom and began to undress. As he turned on the hot water to let it heat, the words kept zooming around his head, and he tried his hardest to ignore them. He looked into thc mirror at his tired expression. The whites of his eyes were reddened, and the lines worn at the sides of his eyes and along his forehead seemed to have deepened. Slowly the steam made his face disappear in the apparent fog about him.

During his shower, Jack decided the only way to get rid of the words in his head was to write them down. But he promised himself this would be the last song he would ever write. With his old, dirty-white bathrobe around him, he sat at the small, scratched table in the tiny little kitchen of the musty, old hotel room. He took a pen and paper and began to write. Beside him was a razor blade, which he would later use to add the final touches to his song, to give it some meaning, some real body.

Everybody gets a second in the sun
I have a feeling my life's just begun
Music non-stop when I close my eyes
It goes around, it's full of compromise
So why don't you dance to the music,
I hear inside my head?
Why don't you dance to the music,
It's the soundtrack for the end.

SPIRIT OF LOVE

Carl E.Vance

Placing another log inside the fireplace, sparkling ashes stir, drifting upwards into the stone chimney. Cascading light from the flames fill the room with amber glowing warmth while outside a blinding winter storm rages, blanketing night's landscape with impassable drifts of snow.

Along the hollow's winding course, icy winds wail furiously up the valley, surging past an ancient wooden rail fence, which surrounds a parcel of land lending itself to the placement of an assortment of ramshackle buildings. Amid the structures, across a creaky porch made from rough-hewn timbers, unrelenting gales descend upon a center-placed dwelling. From its rooftop, swirls of smoke, and lighted ash, quickly disappear in a whirlwind of snow mixed with ice as the wintry gusts ceaselessly bang, and thrash against the cabin's closed rickety shutters. Cold and deadly, the malicious wind appears intent on gaining entrance into the sheltering haven.

Placed near the hearth, outfitted with worn rumpled cushions, sets two rung-rockers amid a sparse variety of other handmade furnishings. Adorning scuffed table tops, dyed burlap scarves are carefully arranged, and upon soot tinted walls, images of ancestors watch every happening from inside their dusty frames. Unaware of years passing, with the constant ticking, and count of chimes resounding from the mantel clock, their eyes cast without seeing, follow the figure arising from the comfort of a hearth placed rocker.

Clad in the era's common, patched, and faded blue bibbed overalls, Arthur shuffles across the room, his walk noticeably bent in stoop, created by the never-ending toil inherited with a farm's daily labor. Pausing, he peers inside an open doorway, leading into the adjacent bedroom, and studies the form of his wife of many years. Frail and old, she lies quietly upon the bed. Only her shallow rattled breath, in conjunction with a slight heaving of the hand-stitched patchwork quilt, gives any indication that she still clings to life.

Into the room, passing the wrought iron bed's rust speckled foot-stead, he makes his way alongside his life's treasured companion. Brushing the strands of soft gray hair from her forehead, he bends forward, and gently kisses her.

"Can I get you anything?" he asks, striving to hide the sadness and anguish from his voice, so as not to upset her, if by miracle, consciousness returned. The only answer forthcoming though, as he reaches to gingerly tuck her coverings, is the wailing winds, and the continued rasp of her breath.

Unmoving were her eyes, and gone was his Jenny's lovely smile. Unaware of his presence, and to the world, Arthur knew his sleeping bride would never waken again. With thoughts of the knowing, no longer was he able to hold back the tears. Softly he wept, and with like voice he whispered, "Sweet beautiful Jenny, I'll always love you."

Succumbing to assured declining affects tethered to age, and the cold chill brought forth by winter, an onset of swift fever overtook her four nights ago while she slept. Hitching the team to the buckboard, before the cock's crow announced first light, a steady crack of whip speeded the burly plow horses toward town, but fetching the local doctor had been to no avail. "Her life is within God's hands now", he said. Keep her in comfort with tending to hearth's grated fire, and to her brow apply coolness with a dampened cloth. That was his prescribed summation before departing upon the journey back to town.

Behind a mask willed in composure, lay the hidden turmoil of the brokenhearted, as Arthur cordially extended his hand to clasp the doctor's, giving thanks, then watched as the horse drawn buggy faded from sight, descending in the distance over the narrow roadway's rise. Turning to enter back into the cabin, noticed were dark clouds forming in the afternoon sky, but unknown at the time was the winter fury, and sorrow they would bring in the days ahead.

Placing the back of his hand on Jenny's forehead, no longer was a fever discernible, but the born intensity of its fiery breath, during its horrid linger, had plunged her into a deep sleep of death. Awaited now, the ticking clock's chime, announcing the appointed hour for death's shrouded angel to carry her away.

"Rest, my love", he said, while trying to hold back the tears seeping from the corner of his eyes. "I need to cook myself some supper, because I'll be no use to you if I don't keep my strength up. I'll be no further away than the kitchen".

Once again, Arthur bends to gently kisses her, then ambles toward the kitchen, pausing long enough to stoke the fireplace, and retrieve some hot coals in the ash shovel for lighting a fire inside the cookstove. With a creak from worn metal hinges he places the burning embers inside the stove's cast iron chamber, and carefully arranges strips of kindling across them. In moments the seasoned wood begins to crackle, and bursts into flames. Little by little, adding more splintery fuel, a roaring fire is soon burning brightly in the stove

Satisfied with the fire, Arthur closes the door, and adjusts the stove's draft to regulate the heat. From the kitchen's small cupboard, where an assortment of home preserves are kept, he slices a goodly portion of ham to fry along with several eggs, collected from the henhouse earlier in the day. Although his evening meal is meager it will suffice, helping restore his needed energy, for tending Jenny's needs.

Across the yard a lone figure stands in the entranceway of the railed fence. Attired completely in black, from hat to shoes, the snow filled wind whips, and furrows the visitor's full-length coat, his eyes fixated toward the faint streaks of illumination emitting from the cabin's ill fitted shutters. Stepping forward, through the opening, he proceeds steadily paced in the direction of the cabin, seemingly unhindered by the accumulation of deep miring snow underfoot.

Sitting down to his meal, Arthur, tries to ignore each loud crashing clap of shutters in the stormy besiegement, but it's almost impossible with their continued successiveness. "Hopefully the wind will ease soon", he thinks to himself, knowing tomorrow, he will have to assess the extent of any damages done by the frigid gales, and attempt to at least make temporary repairs until better weather affords an opportunity for him to fix them properly. He was well aware that the accumulated snow and ice, combined with the wind, and freezing temperatures outside, would make even the simplest restorations into almost impossible chores.

Absorbed in thought, nourished by current, and speculated forthcoming events, another repertoire of banging reverberates through the cabin, bringing Arthur to startled awareness, for the sound was unlike the accustomed flailing of shutters.

A short pause, then it commences again. "The door! Someone is at the door", came the surprised conclusion of thought. Pushing his chair away from the table, in aging hurriedness, Arthur, gains his way toward the door——calling out, "I'm coming".

Reaching the door, and lifting the securing draw-plank. Keeping a firm grasp against the ensuing blasts of frigidness, he carefully opens the door, preventing it from swinging wide, in effort to deny the wind entrance into the cabin.

Looking outward onto the porch, his sight gradually comes to focus being unaccustomed to the splattered light escaping through the doorway, but unrecognizable is the gaunt pallid face of the guest with dark piercing eyes, peering intently from beneath a wide brimmed hat.

Undaunted by his appearance, or the lack of acquainted recognition of the caller, Arthur beckons him to enter. Unthinkable would it be to refuse him refuge on a night like this.

"Come in! Come in out of the cold and stand over by the fire to warm yourself", he said, gesturing toward the blazing glow from the fireplace while re-securing the door.

Removing his hat, and holding it to his side, the visitor without expected hast from someone just entering from the bitter cold, moved over to the fire. Along with his mane of shoulder length hair, shaded closely in color to that of his apparel, neither appeared touched by the snowy wetness blowing beyond the cabin's inner walls, and from beneath snow trodden black glossy boots not a single puddle formed, but in his heightened concern for the stranger's well being, Arthur took no notice to the peculiarities.

Standing with his back to the rippling flames, facing Arthur, unusually long pasty colored fingers from his guest's free hand, made an unnecessary attempt to adjust the white priest's collar, now seen, underneath his outer coat. The motion seemed to be an obvious undertaking to convey his identity, and lend assurances that his intentions bore Arthur no malice.

"Mercy me, what in Heaven's name are you doing out on a night like this, Reverend?" asked Arthur.

"I am about my work", he answered, and continued in a defined assuring

voice. "Upon this night I come seeking those who are in need of my guidance; gathered aloft by the four winds, I've traveled unto your house to offer my assistance. Words have fallen to my ears that a resident within this dwelling is needful of my services."

"Yes," Arthur replied. "Doc. Amsted, who visited earlier in the week must have mentioned my wife to you. She's gravely ill. There's nothing he could do for her. She sleeps, and cannot be wakened, but I'm sure you're aware of that if you've spoken with the doctor. Still, it's so very kind of you to travel all the way from town to see her. I am indebted to you Reverend, but you should have never put yourself in jeopardy by journeying out on a dreadful night like this. There's no telling what type of misfortune might have befallen you".

"The will of thine maker protects those going about His bidding, my friend Arthur", replied the Reverend with the assuredness of his calm steady voice. "I have no fear of that which is part of this world, for it is not here that provides my everlasting keep. I am just a servant sent to gather with me those of the flock, and nothing more".

Noting his guest had referred to him by name, Arthur assumed the doctor had mentioned it, and so inquired as to his visitor's name. The parish in the nearby town was overseen by, Reverend Malone, whom he knew, but he was completely unfamiliar with the man standing before him, so it was likely he was from a province not far away, which the good doctor on occasion visited. Caught in midstream of his thoughts, the Reverend gave answer to Arthur's query, with quietness of his expected manner. "I am called Shepherd", he said, extending his hand in greeting.

Delayed introductions were sealed in a handshake by the fire, with ensuing words leading to the area's traditionally offered hospitality to weary travelers, but Arthur's sincere insistence of allowing him to prepare another fixing of ham and eggs for the reverend's supper, or serve him a hot drink of coffee or tea, was gracefully rejected with a multitude of thanks.

Continuing to speak, Reverend Shepherd added, "My sustenance comes not from the nourishment of man, friend Arthur. I am sustained by that, which is. I exist by the will that forges night and day, and into your house I've come as the guidance, to your seeking. That is my sustenance upon this eve."

Uncertain as to the underlying meaning of the reverend's words, although not unfamiliar with analogies used by soul redeemers. Without interrupting, Arthur listened intently to the overly scored diction with respect due to a man of the cloth, especially this man, whose faith had carried him through the perils presented upon such a formidable night.

As the speaker continued, his eyes suddenly glared studiously toward Arthur, and his words sent a chill down the old man's spine.

"Blessed is this house", he said, "and all who now endure within the confines of its walls. Concern yourself not for your ailing wife; she resides in loving hands upon this eve. Go to her, Arthur, for she has truly awakened, and offers assurances that all is well. Willingly, she embraces the peacefulness, which she is witness to. Hear her words, and allow your own peaceful rest".

Finishing his words, the Reverend stood motionless, and from the bedroom, Jenny called Arthur's name.

Tears streamed down Arthur's face as he stepped past the threshold, leading into the bedroom, and by the light of a twinkling oil lamp sat Jenny in front of the dresser's mirror brushing her long raven colored hair. No longer bearing signs of aging, her beauty was the same as the day they had met, with skin soft and supple. Jenny was once again, the young blossomed girl he had married so many years ago.

"Come to me Arthur", she said, and cradled him to her, as he wept.

"How can this be, Jenny?" He asked.

Looking away, and toward the bed, she pointed to the figure lying beneath the hand stitched quilt, gone unnoticed by Arthur when he entered the room.

A witness to the obvious, his glance fell away from the bed, unable to look at the unmoving outline which no longer heaved with the rasping of breath. Arthur now knew his beautiful Jenny was dead, yet he felt no apprehension or fear in the wake of what should have been mind numbing to the senses, because the specter before him presented an aura of reassurance, along with a tightening of the warm tender embrace.

"It's time for us to go, Arthur", she said. "You are no longer bound to the earth, for I am with you now, and will be forever".

"Go, go where my love", he asked? Not understanding, he pulled away slightly from the embrace to look at her with an air of ponder, but in return she smiled as only his Jenny could smile.

" Please tell me what you mean? Go where, my love?" He asked again.

"My dearest Arthur, unknown to all, while you tended me in sickness, you lay in a shallow within the snow covered field. Given to age, your heart could endure no more. Your passing, came before mine. From death you walked, and in spirit came back to me, and here you still are, my dear sweet Arthur. I love you the same as you've proven you love me. Be at peace now, and fret no more, for once again", Jenny said, "I'm with you".

Into the mirror he glanced, and Arthur saw a young couple held in each others arms.

Throughout the house the eyes of ancestors watched, and for a moment their eyes seemed to twinkle.

"Come children", the Reverend Shepherd said. "Come unto the flock.

Upon the four winds I came, and on them we'll make our journey home." With that, the shutters ceased their banging with their departure.

THE ATTACK
Casey Ponciano

"Mommy, are we there yet?" I asked as I looked outside of the window.

"Christian, I told you to sit down and be quiet," my mother said. I loved my mother. She was very pretty. I always thought she was the prettiest woman in the world. She had long brown hair and dark brown eyes. She was light skin and very petite and whenever she smiled at me, she'd made me feel great, no matter what I did wrong. She was also very cautious with me. I always thought she had eyes behind her head, because when I was about to do something wrong, she'd tell me to 'watch out' or 'don't do that'. Especially when I was in the van. I knew she kept an eye on me from the passenger rearview mirror. Sometimes when I knew she was looking at me, I'd stick out my tongue at her. In return, she'd stick her tongue back at me. We always played around like that.

But that day I didn't listen to her. My father bought me two Hot Wheels and I got off my seat to play with them. The van was very big to me because I was a small kid. Whenever I had toys, I would always roam around the van and play with them. "Mommy and daddy, are we there yet?" I asked again. I was eager to get home because of the road we were driving through. In order for us to get home, we'd drive through a back road called farm road 2528. The road was very scary and lonely because all the houses there were empty and cars hardly passed through it. And it made it worse because we were driving during the night. Home sounded like a better place.

"Christian, sit down and listen to your mother," my father said. I did as he told me. My mother was always easy with me, but when it came to my father, I listened. My father was a serious and very big man, not fat, but muscular. He'd always stayed in shape. Every morning he'd wake me up for breakfast because he jogged for thirty minutes. Even his voice sometimes scared me because it was a deep tone. He didn't try to scare me, but that's they way his voice was. Sometimes my friends never came over because of my father. He had brown eyes and he always kept his hair very short, as if he was in the military. My family always said I looked like him. I was proud of that.

"Okay," I replied. I sat right by the left window and buckled my seatbelt. You see we were driving back from Lubbock because we were grocery shopping.

We lived out in the country, or what some people called it, 'the boonies'. But I loved it out there because it was very quit and peaceful. The town near us was Abernathy, which was a small town north of Lubbock, and because it was small, the grocery stores there were expensive. But in Lubbock, they were a lot cheaper, and my parents always found a way to save money.

As I sat by the window, I looked out of it and up at the bright stars and the moon outside. The stars glimmered and I noticed the moon was an orange color. I always wondered how they stayed up there. They're always pretty to look at. Minutes passed and I got bored so I started playing with my Hot Wheels again. But this time I stayed in the seat. I didn't want father mad at me.

"Daddy, are we there yet?" I asked again.

"We're almost—," but he didn't finish what he was saying because my mother cut him off.

"David, watch out!" she yelled at him as she grabbed the steering wheel. The van jerked as we hit something. My head hit the window on the left side. My mother and my father grabbed the steering wheel and twisted it to the right. My father pressed the brakes and the tires screeched as the van was making a stop. The van swirled to the right side of the road and finally came to a complete halt. Good thing I buckled my seatbelt. We hit something, something big, but we didn't know what it was.

"Dammit!" my father said furiously. I knew he was angry. He made a fist and he punched the steering wheel. I didn't know if he was angry with me, or if he was angry because we hit something. I apologized to play it safe.

"Daddy, I'm sorry," I said.

"Christian, it's not your fault. I should have kept my eyes on the road," he said. That's one thing I loved about him, he'd always made me feel better whenever something bad happened. "Is everyone alright?" he asked.

"Yes. Christian, are you okay?" my mother asked.

"Yeah. My head is just a little sore from hitting the window," I said as I rubbed my head. I knew I would live. It was just a little bump on the head.

"Carrie, Christian, stay in here. I'm going to check what we hit. It was probably a coyote or a wild dog," he said.

"David, please be careful. What I saw was too big to be a coyote or a dog. Please be careful," my mother said. She then grabbed his arm and squeezed very tight. Dad looked at her.

"Calm down, Carrie. You're scaring Christian. Everything's going to be all right," he said as he gently lifted her chin. He kissed her on the lips and tried to make her feel safe, but the kiss didn't work. She was still scared. I smirked at the kissing because I thought kissing was weird, especially when my parents did it in front of me. "Now open the glove compartment and hand me the flashlight," he said. She did so. However, she was very scared that she had a hard time opening the glove compartment and nearly dropped the flashlight while handling it to dad. "Carrie, calm down," my father repeated again. I followed him with my eyes as he got off the van, except the only thing I saw was the flashlight.

It became cloudy outside, the fog settled in, and the orange moon and the bright stars were gone. It became extremely dark and the flashlight looked as if it was floating. "Carrie, I found what we hit!" My father's voice came from behind us. We looked toward the sound of his voice and we could only see the yellow light of the flashlight he was holding.

Mother stuck her head out of the passenger window. "David, what is it?" she yelled.

"I…I think it's dead. It's…it's not breathing. It looks like a dog, maybe a St. Bernard."

But, I knew it wasn't a St. Bernard because no one lived on this road and that dog couldn't survive on its own. Especially, dogs like that. Then all of a sudden we heard howling. At first, mother and I thought they were the coyotes that were out in the country, but the howling sounded a little too close. Coyotes are generally afraid of humans, but this one didn't sound like it was.

"David, please be careful!" mother yelled.

"It's okay, Carrie. I'm going to roll it over and see what it is." I heard him use all his might to move the animal. "It's… on… its… back." It had to be huge. "There, I moved it. It's-, oh my God!" He started yelling and we could see the floating flashlight fall to the ground. Then we heard growling and we heard struggling. Then we heard the sound of something tearing. "Carrie! Carrie! Get out of here—," he yelled, and then the yelling stopped. It sounded as if he was gurgling on something. I became very scared because the only thing I saw was the flashlight rolling back and forth and the yellow light colored with red.

"David?! David?!" my mother yelled. Except, he didn't answer. I started crying after the silence. I knew something terrible happened to him.

My mother started crying. She rolled up the windows from the van. Then she locked the doors. She checked them twice to make sure she locked them correctly, because she was trembling so badly. She tried to turn on the van, but the keys were not in the ignition. My father had taken them. I jumped to the front seat, sat with her, and closed my eyes. She hugged me very tight crying my father's name and rocking back and forth. I continued crying and I begged my mother that I wanted to go home.

Then we heard a growl very close. First it was at the back and then it was at the front. It was extremely dark to see what it was. The growling became louder and louder. Whatever it was came closer from both sides. I wondered if there was more than one. I never opened my eyes. I put my hands over my ears and hoped that maybe this would make the noise go away. I whispered to it, whatever it was, "Please, go away, please leave us alone." Then the noise stopped. Mother and I stopped crying. I thought whatever it was, was gone.

Mother then wiped our tears away.

"Christian, go to the back seat," she said. I opened my eyes and looked at her.

"Are we going home?" I asked as I jumped to the backseat. I was very scared and I just wanted to be in my bed, asleep.

"Yes Christian. I have to see daddy first," she said.

"No mommy," I said and I grabbed her arm. Then I noticed that there was pair of yellow-glowing eyes peeking in from the passenger window. "Mommy!" I yelled as I pointed to the window. She looked toward the window, but she did not see what I saw. The yellow-glowing eyes had disappeared. She then turned her head toward me with a questionable face.

"Christian what—." She did not finish her question. The noise of breaking glass stunned her. It came from the window beside her. I looked at her as she looked at a creature breaking in. She tried to jump to the back seat, but the creature swung an enormous claw through the window and grabbed her by the throat. It pinned her to the seat squeezing her throat tightly. She held on to the creature's arm and struggled with all her strength to get free, but she was losing.

"MOMMY!" I yelled as I tried to reach for her but she wouldn't move. "Christian. Chris—." Blood started pouring from her throat and she started choking when she tried to say my name. Finally she let loose of the creature's arm with her left hand and held her hand out to me, but it dropped like a puppet's hand of no string.

"MOMMY!" I yelled at her once more, except there was no answer. She leaned her head forward and the creature swung the other claw inside. It sliced the back of her neck and blood raged out. I looked at her again, but could no longer see her eyes. Her head was no longer there. The creature had torn it off. Bits of flesh scattered among the seat and then blood gushed out of her neck. She was dead.

All I could do was yell and cry. I cried for my mother and I cried for my father, but there was no answer. They were dead. The only things that I heard were the monsters outside as they growled and howled. "I just want to go home," I told myself, hoping that someone would hear me.

I sat in the middle of the backseat. I lifted my legs and hugged my knees to my chest. I held myself very tight and I kept crying for my mother and my father. I didn't want to believe that they were dead. I closed my eyes and covered my ears again. Then the noise stopped. There was no growling or howling. I knew they were hiding, but I needed to get out of there.

I opened my left eye first and looked around slowly. Nothing happened. Then I opened my right eye and looked around with both eyes and still nothing. I looked toward the front seat to see my mother's lifeless body, but it was not there. I slowly lifted my right hand and reached for the right door, then a creature zoomed at me with its glowing eyes through the window.

I jumped back to the middle of the seats as the creature pounded at the door with its body. I could feel the van rocking back and forth, as it tried to get in. It looked at me, snarled, and showed its razor sharp teeth. The teeth had stains of my parent's blood and the huge snout it had, had also covered in their blood. Saliva and blood slowly fell from the creature's mouth. It wanted me dead. I backed up to the left side of the van as the creature broke the window with its claw. I backed up all the way until I touched the left door. I crossed my arms in front of me and I held myself. I was very frightened. It's yellow-eyes just looked at me with hunger and then it made a deep growling noise. I then heard another window break on my backside. I yelled and I tried to run, but another creature grabbed me. I felt it's hairy arms as they prickled my skin. I felt a sharp pain on my left shoulder. I looked at my left shoulder and I saw blood as it poured down my arm. My left arm went numbed. I heard sirens and the creature let go of me. I looked toward the front of the van, and the last thing I saw was the red and blue lights. I fell to the floor and blacked out.

When I came through, I woke up in a hospital and I was in good health. The doctors thought it was strange of me healing so quickly because on the night of the attack, my left shoulder was severely torn into pieces. But when I woke up in the hospital, they were gone. I wanted to leave, but they wouldn't let me. They wanted me to stay overnight for more tests. They wondered why I was able to heal so quickly. I wondered that too? They also wondered why I didn't have an appetite for any type of food. I told them, I just wasn't hungry. I eagerly waited for the night to come. For some reason, the inside of me knew that when the night would fall, I would be hungry. Why did I feel like that? What killed my parents? I wonder what attacked me?

CAPTURED FREEDOM- PART ONE

Cassandra Marie Carlson

Introduction

I see this pen in front of me and I am compelled to write. I guess I always have been. I have this drawing to, a need to, write. But unfortunately, I only have it sometimes. This need comes only with opportunity and idea. When I have nothing to do but write. During classes, while a bright flash of lightning shoots across the dark sky and cuts off our electricity. I sit there in the dark with only the dim light of a candle to guide my pen to the paper. After that, I need no light to know what

I'm writing. An inevitable fantasy in my mind has been shouting itself out ever since I thought the idea up. But the thing is I've learned to ignore it. The truth is, my mind thinks up a new story every hour or so. All I must do is let them out. Open my fingertips and let the story flow out onto the page.

Captured Freedom

Here now I sit, again. In the dark, but by default. No storm has taken the light. It has left on its own. Chased out by the demons of the night, the ones that lurk around every corner, just waiting. They prod us to confess, give in, so that we must be stuck forever in the darkness, just like them. I sit in this small, damp cell smelling of manure and rotted flesh and wonder how much longer I can hold out. They bother me too, placing false memories in my mind to convince me that I did it. But I didn't. I see visions of beauty too though. Visions that come only from the remembrance of the light. Visions that soon will fade, and I will remember them only vaguely, as the remembrance of a toy I was fond of as child.

They've captured me here again. Trapped me in a corner like some dead rat, gawking at me. I suppose that's what we all are here. Trapped and cold…guilty alone, staring at each other from cell to cell. We stare and stare and think we're the only innocent ones in this hell hole of a place we ended up in, but really we're all innocent. Almost every one of us. But we do what we can to look guilty, because the real guilty ones will eat us alive if they know who we really are…what we really are.

I'm a dead rat trapped in the corner with only one way out…death. But I swore when I first got in here that I wouldn't wander that road. Naïve and brave, I walked among them like a hero, nay, a goddess of theirs. I wasn't guilty. And they all were. Like that light I once spoke of. Not only has it faded, but completely gone out now. Blown out like a weak candle in a howling wind. I thought love was something that could never be taken away, that would remain inside you forever, no matter where you ended up. Oh, once again how naïve of me. There is no love. Only emptiness. No feelings at all exist in this barren world that I now live in. No remorse, regret, or pain. I suppose that's the up side to all of this torture. No pain. Oh, how I remember pain, like a shotgun against your shoulder, it split through everyone, leaving no one untouched. The raspy, cold voice surprises me even now, after so long. No one talks here, with nothing to talk of. We only sit and think. And write, I write too.

The life sentence is upon me. Oh, how I pray to God that they give me death instead. Nothing could be more stolid than being here for eternity, too long to even imagine with the limited human mind. Eternally stuck, apathetic and dead, without contact to anything or anyone who isn't exactly the same. What I wouldn't give to be depressed. But I don't even have that option anymore.

My worst fear has become a reality. I have been sentenced with life. With this turn came the plunge downward. I have now fallen further than the depths of Hades. Satan tried to grasp my hand, but missed as he often does. A darker force pulls me downward now; something much stronger and wiser than Livid Lucifer. A force called life.

MONDAY 22ND JULY

Ceirion James Rees

"All the worlds a stage, and all the men and women merely players: They all have their exists and entrants"

(William Shakespeare)

Monday 22nd July 1996 I woke up at 6.30am to the sounds of my crackling radio, as I did every day. I opened my chocolate brown curtains to a day of grey. Everything was grey, the clouds were grey, the streets were grey, the hills in the far distance were grey, as far as the eye could see was grey. Even the faded reflection looking back at me from the window was grey, but then so am I.

You may know me already, I'm the strange man who lives in the street who calls the police to complain about the noise in your party or the man who keeps your Childs ball that lands in my garden. I'm a loaner, the person who you both despise and feel sorry for in equal proportions, the person who you laugh at and fear and the person who you just can't quite bring yourself to hate.

At 7.45am I got out of the car at my regular parking space, about ten minutes from the factory where I work. About five minutes in to my short journey I came to a road and waited to cross. I was standing next to a young man, he was about 23 and didn't look as if he was from the area, I assume a foreign exchange student studying at the local university.

We stood next to each other in silence, exchanging nothing more than a passing glance to each other's eyes. Then, I don't know if it was, maybe early morning tiredness, but he started to cross the road, seemingly unaware of the car speeding towards him to his right.

Without thinking I put my hand out, in less than heroic fashion, and stopped him. He woke up from his daze suddenly, shaking and breaking a sweat. I asked him if he was ok, he said 'yes' and thanked me in his broken English, and then as if we had never met we crossed the road and went out separate ways.

As I walked in to work that day I felt good, happy even. The more I thought about it, the more I realised I saved that mans life. I knew then, however, that this sense of euphoria would be short lived, and it was. Before the day was out I felt my usual self again. Lonely, angry and ever unhappy.

Thursday 30th January 2002, I opened my chocolate brown curtains at 6.30am to a day that was grey. Everything was grey, the clouds were grey, the streets were grey, the hills in the far distance were grey, as far as the eye could see was grey. Even the faded reflection looking back at me from the window was grey. I put on my new portable television to be met by the sight of the early morning news.

As I dressed quietly, a story caught my eye. I'm not really the sort of person who strays up to date with current affairs, so I couldn't tell you all the details, but I could tell it was about some situation or other that had been avoided, due mainly to the intense negotiations from a forging diplomat, the name of who I didn't catch, thought eyes that's looked at me from the small screen were the ones of the student I briefly met 6 years ago.

I've never considered myself a deep thinker, I wasn't very good in school, or did I go to university, but as I left my house that day and walked with the light winter sun shining on my face, I starred to reflect on it all.

My one action saved the life of a man who, in turn, may have negotiated to save the life of thousands. Of course what I did wont make the early morning news, it wont even make the local newspaper, but to me it felt better than that, it elevated me to a higher place where I had never been before.

Someone once told me that the world is like a jigsaw and we are the pieces. Some are larger than others, some seem more important, some take up the corners and some people just automatically look for first at the beginning of each new puzzle. Some pieces however, are small, pointless and get easily missed. Just fragments in the middle that receive little attention or thought, but are needed to make a complete image, and if just one goes astray it puts the whole picture in jeopardy.

I am the small piece in the middle that can be so vital. I wont win any awards, I wont get any recognition, but I can go forward in my everyday mundane tasks, in my everyday mundane life, knowing I've played my part and that I've made a difference.

Off course I'm still the strange man who lives in your street, but now I'm the strange man who lives in your street who's found his role and fulfilled his destiny.

DOUBTVILLE TO FAITH HAVEN

Clyde Mcdade

LEVELONE

Damon and Joel ages nine and ten, were playing their favorite video game called Doubtville to Faith Haven. "I want to start over! You're winning too much!" Damon had a habit of hitting the restart button whenever his older brother was beating him on the video screen. "I'm gonna tell mom! Why are you such a brat?" Joel asked. "All you do is hog the game and I have to sit here and wait a whole hour to get a chance to go again!" "That's because I'm good at this and you're not!" Joel said. This hurt his brother's feelings. Both had a problem with selfishness and sharing. Their mother had warned them about being a team and not taking each other for granted all of the time. They were on level one, which was one of the hardest. The longer the game the more difficult it became. Joel had to start over. He'd racked up a whole lot of points, but that didn't matter. "Hurry up!" Damon insisted. "You just keep your stupid hands off of the restart button!" Joel hit start and then it happened!

"Where are we?" Damon asked. He looked confused and scared. Joel didn't understand what he had done wrong. All he did was hit the start button and everything went black. "What did you do dummy?!" Damon asked again. This irritated Joel. "Could you shut your big mouth?" He kept looking around. The entire place was covered with blue grass, bright colored trees and bushes. Some had huge pieces of fruit on them. This made Joel hungry. Looking closer he realized something he couldn't believe. "We're in the game Damon!" "Are you nuts or somethin?!" "Look around! Doesn't any of this look familiar?" Damon turned his head in every direction and a sudden fear came upon him. Yet he still tried to deny it. "You're crazy! This is some trick…!" He stopped talking, because the ground shook! Then a growl deafened their ears! "Oh no, it's him!" "Who?!" Damon asked. "The Dragon of Doubt! We've gotta get out of here!" "How did this happen?" He stood his ground as Joel started running. "I'm not going until you tell me how we got here!" "I didn't do anything and you know it!" Joel said. A stream of fire landed close to Damon's feet. Joel grabbed him in the nick of time! The boys ran as fas as they could with the Dragon of Doubt on their heels! "You remember how this is played, right?" Asked Joel. Damon looked behind him. His eyes grew bigger than a saucer as the dragon gave chase. "Yeah! We're in Doubtville and have to get to Faith Haven!" The object of the game was to get from one town to the other or be lost in doubt for life, never fully experiencing God's blessings in your life, due to lack of faith. The Dragon's job was to hit you with his fire so that you'd begin to doubt that God could help you and weaken your faith.

"We're coming to the Cliff of No Return!" Joel shouted. At the bottom of this cliff were massive rocks! They had only one hope as the Dragon of Doubt spewed another shot of fire at them. The boys stopped in their tracks. "Hurry up and say your prayer or we'll be toast!" Damon yelled. Joel said a prayer of faith. Throughout the game, players made their way around by using scripture, prayer, and faith. This would allow them to escape any harmful traps and weapons of doubt and fear, as they went along. "He's only ten feet away!" Damon shouted. The Dragon was blue with orange spots on it's skin. Within half of a second, a large, shiny, and gold slide appeared in front of them! The Slide of Hope! Both boys lunged for it just as the Dragon of Doubt landed and shot more fire! "Whoooaaaa!" They screamed the whole way down, but were not out of the woods yet, when Damon saw the Dragon make his own slide appear three feet from theirs! "He's gaining on us!" Damon warned. "Don't be afraid, remember?" Just have faith in God all the way through and we'll make it!" Joel knew that they were in trouble. How could they consistently work together as a team when they'd been arguing with each other for months? Would their faith in God be strong enough? How did they end up inside this game anyway? All of these questions raced through Joel's mind as he and his brother slid to the bottom. In the distance they could see trees and bushes. Each were brilliantly colored with different types of flowers on them. Hitting the bottom, they rolled at least ten feet before comingto a stop on the yellow grass. Damon's allergies were no help. "Yaaaachu!" Joel got to his feet. Standing in front of them was the "ORACLE OF DECISIONS". This was a large, clear, floating screen that had a question on it with multiple choice answers. He knew that the answer sent them on to the next level. Summoning the many weapons they had as players, Joel called for the "Knock Balls". A bright, orange, fire ball appeared in his right hand he lunged it toward the Dragon! It hit him in the stomach, making Dragon disappear.

Damon continued to sneeze, but calmed down. The steps of another Dragon could be heard in the distance. "Help me answer this one Damon!" Here is what they read:

CHRISTIANS ARE TO LIVE BY:

A. FAITH

B. DOUBT

C. FEAR

D. SMARTS

Which one did they choose?

HER
Crystal Timbeross

The first time she saw him was in the 7th grade in the library. He was a year ahead of her, in the 8th grade, but that didn't matter. He had chocolaty brown hair, spiked with blondish tips, green eyes and he was tall. She didn't talk to him that first day, just crushed on him. Her and her friend Amy nick-named him Library Dude. That's what he was called until February. She was eating lunch on a B-day with her friends Marc, Rachael, Amy and a couple of others when he walked through the lunchroom going from P.E. She called him Library Dude and Michelle asked if she meant Donnie. She told Rachael she thought the one with spiky hair was hot. The next B-day Rachael was talking to her during Spanish and Rachael told her Donnie had asked about her. He asked Rachael who the hot blond was that Rachael was sitting with. Rachael told him and they set up a time and day for him and her to meet.

Next b-day he would skip P.E. and have lunch with her. He never made it, they tired a couple more times, finally Donnie had Rachael give her his phone number so they could talk. After two weeks Donnie asked her out, she said yes. They spent almost 2 wonderful months together. Spending all their time thinking about each other, writing notes, hanging out in the library during team time and talking on the phone until all hours of the night. Once until 4 A.M. Then during spring break, she did the unthinkable. She went to the beach with a couple of guy friends and kissed one of them. Donnie found out, they broke-up, and everything just went downhill. Still she sometimes thinks about Donnie, how he is, who he's with and if he ever thinks about her. She's in the 8th grade now, he's a 9th grader, a fish, at the high school. Maybe one day they'll talk again, see what happens. Yea, maybe one day.

MIRACLE FROM BEYOND

Dallas Cathcart

Kelly just couldn't shake that feeling; it was ominous and very strong. Like a large heavy blanket smothering her. She wasn't prone to putting a lot of stake in the paranormal, but she wasn't a disbeliever either.

It was strange little things happening, dreams, stomach feeling tight and churning all the time. She was feeling nervous and jumpy; it felt as if someone was in the room with her, watching her. Kelly had that deep gut feeling that she couldn't shake off.

The best she could do was try to put the feelings out of her mind, try to ignore them. Kelly sat in the bath relaxing with a hot cloth over her face. She liked the heat and the hot water made the bathroom like a sauna. Even relaxing in the bath she kept fighting the urge to look around. She couldn't help it she pulled the cloth from her eyes and glanced around the bathroom. Kelly jumped 2 inches as she saw something move in the fogged mirror. The shape was blurry through the steamed mirror, but she was sure she had seem something move. It was instant her heart was pounding in her chest. She jumped out of the tub snatching a towel from the rack and wrapping it around her. She was still dripping wet, she slowly peeked out her door into the living room. It was dark and seemed quiet. She tried her best to pierce the darkness; the light from the bathroom shed some illumination. It made long shadows and revealed nothing. After a bit she quickly scampered to the closest table lamp and flicked it on. Now she could see as the living room was now bathed in soft light from the lamp. She took a deep breath as she looked around and saw nothing and nothing was out of place either. She choked it up to her jumpiness and the odd feelings that were haunting her lately. Kelly's focus now switched to the wet carpet under her feet. She realized she was still dripping wet and she hadn't even dried off a bit. She headed back to the bathroom to dry off, but not before she took one more glance around.

Kelly got comfortable with her book; the fire crackled and snapped casting its warm light and warmth over her. She sunk back trying to forget the knot in her stomach, and the relentless nagging feeling of uneasiness as if some one was watching. She was starting to wonder about her sanity. She tried to concentrate on her book, to read and get engrossed in the fiction of her book. It was no use, she couldn't concentrate on it. She again looked up and around expecting to see someone standing there with her in her living room. Of course again there was no one, she put her book on the coffee table and got up and walked around a bit. She opened the fridge and got herself a glass of milk she was getting tired of this. She wasn't able to sleep and her nerves were frayed from jumping a everything. She walked back out to the living room and picked the book up off the couch. She sipped on her glass of milk as she headed upstairs. At the top of the stairs she all of a sudden got a shooting cold chill as her hands and body felt numb. The glass fell from her hand as she spun looking back down at the living room. The book she picked up was on the couch. She remembered distinctly putting it on the coffee table when she got up to go to the kitchen. Kelly couldn't move her eyes from the couch and living room. She felt nauseous as the realization hit her that this may be something more than her nerves or her imagining things. Kelly finally broke free from her frozen state and ran into her bedroom. She closed the door and leaned against it. She tried to catch her breath as her mind raced with all the new possibilities. Kelly began turning on every light and searching every inch of her room. Looking in the closet, her small bathroom, even under her bed. Finally she was satisfied and laid back on her bed staring at the ceiling. She realized she was in for another sleepless night.

She trudged around the hospital doing her rounds, trying to be as pleasant as possible. Kelly was exhausted. She needed a nap before heading to the children's ward. It was hard enough to deal with those young kids with their illness and some of them with terminal disease. Caring for them was rewarding but so hard to see. She wished many a time that she could cure all of them. Kelly didn't have kids but those kids in that ward were all hers. She did what she could for them and it broke her heart when she lost one. This was the price of being a pediatrician. On the other hand their smiles and strength they showed filled her with joy as well. It was amazing how strong those kids could be in spite of their pain and sickness. Even if one could be saved it was a great triumph.

This state of hers couldn't continue, she was tired and her nerves shot. This wasn't any good for the children. She thought they could sense her troubles as well and she needed to be strong and focused for them. Kelly laid down in the staff lounge on the couch for a quick sleep. She awoke about 15 minutes later feeling somewhat better. She stretched and sat up yawning as she shook the fogginess out of her head. She straightened herself up and got ready to continue her day.

As Kelly drove up to the front of her house that feeling returned, then she noticed the light on in her bedroom. She knew that she had turned it off before she left for the hospital. She took a deep breath as she unlocked the door and entered. It took a lot of pushing to get herself in the house. She turned and closed the door and locked it. Then she heard it, an eerie light laugh that seemed almost childlike. It seemed to come from nowhere in particular. She spun around looking for a direction. It happened again it was just audible and definitely sounded like a child's voice it wasn't deep enough to be an adult. "Hello" she called out tentatively, not really expecting an answer. She felt a cold shiver as she headed up the stairs. She saw the light on under her door; she slowly moved to it her hand grasped the handle. She was barely able to function as she gingerly opened the door. Her blood turned cold as she opened the door. In the corner sat a little girl her knees pulled up tight to her. She had her hands wrapped around her legs; she was about 5 years old. It was Jennifer, a little girl that had died in her ward a few weeks ago. Her fear slowly slipped away, the knot in her stomach started to fade. Now a much different feeling started to fill her. A concern and sadness started of overtake her as she stood staring at the little girl curled up in the corner.

Then the little girl looked up at Kelly with sad eyes and she spoke. "Please can I stay here, will you help me," she said the voice seeming to come from all over the room. Kelly felt some relief and warmth as she smiled back at the little girl. "Of course you can stay, and I will do everything I can to help you" she said. Jennifer smiled widely at Kelly with a look of happiness. Kelly didn't even think of how odd this was, she really couldn't help her. Jennifer was beyond any help she could give to her, but it didn't matter one of her kids from the hospital that she had lost had come back to her and she wasn't about to turn away from that. She looked at it as a miracle that she had been given.

A PORTRAIT OF BLACK VELVET

Danielle Ackley-McPhail

Sitting all day in a hard, straight-backed chair, Tammy fidgeted as she absently stroked the soft, stiff skirt of her black velvet dress. Occasionally, big people she didn't know would look at her and shake their heads, looking just like the silly plastic dog in Daddy's car, head bobbing around on a spring. It was hot and she was sleepy, so sleepy her eyes blurred. But she stubbornly looked around, determined to stay awake.

The room was full of chairs like hers, chairs and people and flowers. The people didn't interest her any more, with their dark cloths, pale faces and bobbing heads, they all looked alike. She was interested in the flowers though. Her Mommy loved flowers and so did she.

She couldn't see the front of the room, but there were so many flowers she could see them over the people's heads. They were so beautiful—so many different colors and shapes. She loved flowers. More alert, she amused herself trying to pick out the ones she knew. They were so mushed together that she had to concentrate extra hard to tell them apart.

Still rubbing her skirt, Tammy began her game. In the far corner of the room, in front of the old lady with hair the color of periwinkles, was a bunch of flowers every shade of yellow and orange. First she recognized Tiger's Lilies (a funny name for a flower with spots and not stripes,) then there were golden mums, which they always picked for grandma because Mommy calls her "Mum", and there were the ruffly white flowers that looked dipped in yellow paint—she couldn't remember the name.

Here eyes continued to move across the room and she silently named the blossoms she knew, until she noticed something odd; there in the middle of all the flowers was a big, beautiful box, all glowing wood and shiny gold. All the big people got to go look in the box, but when they turned around their faces scrunched the way hers did when Daddy or Mommy went away from her, which made her sad. The periwinkle lady was crying and everybody kept looking at Tammy, shaking their heads. She didn't like the way they looked at her.

Tammy was no longer interested in flowers; she looked at her skirt so she didn't have to see the sad faces. They made her want to cry to. Seeing her dress of black velvet and the purple-black stain on the hand that had rubbed it smooth, she thought of Mommy and wished she knew where she was. She would be mad to see Tammy's dirty hands, but she would wash them and hug Tammy to her waist so she wouldn't have to see the big people try to smile while they cried, their heads bobbing.

Her Mommy made this dress. She made it just for Tammy, with pretty white lace on the bottom and arms, and white ribbons and a sash. A tiny frown tugged at Tammy's lip. The lace and ribbons were gone, with tiny black threads left behind in their place. Daddy had said in a funny little voice that they had to; he said Mommy would understand. Tammy hoped so—she didn't want Mommy to be mad at her. She wanted Mommy now.

Looking around, Tammy tried to find her Mommy in the crowd. Up by the box was her Daddy, slowly turning around. Moving stiffly down the aisle, he looked so sad. She didn't like to see him sad. Pushing off the hard chair, she tried to go to him.

"Daddy?" Tammy's small voice wasn't even noticed in the hum of big-people voices. "Daddy? Where's my Daddy?"

Moving toward the big box, Tammy's lips trembled with each step. She couldn't find Daddy. No one noticed as she made her tiny way to the front of the room. She reached the pretty box and still no Daddy. Climbing onto the padded bar in front, Tammy peered in, curious about what everyone was looking at. Tammy was confused. Mommy was asleep in there, wearing her dress that she made to be just like Tammy's. Why was everyone watching Mommy sleep? Tammy reached in to caress Mommy's black velvet skirt. She looked so pretty.

"Mommy?" Tammy's voice quivered, without her knowing why. "Mommy, wake up."

As Tammy continued to rub the soft, stiff velvet, arms closed around her and held her tight. Looking up, she saw Daddy's face, red and streaming with tears. He was shaking with silent sobs. Closing her own brimming eyes, Tammy continued to caress both black velvet dresses.

THE PROPHET

Darius Gabriel Bugarin

Ariel began to work hard early. He gathered used bottles, plastics and even pieces of metals that can be sold to help his parents for their daily needs. He's not studying but knows how to read and write. In their place, his fellow-children are always maltreating him. They are spiting on him. They are throwing dirty water on him. Only Jasmine, who's the daughter of the Mayor is nice to him. After his tenth birthday, his parents noticed that he's walking while he's asleep. He's lying on his stomach and extending his arms sidewards. He also cried if somebody's dying, and if there are tremors or accidents happening in their place. He always said that it's the cause of human violence. His parents believed in him. Whatever his expectations are, he keeps them informed. His father made a small sign board placed beside their house to list all his predictions. Many have seen this but are trying to ignore this. Some are laughing and think that they are a family of lunatic. One day, Ariel had seen some of his fellow children. He came and talked to one of them to inform of his feelings and expectations. "Brother, I feel something about you. Please watch out all of your actions and be careful" he said.

But the boy just pushed him and laughed at him. The next day morning the boy was found drowned in the river near their place and they are blaming Ariel of what happened. Until one night, the people tried to burn their house. But the rain falls severely and the place was flooded. The following day, Ariel announces to the people the coming of a big disaster. But the people didn't believe him and mocked him, and stoned him. Two days later the earth began to shake and suddenly, the volcano erupted so violently that many people died. But then, they marched to the house of Ariel and believed that he's the cause of everything, and he deserves to die. The Mayor tried to stop them from marching but they pushed him away. Ariel's parents didn't want him to go out but Ariel said "Don't be frightened. Believe in me and I will be saved". Then he went out slowly, and looked above the sky.

He extended his arms sidewards, and blood was seen to his eyes flowing. Then he stopped walking and looked around the people. The time he closed his eyes, a lightning struck into the big tree and the people were shocked and fell down on the ground. Then their place becomes dark and at once, a light flashed down from the sky to Ariel, and was heard the voice saying: "This is Ariel. He is one of My prophets. Believe in him and you will be free from dangers". It was so silent, and then the people began to realize what they've done. They came forward to Ariel to ask forgiveness. They kneel down to him. But he said, "I am not God. Just believe me and all my expectations, and you will be free from all the dangers". Since then, the people believed in everything he's saying. But then he died but said, "I will be back, to continue the will of God".

GRANITE RIDGE

David Ferrier

I climbed with my brother Chris, up on Granite Ridge, close to the reservoir. We had already made our way through the forestry commission land and had begun the long incline towards the start of the ridge. The weather was good for climbing, cold enough to be comfortable without freezing. It was spring and the leaves had returned to the trees without anyone noticing.

That day Chris wouldn't talk about the war he had just come back from "Its not for you to know" he said. I think there was something he wanted to keep inside. I was only sixteen then and spent most of my spare time playing sports or fooling around with my friends. Wasting the evenings away until school finished for the summer. I couldn't wait to get away from it all.

We both loved the emptiness of the hills. The silence was so tangible we could almost feel it pressing on our skin. The hills had a way of leveling us. My father would normally have come with us but Chris had fallen out of favour. He had refused to defend himself against the rumours and to my father that was unforgivable. The rift had widened after mothers death and Chris's loss of faith in god." I can't believe in divinity after the things I have seen and done." His experiences had changed him.

My brother was an expert map-reader. He always seemed to have a good eye for our position and could work out the timings between points with a reliable accuracy. He always liked to point out prominent features and name them as we walked. I for my part had no sense of direction. My navigation skills inherited from my mother. She could get lost in her own garden. I kept close in behind Chris.

The sweet smell of the spring heather surrounded us as we followed quietly the mist of our own breaths. We both carried with us our rucksacks and walking poles to assist with the climb. There was little wildlife to be seen, apart from the occasional deer in the distance.

We rested together on the southwest slope. There was a wind blowing like a cold tin sheet sweeping over Arran to chill us. We ate in silence, bread and cheese with homemade pickle. We quenched our thirst with a shared coke. The fields below were strewn with a scattering of grazing sheep flowing away from us like a white tide. "Beautiful up here" Chris said.

I was the first to spot a hint of colour almost hidden in the tree line moving slowly towards the sheep. I pointed the movement out to Chris.

"What is it?" I asked screwing up my eyes to see.

"Fox I think "said Chris "After its dinner."

I watched with a morbid fascination as the fox darted from the tree line. A few moments later the white tide was tinted with red. "Jesus did you see that?" I asked turning away. Chris stood up, pulling on his rucksack " Its only nature" he said, "A Fox doesn't have regret or guilt to deal with, it's lucky. We turned our backs on the scene, looking only ahead of us. Trying not to think of what we had just witnessed.

To keep my mind on happier things I told Chris all my news. I hadn't had much time alone with him since his return. I told him all the stupid boyish stuff he hadn't heard for a time. How the football teams were doing, what girls I was chasing and how things were at school. He enjoyed listening to all my stories. I think they reminded him of a time when things were simpler for him.

We reached our camping spot just before the evening sun dropped below the summit. We laid our sleeping bags out on the flat ground. The air was noticeably cooler as we prepared ourselves for a night under the stars. We buried ourselves in the bags as a protection from the evening chill. The two of us lay there, our faces showing. The drawstrings pulled tight around our heads so that our whispered voices sounded muffled. Then, with my stupid young mouth that didn't know any better, I asked him about the rumours. Were the stories true? Did he refuse to fight? Could it be possible my brother was a coward? I just let it all come out, everything. I told him about all the things people, our own friends, had been saying. He just lay there and listened not moving or answering.

I leant over, turning my face towards him " Are you scared of dying Chris, is that it?" " Am I scared of dying, that's what you're asking, am I scared of dying?" he said, "Am I scared of dying?" Then he began to cry silently in a way I haven't seen since we were children "I'm sorry, I didn't" I said "I'm sorry"

He carried on crying unashamedly, the tears flooding from him like a child. I lay there in the darkness, ashamed of myself, watching the stars paint themselves on the night sky. After what seemed like long time his crying stopped. We both lay in silence, just letting the world turn. "It doesn't matter, none of it matters" he said " It's beautiful up here, I'm glad we came, I really am." I heard his breathing deepen as he drifted into sleep. I began to feel alone on the hill. I had a feeling in my stomach, a tinge of regret and something else. The loneliness that boys feel who are forever afraid of becoming men.

INCIDENT AT THE UGANDA MUSEUM

David Tumusiime

After failing to get the job, Ernest Muhindo did not want to return home immediately. He went to the Uganda Museum, which was nearby but found it closed. To pass time, he decided to explore the museum grounds.

He had not gone far when he saw a girl. The girl was seated on one of the museum ground benches under an ageing umbrella-branched tree alone. There was despondency in her face and he guessed that she must have been waiting for someone who had not turned up.

Ernest knew he was not handsome at all but the girl's own deficiency in that matter gave him confidence as he approached her.

It was nine o'clock in the morning in June. The sun was not yet in ascent and there was a cool breezy freshness in the air, the dew only beginning to lift from the grass.

"Good morning," he began. May I join you?"

"Good morning."

He sat down. The wooden bench creaked.

"Such a lovely morning! Why is a beautiful girl like you all alone?" "I am not alone. I was thinking."

"About him?"

"About how it is so nice to be alone."

He was almost completely sure she was a Muganda. She had a broad nose, flat like a pancake. Her whites were a muddy brown, her pupils' black. She had accentuated them with a dark-black eye shadow so that they reminded him of painted ghost masks.

"I love you."

She was startled. A workman passing behind them turned and looked at them before hurrying on.

"Hmm..."

She was pleased.

"Isn't one woman enough for you?" she asked.

"My name is Morris Ssozi."

"You're not a Muganda! With that height, thinness, and that nose?"

"My father is a Muganda, my mother is the one who is not a Muganda."

"I am called Lillian Nakabuye."

She had good breasts, the kind he liked. Not too big, not too small; solid and firm, the tits outlined in the chequered gold nylon blouse.

"You know, beautiful Lil', I can't stay too long. I have got to get to work. How can I see you again?"

She looked at him for the first time. He was not much of a looker. In fact, he was downright ugly. His head was horizontally long with tufts of kaweke, the hardest type of hair to comb. He had almost no chin and all his upper jaw teeth projected over the lower ones and slightly the very thin lips. But he had the most wonderful eyes, laughing eyes full of life's wisdom. Maybe, just maybe…

"I am waiting for my sister," she said.

"Do you often wait for her here?"

He didn't look poor. He was well dressed. Probably worked in an office. He would be a first for her. She wouldn't have to lend him money all the time like she did Abdullah. Maybe, just maybe…

The sun was in the clear blue sky. Beyond the barbed wire fence around the museum, taxis hurtled by full of people. Monday. A new day. A new week.

She got up. He stood up.

Abdullah was not coming. She knew that for sure now. He had all her year's savings.

"Am going," she said. Hesitated. "Am going to see my aunt."

How would she pay the rent this time? Would the landlord accept having sex with her instead? She was going to leave Abdullah.

"Yeah, I've to go also. Where're are you passing?"

He had to get the suit dry-cleaned before returning it to Maurice. Maurice had said he was going to use it soon.

"Mulago road. It's far."

Was continuing at university really worth it? Kampala was overcrowded with unemployed multiple degree holders. The chance Maurice was offering would not wait. Maurice and his gang of thieves had already robbed three banks clean without injuries to any in their group. Maurice had told him they needed another member for the heist they were planning. He could do both, couldn't he? He needed that money. He couldn't continue at university without it without a job to support himself adequately, could he?

"I am passing a bit of that way. I'll escort you, not all the way. I need to exercise my legs before going back to the office."

They sauntered out the museum grounds gate. Walked down Mulago road talking. "More Ugandans should visit this place," he said, "If they do and did, repairing the museum wouldn't have to wait until the museum curators begged enough donor funds."

"But there is nothing to see in this museum. It hasn't changed in so many years. The exhibits are always the same."

"Maybe, but if these museum guys were clever, they would make people see them differently each time. It is all about how you see, like love and the eyes of the beholder."

"But that would be creating a deliberately misleading impression."

"Yes. But it would draw in sightseers who would bring in the money. That's the only important thing." "They would be disappointed when they were being lied to. Then they would not have to come back. The museum would have a worse reputation."

"With money it would put in the stuff people want to see. The people would then have to come back!"

"That maybe too late if they are already convinced the museum only wants to con them."

"I don't agree."

"Would you return the second time after being conned?"

"No."

"See!"

They were at an intersection. She was going to Mulago, he was going to Nakulabye.

"So we meet here tomorrow?"

"I'll be here."

"So will I."

"I really like you. Come, please."

"I will come."

"Will you really come?"

"Yes, I will."

But they were lying to each other and they both knew it. They knew neither of them would come. Or maybe one of them or both of them would come but not at the appointed time but a little later out of idle curiosity and a hopeful hopelessness.

WHO WAS FIRST: EGG OR HEN?

Denise-Annette Langner-Urso

A very long time ago all birds gave birth to baby chicks without laying eggs. They did not need to brood. For the hens of course the pregnancy often was onerous, as today it is for human mums. The hens often felt bad. Their belly, of course, grew with every day of the pregnancy and they walked around as little inflated balls and they gasped for air while becoming thick and thicker.

To tell the truth the hens felt underprivileged, for sometimes they could not even visit their friends because of feeling to bad.

And when the little ones were born the mother hen cared for them while the father went out searching for worms for the little family had to be fed. And often the roosters went out with their friends while the hens cared for the children.

In these old times all the animals were friends and the birds had no animals. Their nest was directly built on the ground beneath a bush as a protection against the sun. The birds were mourning about their destiny and became more and more discontented and cross. It didn't last long and the hens did not want to give birth to baby chicks any more.

The Creator heard about it sooner or later and he was very angry about the birds. One warm summer evening he called all the animals to a meeting and notified them what He had decided because of the common dissatisfaction.

"From this day on until eternity", he said, "you will not give birth to chicks anymore as you did it until today. From now on you will lay eggs and you will have to breed them. I gave you wings to fly and you better look for secure places on top of the trees. Both, hen and rooster should take turns in breeding and caring for food, but it is your decision if you will do it like that. You will have enemies from now on who I will give them appetite for fresh eggs. I never want to hear any more mourning from now on. Now get out of my face, you discontented creatures. I will never make any changes again. " These were His words and he sent them home.

The birds laughed, but soon they had to learn the hard way. Many animals and even men did like their eggs. Even if a nest was built on the highest trees the egg-lovers would find it. And the birds of prey even poke down and took away the chicks as food for their own brood.

Only one of our birds was artful and freed himself of the whole work of bringing up children- the cuckoo. Another punishment for the discontented birds. But the Creator punished him as well. Since then the cuckoo was no more able to feel love or marry, while He fit out other birds with an incredible great love and big hearts for unwanted foreign chicks. And that is the explanation for the question on which was first- egg or hen.

CHILD'S PLAY

Denise Cassino

10:45 pm, June 15 - Somewhere near Longbow, Colorado. "Just piss on it, will ya! Let's go! My old man will kill me if I'm late again."

"Okay, okay, hold on," Josh yelled, unzipping his pants. The stream sizzled and crackled, sending up a plume of smoke from the waning fire. Josh looked up as he squeezed out the last few drops. Stars twinkled against the black backdrop of the summer sky, and he held his breath against the smoke wafting upward. Kicking the smoldering logs with his boot, he zipped his pants and turned to run for the car. "Wait up," Josh yelled as he saw the old Toyota begin to roll away. "Wait up, you guys!"

He glanced back and saw a spark pop from the fire as he jumped in the back seat and felt the car lurch forward. Empty beer cans lay next to the campfire, shimmering in the moonlight while a gust of wind swept sparks and smoke swirling upward into the night sky.

12:30am June 16

I awoke in the dead of night to the wild cacophony of wind chimes thrust into action by high winds that buffeted the tall pines and rattled the new leaves of the aspen trees. A loud bang told me the sheet of plywood had been slammed to the deck by a mighty gust. I rolled over and fell back to sleep.

3:15pm June 16

Now I stood on the uppermost point of my mountain property on a high ledge overlooking the distant Continental Divide and all of the dark green forest in between. An angry, black funnel of smoke billowed upward at a frightening speed moving toward our house, which, along with those of several friends, lay in its path. "I'm heading back. I want to start packing, and I've got to get a hold of The Dunns and The Randalls" I said, turning toward my four-wheel, all-terrain vehicle.

"Look, the fire just jumped the ridge. Oh my God, look at the flames. Oh, God!" my husband David cried, his voice carrying the fear that clutched at my own throat. "Come on, let's get out of here. This thing's moving fast."

I turned the key, and saw David jump on his own four-wheeler parked right behind me. I turned toward the narrow dirt path that would take us back to the main road leading home. I squeezed the gas lever and rolled quickly along, ducking under low-hanging branches and leaning into turns. When we hit the main road, the ruts worsened, and we veered to avoid them. Lack of rain had left the terrain dry, but the winter run-off had made our dirt road choppy and difficult. I looked back and saw David was close behind, but I only saw the car bearing down on my front fender when I turned back to the road and rounded the curve. I hit the brakes and jerked the handlebars harshly to the right, hoping David wouldn't rear end me. The ATV skidded into the hillside leaving my heart pounding wildly in my chest while the squad car slid to a stop in the dust just inches away from my leg.

"Sorry, ma'am. Are you okay?" the State trooper asked tipping his brimmed-hat back, his eyes wide with concern. "Didn't expect to see anyone along here." "I guess I'm okay. You were going kind of fast." "I apologize, but the fire's got us jumping. If you live up here, you need to evacuate. We're clearing out this whole area. Fire's moving quick and the high winds are spreading it. Anybody else live back this way?" "Nope, just us and we're heading home to pack. Thanks for the warning." He tipped his hat and drove on past me, looking for a place to turn around. I shook my head, thinking how close I had come to being squished like a bug on his windshield.

We entered the house and David made phone calls while I emailed friends whose houses might be endangered. The phone rang incessantly as I started packing valuables. I had never made a plan for this occurrence and scratched my head wondering where to begin. David walked in the room with furrowed brow and said, "I don't think we should leave." "Are you crazy? We just watched that fire eat a mountainside in one bite and you want to stick around for more?" "No, I'm just saying, let's just see how this thing plays out. I'd rather have some control than sit down in Denver, wondering what's happening to this place." We mentally flashed on the sweat and labor we'd poured into ten years of refurbishing our old mountain lodge and couldn't bear to see it all go up in flames. I shrugged.

"Okay, let's wait awhile."

We packed a few boxes and poked down an egg salad sandwich. Climbing back on the ATV's, we headed for the ridge. Dusk enshrouded the forest, wrapping itself around us like a gray cloak. Our headlights cast narrow beams on the darkened pines and low scrub oak and berry bushes as we carefully made our way through the woods. Smoke rode the air and the wind whipped our hair as we climbed upward.

Now the fire had engulfed the mountainside and was moving south along the far ridge. Loud booms echoed through the canyons as pine trees exploded their boiling resin, spraying it in a thousand directions, spreading the fire with it. We peered through binoculars, watching houses burst into flames as the furious fire moved indiscriminately across the range, consuming all in it path. The winds gusted around us, sweeping the flames southward along the river. Headlights flashed between trees as cars and trucks pulling horse trailers wound their way out of the forest toward safety.

We arrived home around ten o'clock and had 17 voice mails. Most of our mountain friends had evacuated and were calling to say they were safe. Flipping on the news, we saw the fire chief calling for smoke jumpers and slurry bombers to try to contain the inferno which had already consumed 8000 acres and with them, 14 homes. The fire was completely out of control, with little hope of speedy containment or heavy rain, and new spot fires were cropping up here and there. We dropped into bed, saying an extra prayer. As I lifted my head from the pillow I could now see flames in the distance. We slept restlessly and rose early to the sound of airplanes overhead.

10am, June 17

The air was thick with smoke, and we could taste it in the backs of our throats and smell it with each breath. The fire had spread and now billowed black and ominous in two directions. Small aircraft buzzed the hot spots dropping their liquid loads of red slurry in a wide swath as they passed low over the forest. We rode back to the ridge and found blackened devastation where a proud pine forest once stood. Smoking quietly on the smoldering hillsides lay the sad remains of burned-out homes. We drove slowly toward the main road and found our friend, John Randall, and his son, Josh, tying down the load in his truck.

"You going?" David asked. "I'm staying, but I'm sending Josh with his mom down to Indian Hills until it's over." He looked skyward and said, "Must have been dry lightening, or some jerk with a campfire. If the wind turns and whips up that canyon, we're done for. What about you guys?" "We're staying. I guess after today, once you're out, you stay out. They're setting up checkpoints at all the main intersections. I just feel better staying up here. Keep in touch and call if you need help."

We waved as we rode off. The other houses along the road were closed up, horses taken from their corrals and vehicles gone. No dogs barked as we passed. We were eerily alone on the mountain. As we neared home, our dogs barked and, we saw the flames had jumped the creek road far below. If the winds turned north, we were directly in the fire's path.

****

As we drove off, we didn't know that Josh's heart was aching and the taste of fear was thick in his throat.

"Dad, Dad, I need to tell you something."

John turned and looked into his son's frightened eyes.

"What, Josh, what is it?"

Tears welled up and broke over the rim of Josh's eyelids, rolling sadly down his cheeks.

"Dad, I think we might have started the fire."

He bent his head and held his face in his quivering hands.

****

The winds died down and the slurry bombers kept at it. For two days, they roared overhead with small, single-engine guide planes leading them into the blaze. It was like stories of the London blitz with the steady buzz and drone of planes passing every five minutes followed by the helicopters hauling huge buckets suspended by cables, which they dipped into a small lake at the base of the fire. Rain followed and the fire smoldered for a couple more days while the fearlessly dedicated firefighters worked round the clock to douse the last of the hotspots.

11am, June 21

We drove out together after six days. As we hit the main road, we saw a sheriff's vehicle waiting to turn onto the road. In the backseat sat Josh Randall and two other teenagers. He bowed his head and averted his eyes from ours. Behind the sheriff's car, his parents followed. We nodded an acknowledgement of their sorrow, knowing the hell they were about to endure was only second to the hell that had rained down on our valley. I reached over and took David's hand and squeezed, knowing we were lucky to have survived intact. I thought of all the families, the homes, the pets and wildlife that did not survive, the lost beauty of our forest, and I couldn't help but remember the last line of the movie, "A Bronx Tale."

"The choices you make today, affect you for the rest of your life." If only that lesson were not so difficult to learn.

RAIN

Donald Edward Kidd

As I drove up and down the lazy Missouri hills, I daydreamed to pass the time. I also counted the dead animals along the roads, which wound like a roller coaster in the western part the state. I was heading home from school in Kansas City to St. Louis for the weekend, although it was only Thursday.

I daydreamed about Jennifer, my first love, who had dumped me earlier in the week. I vowed never to go near a blonde again. I couldn't concentrate on school so missing Friday's classes was not much of a sacrifice. I ached in my gut, thinking at one point I was seriously ill, until my roommate told me it was only lovesickness. Four hours is a long time to waste driving across the state with nothing to do. I thought about how to win back Jennifer, though deep down I knew I couldn't. In a fit of anger I called her a terrible name. She had seen my dark side and ran away crying. I was crying myself a few days later when it dawned on me she was not coming back. She didn't take long to get over me. I saw her in the library a few days later with a nice looking, athletic guy. I was just average looking, average looking with a bad temper.

It wasn't long into my daydream when it started raining. It rains a lot in Missouri. The farmland doesn't look so nice when it's pouring outside and you're down. My only plan was to just keep going: keep driving, keep going to school, and keep breathing, until I could function again. I didn't want to give up my peace of mind for the sake of a girl. My mother taught me that, before she went on to a better place, dead at forty from cancer she got from breathing asbestos fibers where she worked. I sure missed her.

Fifty miles west of Columbia, which was near the center of the state, I saw someone along the side of the road. They were soaked. I slowed down the car, and as the brake lights came on the stranger broke into a trot towards me. "Hi, I'm Kat," the stranger said, getting in and huffing slightly from the run, "You don't know how glad I am you stopped."

"You're a girl," I replied.

"Well, yeah, I'm glad you noticed. You're not a pervert are you?" She leaned closer to the door.

"I might be if I were in the mood. You want to get out?"

"No. You don't look too bad." She looked me over as I pulled away from the side of the road slowly, then she relaxed. I sensed it more than saw it. I stared at the monotonous road ahead.

"Do you have a name?" she asked.

"Yes."

"Are you going to tell me your name?"

"Yes."

"Today?" she asked, playing along, like a child asking twenty questions.

"Yes."

"Does it start with a 'Z'?"

"Yes," I continued in an emotionless monotone.

"Is it 'Zebra'?"

"Yes."

"Is it "Zipper?"

"Yes."

She looked in the back seat and saw my duffel bag.

"Do you have a towel in there?" she asked seriously.

"Yes."

"Can I use it to dry off?"

"Yes."

She reached into the back and dug around until she found an old gym towel. I hadn't the heart to tell her how many months it had languished in my gym locker, soaked in stale perspiration, until I threw it at the locker door one day and it stuck to it like a piece of cooked spaghetti. I think I washed it since then, but who could remember things like that.

She toweled off her long auburn hair, like a goddess stepping out of the shower after a marathon love-making session. At least, that's what I imagined. Jennifer and I hadn't got that far when we were so rudely interrupted by my caustic immaturity.

"You look like a hippy," I offered.

"I prefer the term 'flower child'." She continued to dry her hair, which had been partially covered by her jacket hood. She looked out at the scenery. I glanced over and saw a mole just below her lower lip. She reminded me of Anne Francis, a gorgeous blonde on TV, I'd had a crush on. She had a mole, too. "There's not much to look at in Missouri," I ventured forth, feeling guilty for not being better company. "Look," she sighed, turning to face me, "I don't want to go into my whole life story, just because you gave me a ride. Not that I don't appreciate it, I do. It's just that..." "Forget it," I whined, a little too indignantly, immediately feeling bad. "Sorry, my girlfriend broke up with me this week. I'm in a rotten mood."

"You shouldn't let someone else dictate your life."

I looked over at her and tipped my head a little, my standard look of disbelief. "All right," slipped out of her mouth, as she gave up on conversation and rested her head back against the seat. She closed her eyes.

Stirring from sleep an hour later, she sat up groggily. I had enjoyed watching her sleep for that hour, even entertaining a fantasy or two about her. I wished she was at my school and she was my girlfriend.

"I'm too old for you," she said, more awake than I figured.

"Shit, I'm eighteen," I replied defensively.

"I'm twenty. That makes me much older than you."

I gave her my tipped head look again.

"I'll admit you're cute, in a goofy sort of way. Mind you I wouldn't go out with you, but maybe a younger sister, if I had one."

"We don't even know each other and already you're breaking up with me," I complained.

"Yeah, but you were thinking about me weren't you?"

I blinked. That was my answer. I had absolutely no ability at lying so I stared ahead, always the careful driver.

"It's okay. You're a guy. Eighteen-year-old-guys are hornier than a barnyard owl."

"How much is that?" I queried.

"Pretty damn much!" she laughed and I couldn't help cracking a smile.

"I bet that hurts," she said, acting motherly all of a sudden, catching me off guard.

"What?"

"When you make that weird face. I think some people call it a smile," she teased.

I responded by shaking my head.

"You liked it, admit it," she smiled and her mole turned upward a little, following her mouth. Her teeth were beautiful. I noticed things like that.

"Yeah, yeah," I said, as matter-of-factly as I could, although I didn't feel as calm as I acted.

"I used to like sad men. I don't any more." Gone was her smile, replaced by a forlorn expression I hadn't seen before.

"I'm not sad. I'll get over it," I defended, although I didn't have any conviction in the statement.

"It's your life. I just think it's silly to spend all your time regretting."

"A week isn't a lifetime."

"But you see, it is. That's the whole point. A week turns into a lifetime. Then, you look in the mirror and your life is almost over and you realize you've been feeling sad your whole life, missing out on important things in the process." She sounded like my mother, just then, saying something only my mother would say. I pulled the car over on the shoulder and stopped. I began to cry.

She didn't say anything, just rubbed my back and neck and shoulders while I let out five years of pain, pain at knowing my mother was gone forever and I was alone in the world. She handed me the old gym towel and I laughed, while still crying.

"What's so funny?" she asked, looking at me like I was keeping a secret from her she ought to know.

"Nothing," I answered, while sniffing as the torrent subsided.

"Just breathe," she coached, making exaggerated breathing motions as if teaching me.

I laughed again at her seriousness. She feigned insult by pulling her hair back and making a disapproving noise. But I knew she was pretending, and she knew I knew.

"You are much older than me," I said, as complimentarily as possible, emphasizing the 'are', as if it were some great revelation from ancient Egypt that I'd discovered single-handedly. I pulled back into the road.

We didn't speak much after that, not because we didn't want to, but because we were comfortable in our silent bonding, our comfortable cocoon of mutual respect. God knows I didn't respect women, only chased after them as objects of lust and fantasy. I learned from Kat, that that was not good enough.
As I pulled up to a bus station, she knew what I was doing; making her take a bus so she wouldn't have to hitchhike. There were a lot of perverts out there. She meant something to me now and I intended to do some little something to keep her safer. "Write to me at school, okay?" I asked, choking up a little. "I had a brother. He died when I was ten. He would be just like you if he'd lived. I'm sure of it."

She touched my cheek gently where a single tear had begun to creep slowly downward, then slipped away, clutching her bag and a scrunched up piece of paper with my school address on it.

I watched as she took a seat near the window and looked out at me, staring at her long gone brother. Then, the bus pulled away, churning up the gravel on the roadside until I could no longer see it, but only smell the strong fumes of gas, which hovered like an invisible mist.

It started to rain again.

OUR RAISON D'ECRIRE

Duncan Reeves

Last Wednesday, I sat before a computer completing Anybody's Patriot, the project that I had strived to finish on and off between college lessons for the past six months. I was part way through the final chapter when a voice said behind me;

"What's that, Dunc-Star?"

"A story," I replied.

My friend, Henry, looked over my shoulder at the number of pages I had written. "108 pages? (Fill in various expletives - use your imagination, you won't be far wrong)!"

Pretty soon the small group of people around me knew I thought I was an author. Then someone asked a question. "Why did you do it? Is it something like an English project?"

"No."

"Enrichment."

"No, I was just bored one day and started to write."

That's not exactly true. I do write when I'm bored, but there are also a lot of other reasons. I mean, I could read a book, or play on the Playstation (except that's in my brothers room at the minute) but instead I choose to write.

Well; why?

I think there are a few reasons, all of which are present in some form or other on Nicestories. I think the most morally correct and fulfilling is to write about one's own experiences, to share your own good times and bad times with the rest of the world. Mmm, interesting. I can't say I have ever written like this, but I assume that it will be relatively easy. You have everything laid out in front of you, you just need to transfer it to paper. But why do this? It may be that the feeling you experienced was a one in a million, and that you wish to make others feel like this.

It may be a warning to others, not to get one's self into such a scenario and feel quite as crappy. Or it may be some psychologists trick (I don't do psychology, so don't blame me if I'm wrong); isn't it said that talking about a traumatic scenario is better than trying to forget about it? As I said, I'm using my imagination to explore this area.

Probably the second reason is the opposite of this. Maybe one would write about a scenario that one would wish to find one's self in. I wrote a story like this once, a long time ago. In your fictitious world anything can happen to your fictitious self. Save the world? why not? I haven't anything better to do this afternoon! James Bond look out, here comes Duncan Reeves!

Unfortunately it can have a habit of getting corny quite easily if you write about the wrong thing. Reading it back to yourself, it sounds too cheesy to publish on a site like this, wouldn't you agree? Most first person stories are literally ego boosts (but for a few exceptions), and basically one cannot live on dreams of a better life.

Now we proceed to the motives that are a little more detached. One can write about a possible scenario, such as a potential conflict, for instance. No? What about a certain type of hero? or establishment? or villain? principal? anything. I find this as the principal home of fictitious writing, because there is no limit to where you can go. You write a hero into a conflict in a mystic land with a special task etc etc.

And why do this? Perhaps because you become the character. It is true, even if you are writing a series of television programs, a novel or just something on the back of a bus ticket. Your hero becomes cool, unstoppable, handsome as hell, agile, everything you want to be. Yes it is another dream but it has the potential to become the great adventure of another man, and that makes it better when you read it back, because even you are left with the thought; 'Bloody hell! I need to become this cool.' Is it still a dream or is it now motivation? Your character becomes an ultimate version of you and you strive to become your character. Plus, on the side, you get to explore a range of different possibilities - the future, the past, what will happen if..., how will someone react when... - and other people get this insight as well.

All in all, there seems to be a common theme. Have you picked it out? Our raison d'ecrire is to share - experiences, insights, visions, feelings, anything that springs to mind. You hear talk of how human nature is dominated by selfishness. Is it possible that with this spirit of sharing, the writing community has broken away from this maxim?

Writers are a breed unto themselves in my view. Writing and creativity is the one pastime that can be done and thought of at any time in any place. It expands your thought processes all the time, as opposed to something slightly more restrictive like sports. Sure, it is bad for your health, but in moderation it can be the most rewarding of activities. Writing is a drug - overdose and you'll suffer the side effects, but take just enough when you need it and you can fly with the birds.

Definition; a writer. One who writes stories, poems, articles and other literary works.

Job specification; a writer. Must be imaginative, smart and with the ability to express themselves perfectly. Must be capable of complete lateral thought - so lateral it bends back on itself. Must be versatile, dedicated, and a touch of eccentricity wouldn't go amiss. Offer open to anyone who can string two words together.

How many people do you think could take that up? Personally, I'm left with the impression that writing is a tool for the selective elite, but then it depends on what you like. Really, all it takes is the last point to be a writer, does it not? Could it be that there is a writer in all of us that is hemmed in by a person's misconception of what a writer must be? A misconception founded on observation of the writing community?

Such a shame.

What is there left to say? Write! Write and be free! Explore the avenues of your mind! Journey into darkness with your trusted companion, your faithful weapon and your pen ready to write it all down! Charge straight back out again, your foes vanquished, you mind expanded, your pen dry and your paper filled with the stories of countless adventures and emotions that no one will believe. There are over six billion people in the world today. No matter how unique you think you are, you can only be so unique. There are people out there who are you in a different scenario. Write for them. Write for the joy of writing! Write simply because no one has written anything like it before! Write because you think you can do a better job than what has been done! Find your own raison d'ecrire and don't stop until you too are one of the selective elite, and you'll find we're not quite as selective as once you thought.

Adventures, exploring, romance, emotions you have never felt before, all of these and more stand before you, more even than the selective elite can identify. Do you have the courage to step forwards and take them in your stride? Do you think you can free yourself from this world, experience the joys of a lifetime and bring others with you? Anyone can. As with every good hero, you start at the start and you work your way up to the point of international bestseller, and then you'll know - when you hold the Booker Prize for Best Book - what it feels like to save the world, or be loved by someone you really do love.

You can't get the prize unless you're in the game, mates. Write! You won't stink forever!

Sorry, I must dash. I've got a couple of magical kingdoms to save with the steel of my sword, and there's one of them nuclear bomb thingys I have to disarm, and at the end of all that I've got to go and romance the most beautiful girl on the planet. Oh well, a hero's lot is never done, eh?

Heh heh, give me five minutes!

A MAN ONCE A MACHINE
Dylan Skriloff

There once was a man. A short stupid man, bald headed to the maximum. He used to play the orangutang to the guillotine, meaning he loved to go shopping with his wife. Bald headed, he would buy three times the laundry to wash, just to watch his beloved wife three times over wash the same again laundry/ wash. Three times Three is nine, and this is how many times through they would go, two times into the dryer, three times into washer, each load and in. And so this went on, and it was a most splendid love affair, until one day later that same day he met an even fairer finer girl.

This new girl would often times find her finger fried with the fine wine of a newfangled automobile. In other words she loved to feed the geese. And so they went everyday with their bag of wonderbread deathbread, and theyd feed the geese until one day, one ended up dead. Nonetheless, the two did wed, but most sadly on their nuptial day came a villain and with a blade, he split her chin down to her waist, and as she bled he scooped out her insides with a spade. That was certainly a very sad day. The man cried three tears and slumped away.

And sad he was four years and three, for none knew who the villain be, but all was cleansed when within his reach came the answer of his long sleep's wish. For the policepersons found a brand new clue, and guess who came all dressed in blue. It was his old first wife, and he still adored her still, she came and forgave and gave him a bag with a DNA sample and said... Lets do some laundry.

Dirty laundry indeed, and they riled in greed, and sweat and vomit and created a swamp within it to mail it to mom, it would have to be real nasty and green and contain the spleen of a human machine. A stupid robot, dead from birth onward, wrapped in paper, pussing the death of a tree, wrapped in paper, and afraid of everything that never could be. And upon a bloody mattress, they reached for silence and were delivered a message.

"Life is not for the squandering, nor is it for cramped spaces, or only laundry. Just calm down and open yourself, just calm down and open yourself, you are alive, you are real, and you do not need to play this game anymore. You do not have to die this way anymore. You are the real thing, you can fly through a heaven within and never stop to retrace your steps, for stepping through love is like stepping through your very own steps, and noone will know whos you or whos who, for everything is there, and there is only one thing to share and only one thing to do. And thats you."

And so they were touched, and in splendor would walk, never again to hurl a curse or judge a stupid head, and they walked and they touched and they would open ones brain and crawl inside and open again, and it continued forever and soon all death was abolished, and everyone floated on a massive curtain of air, that was golden but white and shined in a light a million times brighter than light. And it went on forever, and it never ended, and if only we could all feel that way RIGHT NOW.

LIFE IN THE SUN

Erma Hernandez

She woke up from the anesthesia with a sudden alert of hysteria. "My baby! Where is my baby?" she cried and screamed as she tried to remember where she was. She heard the sound of a woman's voice saying her name softly and asking her to please wake up. Finally, beginning to understand the woman's request, she opened her eyes and knew instantly where she was. She had just come back from surgery; the surgery that had determined her baby's demise.

They rolled her back into her hospital room as she grasped for air, still sobbing uncontrollably. "My baby is gone," she whispered repeatedly with a look of panic and pain across her tired face, as the nurses hooked her up to an IV and took her blood pressure. She looked around the room, with her tear-flooded eyes and realized she was alone. He had left her during her time of need, when she needed that love she had known with him for so long.

"Jade, sweetie, here is some soup. You need to eat. As soon as you look and feel better, we will let you go. But, until then you've got to rest." The nurse spoke as she moved the food tray to Jade's chest. "If that is the case, I'll have to stay here forever", Jade thought to herself. At this point, she could not see herself ever being able to feel better. After all, she had lost the two greatest loves of her life.

The nurse left shortly after making sure Jade was strong enough to feed herself. Jade sat quietly in her stiff hospital bed playing with the chicken broth that sat in front of her chest. Wide eyed and scared, Jade could not help but think about Steve and little Kaleb or Kayla- whatever her child should have been born. Just a week earlier she had had it all, a wonderful boyfriend whom she declared her hero and a beautiful child tucked away in her little belly. Now it seemed that was lifetimes away. She began to cry softly and couldn't help but wonder who she was and if she was going to ever know again.

With her head down, and her shoulders sulking, she felt a gentle hand touch her right foot. Her mom stood at the end of the bed, smiled and then asked how she was doing. Jade looked back down and continued to cry. Her mom lightly grabbed her foot and went to sit in the chair that sat at the side of the bed. Jade sat there, wanting to speak to her mother, cry to her mother and ask her to please hold her. But, there was a barrier and it was as if Jade was almost afraid to speak.

They sat alone in silence for what seemed to be hours. Jade lay in her hospital bed, eyes closed, thoughts racing. She tried countless of times to fall asleep, in hopes that she might never wake-up. Her mother sat in the chair beside the bed watching silly court television shows, trying not to laugh at the class of people brought onto the show. The sounds drumming from the television were distant in Jade's mind. The only thing she could hear was the sound of Steve's laughter and the sounds of her weeping intertwined. Ironic, isn't it? She thought as she desperately tried to piece her broken relationship together trying to make sense of it.

After minutes of selfishly thinking about the failure of her relationship with Steve, she remembered the amazing being that once grew in her tummy. She moved her hand from her side and laid it flat on her once bulging stomach. For almost an instant she had forgotten why she was even at the hospital, and why her relationship had ended. A sudden wave of guilt flooded her heart, remembering that is was all her fault. She was the one who cried, she was the one who yelled, and she was the one she stressed out her body enough to kill her incredible creation. A voice continued to whisper in the back of her mind, "It was you. This is all on you", long enough to make Jade believe that she was the one to blame and that an innocent life was on her hands.

A while later, her thoughts and inner arguments had led to not even wanting to think any longer, so she finally drifted off to sleep despite her fears of dreaming. A little while later she heard a familiar voice telling her that she needed to wake up now. She slowly opened her eyes, and for a moment she considered her living nightmare to actually be a nightmare, and it would no longer torment her young soul. Then, she turned her body around and saw a nurse with a silver tray carrying pills, needles and a cup of water. Her living nightmare was continuing and hope had quickly escaped her body. "Jade, you're ready to go home", the nurse spoke while hastily sticking needles here and there and shoving pills down Jade's throat.

Blankly looking into space as the nurse man-handled her feeble body, Jade couldn't help but think. She wondered where her home was and if she was ever going to find it. In the past week her life had fallen apart. The laughter that filled her soul, the happiness that shown through her eyes, had suddenly disappeared without leaving a trace of where it had gone. Every breath she took was once for love, hope and faith. That was a time when she believed in life. It seemed that reality was now suffocating her and there was nowhere and no one she could turn to for fresh air. She couldn't help but ask herself why it had to be her and why she was being punished for being an optimistic.

As soon as the drugs were settling into Jade's system and taking her into a 'happy place', the nurse instructed her to change her clothes and that she could finally go home. The nurse and her mom helped her from the bed and left the room as soon as they saw that Jade was stable. As she was getting her things together, she felt her purse vibrate. At first the thought of a moving purse terrified Jade, but then she abruptly remembered that it was her cell phone. She reached into her pocket and pulled out the jiggling phone. She looked to see who was calling and saw that it was Steve. She hesitated for a moment to answer the telephone. Then realized who was calling and who she still loved. She decided to answer the phone.

"Hello?" she answered in a dazed voice. Steve replied with a simple 'hey'. "How did everything go?" he asked, almost sounding concerned. "I woke up from the surgery crying for my baby," Jade answered in hopes for a sympathetic response from the love of her life. "Oh, how sad", was what the boy who once would die for Jade's love, would say. "Well, I just wanted to see how everything went. I'll talk to you in a few days to see how you're doing." There was a long pause, "you there, Jade?" Steve asked. Jade wanted to ask him the same thing, but with different meaning. "Yes, I'm here. Okay. Um, I'm sure I'll be fine and, yeah, I'll talk to you in a few days." There was another pause as tears began to fall from Jade's eyes. This time her sobs were silent, for she would not let Steve know he had broken her heart. "Alright, well I'll talk to you later then. Bye", Steve said, not knowing what his insincerity was doing to the girl he once cared for.

Before he could hang up, Jade spoke up. "Steve?" He answered her with an irritated voice and told her that it was time for him to go. "I know. Can you just do one thing for me?" "What's that?" he asked. "Tell me you love me. Please? Even if you don't anymore. Just lie. Please? It'll make me feel better." She couldn't believe that she was presenting her vulnerabilities to him so openly. But, at this point in the day- and her life, there was one thing she wasn't confused about, and that was her feelings towards him. Steve answered quickly; "Don't do this, Jade, not today or ever again". Her tears began to flow heavily and her cries grew a little louder, as she heard him hang up the phone.

She sat at the edge of the bed. Her eyes were closed and her thoughts were at a halt. The only thing racing in her head was the sound of Steve's voice as he said "….not ever again." The thought of moving on without him devastated her and she felt as if she had nothing else to live for. Staring blankly at the wall in front of her, she had an abrupt flashback that caused the tears to stop rolling down her already stained face. She blinked rapidly and lifted her tired body from the bed. She continued to dress and as she put on her gray draw string pajama pants, a small smile came upon her face.

She walked over to the window, tugging the shirt of Steve's she planned to cuddle in on the way home, over her head. She peered out the small window that seemed to give the hospital room life. She saw the bustle of common day life as people of all races, sizes and ages crowded the incredibly busy Los Angeles street.

She looked up to the sky, to the sun and the clouds, and for an instant it seemed as if the Sun was only shining on her. Squinting her eyes, she embraced the warmth and ease of the sun beams that gave life to every living thing on Earth. For a moment, she felt as if it was giving her all the life it had to give. And without shying away, she excepted it, letting the warmth flood her soul and begin to birth a new hope that had once lived deep in her spirit.

She continued to smile as she walked away from that window and started to gather her things. She turned back around to the small window that the sun shone through, letting life into the hospital and into Jade's heart. She whispered "thank you". She wouldn't ever be able to describe that sudden wave of enthusiasm, but she knew she'd never let it leave again. And that was enough inspiration for her to begin the long journey of recovery.

MOUSETRAP MADNESS
Floriana Hall

When a teacher assigns an unusual homework project, it can sometimes create havoc with the whole family. That's what happened to Shelley, a fifth-grader who was one of the top students in her sixth grade class. She mastered reading, math, English, social studies, and all the rest of her subjects. However, designing and building a car was out of her element.

The assignment for the whole class was to make a racing car out of a mousetrap. The teacher wrote that she hoped everyone would have fun with this project, and they could use objects found around the house. Parents were required to help.

Unfortunately, it was anything but fun for Shelley, an only child, and her parents. Neither parent was mechanically inclined. Her mother could wire up a VCR or cable, but her dad really knew nothing about building anything, and declined helping with the assignment. He didn't even own the necessary tools.

After purchasing the mousetrap, they tried to find wheels, axles, etc., around the house. They searched and searched the whole weekend. Of course, there weren't any. Shelley called her grandma and she suggested that they buy a wooden car kit, for neither grandma nor grandpa were handy with tools, either.

Shelley's Mom bought the kit. They put the mousetrap and part of the kit together, but their improvised car wouldn't roll, let alone race. They couldn't figure out how to attach the string that mobilized the car. Shelley decorated it with lipstick and various decals and was prepared to turn it in the next day, regardless.

After arriving at school, her best friend, Leah, showed Shelley her car, which raced along smoothly. You see, Leah has two older brothers, one of whom helped her create it. They found all the equipment around their home. Shelley inquired of Leah, "How did you get the string attached to make the car race?" "Here, I'll show you," replied Leah, and she remembered exactly how her brother attached the string to propel the car. She fixed Shelley's racing car and 'Voila,' it was rolling along smoothly, also.

While Leah was checking out Shelley's car, the teacher passed by and remarked- "That's a good looking mousetrap car, Leah."

Leah answered, "This is Shelley's car, Mrs. Watson."

Mrs. Watson gave every student an extra day to perfect their particular mousetrap car. The race was held two days later. Shelley was thrilled when her car won the first heat. However, Leah's car won the next one. The over-all winner was a boy who was handy with tools and had made race cars for his Scout troop with the help of his dad.

Shelley did get an A for effort and her unique design and was satisfied. Her mom and dad are hoping she won't get any more similar tasks for homework.

DOMINATION

Honor Alisha De'Mandoren

One

They were dead. Not two hours ago she had laughed with them over breakfast and planned on what she would do during the next ball. Would she be able to dance this time? *I will never see them again.* Sitting at her balcony windows she hugged one of her bears to her tightly as she watched the rain slide down the panes. Tomorrow she would be fifteen. Papa had complained that he would have to marry her off soon because she was becoming an old spinster. She had laughed and protested that fifteen was not old.

In a few days, I will marry. Would you have wanted that Papa? I know that you had planned for me to marry Alexander. Would you have married me off so soon?

Rocking back and forth she held her bear and watched the rain as it slid down the panes.

"What do you mean 'marry'? The chit is barely fourteen."

Fantel took another firm grip on his temper, trying not to cosh his twenty-four year old son. He had never struck the boy before, even when he had needed it. *Like now.* "Alex, I know that you don't want this, but I made a promise to her father years ago that the two of you would marry. Besides that, she is actually fifteen and will be a ravishing beauty in two years. All that I ask is that you marry her now and give her the chance to become a good wife to you."

"*All*? I'm not even twenty-five! I have another three years before you can leg-shackle me to anyone. You gave me your word on that!"

"The situation has changed." Fantel said impatiently for the fourth time. "She is alone now, orphaned. You would be able to care for her."

"Oh? And what do I gain from this marvelous wedding? Some scrawny-faced brat that will cry over the smallest thing?"

"That is enough! I am your father, and you will obey me or as God is my witness I will thrash you within an inch of your life."

"You?" A sneer of contempt twisted the young man's face. "You've never hit me."

"Perhaps I should have. You've been spoiled dreadfully Alex. Any decent man would—"

"Decent? Now I know that you've gone loonies. I'm a scoundrel, remember father? Not to mention a libertine, a rake, a blackguard, a drunkard. I'm even a gambler. Do you want to know how much of my inheritance I've lost today?"

Lord Fantel, Viscount of Pemberly, lost all patience with his son. Grabbing both lapels in his hands he raised the slighter form of his son until he dangled a foot off the ground and shook him. "If you don't marry her, and treat her well, then I will stop redeeming all of your debts. That includes the ones to your mistresses. Do you understand?"

The bloodshot blue eyes—his mother's eyes—widened in panic. "Now wait a minute—"

"Do you understand?"

There was no hope for it. Alex swallowed the rest of his arguments and choked out "Yes."

"Good." Resisting the urge to throw his son against the room he lowered him to the floor. "Now go get cleaned up. She'll be here for the ceremony in four hours. Even you should be able to look presentable in that amount of time."

Celeste tugged nervously on her gloves, adjusting the fit over each finger carefully before starting the procedure all over again. It was the only aspect of her appearance that she could fidget with. She was wearing a demure gown of blue silk, and while silk was very beautiful and soft it also wrinkled quite easily. Her abigail had given her firm orders to touch the gown as little as possible. The same went with her hair that was—for once—done in ringlets that spilled over her shoulder. She rather thought that the blonde curls over the light blue made her look older and more mature. *Perhaps my new husband will think so too.*

Finally, they arrived. Celeste managed to contain her impatience as the footman came and opened the door, offering a hand to help her down. She took it gladly, for the shoes that she was wearing were *not* designed for comfort. The high heel in the back made climbing in and out of carriage a hazardous venture. Smiling at him in gratitude she gathered her courage, squared her shoulders and walked up to the house. Before she could knock it was opened by the butler. He looked so much like the *beau ideal* of a grandfather she relaxed slightly.

"You are Miss Harrison?"

"Yes. I am here to see Mr. Fantel." There, that had sounded quite confident.

"Of course. If you will follow me?"

She handed him her bonnet and gloves before following him obediently into the drawing room. There she finally saw the man that she was meant to marry.

He wasn't overly tall, but far from being short. She noticed with delight that he had the same shade of blue eyes that she did, but there the comparisons ended. Black hair cut in the latest fashion, a solid build that didn't—quite—look like muscle and a sullen twist of his lips. By no means could she claim that he was without appeal, but from the set of his face he looked more like a schoolboy being reprimanded than a groom on his wedding day. She curtsied to him but received only a curt nod in acknowledgement. At that brusque gesture her heart sank. *He doesn't think that I am old enough. He's only marrying me because he has to.*

The rest of the afternoon passed in a haze. Looking back she barely remembered exchanging the vows with him before she was swept into a waiting carriage, facing the man that she was married to. London had passed before her sightless eyes, yet she dare not look anywhere else for fear of her gaze landing on her husband. One look at his black rage had convinced her to remain silent. Not daring to even glance at him she clenched her gloved hands together and wept silently.

They rode on for eternal minutes before Alex thumped the top of the roof with his cane. "Stop here!"

Obediently the carriage pulled over to the side of the street and stopped. Climbing laboriously to his feet—the brandy that he had consumed earlier still was affecting his judgement—he stumbled from the carriage and straightened his waistcoat. With a loud sniff he ordered curtly, "Drive on."

The two drivers immediately exchanged startled glances. "But my lord—"

"Are you deaf? I said drive on!"

The tears came harder as they pulled away. Celeste didn't bother to lean out the window for a last look at her husband. As far as she was concerned, she never wanted to see him again.

She knew that he was coming. Lord Fantel had written and told her that his son had experienced a change of heart and was coming to reconcile everything with her. She didn't believe it for a minute. After four long years of marriage of not seeing—or even hearing from—him, she knew that it was a lie. So when the door to the library burst open she did not leap to her feet but finished the last stitch in the embroidery and raised her head calmly.

Alexander had expected a number of things, but the vision of his wife framed in firelight was not it. *My God, she's beautiful.* His eyes ranged hungrily over her, taking in every detail from her honey-kissed blonde hair to the delicate slope of her neck and the sight of her matching blue slippers that peeked from underneath the skirts. Then he caught her gaze—had any woman had such large blue eyes? —and froze. "Celeste."

"Well at least you remember my name. That is something. You even remember where your country estate is—which is nothing short of a miracle. Or did your father remind you where it was?"

Her tart words snapped him out of the spell of her beauty. Frowning severely he stepped inside and slammed the door behind him. "You have no right to speak to me like that. I am your husband."

"No, not really."

His whisky ladened brain took a moment to decipher that. "You were a child, Celeste. Did you really expect me to bed you?"

"You could have at least stayed with me. I had just lost both parents. I didn't need to lose a husband as well."

The face that many women in the past had praised turned ugly in rage. "Stop. I don't want to hear another word. I'm here now, and ready to make you my wife in fact. Now, come with me."

"No."

"What did you say?"

Setting the embroidery hoop to one side she stood to deliver her words coldly. "I said no. You are familiar with the word, are you not?"

All thoughts of forgiveness were wiped from his mind. He would take her, and then she would see that he was not going to play games with her. "You arrogant little whore, if you think that I am going to—" He stopped abruptly as a cocked dueling pistol appeared from behind her skirts.

"I should warn you that I am an excellent shot. And at this range—what would you estimate that it was, five feet? —I am hardly able to miss." Celeste kept her tone exquisitely polite as she raised a brow in query. "Now, you were saying?"

For the first time in his life Alex restrained his temper. "Put down that gun."

"And let you rape me? Tsk, tsk. I'm afraid that won't do at all."

"I'm your husband. It wouldn't be rape."

"I'm not willing to go to your bed, wife or no, so yes actually it would be rape."

A horrible suspicion dropped into his brain as he stared at that gaping muzzle. "You knew that I was coming, didn't you?"

"Of course."

"Then why in the devil did you stay?"

"Just one reason." Gliding to the desk without dropping her gun from his chest she turned a sheet of paper for him to see. "This. An annulment for our marriage."

"You want me to sign it, I suppose."

"Quite frankly, yes."

Alex stared at her, this girl that was his wife. No, not a girl but a woman. A woman of fire and spirit. Never before had he seen such a creature but he was married to her. And he refused to let her go. Pride dictated that much at least. "No, I don't think so. I want you too much to sign that thing."

"You mean that you are letting your sex dictate your actions."

Alex only leered at her, determined not to be cowed behind her empty bravado.

Celeste saw the shift from fear to smugness in his eyes and groaned. *Why can't he make anything easy?* "Very well. Let me put it in a different way. You have five seconds to sign this or I will shoot."

"And kill me? Nonsense. Not even a woman could be that stupid. You would be hanged for murder before the week is out."

"Who said anything about murdering? As I have already said, I am quite an excellent shot and at this range it is rather hard to miss. Which shall it be *husband?* The leg or the shoulder?"

"That is quite enough from you. I refuse to be threatened in my own home—"

Celeste overrode him by raising her voice slightly. "No preference? As you wish." Taking aim she calmly fired at his shin.

Alex didn't feel anything for a moment. That respite lasted as long as it took the ringing to leave his ears. Then a flash of pain hit him before his whole leg started to burn. Screaming shrilly he collapsed on the rug, clutching the bloodied hole in his leg. "I don't believe this. You actually shot me."

"Of course I did. I am a woman of my word. Now, are you going to sign or do I have to put another bullet in your shoulder as well?" She fervently hoped that he would regain his senses. The sight of all the blood on the carpet was making her feel queasy.

"You're mad. A raving lunatic."

"Perhaps. Do you need a pen?"

Alex stared at her, but was not going to press the issue. She had already demonstrated that she was not to be pushed too roughly. He accepted the documents with a trembling hand and scrawled his name across the bottom line.

"The bottom sheet as well, if you please."

Casting her a black look he flipped the first page over and signed that one too.

"Thank you." Carefully she edged closer to him and picked the documents up before retreating to a safer distance. "Now, I would suggest that you have someone fetch a physician. You are losing a good deal of blood."

"Curse you." Alex gritted out. "Where do you think that you're going anyway?"

"As far from here as possible." Giving him a mock curtsy she swept regally from the room. The footman, primed by the shot that he had heard earlier, already had the door open and the carriage waiting outside. "Is all of my luggage aboard, Jeremy?"

"Yes, milady."

"Not anymore." She corrected cheerfully. "It is plain Miss Harrison now."

"Yes, *ma'am.*"

Laughing her approval she bounded down the steps and into the carriage. As the carriage lumbered down the winding drive she cast one look at the moldering estate that she had lived in since she was little more than fourteen. "Farewell, dungeon. And may we *never* meet again."

SAYING GOODBYE TO UNCLE RICKY

Ian Stuart

The five F4 Phantoms came over low and slow, dragging a curtain of thunder behind them. They were in a tight arrowhead, with a gap off the leader's starboard wing- the missing man formation.

As the thunder faded, the top sergeant of the honor guard barked an order. Three volleys rang out in the misty air. It was time to say goodbye to Uncle Ricky.

They invited me back afterwards to the officers' club for beer and sandwiches.

The base commander gripped my arm.

"He was a great guy," he said, "Ricky Haven was my boyhood hero. He was a real aviator. Hell- he was the reason I joined the service."

"Thanks," I said, "That's good to hear."

The colonel took a pull at his beer.

"You know him well ?"

I shook my head.

"To tell you the truth he wasn't my real uncle. My old man met him years back and they became buddies. I met him a few times when I was a kid."

The Phantom boys started kicking up a bit of a ruckus at the back of the room, building a pyramid of beer cans. "Excuse me," said the colonel, "I got to have a word with those boys. They're staging back to 'Nam in the morning."

If my old man hadn't piled his Cessna into a mountainside two years before, then things would have been different. But I was Uncle Ricky's sole heir. Not that there was much to inherit-a bungalow, the lawyer said, and about fifteen thousand dollars. Not much for a retired Air Force colonel.

I stayed overnight in a motel and went out to the base next morning to look over the bungalow. It was a hundred yards away from the end of the active runway. The air was heavy with avgas and burnt rubber. As I walked up to the front door I could hear the Phantoms winding up on the flight line.

Inside it smelled of old age- back rub, shaving soap, and that sweet smell old people have. The sitting room was neat and bland- pastel shades and anonymous good taste. Uncle Ricky must have had an interior decorator in to fix it for him. The bedroom had nothing but a steel frame bed and a service issue cupboard. I opened it. Headache tablets and a bottle of Zantac.

Then I went next door to the den. This was where Uncle Ricky had lived.

There was a big tv in one corner and a worn leather recliner. The walls were covered with photographs- Uncle Ricky in the cockpit of an F86 Sabre, Uncle Ricky standing by the mainwheel of what looked like a Dakota. There were plenty of books too- mainly ornithology. It looked like he had a particular interest in hawks.

It was mid-morning by now, and hot, even though the air conditioning was on. I was feeling hungry, so I went through to the kitchen to see what was in the freezer. He hadn't left much behind- a tub of frozen yoghourt and one of those zip up freezer bags.

I knew the moment I picked it up that there was something wrong about it. It was somehow too square and heavy to be edible. I took it over to the table and unzipped it.

I wasn't surprised that Uncle Ricky had a gun. There are plenty of Air Force officers who "forget" to hand in their side arm when they leave the service. But not many of them keep a Model 1898 Mauser stashed away with the pizzas and the frozen peas. I mean, this is one big gun for a start, with the sausage shaped grip and this square magazine. The other thing is- this gun is really old. It was going out of style when the First War broke out.

I unclipped the magazine and worked the action. It was a touch stiff, but every surface had a thin film of oil. Oh- and the magazine was full-Uncle Ricky wasn't taking any chances.

I turned to the other stuff. It looked like documents and photographs. I found a pilot's license in the name of Frederick Richard Haven. The young guy in the photo had lines at the corners of his eyes, like he'd been staring into the sun too often. The license said he'd been born on December 12th 1894 - that would be about right. Uncle Ricky had been about eighty when he died. But there was something about the date that rankled. He wasn't born in December- he was born on April 21st. I remembered that because it was my dad's birthday. They used to send each other jokey cards every year.

I carried on looking through the pile.A wad of fuel vouchers made out to Rittmeister Mail Lines and dated 1923; a shot of some early rocket plane with a white paint job and stub wings. Some guy called Chuck had scribbled his name on the back. One thing really puzzled me. It was just a plain white postcard on which someone had scribbled " Yoo Too huh, Ricky ?" It was signed by someone called The Skunk. More photos- taken out east- with Asian guys standing next to a pile of sacks with a C46 in the background.

Then I found the medals. They were just stuffed into a plastic wallet- a couple of Iron Crosses, and a neat little Maltese cross in blue and silver enamel. Where had he come across stuff like that ? I spread the whole lot- photos, documents - out on the table and tried to make sense of it. Where was his flying log book, for example ? That would fill in some of the gaps. It was like having half the pieces of a jigsaw puzzle.

Maybe it was the hum of the air conditioning. Maybe one of the big tanker jets came over at just the wrong time. But I never heard the door click open, never heard footsteps across the sitting room.

"I think you have found the material I require."

He was standing in the doorway, a middle aged guy in a rumpled tan suit, carrying a briefcase. He wore those half glasses on the end of his nose like professors do. He looked tired, like he'd just got off a long flight.

"Who the hell are you ?"

"I am the librarian of a...government agency, Those documents

concerning your uncle are a national resource. It is my job to take possession of them."

"Got any ID ?"

He looked at me pityingly. "Who do you think I am, Mr Patterson ? The tv repair man ?" While I stood there, wondering how he knew my name, the little guy went over to the table and started gathering all Uncle Ricky's stuff together. He snapped open his briefcase. He had a banana in there, and a packet of what looked like walnut and apple sandwiches. And a Browning 9mm automatic.

"You can't just steal this stuff !" I said, "I'm calling the cops !"

"Phone's cut off," he said, without looking round.

My hand moved towards Uncle Ricky's big Mauser. The Librarian caught my eye. "Now that," he said slowly, "Would be really silly. All this stuff is going to Washington. It will be dealt with there by a very senior government official - we are talking National Security Advisor here- and he will reach a decision. That will be communicated to you in due course." His mouth twitched in a parody of a smile.

"Would you mind handing me the gun ? Pick it up muzzle first, if you don't mind"

The Mauser disappeared into his briefcase, along with the medals. He snapped it shut.

"Thank you for your help, Mr Patterson. Sorry to have disturbed you at a time of family grief." And he was gone. I heard the front door click behind him. I went over to the window. He climbed into an anonymous Black Ford and drove off.

I sold the bungalow in a week and flew home. Nothing happened changed my job and moved house. The little guy in the tan suit began to fade in my memory. Sure, there was a story there- but there was nothing I could do to uncover it. The guy in the suit had taken all the evidence.

Eight months later I got the call.

"Mr Patterson ?"

"Who is this ?"

"We met last summer in Florida."

I knew his voice straight off.

"What do you want ?"

"Your Uncle Ricky"

"Yes"

"We have a decision. Doctor K looked over it on one of his peace shuttles. We need to meet."

We met in an anonymous hotel room. This time the suit was grey. He still had the glasses perched on the end of his nose. He pushed a piece of paper across the desk.

"Sign this please."

"What is it ?"

"An agreement to keep your mouth shut if we return your uncle's belongings.."

"OK"

"For twenty five years."

"You trust me to keep quiet that long ?"

"If you don't- then we'll know where to come looking."

I signed the paper. He put it in his briefcase. All the stuff was there- the photos, the medals, the Mauser. The Librarian leaned back in his chair. "Ok," he said, "I'll tell you the story. Lieutenant Colonel Frederick Richard Haven was one of the greatest aviators of all time- and a US intelligence agent for over forty years."

"I thought he was ...just a pilot.."

"He was - one of the best. Started in the twenties running a mail line across the southern states. It was tough in those days- little single engine biplanes with no radar, no ATC- the three other guys in his company crashed and burned."

"What about the war ?"

The Librarian fanned out half a dozen photos on the table. Uncle Ricky and various fighter planes- except they all wore either the swastika or the Japanese meatball.

"Test flew captured enemy aircraft."

"And after the war ?"

"He was one of the first pilots to join Air America. During the Korean war he flew electronic reconnaissance missions over the north. Then he hit the big time."

The Librarian put another photo on the table, like it was a winning card. It showed a sleek black jet with long, thin wings. "Uncle Ricky flew the U2?"

Then I remembered the card- "Yoo Too huh Ricky ?" "Ricky Haven flew the first mission over the USSR in 1952. We didn't know squit about what was happening over there in those days. That guy brought us the crown jewels."

He gathered the photos into a neat pile.

"He flew four missions for us. Took off from Turkey and landed in Norway. Damn near three thousand miles. Then Francis Gary Powers got himself shot down and we had to close everything down- especially your uncle."

"Why him especially ?" "He was German. Think of the implications. The USA send a German to do their spying for them. The Cold War would have frozen solid. Hell, they might even have gone to war over it. They were crazy enough in those days." "But that was years ago," I said, "He came to America with my dad just after World War One. They were immigrants together."

The Librarian shook his head. "Not after. During ." "I don't understand."

The Librarian took out the three medals and the Mauser and laid them on the table. "How did he come by these ?" "I don't know."

"He earned them." He picked up the little Maltese Cross. "Know what this is ? This is the Pour Le Merite, awarded by the Kaiser himself to soldiers who showed the most conspicuous gallantry. Rick Haven was a member of the Imperial German Air Service. He was the very best. Shot down eighty Allied planes- then saw which way the wind was blowing and decided to defect. He made contact with an Australian intelligence officer- your father. And on the 21st April 1918 he flew across the lines and landed twenty yards away from your father's command post. It was that easy."

"But what about the Germans ?" "Your father faked his death. There were plenty of corpses to take his place. A whole heap of publicity- post mortem- funeral- photos dropped over the German aerodrome the following day.." "I've just realised," I said "The 21st April was Uncle Ricky's birthday."

"It was- in a way-" said the Librarian, "It was a new start, anyway. We kept him under wraps for a couple of years but he was working for us from that time on. Forty years a spook. Not bad huh ?" "He snapped his case shut and stood up. "All this is yours, subject to the agreement you've already signed. Any questions ?"

I couldn't think of any. "Then I'll bid you good day." His hand was on the door handle when he turned back. "Oh- one other thing....would you like to know his name ?" "I don't understand ," I said , "He was Frederick Richard Haven..." "No," said the Librarian, "That was an Americanisation ."

"Well ?" "It was Manfred von Richthoven. Some people knew him as The Red Baron" The door clicked shut behind him.

THE TRAIN RIDE

Inessa Cutler

Standing on track two at the train station, I was waiting for the eight oh three morning train into the city. I was on my way to work for a 10 AM meeting with my manager to discuss my review of a project that I had recently completed for a previous client. I looked at the navy blue watch on my wrist and it clocked eight o'clock on the dot – I had another three minutes to go. Fidgety, I leaned over and look down the train track, to see the glistening lights of the train's headlights.

An announcement from the PA system came on from above "The train to New York City will be arriving in two minutes." The train ride was going to take about an hour –give or take a few minutes and I didn't bring anything to do to kill the time. I would usually stare out through the window at all the scenery that we brushed by – cars that drifted slowly as they stopped for each red light at the crosswalk, the shopping centers filled with every kind of store imaginable, and of course the many parking lots bustling with cars pulling in and out of parking spots, but during rush hour there was little chance of me getting a seat by the window.

The train from Massapequa to New York pulled in at exactly 8:03 on the dot and the doors opened wide. The mob of people moved closer to walk through the train doors on their way to another busy day of running around. I walked through at the tail end of the group of people waiting in line, taking little steps so as not to push anybody. The train was pretty crowded and everybody who got on before me took up every seat by the window. As I looked around, I saw many faces, none of which were familiar, of professional people, moms hauling their kids, teenagers playing hooky, and shoppers eager to spend their last dollar.

I made my way down the center of the train, sitting down next to a man who was smiling while reading the comics of the local paper. He was a middle-aged man wearing a gray overcoat over a dark blue business suit. A freshly pressed white shirt peeked through just underneath his speckled black and blue tie. His freshly trimmed haircut was nicely tucked behind his ears. His dark brown eyes were covered with wire rim black glasses. After taking off my coat and putting my pocketbook on my lap, the train conductor came over and was standing beside me. I looked up to see a silver haired gentleman dressed in the train uniform. His thick belt, falling down to his hips, contained reams of ticket stubs and change coins of pennies, nickels, dimes and quarters. His tired eyes revealed a man who has been up since the wee hours of the morning, checking tickets and riding the train. "Ticket, ma'am" He asked.

I started rummaging from my purse to find my wallet, which contained the train ticket that I had purchased prior to boarding the train. Pulling out my ticket from the change purse in my wallet, I handed it to the conductor. The conductor punched the stub and placed it on the ticket slot on the seat in front of me. "Thank you, enjoy the ride," He said as he walked off to check another passenger.

With nothing to occupy my time, I looked down over my right side at the comics' page that the man was reading. The comics' page contained the latest comic strips from For Better or Worse to Heathcliff to Ziggy. Along with the comic strips, the horoscope, puzzles, and word find sections were on the right side of the paper. Since my favorite comic strip was Cathy, I strained my eyes to try to read it at the opposite end of the paper from me. The man looked up, his eyes began squinting as if he was saying, "What are you doing?" Embarrassed that I intruded on his morning ritual of reading the daily paper, I smiled and asked him, "Anything new in the world?" "Naw, just your everyday news about everything goin' wrong in the world," He responded with a wry look. "Any more news about what's happening with Enron?" I questioned him, trying to make conversation.

"Well, the justice department is still trying to get David Duncan, the Andersen partner to admit his part in the whole thing." He responded, sounding like he kept up with day-to-day events.

I had been working for Andersen for several years as a Consultant in their system integration group. Struggling with the low morale at the office, I was on pins and needles, checking the newspapers on a daily basis. Ironically, I received more information from the papers than I did from the partners at the office. "You know, I work for Andersen. This whole experience has been really interesting. Nothing like it has ever happened to me before." I explained to him. His eyes brightened with empathy and curiosity. "Do you know what is happening to you guys?" He inquired.

"Naw, unless you are a partner, nobody really tells you anything except to sit tight. It really sucks when you don't know what's happening." I told him, my face tensing from the frustration that I was feeling.

"That really is a shame. Andersen people are really good. I have worked with a few of them in my time. Which group are you with?" He probed, while closing the newspaper and looking intently into my eyes.

"I am with the consulting group and things have really quieted down ever since this whole has started. Since the clients don't really know what is happening either, they don't really want to sign up for us to do any major work." I remarked on the state of the company.

"I can understand that. By the way, my name is David. Nice to meet you." He said holding out his hand. "I'm Inessa." I replied, returning a firm handshake. Energized that I was making a new friend, my worries about Andersen faded for the time being. It was always a good thing to make contacts; you never know when you will need a stranger to help you out.

"I work over at the NY Times in their editing department. We hired Andersen to conduct an overhaul of our computer system. They really worked their butts off."

"Yeah, that's kinda our job and now it's coming to an end. But it must be interesting to work for the NY Times. Do you do any reviews?"

"No, I just edit other people's work but we do have one lady who writes reviews of restaurants. She usually wears wigs and thick glasses so that restaurants don't recognize her and give her special treatment. She usually takes several people from the office with her to try all the different foods. She also usually goes out to the restaurant for several meals on different days. The thing that restaurants struggle with most is consistency. Depending on the chef, the same exact meal can be slightly off."

"That sounds fun!" I exclaimed joyful that somebody had a fun job to do. "Yeah, she likes it. The only thing that she doesn't like is hiding behind a wig. She doesn't get as much recognition for her work." He explained nodding his head. "I guess that's part of the job, Have you ever gone with her?" I questioned. "No, I'm too busy but she sometimes brings back with leftovers which are usually pretty good." "How long have you been commuting into the city?"

A one-way commute takes at a minimum an hour and forty-five minutes door to door. It can get pretty draining after awhile. It's four hours of your time that could have been spent watching two movies, making a fine cuisine, or catching up on the housework that you have been procrastinating on. I have always been curious how people make decision about their lifestyle – what works, what doesn't work and why people go on a chosen path.

"About ten years. It sucks but it's where the opportunity is. There aren't too many newspapers out here on the island. There is only one -Newsday but when I couldn't get a job there, I applied at the NY Times where a friend got me in the door. It also pays pretty well, too."

"It's all about connections, isn't it?"

"Yup. What about you?"

"I commute on and off depending on what is going. I usually work at client sites that can be located anywhere – even other countries." I said matter-of-factly, smacking my lips.

"Really, have you ever traveled internationally?" He sounded excited at the thought of travel to far away places.

"No, mostly the states. I have to admit it though; it gets pretty old after a while. All you see is the hotel and the office. It's not fun." I clarified killing his excitement level.

"How does your wife feel about all that time that you spend commuting into the city?" I asked, looking at the ring on his finger.

"She understands, but we have a little girl and I miss those days when I hear my wife tell me about my girls first words or first steps. I have a picture, do you want to see?"

"Sure" I said.

He pulled out his black wallet from behind the back pocket in his pants. Opening up the silver clasp, he took out a picture from behind his NY state driver's license. When he handed me the photo, I saw a brand new picture of a little girl sitting down on a pink blanket while clasping the end of it with the small fingers of her right hand. She wore a frilly white dress with red and blue flowers and a matching sash around her waist. Her mouth was open wide to show a large Cheshire smile and exposed two center teeth. Her eyes, beaming with happiness were looking straight into the camera.

"Cute! What's her name?" my high-pitched voice announced, giving him the picture back.

"It's Jacqueline! She's eighteen months and getting bigger every day" He said proudly while taking back the picture and neatly tucking it inside his wallet. After flipping through his wallet, he took out a small white piece of paper. "I want to give you this, in case you need anything." He was holding his hand out to give me his business card.

"Thank you," I nodded. I accepted his business card and carefully placed it where I knew I could find it – the dollar bill slot of my wallet. I was hoping that I wouldn't need it but you never know when you will need someone to help you with a job.

"I have mine somewhere in here," I said reaching into my purse to give him mine. I found it tucked behind a side pocket in my pocketbook.

"Here it is." I handed him my Andersen business card.

"Thanks." He placed it in his wallet along with the rest of the many business cards that he was carrying.

"Do you have any kids?" he asked, raising his eyebrows, while turning his head to the side.

Since my mother had been nagging me for several years about having kids, I never really liked having that question thrown in my face. Many people think that having kids is the answer to life's big question but I just believed that just like anything else, they are part of life.

"Not yet, maybe in a few years. I'm married but me and my husband decided we weren't quite ready." I sighed, hoping he would drop the subject.

"That's ok, you still have time" he commented.

"It's kinda hot in here," he said as he stood up to take his cvercoat off.

I stood up and took a step toward the center of the car to give him some more room to stretch his arms. David's large hands quickly pulled each sleeve of the pressed overcoat and folded it up as he laid it on the overhead bin. When we both sat down on the seats, I was considerably curious about his desire for kids. "Did you always know that you wanted kids?" I challenged him. "Well, my wife did. I didn't really know what I wanted but we got pregnant." He replied, admitting that it wasn't on his top ten list of things you want out of life. "Ironically I don't really get to see her all that much. It's one of my biggest regrets." He admitted, his heart gasping in regret.

I was considerably surprised at his blatant desire of not wanting kids because from the look in his eyes, it was what he was the most proud of. It wasn't the job or the money but a bouncy little girl that brought a bright ray of happiness into his otherwise unfulfilled life. How sad that he envies his wife for being a stay at home mom. I guess people just don't appreciate what they have until it's too late. "New York City, next and last stop," yelled the conductor as he walked past me. "Don't forget to take all your belongings, Please take all your newspapers and coffee cups and place them in the receptacles on the platform. Thank you for riding the Long Island Rail Road and hope you enjoy the rest of your day." The conductor continued yelling loudly for everyone to hear.

"It was annoying to hear it every time I took the train. I mean really, isn't once enough?" I thought.

"I guess we'd better go," I said, getting up to gather all my stuff.

"It was nice meeting you!" he responded.

"You too, maybe we'll bump into each other again sometime."

"Maybe". I waved goodbye.

I pulled my pocketbook over my shoulder and quickly skirted in between the line of people walking toward the exit doors. The train was slowing down as it pulled into track seven at New York's Penn Station. When it came to a halt, the wide doors opened and the pitter-patter of feet started bustling out of the train. The passengers were carrying subway tickets ready in hand for another train ride. David was walking behind me as I stepped off the train and walked toward the escalator. When I reached the top of escalator, I had lost him in the crowd of people trying to survive another day.

I never saw David again but he gave me hope that you never know where you will find happiness. Life is an unexpected journey of hopes, dreams and surprises. You never know where you will end up, but you always need to make the best of it and remember not to take anything for granted.

ME TOO...

Irving Bronsky

PTSD In The Bronx, New York and Tumpalega, Alabama – A New York Psychiatrist Journeys to Alabama to Help Vietnam Veterans recover from their Post Traumatic Stress Disorder.

CHAPTER 1

Fifteen veterans are in the group at the Tumpalega VA hospital and they are waiting impatiently for it to start. My assistant in the group, Chaplain Mike Dills, the administrator of the PTSD program is in no hurry. He is a ground war Viet Nam veteran, a pastoral counsellor, and in the US Air Force active reserve. Like starts this morning's group by collecting the attendance forms from the 15 patients and signing them. He is a gentle man, in his late forties, slim build, pleasant of face; his wire-rimmed glasses set low on his nose are his most distinctive facial feature. He is polite in manner but from time to time he can be tough in his speech and behavior. He is that way now, as he signs the attendance form and talks about the rules of the program. He talks to them about maintaining discipline in the program and following the rules.

It is Friday morning and the vets are complaining that they aren't allowed to leave for the weekend home visit before two p.m. He swings his finger-pointed arm around the group, speaks crisply with his soft southern accent, he says, "Listen up you guys. Friday is a therapy day and we don't want you to lose it, you hear? There's precious little enough time as it is, with only five weeks to the whole darn program." He signs the last of the forms and looks sternly around the group, frowns and says, "You all know you've not been policing up the room after groups." He looks towards me and adds, "Dr. Bronsky and I don't want to go around picking up after you guys, cause you leave your coffee cups and soda cans behind you."

"Me too."

I am sitting quietly, watching and thinking about how I will start the group. I'm sixty-five years old, bald, with a handlebar mustache, a straight nose and hazel eyes. I'm six foot two, overweight, and I have an ease and confidence about me that is obvious when I work with patients, or in groups. After working with the vets for more than a month I came to realize that the American PTSD is different in some ways than the Israeli form of PTSD.

I learned to treat PTSD by working with hundreds of Holocaust survivors and their families, and with the Israel Defense Forces soldiers, some of whom suffered from PTSD. I was a psychiatrist in the active reserve and served in four wars. A few months ago I journeyed from Haifa, Israel to the Tumpalega VA hospital in Alabama, to set up and run the PTSD program. I "came home" after living and working in Israel for twenty-five years.

The Israelis never suffered the humiliation of being rejected and neglected after they fought for their country. They were not political scapegoats and they were given immediate psychiatric treatment soon after they began to shows signs of PTSD. The southern American vets grew up with an abundance of violent activities: hunting, fishing, sports, drinking, fighting. Many of them were frequently beaten as children. I heard the following sentence from many of them: "My daddy was real mean when he was drunk. Sometimes he made me go out and cut a big switch to bring him so he could beat my butt. If it wasn't big enough then he'd go out a get a really big one."

All veterans suffering from PTSD have recurrent nightmares, flashbacks, rage reactions with frequent violent outbursts, anxiety and panic attacks, paranoid attitudes and depression with suicidal tendencies. But the Israeli vets have almost no history of alcohol and drug abuse; the American vets have had frequent arrests for drug abuse and violent behavior.

In Nam they faced death and destruction almost every day; they lost close friends as well as comrades-in-arms in tragic and dramatic fashion. For example, two marines were bringing supplies on to the shore in the Mekong Delta when one of them had his head blown off, spraying his buddy with blood, bone and brain. Since then this survivor has nightmares three to four times a week in which he relives this terrible trauma.

Many of them have killed enemy soldiers and Viet Cong, but they also shot innocent civilians. "We couldn't take no chances in the some villages so we shot up all the hootches. If there were women and children in them that couldn't be helped." One vet lost two of his buddies to a booby-trapped Coca Cola, sold by a nine year old girl. The next time a Vietnamese girl came near his squad to sell the thirsty GI's a cold drink, she was cut down by three of the squad when she was 15 meters from them. A few committed atrocities such as running over civilians who slowed them down while in a convoy. One technique the VC used was to push civilians, including women and children, in the path of a convoy to stop it for an ambush.

These traumas are alive in their conscious minds, and repeatedly haunt them in their nightmares. During their waking hours they have flashbacks, (nightmares occurring in the form of a violent daydream,) triggered by any loud sudden sound or someone suddenly coming up behind them. If they go to public places such as restaurants they sit with their back to the wall, facing the door; they do their shopping at 2a.m. when there are few people in supermarkets. One vet was cruelly taunted at his place of work by a group of his co-workers; they would drop a large piece of metal and his inevitable reaction was to duck for cover or run out the factory in panic. He was a quiet, introverted, a good worker but had to quit because management also thought it was a lot of "fun to see him run."

They are survivors in real or imagined situations where they feel the least threat, showing it in their cursing, in the threats of violence, and occasionally being violent. A common way for some of them is to release their rage and anxiety was by going into a bar, pick a fight, very often winding up the loser, punched out, or in jail. I treated three vets who went to jail for manslaughter because of bar fights that ended in murder.

It was only after I came to Tumpalega that I realized that I too suffer from PTSD. When I was three years old I was run over by a car and suffered a fractured skull. The doctor told my parents that I have a fifty-fifty chance to live. I was hospitalized for one month, tied down to the bed for the first two weeks: "for bed rest,," they said. The "accident" was the label applied to me by my family to describe my behavior when I did something wrong or they thought I misbehaved. "Sure, it's the accident that made him crazy." Sometimes there was an additional zinger: "I think we should call the ambulance to take him to the Bellevue Hospital crazy ward." Before the accident I was a curious, bright child nicknamed Little Jack Dempsey. When I came home from the hospital I was hyperactive, aggressive, frightened, a nail-biter, and had recurrent nightmares about dying. I still have occasional nightmares but I am able to get out of them more quickly. And I not only survived but I overcame a lot of my PTSD.

Suddenly, I am aware of the silence in the room, embedded in the loud thrumming of the air conditioning. Out of the corner of my eye I notice that one of the vets is nervously tapping his finger on the notebook sitting in his lap. Mike asks the vet, T.J., "You all ready to talk about your flashback?" Today is T.J.'s third session in the group and he has yet to speak of his PTSD symptoms. Yesterday afternoon he was watching a cowboy picture on TV on the back porch of the ward with the rest of the group. When the shooting started he had a flashback and began acting as if he was back in Nam, crying, in panic, hiding under the table, shouting "Incoming, incoming." The other vets calmed him down and took him to the nurse. She sent him to see me and I worked with him in an individual therapy session. I had interviewed him on admission a week before: he was in his early forties, had been a pre-med student who quit the university after two years to enlist in the marines so he could fight in the Viet Nam war. In the interview he was anxious, cooperative but very reluctant to go into any details of the traumas he suffered in Nam.

Now, in the group, T.J.'s hands are shaking and his body is very tense. He is a tall and thin, with a shaggy mustache which partially covers his mouth and a neatly trimmed Van Dyke beard. He wears thick-lensed glasses that tend to fall down his nose. In a voice crackling with tension and rhythmically wringing his hands, he answers Mike's question. "Yes, I am ready to talk. I had a session with Dr. Bronsky yesterday and we talked about it."

He pauses, takes a deep breath and lets it out slowly, putting the pen and notebook down on the floor besides his chair. He takes off his glasses, wipes them slowly with a crumpled, soiled handkerchief that he pulls out of his back pocket. Putting on his glasses and clearing his throat quietly, he says, "I saw how some of the guys got help when they talked about some of the stuff they're hung up on and I think it helped them. But I'm a little afraid."

After a brief silence my voice sounds loud as I say, "I know you're afraid because you're probably going to talk about something you kept bottled up in you for almost 25 years. It was only yesterday that you spoke to me about it. I don't think you'll have a flashback and if you did, you'll get plenty of support from Chaplain Dills and me. I'm sure the guys in the group will also be available 'to protect your back.' Besides, I believe you have too much strength to let it blow your mind." He nods his understanding and agreement, as does the Chaplain, along with most of the vets in the group.

Raising my hand slightly off my lap in a 'stop sign' I say, "Before you start, I'd like to ask the guys here I have already worked with if they thought that sharing the experience of their traumas from Viet Nam was worthwhile." I look around the group and make eye contact with each patient who had taken the risk and talked about a traumatic experience in Viet Nam.

Tim, sad-eyed, slow talking, clean-shaven and very neatly dressed, relived his experience of handling many hundreds of bodies, bagging them, tagging them, shipping them back to the U.S. He had mind-promised the bagged bodies that he would never forget them. Since returning home he has been obsessed with his promise, that has become intrusive and obsessive thoughts. He describes them as being "like a like a broken record, going round and round in my mind, especially when I try to sleep." He visualizes the body bags a number of times a day but if he feels threatened by someone, he imagines him dead and puts him in a body bag. Tim sits very straight in his chair, clears his throat and says to T.J., "Do it man, I know it helped me."

Bobby is small and thin with a high-pitched voice. In Nam he had been a 'tunnel rat': he explored Viet Cong bunkers and tunnels. When he worked in the group he sweat profusely as he relived the experience of being in the middle of a platoon, his two best friends walking point, the lead man and the second man. They were ambushed and the point man was killed immediately and the other one seriously wounded. He was crying out to Bobby for help, but he couldn't get to him because he was pinned down by the murderous crossfire. It would have been sure death for him if he had tried to get to his friend. After his platoon broke the ambush Bobby found his second friend, dead from a bleeding wound in his leg. If he had been able to get to him on time he could have saved him with a tourniquet. He has been suffering from survivors guilt ever since. He barely raises his head to look at Tim and mumbles in a little voice, "You done said it for me, okay?"

Kyle, obese, is emotionally labile. He was an army corpsman. When he talked in group he cried, grimaced, walking around as he relived the trauma of losing his best buddy in a fire fight. He was unable to help his friend because he was too far away to answer his cries of "Medic," and he was too busy caring for the many wounded around him. The next day he found his dead friend with bamboo sticks in his eyes and his genitals in his mouth. He leans toward T.J., then points with his head in my direction, "Trust the man. You're my brother. We were both there. We'll watch your back."

Don is grey-haired, very big, muscular and very suspicious. His eyes are usually half-lidded and he glares aggressively at the person he is talking to. He often describes himself as a 'trained killer.' He is very bright but hides his intelligence by saying, "I'm just a little old country boy." He didn't allow himself to cry when he shared his experience with the group. He raged and then crushed an empty soda can under his big foot before he stomped out of the room. But he was back in five minutes to finish up. His talked about his buddy 'The Wildman,' saying "We was both wildmen in them days. You better believe it. When we come off patrols we'd get drunk, fight, tear up whorehouses." His buddy was gravely wounded when he took a grenade hit that tore off his face, leaving a pulpy red mass, his blond hair stayed clean and bright. Don had the same bright blond hair. "Shit T.J., you can trust this damn Yankee. Just a little, hear?"

Bubba, looking like an All-American football player is a chronic alcoholic and has a long history of being violent, in and out of jails, and in and out of jobs. When he shared with the group he was grim, almost growling in a low voice; his white-knuckled fists pounded rhythmically on the chair arms when he talked about his buddy on the navy river gunboat. After the war they were going to his friend's hometown, Chicago, to visit the Playboy Club. His friend was a member of the club and often told Bubba what they would do with the big-busted bunnies. The day his friend bought it, Bubba was at sick call because he had a fever. His friend, who was usually the after gunner, replaced him at his forward post on the fifty-millimeter gun. He took a direct hit with a rocket that disintegrated him. Bubba has an almost overwhelming survivor's guilt. He points his finger at me and looks at T.J. "Dr. B. is okay. He's one of us. Go to it. It don't mean shit anyway."

T.J. is different in his demeanor and speech than the others in the group. Almost all of them grew up poor in rural areas, didn't finish high school, were driving farm vehicles, cars and motorcycles before they were sixteen years old. T.J. came from a large southern city; his father was a college graduate and a high level civil servant. He begins to speak tensely but clearly, telling the group that he had been a pre-med student but quit after two years to join the marines. "In those days I was a patriot and I joined up to serve my country." He met his friend Richard who joined around the same time and they became fast friends. T.J. took to calling him Dicky Lee, a private joke between them, christening his Boston catholic friend into the southern Baptist faith. In the individual session the day before, he spoke tearfully and lovingly of Dicky Lee, whom he described as "my best friend, like a brother, the best partner anyone can have in life. We went out bar hopping, to whore houses. We had plans that after the war that we'd go to medical school together and open a private practice. We were going to be partners."

"For two years we were together all the time, studying and then working as medical corpsmen in navy hospitals. We were really good and got to be qualified operating room technicians. When we got our orders to go to Viet Nam we made a pact. If one of us got hit bad" - He stops speaking because he is choked up. He gulps, resettles his thick glasses on his nose and then he says, "Like if one of us loses a leg or something, then the other one won't let the dying man suffer. We had seen so many wounded marines, without arms, without legs, burned, blind." Very quietly he adds, "Neither of us believed we would have to use this euthanasia agreement."

In Viet Nam the two buddies separated, corresponded regularly. They didn't see each other for almost a year. T.J. was stationed at a big field hospital that received helicopter loads of wounded and dying. Because there was a shortage of medical doctors when the wounded and dying came in he did Triage. He explains this to the group, saying, "This is a fancy word we use in emergency situations where usually the doctor has to use his clinical judgement to decide what to do with the wounded. There were three kinds of wounded: those you knew were going to die, no matter what. We eased their pain and we left them to die; the lightly wounded didn't need immediate care and were ignored." He pauses for a moment, looking up at the ceiling and then says bitterly, "It was the big in-between group we had to treat first so that we could get them back to the killing fields as quickly as possible."

T.J.'s voice breaks and the dam of tears breaks and he cries. There is some stirring to my left and I am handed a tissue box to pass to T.J. He pulls one out and with a shaking hand, wipes his eyes without removing his glasses. He crumples the soggy tissue and carefully puts it into his lap. I ask him if he wants to stop and he responds by taking off his glasses, wiping them with a clean tissue saying "I'm going all the way."

Yesterday I taught him a relaxation exercise and now I speak, using the same voice, slow, rhythmic and quiet: "Why don't you take a deep breath...and then let go...slowly...as you breathe out." He starts to do it but then says angrily "I was playing God and I didn't want it, but what could I do? We had too many wounded and dying and not enough doctors. They said I had to do the triage so I had no choice." His anger disappears in a new flood of tears and sobbing. Several vets make a move to go to him but I shake my head no. They are angry with me but do nothing.

Slowly, he stops crying, sitting with his head hung down. I tell him, "Time out." He looks up at me, surprised and then he understands, nodding. In the private session I taught him the meaning of a "Time out": Stop what you are thinking about or doing and regulate your breathing to be slower and deeper. Then you relax any tense parts of the body you are able to. At that point you can choose to go on or to stop.

There is no movement in the group and the silence in the room is almost perfect. Through the closed window behind T.J. I see a tractor lawnmower clumsily moving in and around the scattered trees; it is cutting the weedy lawns. I hear the distant hum of the air-conditioning, faintly intruding. T.J. begins to talk and cry, talk and wipe, occasionally choking up with anger and helplessness as he describes what happened. Three medivac choppers come in. bringing many wounded and some dead. T.J. is running from marine to marine, efficient and effective, smoothly triaging the wounded, ignoring the dead and the lightly wounded. Then he trips over a squirming, moaning marine and he falls to the concrete. He begins to get up when he notices that it is a legless, dying Dicky Lee.

A moan-wail is torn from T.J.'s mouth. The vets on either side of him reach out to him as he folds into himself, putting his head down, bringing his knees up a little, hugging them to his chest, rocking rhythmically. I fight back my tears, hesitating about intervening, and then I remember that T.J. wants to go all the way, and I decide that he can make it. I don't intervene. The group is restless, most of them tearful, some crying, none loudly. Mike is concerned and looks questioningly at me. I indicate that I am in control and he sits back in his seat, sighing. I wipe my wet eyes, look around the group. Most of them do not make eye contact with me. The intensity of T.J.'s reaction has waned. I speak quietly, emphatically. "T.J.? Can you look at me?" He nods. I lean towards him and ask, slightly more emphatically, "Here? Now?" Slowly, he unfolds and looks up at me. I ask him if he knows who I am and what's happening and he nods, almost imperceptibly. "Do you want another time out?" He shakes his head, no. "Fine. By the way, we are all here, if you need us." I make a sweeping gesture that includes everyone in the room. There is a responsive, quiet chorus of yeses and heads nodding in support.

"Why don't you finish the story," I say and then pause... Here...now...you...us...all of us together." I take a deep breath, hold it for a second, and let the air out slowly. He takes a deep breath and lets out the air, loudly, into the heavy silence. He begins to speak, unmindful of the tears raining steadily down onto his shirtfront. "Dicky Lee was semi-conscious but he knew it was me. I put him against a mango tree and then I did what I had to. I gave him enough morphine to put him out of his misery and he relaxed right away. Then he stopped breathing." He looks at me with unseeing eyes, the tears streaming down his face. Three patients go to him, one hugs him, and the other two put their hands on his shoulders. One of them whispers something to T.J. and he nods his head. He is still crying quietly. The three return to their seats.

He stops crying and looks at me, indicating he wants to say something. I nod at him and he says, "I wrote to his parents that he died quietly in his sleep but I never told them the whole truth about the injection. Five times in the last twenty years I went to his home in Boston. Each time I got to the door but I couldn't ring the bell." I say, "I've got an idea I'd like to share with you." He nods almost imperceptibly and in a quiet, soft voice, says, "I'm with you. Go." "In my imagination I heard you speak about God to Dicky Lee, in three different ways. In the first way you said to him, 'Thank God I was able to keep my part of our pact.' In the second way you said, 'Thank God I was with you so you didn't die alone.' And the third way, 'Thank God you've gone to heaven and your suffering has stopped.' " In child's voice he says, "Do you really thinks so, Dr. Bronsky?"

"You bet your ass that I do. And I'll tell you something else. I had a wild thought a few minutes ago and I'm going to show you what it is. I might get hurt but I'm going to do it anyway." I get up and whisper in the ear of the patient sitting on my right, "What I am going to do has nothing to do with you. I'm going to use you so be ready and above all don't feel guilty. I know exactly what I'm doing." I take a step in T.J.'s direction, and I purposely trip over the patient's foot and fall heavily to the floor. The rug cushions my fall and I roll onto my back, shaken up, momentarily confused, but unhurt. I take a deep breath and as I let it out I say, "I purposely made myself trip to illustrate a point. After the fall I know I can get up and I can stand on my own two feet." I pause for emphasis and then I say, "Dicky Lee, through no fault of his own, couldn't stand on his own two feet because his legs were gone. But you can."

T.J. begins to cry and some of the group murmur about stopping but T.J. says, "No, no. Let him go on." I say to T.J., "Your legs are okay, and you can stand on your own two feet. I am asking you to use them to help me get up." He gets up, unsteady on his feet. Hands reach out to support him. I say loudly to the helping hands, "Let him stand on his own two feet." He sits down heavily in his chair. For a moment I have some conflicting thoughts about stopping but then I feel a big lump in my throat and my eyes flood with tears. With a voice near cracking, I say, "Choose to do it, T.J., or choose not to. Either way is okay with me." What I am really saying is that I too need help from him, but it doesn't come out that way.

He gets up, swaying, and then staggers towards me. I reach out my arm and he takes my hand in his. I use his support to sit up. For a moment I rest my head against his thick thigh. Then I look up at him and say, "Either you got the strength or you don't." He takes a step back and still firmly holding my hand in his he pulls up strongly. I am surprised by the ease with which he helps me to my feet. We hug, T.J. squeezing tight and patting me on the back. I hold him gently and stoop down a little to rest my head on his shoulder. Then I feel weak and begin to sway. He tightens his embrace and I stand more firmly. He says loudly, "Thank you, thank you, Dr. Bronsky." Tears choke me but I manage to say, "Thank you, T.J.." After a few seconds we separate, he strongly squeezes my arm and he goes back to his seat, walking steadily. I speak to his back, saying, "You're coming home, T.J. Welcome home."

I sit down, bent forward from the waist, my head down, staring at a small imperfection in the carpet. My lips are quivering and the tears are filling my eyes but I can't let go. Don, big, muscular, ham-handed, gets up and walks to T.J., who stands up. Don says, "You're a man, god-damn it. You sure are one hell of a man." He takes T.J.'s small hand in his huge one, pumps it up and down several times, shaking the dry-eyed T.J. They hug and rock, separate for a second and then hug and rock again. Don goes back to his seat and a number of veterans go to T.J. and shake his hand. He is peaceful, breathing quietly.

The tears in my eyes overflow and the chaplain asks me if there is something he or the group could do for me and I let go and burst into tears, deeply sobbing. I have wanted to cry like this for many years but was unable to let go. Sixteen years ago our first born, a son, almost eighteen years old, died of leukemia. Since then I've cried a number of times but I never let go as I do now. For a minute I have spasms of sobbing, and a growing sense of purging release. When I regain some of my composure I tell the group why I let go. Don gets up and we hug. Then Tim comes to shake my hand, saying slowly, gently, "Doc, I got to hand it to you. You're okay. But don't you think you have to come home too?"

The man on my left holds my hand. The man on my right puts his arm around my shoulder and I put my head on his shoulder and I am racked by a new burst of sobs. After a minute I stop crying, feeling peaceful and sad. Mike nods at me, says quietly that it is time to stop the group. Everyone gets up except me. Several vets come over to shake my hand, one tells me, "You're a man." Another says, "Even though you ain't been to Nam you belong with us, Doc." I look up, seeing that Mike is the only one left and he's standing a few feet away from me, waiting. I get up and we hug and I say to him, "Thanks, Mike." He says, "God bless you, sir."

Later that afternoon, after I finish my outpatient clinic I come out of my office, and T.J. is sitting in the empty waiting room. I am uncertain, thinking that something is wrong. "What're you doing here, T.J.? Are you all right? "He smiles softly, saying, "I'm fine. I came to see if you are all right." I sigh loudly, nod my head, tears in my eyes, and then say, "I feel as if I've been walking around with a heavy weight on my shoulders and now it's not there anymore." He takes my arm, holding it gently and says, "Me and the other guys were talking about you. Like we were worried about you." We sit down in the waiting room and I tell him the details of my son's illness and death. We both cry quietly. He offers me his hanky but I shake my head, wiping my eyes with the back of my hand. He takes my hand and wipes it with his hanky.

He says, "I'm glad for you Doc. Another reason I came over was to tell you that I called Dicky Lee's parents, told them what happened and said I'll be coming to visit them after I get out of the hospital." He nods his head vigorously and says, " I feel much better."

"Me too."

AN ICK FILES CHRISTMAS

Jeanne Owens

Christmas Eve. The day most men wait for to do their Christmas shopping. And handsome, dark-haired Special Agent Kenneth Aida was no exception to this.

It was a cloudy day. The sky looked like it could snow at any minute. But the weather forecasters on the TVs displayed in an electronics store window that faced the street said it would snow in Hell before it snowed in Washington, D.C.

"Yeah, right," Aida muttered as he walked past the window and wrapped his jacket tight about him against the cold. "And since when have you guys ever been right? We'll probably end up getting a blizzard." He then walked into a jewelry store.

He looked at the display cases, and found the ones with the rings. He then stood there for a while, looking them over, and over, and over. He stared longingly at a particular diamond solitaire ring.

"$3500," he thought sadly. "I wish I could afford it. Becky would love it. I know she would. And she deserves such a beautiful ring. But we federal agents don't get paid diddly for all our hard work."

A salesman walked over to Aida.

"May I help you, sir?" he asked.

Aida shook his head. "No, I don't think so. Not unless you can lower the price of this ring down some."

"How low did you have in mind?"

"Say…to about $500?"

"Uh…no, sir, I'm afraid not."

Aida sighed. "I thought as much. Well, thank you, anyway."

Aida walked off, muttering to himself. "There's no way I can afford $3500 for that ring. Not since buying my Mustang. But…I really, really want to get that ring for Becky. But how?"

He walked down the street, to where he'd parked his red Mustang covertible in the only available parking space at the time: the side of the road a block down. He stood there, staring at his car. "I hate to say it," he said to himself, "but the only way I can afford to get that ring is if I sell the Pony. So, which is it going to be, Aida old boy? The sports car? Or Becky?"

It took him no time to decide. And in even less time, he was driving around, looking for a car lot.

Aida came to a stop at a stoplight. As he sat waiting for the light to turn, he saw a pudgy old man with long white hair and beard running down the sidewalk in a hurry. He seemed frantic about something. Aida had a feeling something was up, so he pulled the car to the side of the road and go out. He hurried up to the old man's side. "Hey!" he said. "What's wrong, old man? Can I help you?"

The old man slowed to a stop and looked at Aida appraisingly. "Yes," he said after a moment. "I believe you can help me, Agent Aida."

Aida stared at him in shock. "How...How do you know my name?"

The old man ignored his question. "I'm chasing after some punks who robbed me."

"That so? Well, then. I can certainly help you with that. Which way'd they go?"

"Down this street. They turned a corner up here somewhere."

"All right. Let's go!"

Aida and the old man hurried down the street. The old man pointed out the corner the thieves had turned down, and they turned there.

The corner was a deadend alley. Aida and the old man came to as stop in the middle of the alley.

"What now?" the old man asked.

"Well," Aida said as he looked the alley over. "I see three possibilities."

"Possibilities?"

"Yes. There are three doors facing the alley, and no fire escapes. So, they had to have ducked into one of the doors."

"Ah. I see. Yes. Very astute of you, Agent Aida."

"Thank you." Aida paused. "Hey! How do you know who I am?"

The old man ignored him. "Well, which door shall we check first?"

"Well, how about the closest one?"

"All right."

The two men then opened the door directly to their left...and looked in surprise at a brick wall.

"Hmmm...I don't think they went in here," Aida said.

"No," the old man said.

"I guess they built over this doorway." Aida shut the door. "Okay, then. Next!" They walked down and across the alley to another door and opened it. A naked man and woman on the floor, in the middle of...business...looked up at them, startled.

"AAAHHHH!!!!" the woman screamed as she tried to cover herself. "HEY, YOU JERKS!!" the man yelled. "DO YOU MIND???"

"Uhhhh...."Aida said, blushing madly. "You two didn't happen to see... Umm... Nevermind. Sorry."

Aida shut the door. "Third time's the charm?" he said.

"Apparently so," the old man said.

They walked to the door at the end of the alley and opened it. Two young boys peering inside a big red velvet bag looked at them.

"YOU!" the old man said. "Give me back my bag!"

"Uh-oh," one boy said. "Run for it!"

The two boys abandoned the bag and ran off. However, since the only way in or out was the door, they had to go through Aida and the old man. Aida easily grabbed hold of them.

"What do you want to do with them?" Aida asked the old man.

"Let them go," he said. "They're just kids. And it's Christmas, after all. The season of love and forgiveness."

"All right. If you want. It's your stuff they stole. If you don't want to press charges, it's your perrogative."

The old man nodded, and Aida let the two kids go. Then the old man retrieved his bag.

"Thank you for your help, Agent Aida."

"It was no problem, sir. Just glad I could help. By the way, could you PLEASE tell me how you know my name?"

The old man ignored him and reached inside his bag. "Here. Take this as a thank you."

He handed Aida a small square box wrapped in Christmas paper. The tag on it read: Merry Christmas, Kenneth Aida. From Kris

He looked up from the package. The old man and the red bag were gone without a trace.

"Kris?" Aida said. "No. It couldn't be."

He tore the wrapping from the package, revealing a ring box. With wide eyes, he opened it. Inside the box was the ring he'd wanted to get Becky. Aida fainted.

Outside, it began snowing.

Christmas morning, Aida went to the apartment of his partner and lover, Special Agent Rebecca Rogers. Nervously, he knocked on her door.

A young, pretty redheaded woman answered the door and smiled at him. "Good morning, Kenneth," she said. "Merry Christmas."

"Merry Christmas, Becky," he said with a smile in return.

He followed her inside and to the living room.

"I brought you a present," he said as she sat down on the sofa and reached over to the coffee table to pour a cup tea.

"Oh, that was sweet of you, Kenneth," she said. "You didn't have to, you know."

"Of course I did. It's Christmas. So, do you want it or not?"

"Silly! Of course I do!"

He reached into his pocket and pulled out a small, wrapped box. He handed it to her.

Excited, Rogers opened the present. She gasped as she saw the ring.

"Kenneth! It…It's beautiful!" She took a second look at. "It…It's an engagement ring!" she said in surprise.

"Yeah," Aida said. "I know. So, will you…"

"Yes!" she said, jumping up to hug and kiss him, not even giving him time to finish the question.

BLADES OF TERROR
JirQUEST

He stared at the electric fan, his eyes not wavering once as he deliberately examined the blades. Everything appeared fine. Greyish and translucent blades that seemed contented to be caged in. Yet, he knew something was not right. He could feel it. He could sense that malevolent influence coming from the electric fan. From the blades. The very source that caused his Auntie Chong to lose her fingers. And now, it stood serenely about 5 metres away from him. A harmless object that was supposed to cool people down if the heat got unbearable.

He gazed at the structure of the fan. A long, narrow body which held the buttons, and a broad base to go with. A metre in height, it was like every other normal electric fan.

He did not know the exact details of the incident, but when he visited his aunt in the hospital, she mentioned something about the fan being hypnotizing, that it called for her to reach out and touch its blades.

He wanted to reprimand her for conjuring such a ludicrous excuse, but she had grasped his arm tightly, her eyes all teary and bulging in enormous fear. He had to believe her then. However, his skeptical nature forced him to do a little investigation on the previous owners. What he discovered, convinced him that his aunt was not hallucinating

The first owner, Mr Kang, lost his fingers one night after coming home from work. He had rested on his couch - dead-beat from carrying large boxes of computer hardware all day - and was about to go into a deep slumber when he heard a voice. It was feminine, very sweet and alluring. It was calling for him, asking him to open his eyes, and switch on the fan. He did. And as he reached forward, he felt a push from behind and his fingers went straight in the tiny slots and got mangled.

The second owner suffered the same fate. Except that both his hands were affected. Martin sighed. He turned to the table beside him and retrieved the notes. He looked over it again, trying to find out what were the common characteristics of the victims. Nothing visible to his eyes. He closed it and pinched the bridge of his nose. Something was wrong with the fan, yet there was nothing he could do about it. His auntie had lost her fingers for no reason, and the only thing he could do for her was to gather a useless stack of history notes.

Then he thought he heard something. It came soft at first, nothing more than a little whisper. And it became clearer by the second. Someone was calling his name, repeating it in a musical-like tone.

"Touch me... Come forward and touch me. Feel me... feel my smoothness.

Hurry up Martin. I want you to feel me."

Suddenly, he felt drowsy, his eyelids became heavy and his mind swirled. He could no longer think straight. He needed a nap, to sleep away the giddy sensation. He felt himself getting on his feet, swaying back and forth unstably as he edged forward, shuffling. He heard a click sound, and the wind blasted his hair as he continued moving towards it. Around him, everything turned black and a spot of light appeared. A light that transpired across as tranquil and full of warmth. He felt a longing to touch it, to raise up his hand to caress the light. And he did.

Martin howled in pain.

TWO ULTRA-SHORT STORIES

John R. Guthrie

(I) SEX

"Earl, sound like you gonna need to talk with her. Faking an erection's next to impossible." "Doc, you just don't understand. She's young, just started drawing her social security. And she's something, Doc, really something, in bed, I mean. When she gets going, oh boy! And she's got a shape, you know, she's really BIG on top." He held his hands before his chest to indicate melons, then brushed his hand through white hair, hair which was full despite nearly eight decades. His knobby fingers ended up kneading the back of his neck; blue eyes, washed out and pale looked into the distance as he continued.

"You see, I'd been by myself six years until I met Muriel. My kids live all the way across the county. My daughter called from San Diego two years ago to borrow some money, but besides that I hardly ever even hear from either one of them. Too busy, I guess. So I mostly just hung around home. But since I met Muriel, things've been different. My boy in Los Angeles, he's Mr. Big now, has his own company. He came home a while back from California, just walked in one day. I hadn't seen him in nearly five years. He said, talking so pitiful, Dad, you been all by yourself since mom died, so I just took time to come and see you.. Know what I said? I said, well, make yourself at home, Son. We'll talk about it when I get back. I got a date. Then I left. But once she finds out that I can't even…." "Yeah, Earl. It's tough to think about, isn't it? But you never know…"

"That surgeon, he got the cancer, but he got my nature too, just like he said he would. After I had the surgery, though, I just couldn't go around Muriel. See, I even used to have to close the bedroom windows before we went to bed so the neighbors wouldn't hear her when we got going. Finally she came by my place when I got home from the hospital, came right in, me lying on the couch. Boy, she was pissed. She said, what the hell's wrong with you? I'm not good enough for you any more? So I told her, Doc. Told her how I figured she wouldn't want me no more, 'cause I couldn't do anything. Know what she said, Doc? She said, real soft and easy, Earl, listen to me! When I had my surgery, they took everything out. I hadn't felt a thing down there for 15 years. I said, but you were so, so… She said, that was just for you, Earl. And you're still just the man I need. Now ain't she something, Doc? Ain't she really something?"

(II) CHRISTINA

One day when spring returned to the Carolina Piedmont, Christina came to the clinic to see me. She was a little bent in her back from working in the cotton mill all those years before the mill closed up shop and headed south for the cheap wages of Mexico. She had wrinkles, and her hair was graying. She took Maxzide 75/50 for blood pressure, just a half tablet every morning. "132 over 86. That's great. And you look like you're feeling well," I said.

"Doc, I do. You know how bad off I was when the bad thing happened, but I got better, and I'm busy with the girls." The girls, Amy and Courtney, 11 and 13, were sitting outside the exam room, all giggles, denim, tees and Nikes. The bad thing that had happened a few years previously involved their parents, Christina's son-in-law and daughter. You couldn't help but notice that those two, Jesse Ray and Valery were cute together; kissy-kiss still, even after a couple of years of marriage and two kids.

Christina heard them arguing that evening, but she'd heard it before, so she settled down in the front room to watch Wheel of Fortune on the TV. Then she heard the smacking sound that a .22 makes. When she ran into the back room, the room that had been a porch but she'd had it framed in for Valerie and Jesse Ray. Jesse Ray had four bloody claw marks across his left cheek. He was frozen in place, his mouth half open, looking at the pistol in his right hand as if it were a serpent, not saying a thing. Valery was lying in the floor looking straight up and she wasn't moving either, and blood oozed from a wound above her left eye. Later, nobody remembered what the argument was about, not the children, not Christina, and not Jesse Ray. Still Valery was cold and dead and laid out in a stainless steel filing drawer waiting on the pathologist with his sharp knives and his bone-shears to make a canoe of her corpse so he could dictate his report into the mike suspended by a cord above the autopsy table.

"I never spoke ill of him," Christina had once said. "I take the girls to see him once a month. We always take him something. They don't treat people good down there, you know. I told him when you get out, you have a place to live with us. It was all he could do to keep from crying. He said Mama Chris, I don't see how you can be so good to me. I said, Jesse, those children are part you. I couldn't do bad by you without doing bad by them, too." Everybody had something to say about how Christina handled the bad thing, her taking the children once a month down to that place where they don't treat people good, and taking him cookies and such. All the neighbors put their two bits in. The sheriff said Jesse Ray was there to be punished, not to be coddled. The preacher said Jesse Ray had sinned, and the wages of sin are death. But the sheriff always says what he thinks will get him elected again next time, and the preacher's stories haven't meant much to me since I quit believing in the tooth fairy and such.

THE FINAL DAYS OF HARRY STEGMAN

Joseph Aprile

The fall was unusually bleak on Elizabeth street. The fallen leaves were outnumbered by the clutter and refuge left over by the many pedestrians that made their way along the busy thoroughfare. It was on this street that Harry Stegman lived. Harry lived in apartment No 6, three flights up in a six floor walk-up. The stairs always seemed to be in the shadows, and they made peculiar creaking noises when anyone walked upon them. Gladys, a tenant living surreptitiously with four German shepherds on the first floor, could identify all the tenants by the particular pitch and rhythm of their footfalls on those stairs. Harry was heavy footed, and his sounds were distinctive.

Harry was a retired merchant marine and lived frugally on a seaman's pension. His apartment was a rat hole like the rest, but he enlivened it with the colorful memorabilia of his past. During his lifetime he had experienced the devastating effects of the great depression, and the social dislocations resulting from the emergence of modern technology. He, therefore, fashioned his apartment into a kind of personal sanctuary.

Artifacts from around the world adorned Harry's flat without regard to any accepted norms of interior decoration. Delicate wood carvings from the Philippines, beautifully woven wall hangings from Liberia and a luscious happy Buddha from the east were there as evidence of a lifetime of ceaseless wandering. These objects earmarked a time that was well in the past. For Harry was now old and sickly, plagued by an arthritis that had its origins in his youth during his many crossings of the North Atlantic. Also, Harry, having been captivated by a seaman's promiscuity, had repeatedly contracted gonorrhea, and it was only in his later years that these excesses made themselves felt. His liver was beginning to trouble him as bourbon was Harry's most trusted ally. This flat had become for him his latest ship, and he as its captain tossed about in a sea of dreams and memories.

On the wall opposite his bed hung a very special photograph of himself as a young man in Boston with his sweetheart, Sally Ritter, by his side. Sally had the misfortune of marrying Harry whose heart always belonged to the sea. Whenever Harry looked upon that photograph he did not feel regret, but a kind of knowing melancholy. How those youthful dreams so quickly withered, how the force of personality drove one to such extreme behavior, abandoning love for the inexplicable urge.

They were married just two short years, not quite long enough for a relationship to mature, but long enough for the ending to leave deep and lasting wounds. He never was to hear from Sally again. He never was to return to Boston where his soul took its character; where those dreary overcast skies imprinted a somber moodiness; where the great sea enveloped his burgeoning mind. Harry was alone but content with the secrets that prowled about in his aged soul.

Each morning at the first intimation of dawn, Harry's eyes would open, and his hand would automatically reach out for the pint of bourbon that sat by his bedside. In a most enchanted and graceful motion, Harry would reach out for the bottle, begin to pivot himself and assume a seated position while his free hand embraced the empty glass nestled on the drawer of his night table. It was a ritual which established a tabernacle for his sanity in the unrelenting chaos about him. With his glass of bourbon in his hand, Harry felt the courage to get out of bed and approach the one dingy window that faced the street. The physical pattern was well entrenched, for Harry would not wet his mouth until he had witnessed, for himself, the light of a new day. With a steeled commitment, he would then drink it down in a singularly poetic motion. This was his way of giving thanks.

Harry would move his chair to a position opposite the front door and sit in a position of waiting. He kept no newspapers or books with him, and, as he sat motionless, no thought of any substance entered his brain. Harry was capable of assuming this state of mental quiet only after having spent many years learning the self-discipline required for deep meditation. He learned the essentials of this practice during his travels to India. Generally, Harry maintained this meditative posture until either a knock on the front door startled him or his stomach made its inevitable demands.

Although Harry was essentially a recluse, he was not friendless. The internal complexity of his person expressed itself in discreet and distinct compartments. It was in these compartments that Harry placed well chosen friends. Sam Pontius, who owned a barber shop down the block, was an aged friend with whom Harry could discuss philosophical matters. They rarely agreed, but they shared a mutual respect for each other's intellect. For them, their relationship was a substantial though weak light that shone upon their lives. Sam was a widower living on limited resources. His children all lived far away with families of their own. Sam was a career army officer who had seen action in both World War II and the Korean War. He had been enamored of the military life, and a zealous patriot until his only son was killed in action in Vietnam. Edward's death was particularly painful for him, and often plagued his thoughts.

It was not unusual for Harry to be awakened from his morning meditations by Sam's characteristically aggressive knocking. "Come in," Harry beckoned. Sam entered.

"Harry, you old decrepit I've caught you snoozing again." At this Harry shrugged his shoulders playfully.

"What's happening Sammy?" Only Harry could call him that; it was a hallmark of their intimacy.

"Let's go out and get some breakfast before it begins to rain."

"Sounds good to me."

Together they walked slowly and with considerable dignity towards the pier. The wind blew their stiff overcoats into undulating patterns against the relief of the old wooden houses and the great stone church that marked their progress. Old and retiring seagulls held their posts with that snobbish indifference to humanity that is so characteristic of their race. Their cousins, the pigeons, bickered among themselves over the crumbs thrown to them. Sam always kept some old bread wrapped in plastic inside his coat pocket and perfunctorily reached out and flung the remnants to the pigeons while engrossed in conversation with Harry. Sam was usually of a serious temperament, and Harry could tell when something was disturbing him. "Sam something's bothering you what is it?"

"Harry, you've heard it all before. I don't want to bother you with it."

"Oh come on Sam! What's eating you."

"I used to consider myself a romantic, but I've grown cynical. I'm not as sure about humanity as I used to be."

"What do you mean Sam?" Harry asked.

"Well you know how much I follow the news. I used to consider myself a patriot. But after my Edward was killed, I just don't know any more. I still feel responsible for his death."

"But Sam it really hasn't been that long."

"If I hadn't been so outspoken about God and Country maybe Eddy wouldn't have volunteered. And maybe he would still be alive today. Harry its hard having to bury your own son. It just ain't natural."

At this point Sam's voice had became tremulous, and his voice dropped off into a deep silence. Harry feeling his friend's pain gently put his arm around Sam's shoulder. "Sam, that must have been hard. But you shouldn't be so tough on yourself. Sure you could have acted better if you had known the future. Look, you've been pretty lucky to have had a son and to have all those memories. I have only myself to look back upon."

Sam looked up at his friend with an appreciative and loving glance. He felt as if a heavy weight had been lifted from him, and for that brief moment the cold did not touch them. Together they continued their walk carrying a warm silence between them. The Seaside Restaurant was now in sight at the bottom of the hill. Harry and his friend entered and sat down at the counter.

"Good morning gentlemen," the young waitress greeted them, approaching with the morning paper.

"Hello Trudy," Sam responded, reaching for the paper. Trudy epitomized that vivacity and optimism of youth that is both endearing and contagious. Both Harry and Sam appreciated her vitality and felt its beneficial influence. "Trudy," Harry said "bring us some coffee."

She soon returned with the coffee and asked, "Should I bring you boys the usual?"

By this time Sam was totally engrossed in the paper, and Harry ordered for the both of them.

As they were eating their breakfast, Harry sat facing a huge picture window that looked out over the waterfront. His eyes would gravitate towards that view. Sam, on the other hand, was buried in the sports page. They were both off in their own private worlds, but inwardly appreciative of each other's company.

When Harry was finished with his breakfast, he quietly arose from his seat, placed some money by Sam's side and said, "Sam, I need to be off right now. You take care, and I will see you soon." Sam looked up warmly at his old friend and said nothing. Harry indulged his need for solitude with a brisk walk along the waterfront. The smell of the sea and the salt winds and the lumbering vision of the big ships delivered to his mind a panorama of sensations that seemed to reflect the true nature of things. As he stood with his face thrust toward the wind, his eyes filled with a subdued light reflected from the heavy water-laden clouds. Seagulls paraded about their false aristocracy while beneath this pretense lay the slothfulness of poor fishermen. His mind thrilled to these sensations not only because of their familiarity but because such images had a way of stilling Harry's mind and quieting his anxieties. It was during such moments that Harry could feel the power of reality exposed and undisguised . It was during such moments that Harry could foresee his death with an objective clarity. He could sense the frailty of his aging body and knew how it longed to lie down forever. Paradoxically, it was after such close encounters with himself that Harry was infused with a new vitality, childlike and, seemingly, invincible. His gait quickened, his breath deepened, even his heart beat less laboriously as Harry made his way back to his rooms.

He spent the rest of that afternoon reading and took a brief nap. When he awoke, his thoughts fell upon Sue. He was familiar with her working schedule and knew that tonight she would be at the All Nite Cafe. Harry got himself bathed and dressed and ready for what he hoped would be a memorable evening.

The All Nite Cafe was a notorious hangout for landed sailors. About the darkened room, dominated by the bar, were cheapened ornaments of the seafarer's trade. Harry cared for none of that, but headed straight for the bar where Sue was working. Sue had an imposing figure, an apparition from one of Chaucer's bawdy tales. Her features portrayed an expression that was suggestive though reserved and cautious. She was not a woman who was stupidly cautious for she was also cunning. It was a cunning smartly draped with a woman's charm and guile. Sue pursued her own interests in a way that did not deny pleasure to others. She was certainly admired.

As Harry stepped up to the bar across from where she was working, Sue greeted him, "Hello Harry, how are you these days?"

"Fine, very fine," Harry responded with a broad beaming smile on his face.

"What will it be then?"

"Well, for now a Seagrams and Seven will do."

As Sue moved about to fill his request while interacting with the other customers, Harry could not take his eyes off of her. She was well aware of this attention, and found it quite flattering for she liked Harry a great deal. When she returned with Harry's drink, Harry leaned over the bar and said, "Sue, honey can you go out with me tonight?"

Without changing her general air of commercial deference required of women in her position, she responded, "Pick me up at eleven, that's the end of my shift." At eleven, Sue met Harry outside in the parking lot. She walked quickly to his side and placed her arm through his, "Well, Harry where will it be?"

"How about the movies?"

"Oh come on Harry!," she responded. "I know what you want to do with me.

Take me home."

Harry smiled, "All right, love you certainly are a prize!"

As they were walking to Sue's apartment, Harry became thoughtful. The nearness of Sue to him together with the subtle influence of the night air, aroused in Harry's mind a deep melancholy. Suddenly, he turned toward Sue and asked, "What do you see in an old fool like me anyway?"

Seeing the grief in Harry's face, Sue responded, "Harry I care about you. You are a close friend and have always looked after me. You're being extremely silly to think like that."

Harry put his arms around her, and kissed her with a tender yet wildly possessive impulse. When they arrived at her apartment, Sue went to her bedroom and turned on the light. "Harry," she said, "I won't be long, make yourself comfortable," and she went to the bathroom. As Harry was undressing, vivid images of the women he had known traversed his vision, and seemed to form a chorus line. They danced for him while singing, "Harry, Harry we love you Harry," over and over again. When Sue finally returned from the bathroom, she found Harry sitting on the edge of the bed with a bemused and distant expression on his face.

"Harry, what are you daydreaming about?" she asked.

At first Harry was not going to say anything, but he knew better than that. He related to her the substance of his thought dream. Sue looked at him intently, and then spoke, "You old philanderer!" She leaned over on top of him and together they fell into bed. They made love with admirable adeptness for their age. In this way, night passed quickly into day separated by a most tranquil sleep.

Impassioned love among older people, unlike in their younger counterparts, is not usually followed by that starry-eyed awe that seems to obliterate all reality except that which gravitates about the loved one. Both Harry and Sue were well honed by reality, and respected each other's strong sense of separateness.

"Well Harry," Sue spoke as they both awakened, "I haven't had such a good time in a long while, but I must be going." Harry would have liked to detain her in some loving way, but did not follow that impulse. They both dressed quietly, and left arm in arm. Harry walked with Sue to the cafe, delicately touched her cheek as he left her side, and proceeded towards his own place.

"There is something unusual about this day," he thought. The daylight seemed strangely subdued; it seemed to possess a solemnity and sacredness. The world seemed more luminous. Harry felt that this was a special day although he was unable to determine why. He touched the edges of stone on the church as he passed, the bark of some kindly oak trees, and he even ventured to touch the vibrant hair of a child as she skipped passed him. Everything seemed more electric to his senses. Harry noticed that he was smiling, and that the people around him were smiling back. "What an amazing life," he thought. When Harry had climbed the stairs and entered his apartment, he felt suddenly exhausted. This sensation did not seem to originate in the bones or muscles, but from somewhere else. He sat down in his familiar chair. The next morning, Sam found his good friend Harry. The old sailor had died. His long and remarkable journey had ended. Following Harry's instructions, Sam had the body cremated, and as he was pouring his friend's ashes into the sea he said, "Harry, this is where you belong."

HOW NOT TO DOCK A BOAT
Joy Bennett

My husband and I are beginning boaters. He is doing quite well, learning how to steer, taking care of the mechanical things, but I am having an inordinate amount of trouble learning the ropes. On top of that, we tend to fight a lot in new situations, kind of turf warfare, so our boating experience can be described so far as adventurous at best.

This is how we typically dock the boat. I say a prayer, especially if it's windy or rainy. He yells, "Get the lines ready!" I panic, trying desperately to remember which line. He says, "Get the bow line!" I take a few minutes to recall which end of the boat is the bow. By that time I'm already late for the next critical thing I have to do, which is get the spring line (whatever that is) ready too. At this point, we are usually somewhere within six feet of the dock. This is the where I desperately start to run around and yell "Cut the engine, cut the engine!" This is my reasoning. I figure our best bet is to throw a line, any line, close to where our beleaguered boat neighbor is standing in the rain, kindly trying to help us dock yet again. If the line should go into the water (as it inevitably does), and into the propeller, if it should wrap around the propeller and damage it, it will cost us $1,000 for a new prop. However, if the engine is stopped, even if the line goes near the propeller, it can't possibly damage it, because the prop wouldn't be moving.

Our boating neighbor has another idea. He patiently tells my husband to maneuver the boat a little closer. At that point I say another prayer, and hope I'm not hit by lightening even if it's raining just a little. Somehow, maybe because by that point usually someone on the dock somehow has managed to get a line, although I'm never clear exactly how that miracle happened, we are pulled in closely enough to the dock. Mercifully he does finally cut the engine, and we are tied up once again to safety.

A loud cheer goes up. I proudly loop the bow line around the dock post and then tie it again to the cleat on the boat. (My husband was inexplicably agitated when he found out about that one.) I inspect the cabin for property damage or injuries, and remind myself yet again why we bought a boat: to relax.

Some people have no business being on the water, and I'm afraid I'm one of them.

APPLE BLOSSOMS, OLD MONEY AND SEX

Julie Failla Earhart

Bill stepped off the elevator, dropped his disposable cup in the trashcan and headed slowly down the long, carpeted hallway. His luxury suite was at the end and his private office commanded a breathtaking view of the red brick building next door. As he reached the halfway point he stopped to take a drink from the water fountain; it was the only one in the nineteen-story building that had ice-cold water. The cool wetness came as a much-needed relief on this scorching, stifling August afternoon. As he drank, his lips delicately pursed over the arching silver stream. In his peripheral vision, Bill saw a woman exiting through the plate glass doors of his executive offices.

As the woman sauntered toward him, Bill sensed something familiar about her. He stood upright, straightened his silk, peach-colored tie, and began walking toward her. Bill felt every nerve in his body spark and tingle as he took in her square jaw and pageboy hairstyle. He felt his penis stiffen, and he slowed.

The woman took small steps, steps that were out of synch with her large bone structure. She didn't seem to be in a hurry. Now there were ten feet between Bill and this goddess-like creature in the tomato-red dress. She had auburn hair with golden streaks, a full bosom, long legs and carried a large, black bag, slung carelessly over her left shoulder. There was something in the sway of her hips that created an urgency in his groin, something that caused all the butterflies in his stomach to beat their tiny wings hard enough to create a gusty wind.

Five feet separated Bill and the woman. Bill rarely made eye contact with anyone in the hallway, preferring to watch the tassel of his slip-on wingtips gently bounce. Now his eyes were drawn to the thick lashes coated with mascara that framed mottled-blue eyes.

She smiled and nodded. A husky "good morning" tumbled out of red-lipsticked lips. Bill nodded in response, unable to make his vocal cords respond. He stopped when they were handshaking distance apart, but she kept walking. Her scent—a mixture of apple blossoms, old money and sex—settled in his nostrils and cloaked his body like a warm blanket. Bill knew he knew the woman. He couldn't place the face. Or the jaw. Or the lips. Or the legs. But those eyes; he knew those eyes.

After she had passed, he watched her reflection in the fifteen by twenty-four pane of glass that separated his world from the rest. He couldn't take his eyes off those legs. The calves were sinewy and rested on delicate ankles. The juxtaposition would seem unsightly on any other woman; one that more than ordinarily attracted him. The red dress did nothing to soften them, only accentuating the fullness of her thighs.

Bill reached for the handle of the glass door just as the woman punched the down button for the elevator. With a light ding, the steel gray doors parted. Bill watched four men exit. As the remaining occupants stepped aside to allow her inside, Bill jerked his hand away from the door, turned and ran back down the long hallway.

The doors were almost closed. "Robert?" He pushed the down button several times. The elevator doors slowly began to re-open. Bill and the woman stared at each other. Her husky voice whispered, "Ellen. It's Ellen now. I've missed you." Before Bill could react, the doors closed and the elevator cables swooshed. Bill looked over his shoulder, down the long hallway. He stared for a long time. Then, behind him, the elevators opened with a slight ding. Bill took a deep breath. Even his heart seemed to stop as he hoped for the fragrance of apple blossoms, old money and sex.

A CURIOUS WORLD

Kathryn Gabrielle

There are wishes that must never be whispered aloud and there are also a few "magical" words that must never be spoken. Words that most people throw around easily. Words like "curiosity"and "silence"and "happiness". To speak these words and feel the meaning resonate just like a song. The words reflect in the sparkle of the eyes, the lilt in a voice and the blush of a cheek.

What does it feel like to be on that other side of the looking glass just like Alice? Alice was brave and curious. I need to leave fear behind and be curious too. I don't know of anyone who has been there and come back to tell the tale. It must be that wonderful that no one ever wants to come back here. It surely must be filled with music and flowers and love. My side is full of problems, noise and pain. Is there a catch to it? Is there a difficult riddle over there yet to be solved? Am I the one to do it? Can I solve the mystery of a land that I can never see or experience? I must find that beauty for myself.

I envy Alice. She found out.

The glass feels soft and I feel like I can almost put my hand through it. A mist creeps up around me as I step forward into the looking glass world. I am beyond the looking glass into another world of illusion and fantasy have left behind my world of pain and life. I see only pinks, blues, greens and whites. I see a backward copy of the room I left behind. There is a lovely fire crackling in the fireplace and I may sit by it as long as I wish. There is no one here to tell me that I can't stay. Even the grandfather clock that ticks so happily in my real world room is different here on the other side of the looking glass. It has a face on it and I swear it winked at me. There are pictures on the wall and the eyes follow me and I hear a voice speaking. The eyes of the pictures are at this moment watching a very intense chess game going on in the middle of the room. Every now and again one of the pictures would shout "Hooray!" for a queen or knight or king that had just made a move on the chessboard. What a curious world!

On the table in the middle of the room is a chessboard with all the pieces moving by themselves. A game is going on but there are no people to play it. The game pieces are playing against each other. If I listen very carefully, I can hear the King and Queen directing the white knight and black knight to move diagonally to protect them from the opposite "army". What fun!

This seems an ideallic world of forgetfulness and peace. Alice was brave and curious. I need to leave fear behind and be curious too. I don't know of anyone who has been there and come back to tell his tale. I have stepped inside the world of the looking glass and it is such a world that I have never seen before. There is music that fills the air and this lovely air has the scent of chocolate chip cookies and hot cocoa. It reminds me of a cold winter day when I was a child. A wonderful day that I went sledding with my friends. It seems I am re-visiting my childhood here. I am smiling.

There are many mysteries to this room on the other side of the looking glass. The real mystery is that one must look in between the lines of the songbook that is propped up on the piano. I walk over to the piano and start playing the lovely tune. Suddenly, the chess game stops. I hear a shout from the King piece. "Stop that racket!" Who are you?"

"I am me." I respond.

"Who are you? ", the King piece repeats his question.

"I just told you."

"Come here." Says the King piece. "Join our game. You must play chess and save the Queen from being captured by the Black knight."

"But I don't know how to play chess."

"Don't know how?", the whole chessboard of pieces laughed out loud.

"Why everyone with a brain knows how to play chess and you claim you don't know how?"

"How did you get here?"

"Through the looking glass."

"Why did you come?"

"I was curious about your beautiful world and I just had to be a part of it."

"To be a part of our beauty and world you must play the game. Come join the chess pieces and win this game for us. If you beat the black Knight, you shall be crowned the white queen."

This whole looking glass world is a paradox of everything and I cannot seem to make any sense out of it all. It is in the silliness of it all and the illogical nature of the looking glass world that I love so much. I must look for the answers to the many puzzles that just beg to be solved. There is real beauty here but is in hiding. It lies between the pages of a 1,000-page novel just waiting to be discovered. Or it may lie in the warm breeze that I welcome dreamily through the window. I smell the scent of lilacs lofting in this sweet air. I inhale deeply and smile.

A person could live happily here in this dream-like world. A person could make better choices in a place such as this. In this looking glass wonderland, I want to be a Queen or perhaps, a Princess. I could most definitely be a Traveler, an Artist, or a Sculptor. I wouldn't be someone ordinary. I am here on the other side of the looking glass on a far away island watching the palm trees in the distance and just waiting for the dawn. Waiting.. waiting.. for the silence to embrace me. I would close my eyes and experience the beauty of the silence. Moments like this are unforgettable especially when you exist in a noisy vacuum called a city. There are no cities here. No hot, stifling cities. There is breathing room and lots of time to play chess and dream. I want to lay my weary bones on a country meadow and walk barefoot through the babbling brook. Then I will spend the rest of the days picking daisies, roses, lavender and daffodils in a basket made up of silk dreams. I stop every once in a while to pick strawberries. Now it has started to rain. A million drops of rain wash away my sorrows and pain and bring a smile back to my life. Why do I jump in the puddles?

Because I can!

On the other side of the looking glass, I see my own reflection and I smile. On the other side of the looking glass, I am curious, kind and good. I am happy, loving and joyful. I am the Queen of the chessboard games. I seek the beauty of this looking glass world. It stirs the curiosity in my heart. I find my own peace of mind and a curious sense of wonder in this lovely world.

BREATHING

Kathryn Lynn Wilson

He could hear people breathing. Constantly. Down his back as he sat on the subway, across the counter of the deli in his face, walking down the street, from person to person, the accumulation of all the breath merged into one, until the entire city was breathing one suffocating heave. Everywhere he went the warm streams attacked his space, wrapped around his legs and face, and at times he swore he could even see the ribbons of breath invading like a swarm of maggots leaching at the corpse of the city. Writhing and squirming in and out the noses and mouths.

The one and only time he had ever kissed someone was before the fear had grown to its height. But even then, he asked her to hold her breath for a couple of seconds. It was a pitiful kiss, one hand behind her neck and the other trying to subtly plug her nose. He couldn't even enjoy it being so afraid that she would start breathing again. Her hue changed from crimson to blue as he held her tightly in his grip. She pushed him away gasping for breath, close to fainting. She told him it was over and that he was crazy.

Holding down a job wasn't an easy trick either, because the stale, workaholic breath of a boss was the most repugnant. It doesn't go over very well when an employee cuts off his boss mid sentence, cups the latter over the mouth, and dry heaves to the side. Why his superiors always made it a point to breathe directly at him he could not explain. Trying to outsmart himself, he figured a job with little human contact was his cure. So he acquired a job with a telephone customer service center, imagining this would distance him from his foe. He soon realized that even worse than feeling the breath was hearing it, especially accented by the microphone of a receiver. Hearing was creepy to him because the source of breath was hidden, ready to jump on him at any time. That ominous shadow that stands behind the wires, breathing heavily through the phone like Darth Vader in his low raspy heave, made him nervous. He stayed for a day and a half. On his last phone call an old woman with nasal congestion called in and as she spoke his ear grew suddenly moist. Confused, he threw the mouth piece to the floor, the muffled voice of the woman still talking, like a sunk submariner. He stared at it for a second while wiping his ear and left, never to return. After that incident he refused to return to work and he called upon the government to rescue him. He believed that the breath-maggots had crawled their way across the wire and squeezed through the holes of his ear piece.

He was jobless, friendless, and comfortless when he received the morning paper on April 6th. He peered out his key hole and waited for all persons to pass before he cracked open the door to grab it. With one swift motion, he snatched it and slid back inside. Inside his box shaped apartment was small but clean, and he made it a point to purchase only white furniture and accessories. He figured it was easier to detect filth on such a contrasting background and it pleased him to know that everything was spotless. He felt safe here, especially because he had never allowed any one other than himself to attain passage into his germ-free, people-free apartment. Perhaps the only person besides himself to set foot in it was the cleaner he had hired to disinfect every square inch of the place. The morning paper was the only foreign object besides food that was allowed daily passage, and this was always discarded promptly along with the surgical gloves he wore to handle it. He paced across the cold white tile in a rhythmic way almost like he was playing hopscotch. He would not allow carpets because of their tendency to collect and accommodate bacteria and this kept his place cold, another thing he was satisfied with. He sat himself softly upon his white couch and began eating his cottage cheese when he came across the horrific story. His fingers grew cold around his dish and the paper trembled a little. "SERIAL KILLER IN OUR CITY!"

He dropped the paper with its foreboding black letters that scattered its remnants across the chilled white tile. Thomas eyed it suspiciously as if the very inside of the paper housed the killer himself. He stepped a pace back from it, still staring. His face was titled to the side, like a querying dog, analyzing the portrait that printed itself on the top page of the brown tinted paper. He had seen that man before. He knew that man. That man had breathed on him before he was sure.

He thought about going to the police, but he didn't know what he would tell them. "Hi, my name is Thomas, I've seen the serial killer before...I don't know where he lives, I don't remember where I saw him, I don't know his name or what kind of clothes he wears, but mark it...I have seen that man before." He refused to put himself in such a situation. The thought also entered, that the killer was probably there watching the police station, eyeing and memorizing the bodies that entered and left...even following some. He couldn't risk it. Not for *them* he wouldn't.

He sat on his couch contemplating what he should do while his right knee bounced nervously and his left hand in a fist shook frantically near his mouth. He was worried about the paper. It still lay there strewn across the floor leaving its dust every minute. Thomas was afraid, because it had been there so long, that if he pulled it off, there would linger an imprint of those inky letters across his floor to haunt him infinitely. While he thus thought a knock came to the door. So acutely aware he was that it seemed even before the knock reached his ear he was already couched behind his couch in a pouncing position. His ears perked up and the knock came again but this time it sounded in Thomas's ear almost as if in slow motion... "Thawuuuump, Thawuuuump," and again, Thawuuump." Thomas shuddered with each one and his eyes winced as if the knock was inflicting some physical pain. His muscles were tight and the knock relentless...it came again..and again. Finally a voice emerged.

"I know you're in there."

"Thawump...Thawump."

"Do you want me to kick down this door, or are you going to come and get it?" Thawump, Thawump.

"C'mon!! If you don't get this door right now, I 'm going to..."

A sigh was heard, and then a quiet mumble. "C'mon you freak, open the damn door." Thomas easily heard it so aware he was of each syllables and even behind the couch the breath was coming... searching for him. In one last desperate attempt the voice called again.

"THOMAS! If you don't open this door right now, you *will* have to find someone else to get your groceries for you!"

Thomas came out of his trance enough to realize what was happening. In the sternest voice he could muster he yelped.

"Who are you?"

"Thomas you know who I am, I have been coming here for ten years now, every Sunday at 3:00pm I come and I deliver you your weekly groceries from the organic market." She paused and waited in silence. Still frustrated she continued on.

"Come on, lets get this over with Thomas. Every week you come to the peep hole. You take a long look at me until you realize that yes you do know me. Then you unlock, not one but two of the deadbolts...you stop there look through the peep hole again and then I say to you as you told me, 'My name is Margaret Sullivan, my code is F-I P-I Alpha, 0038. I work at the Organic Market, you pay me $10 dollars a week for the delivery of your groceries, $5 extra to wear the surgical mask." Then you undo the last deadbolt and I hand you the groceries and the bill to be mailed to me by the following week."

While she was talking Thomas had emerged from behind the couch and went through the exact motions she described. He unlatched the last bolt and opened the door to the plump woman of no more than 5 feet. Her hand was placed upon her hip and her lips pursed when Thomas met with her face. However, this time Thomas did something out of the ordinary, instead of frantically pulling the bags inside in order to not let as much germ enter, he stood there and watched the old lady for a second almost in a paralyzed stance. His eyes fixed upon the top of her head and watched her carefully and methodically. His eye formed a thin milky glaze over it and he analyzed her hands even the veins upon them. He then glanced out further, past the woman upon the sooted concrete and scanned the land methodically. This place was horrifying, unkept....even colorful. He wished to take a giant bucket of white paint and spread it across the whole city. It was then she finished and she peered up at him.

"Thomas."

He looked upon her again.

"I'm finished I'll see you next week. And please Thomas I can't knock for 10 minutes anymore, I have to get back to work you know. I need you to remember that I come at three on Sunday."

There was a pause.

"Okay Thomas? You need to remember."

He glanced at her with his milk eye, "Don't come anymore," he said in a blunt tone.

"What?"

"I said, don't come anymore. I can't have you coming to my house anymore. It's too dangerous for my health. I need you to leave me alone."

She was upset and enraged at his ingratitude. She was the only one at the shop that could put up with him. He could starve for all she cared. She slammed the bill into his hand, tore off her surgical mask, ready to scream at the little scum. But she couldn't find a voice to scream at this pitiful creature, and articulating her anger would be of no use. She closed her eyes, took a deep breath, and nodded her head.

"Fine." she said and walked away. Thomas slammed the door and began the deadbolts. One, Two, Three. He checked them again. One, Two, Three. He looked through the peep hole to make sure she was gone. He returned his focus to his box, ran to the bathroom, into the shower, and began to scrub.

Two hours later he emerged in a full armored suit ready to attack his groceries. He placed them on the counter and began to file them out in an disciplined procedure. He knew his food well, he had been living off the same ingredients for the last 5 years. That is how he knew that when his hand was supposed to be grabbing the large gallon of purified water on the right side of the third bag, instead feeling something small, he threw back his arm and peered into the bag. His purified water was missing! How could she have forgotten that? She knew that was the one thing he had to have. He couldn't survive without water. He began to feel hot and he imagined that she did it to spite him. He felt the panic rising in his throat and he clasped his head in frustration. He let out a small pitiful wail. How could she do this to him? Not now... not today. He pressed his back against the counter and slid to the floor still hiding his face behind surgical gloves. His eyes filled with a few tears that slid past his frightened face. He remembered the paper, he hadn't picked it up yet. It still lay there across his floor, laughing at his face now that he had to go out *there.* He had to go out *there,* where there were killers and rapists and...people breathing. He pulled his fragile body off of the kitchen floor and stood straddled over the black print. With wide eyes he memorized the face...if he had to go out *there* he would remember it just in case. With surgical gloves and some small scissors Thomas carefully cut the hollow face from the paper and placed it in a plastic baggie and placed it in the front pocket of his jacket.

He tried to dress himself as normal as possible to detract getting any attention from breathing people, but his wardrobe was limited...to white. So he wore a casual white shirt, with some white sneakers and a pair of white sweat pants. He looked in the mirror and tried to appease his mind. He thought that if the blacks could get away with outfits like that why couldn't he? The only problem he didn't take into consideration was that his skin was almost as white as his outfit, and his eyes were still filmed over by a milky substance.

The day was falling by the time he was ready to leave. A gray deposit left its mark upon the winter sky like lead does after it's smeared. Rain was coming. The closest supermarket was on the 10th floor of the new high-rise just two blocks down. An odd position for a supermarket but they had raved at how *modern* the idea was, and afraid of being traditional, people accepted it. Thomas had read about its opening in the paper about a year ago and it would be the first time he would be visiting, he prayed it was still in business. The moment he stepped out his door his eyes began to pan the streets...for the face. He reached the main street and walked quickly down the grimy sidewalks. Back and forth his head spun watching and occasionally dodging the breath that came his way. He looked like a boxer getting pumped for a fight, bouncing and jumping from side to side. His attempt at going unnoticed failed and his white shoes were leaving traces everywhere. He continued on faster now into a light jog, verging on the edge of running. Suddenly a burst of fear overcame him and he began to run fast now and he continued in this frenzy all the way to the building and down the long empty hall of its entrance. He reached the elevator and fumbled around in his pocket for his hanky which he found and pushed the "up" button. He was panting now to catch his breath and already his entire ghostly figure was gasping in exhaustion. A bell rang above him and the arrow key flashed a green button. It startled him at first but he understood when the doors widened to let him through. He walked across the threshold into yet another box, this time metal, and when the doors shut behind him he wished he could take it back.

There was another man in the elevator. He must of been there already and in his exhaustion he had failed to notice him in the corner when he climbed in. How could he of missed such an important detail? Why was he shoved so far into the corner, he thought? Is he trying to hide something? Thomas peered at the man out of the side of his eye and took serious note of his figure. He was 6 foot, lean, with dark hair. He was watching the ground intently and Thomas could only see a fourth of his face. The picture from the paper flashed in black and white across the eyelids of Thomas, every time he blinked. The nose fit, he was sure. The picture had described it perfectly, long and skinny with a big knot at the bridge. And out of that nose the warm stream was coming....searching for Thomas and he pressed himself against the metal door. All of this happened rather quickly and now the elevator began to ascend. Thomas's nerves grew tight and his breath restricted, the breath maggots were everywhere now. They infested the walls, searching the metal for an escape. Thomas was being shut in on all sides, confined in a box were every moment the air was growing thicker his muscles grew weak and smoke clouded his head. The man glanced his eyes upwards without moving his head. Thomas began to squirm and clasped the metal harder. He pulled his hanky out from his pocket and covered his mouth and half his nose, wheezing short high-pitched breaths. The man grew concerned. He moved his head upwards looking at Thomas with a slightly furrowed brow. This time Thomas got a good look at him. The smoke cleared from his head and Thomas knew it was him. The man inched towards him with an outstretched hand and Thomas inched further back. A primal survival instinct took over his body. This man meant him more harm than his breathing had already inflicted. Rage and terror boiled through Thomas's blood rising from his feet and forcing its strength to the tips of his hands. Thomas surged forward and clasped the mans neck and bit by bit squeezed the raging blood from his fingertips into the mans throat. His hands shook violently and Thomas's milk eye grew still staring at the man with a numb stare. The man's eyes rolled backwards into his eyelids and his limbs grew lifeless. Thomas released and with a heap the man hit the metal floor with one resounding thud. He punched the cancel button on the elevator and stepped carefully over the body on his way out. He scrambled down the concrete stairs in silence making no discernable noise and made his way out onto the street again. It was a moonless night and the rains had begun to fall. He pulled his white sweatshirt over his head, covered his pale hands, and began to lightly jog. Beneath the half light of the street lamp, Thomas frail hollow figure ran, a white form with an even larger shadow that he barely escaped with each step. Beneath his hood, his nose pointed through, long and skinny with a knot at the bridge. His chest heaved in and then out, with every heave a small white tail emerged from beneath his nose, a small distinct ribbon of breath, that turned white and sailed away when it reached the cold air. He ran faster now, he was in need of a good scrub.

LET'S GO FLY A KITE

Katy Picard

The man set the excited little girl on the sand. She childishly sprinted down to the vast ocean. Seagulls called above her. Waves teased her toes. She giggled wildly and turned to smile happily at her father. She took her cheerful orange pumpkin bucket and began filling it with various rocks and shells. As she skipped along the shoreline, she came across a starfish. She gingerly picked it up to examine it. It wiggled in her hands. Her light blue eyes filled with laughter. It tickled her and she was going to keep it. She set the starfish on the edge of the water. "Stay right there," she commanded. She went into the water a little ways and filled her bucket carefully, making sure that her precious jewels wouldn't spill. She returned to her newfound friend and placed the starfish into her treasure box. She continued on her way, stopping frequently to stoop over to touch another glorious adventure.

Her father called her over, a large, bright colored kite in his hands. She dropped the bucket, forgetting it's valuable contents, and ran to the arms of her hero.

They flew the box kite all over, higher, and higher, as the little girl requested. Sunbeams bounced off the bright material and cast shadows across the bucket. Suddenly, the wind began to toss the kite further and further over the ocean. The tension in its string grew. Finally, the little girl's grip on the kite slipped and the string went racing alongside the ocean. It hit the bucket with a great deal of force, which sent it flying across the shore.

~*~

The starfish was thrown over itself and landed roughly in the damp sand. It sat for a moment, motionless. Then it began to move each of its five legs, as if checking to feel them all there. Of course it was a relief to be out of captivity, but it had to be sure. The starfish silently began the long journey to its home. It moved quickly and accurately, avoiding the gull's shadows as they soared on the sparkling dust. The sun beat down on the starfish, making the trek harder as it went along. Suddenly the starfish felt damp sand beneath its body. It congratulated itself, but not for long. The ground vibrated with the little girl's frustrated stomps. She approached the starfish, and almost stepped on it, but her father whistled to her. She stepped back and turned to her father. She protested and whined as the starfish quickly scurried to the water. The relief of the salt overcame the starfish. It sighed internally and spun itself deeper into nothingness.

Her father promised the little girl another kite and she reluctantly accepted. As her mood grew lighter, she began to pick up where she had left off. She picked up her bucket and searched for the starfish. She looked to the water and caught the last traces of her friend, speeding off. She shrugged her shoulders. It was only a toy. She could always get another one. The rocks, on the other hand, were more important. She grabbed them in handfuls now, and shoved them into her bucket. Her hair blew lightly with the calming wind. Her father came down in the sand and scooped his little girl into his arms. They walked back to their car. And then they were gone.

STRANDED IN A SUPER 8 MOTEL: TWO DAYS IN IOWA

Kenneth F. Pearson

The lounge at the Super 8 Motel in Stuart, Iowa, was eerily quiet at 2:15 that morning. The snow had been breathing heavily down on us for only about six hours, but already there were over twelve inches on the ground. The wind was gusting around seventy miles-per-hour and the snow, being as light as baby powder, made the storm one of the worst in my short memory. While attempting to drive, I couldn't see the front of the car, let alone any of my fellow motorists. To see the road was virtually impossible, and when I could see it, the road was a white path to nowhere. This was the reason for Rich, Jen, and I stopping over for the night.

We were coming home from a week long trip to Fort Collins, Colorado and I was ready to go home. Rich and Jen had annoyed me for most of the trip, and I needed a well-deserved break from them. I drank heavily that week, trying to ignore them or at least trying not to remember I was with them. The night we stopped at the Super 8 Motel, I became fairly intoxicated from drinking at the bar in the motel lounge most of the night.

I removed myself from the lounge and made my way into the motel lobby, where I sat impatiently trying to figure out how the hell I was going to get home the next day. The weatherman had predicted the storm to last about three full days. After the nightly news, I watched infomercials. They kept me company. There was a very good infomercial for an oldies CD, which I would've purchased if it weren't for the fact I only had twenty-eight dollars in my pocket. The CD was mostly a compilation of 50's music and I figured it would make a good gift for my mother. The desk clerk kept eyeing me suspiciously, then looking away, pretending he was counting the money for the night, but no one should be counting it for that long. He never said a word to me. Maybe he was nervous I would try something. I guess he figured since I'm from New York, I must be a criminal. I'm sure most people in Iowa think of New Yorkers that way.

I left the lobby at around 4:15 that morning and walked across the street to a twenty-four hour Citgo gas station. There was a newlywed couple working the front counter. Marcia and "Stank." I don't know where he got the nickname from, but by the looks of him, it didn't leave much for the imagination. They made me sick to my stomach watching them flirt with each other, but at least they were good for a conversation. "Stank" was excited when I spoke with him. I'm sure working with his wife day in and day out made it enjoyable to have a new face to converse with. He was thrilled when the conversation focused on his town. Turns out, it's the town where they filmed "The Bridges Over Madison County." I almost peed my pants from laughing so hard when he told me. He was insulted at first until he realized I was from New York. In turn, he sarcastically inquired as to whether or not I was going to rob them. "T'ouche, gas man, T'ouche." The conversation continued on for another hour or so, until I felt the need to sleep. I asked if I could sleep there, as I was not looking forward to going back to the motel room with Rich and Jen, but they kindly declined and wished me a safe trip home. I thanked them and stumbled across the street through the snow. I fell asleep on a very comfortable couch in the lobby of the motel. I was cold, but I refused to go upstairs to my motel room.

Early the next afternoon, I woke to Rich and Jen glaring down on me. My head was throbbing from the beer I drank the night before and they were the last thing I wanted to see when I woke. They had been ready to leave for about half an hour, but according to them, I was nowhere to be found. They knew I would have to shower, so that aggravated them even more. I purposely took my time, but then sped up as I realized it wasn't snowing quite as hard anymore. The winds were still gusting at high speeds, but I was sure if we could get out of Iowa, we'd be home free. I quickly packed my bags and took a half-assed shower. It was nice to have that warm water spraying down on me. It gave me a renewed sense of urgency. When I was done, we checked out of the motel and continued on our journey home.

The three of us packed into a 1995, two-door Honda Accord. Rich and I took turns driving and Jen just sat in the back complaining about everything. I think she enjoyed listening to herself talk, so when I drove, I made sure the music was blasting through the speakers, so she couldn't complain to anyone. We were traveling on Route 80 at about forty miles-per-hour, fighting the snow, the plows, the trucks, and other drivers. The light snow still made it difficult to see, but not impossible. We commented to each other about the number of trucks stranded in ditches off the road, knowing to ourselves that they must have been cruising at quite a high speed to end up there. That was the extent of our conversation when I drove, though.

Rich and I switched roles and he took the wheel for awhile. I just gazed out the window while he drove. He began talking to me about Zen Buddhism and Jack Kerouac and how "The Dharma Bums" changed his life. He thought it would be a good idea for the three of us to move to Colorado together. His dream was to emulate the life of William S. Burroughs. I started giggling to myself at the possibility of living with Rich and Jen. Rich could be the junkie, I could be the drunk, and Jen could be our "yabyum" partner.

It had been fours hours since we left the Super 8 Motel in Stuart, but we had only traveled about one hundred and twenty miles. It was actually a miracle we had gotten that far, but I still wanted to move much quicker. Jen had silently decided to herself it would be a good idea for her to lather her body with lotion. The lotion gave me an allergy attack, so I fought back by allowing my rectum to add a night's worth of stale beer into the recycled air. I listened to her complain about it for a second and then tuned her out. I went back to gazing out the window. I noticed a herd of cattle having sex in the ten below zero temperature, trying to keep warm, I suppose. I'm not sure if it was my mind playing tricks on me or if I had actually seen it. Either way, it answered my question as to the way cattle have sex.

I took my eyes away from the outside world and started to look at maps. I was trying to plan an alternative route, but the moment I did, the snow began falling harder, the wind increased, and cars began swerving all over the road. I witnessed one car accident, then another, then another. I witnessed a total of four accidents in a matter of fifteen minutes. I began noticing state troopers at various exits, trying to pull people off the road. I thought if we could just get by them, we'd be able to continue driving. I kept telling Rich and Jen to just look forward and not to make eye contact. All of a sudden, we were in dead stop traffic. A big, blue eighteen-wheel Werner truck lie jackknifed across the highway. It was just after the exit to Coralsville, Iowa. A state trooper waved us off the side of the road and said, "How ya doin' gints, ma'am. Sorry, but we done closed the highway. Go 'n git yerself a motel room 'cause the road a'int gonna open 'til tamorra." All I could think was, "Goddammit, not another motel... ...IN IOWA!"

THE DEBTORS

Kenneth Ormsbee

Stephen Colling died twice.

The first time was an accident, at the age of eleven. Every winter he and his parents would take up residence in northern Florida, inside a refurbished Civil War mansion. Stephen loved to watch the machines crawl through the cotton fields, gathering up the white pugs with their steel paws; and, when his mother would flap her thin hand, ostentatiously shooing him away from the "horrid machinery," he would traipse down to one of the several water holes dotting the plantation.

Today was no exception to the routine, and Stephen soon found himself wandering around the perimeter of a stagnant pond, just south of the large Victorian mansion. In his youthful exuberance he was able to ignore the fetid air, enjoy the ordinarily aggravating bugs as they bolted in and out of the water, and relish the tough of the slippery, lime-green moss. He could not tolerate, however, the fiends who inhabited the swampy area - the very ones who hid under his bed at night. These monsters loomed everywhere and Stephen soon forgot the joyful subtleties of the swamp, and his eyes darted back and forth erratically. He could feel the sultry breat of one of the imagined creatures on the nape of his neck; and, in response, swatted nervously behind him, edging closer to a gnarled tree hanging precariously over the tinted water.

Without realizing his actions, he sidled onto the slimy, lichen-covered wood, oblivious to the groaning sound of the roots grasping the bank. Before the monster could snatch him, the wooden fingers let go of safety and Stephen, with a panicked gasp, found himself immersed in the greenish water. Five years of private swimming lessons did him little good, for his leg was impacted between a rock and the guilty tree. No amount of struggle could give him freedom and his body soon felt a last shudder and went limp.

Stephen's mother, endlessly searching for him in the past and present, spotted his lifeless floating hand and screamed in horror. Her attendants were not far behind her cry and they endeavored to pull Stephen from the water. The audible cracking of bones escaped the attention of his rescuers as his leg twisted unnaturally out of the entrapment. His mother turned her head affectedly, unable to bear the thought of losing this, her only heir. She was apprehensive at the thought of ever making a new one.

One servant pumped Stephen's soaked chest, while others displaced the stringy seaweed that covered his person. All efforts seemed futile; and, and after a few last attempts at resuscitation, they gave up, turning away at the very moment a cough slipped from the shivering body and the eyes opened wide. The only thing Stephen remembered of the incident was the wonderful floating sensation and then the horror as he was uninvitingly sucked back into his frame.

Now at twenty-three, Stephen hobbled along the streets of windy Chicage, a trusted cane ever in his grasp. He gazed admiringly at his third leg. The pointed tip was encased in gold, and polished wood, now stained deep red, was carved by request from the very tree that took the life from his leg.

For only a moment he stared at the cane, soon returning to an ever-vigilant watch. He was rich; he fully realized the fact after his parents died two years previously when he was inundated with invitations of service from lawyers, doctors, politicians and corporate brokers. Thereafter, the monsters of his childhood took the shape of greedy lawyers, avaricious businessmen, and beggarly charities. Stephen soon concluded that the entire human race sought his money. The innocent looking child holding fast to his father's leg, the hot dog vendor with the grating accent, the woman draped in black with a shiny cross around her neck - all of them were envious of his wealth, covetous to the degree of theft.

Stephen entered his building, eager to get to his office, the place where he signed carefully scrutinized forms and kept his money painstakingly active. He passed the front desk clerk, who clipped a hello and tried to act like she was busy doing something. Stephen glared at her suspiciously and shuffled briskly to the stairs, the elevator always to full of pressing people.

When he reached his floor, he pushed the door aside and limped into a bustling office. A money-grubbing woman smiled at him in passing, a steaming Styrofoam cup of coffee in hand. She was an exception. No one ever spoke to Stephen, and only a select, naïve, few dared smile at him. So he was understandingly surprised when Harvey, the poor, balding secretary muttered a few words in his direction.

"The young woman you met at the party the other night is in your office. We tried to get her to leave, but she wouldn't listen. She is Walde Worth's daughter, after all," he stammered. "We couldn't very easily turn her away."

Stephen's brow furrowed in annoyance as he walked away from Harvey's pitiful attempt at sucking up. There was only one plausible reason for her being there. Stephen clamped his jaw tight. He would rid his world once and for all of this rapacious wench who had been doting on his wallet for years. He swung open his oak doors speedily and stalked into his spaciously well-lit office. Too late did he realize that he was alone with another human being.

She was dressed in a short, bright-red skirt and jacket, the latter covering a glimmering white blouse. Her heels added an inch to her height and her fashioned hat cast and imposing shadow across her face, red lipstick contrasting the darkness. Before he could act, he was trapped in the depths of her eyes. Immediately, he could see her desire for his riches. "I know what you want!" he shrieked, edging as close as possible to the nearest wall.

"I like a man who knows what I want," she purred demurely, casually stepping closer. She placed her thin hands on his chest and moved to touch his lips with her own.

Panicked, Stephen turned and raced toward the door, grasping the handle with a shaky hand. He could feel her breath at the nape of his neck as he rushed from the room. In a daze he staggered to the elevator; it was worth the risk this time. Soon after, his cane clicked rapidly on the sidewalk. He turned into an alley and ran headlong into a gun.

"Hey, buddy, gimme yer wallet, or I'll blow yer guts to Toledo," the unshaven vagrant blurted.

"Never!" Stephen gasped, raising his gold-tipped cane to bat the fiend away. He heard a muffled pop and felt a wrenching in his stomach. Doubling over, and striking the ground, he could vaguely feel rough hands searching his pockets. He mumbled, "My money."

The disgruntled vagabond, satisfied with a pure leather wallet in hand, searched its crevices and cried, "A lousy five dolla' bill! No credit cards! No nothin'! What kind of paranoid freak is this guy?" His hand crumbled the bill and he threw the wallet to the pavement.

From what seemed far away, Stephen heard the man hustle away in the distance, and shuddered one last time, his hand gripped tightly around the tip of his cane, hiding its color.

THE LAST NORMALITY

Kevin Patrick Necessary

The man shuffled into the room, not really wanting to be there, but reluctantly, and on the advise of his doctor, his friends, his wife, he had accepted the fact that he should go.

Nervously, he looked around, gathering up his surroundings in one sweeping gaze. There was nothing that he missed, from the utter emptiness of the room, minus the seven chairs arranged in a circle, six of which were occupied, to the wooden beams supporting the ceiling. Every footfall he made echoed in the cavernous room, keeping pace with his beating heart.

He'd always known he'd had a problem, but had never come to accept it. As a child, he just wasn't like the other children. He never fit in. As an adult, he'd had to cope with his family, his friends and co-workers. No matter where he was, how old he became, he just was not like everybody else.

One of the six other people, a woman, came over to him. She wore a sticker nametag on her blue sweater, its baggy arms and midsection looking made the garment look too sizes too big on her small frame. Her name, he saw, was Kathlene. She smiled at him, a big, fake smile, one that she probably gave everyone who came to the support group.

"Hello, are you Jack?" she said, her voice high and sing song.

The man just nodded.

She handed him a nametag with his name already on it. "Good. This way, please. Come, join us."

She ushered the man over to the circle of chairs. He stepped in, sat down, looking at the faces of the others who'd come, the others who knew they weren't like everyone else. There were two other women, and three men. Some looked happier than others. One looked down right depressed. Two had blank faces, absolutely devoid of emotion. Jack felt like he'd just stepped into a prison, his own personal cell, his own private hel. The woman, Kathlene, sat down and turned to face each of the people in the circle, one at a time. The damnable smile on her face never left. Such big teeth you have, Grandma, thought Jack, looking at that smile.

Kathlene clapped her hands together. "Well, it's so good to see you all again."

Again, she turned to face everyone present in the circle.

"As you can see, we have a new member to our group today. Why don't you tell us who you are and why you're here?"

Jack stood up, his hands anxiously brushing at his sides. He looked down, eyes avoiding the gazes of the other six gathered. He cleared his throat before he spoke.

"Um, uh, hello. My name is ... my name is Jack. And I'm here because I'm normal." "Hello, Jack," came six voices, all in unison. It freaked the hell out of Jack. They're like cattle, he thought sarcastically. Dumb, damn cattle.

Jack took his seat.

Kathlene smiled, her focus totally on Jack. "Jack, since you're new, why don't you tell us why you're here."

Scratching the back of his head, Jack looked up, then, finally, at the faces of the other members of the support group. His gaze lasted briefly; as he began to speak, he lowered his eyes once again.

"I, uh, well, I have always known that I was normal. That there was nothing wrong with me. I didn't have manic-depression, or even regular depression. No A.D.D."

Jack turned his head, his eyes darting up and then down and then up again, trying to gaze everyone's reaction to what he was saying. Nothing, he saw. They'd probably heard it a million times before.

Jack continued on: "As a child, I was always less creative than the other kids. They could all draw or write or play music. I couldn't. I was just a normal kid. I didn't feel isolated, or draw within myself. I was just me. No mood swings. Nothing.

"As I grew older, it was the same thing. I remember taking this art class, my senior year in high school. Most of the kids in there were brilliant, absolutely astounding. And then there was me. Just a regular Joe. Yeah, there were always a few of us who felt left out, who couldn't do anything. We just hung together. We didn't know what was wrong with us, and we were afraid to say anything. But we all knew that we were different."

"How do you feel now?" interrupted Kathlene. "What's your life like now?" "Terrible. It's just the same as when I was a kid."

Jack stopped, his breathing deep. Like everyone else, he'd spent years with a therapist. Of course, he'd never felt the need to talk to anyone. But it was just something you did, like go on picnics or church on Sundays. Jack had never come this clean before, never told this much, not even to his assigned doctor.

"After college, I got married to a beautiful woman. My wife, she was-is-bipolar.

I got a job at a local firm, and for the first time, everything seemed to be going well. Yeah, I'd get upset at my wife's mood swings. But that's normal, isn't it?"

No reaction from the other five. Kathlene just smiled. "But things started going bad about six years ago. That was about the time my firm landed a huge project, and I was put in charge of it. It was also the time that my first son was born."

Jack wrung his hands together, his palms balmy and sweaty. "I thought I was doing well with the project. It was an account, and we had four years to make it work. I thought that I could handle it. I guess I was wrong.

"By the time the fourth year came around, my boss took me aside. He asked why the results were substandard, why I wasn't being more creative. I told him I was doing the best I could with the resources provided. But that wasn't good enough for him. I couldn't handle late nights, or all-nighters, and, looking back, the quality of work was just, well, normal. I was replaced, and over night, the guy who took over for me, well, he turned the whole damn thing around."

He cleared his throat again. "About that time, my son was diagnosed with having bipolar disorder, just like my wife. And that really did me in. My wife sheltered him from me, refused to let me see him or play with him. She'd always tell me that she didn't want someone who was 'just a normie' handling our son's budding creativity. He was four years old damn it-sorry."

Kathlene reached over and patted Jack's knee. "It's all right. This is a place to get our emotions out."

Jack offered her and the rest of the group a small, sheepish smile. "Sorry. Thanks. Anyway, she then began secluding me from our second son, who was two. I was just too normal. She didn't want to take any chances. 'We have to keep their condition in mind at all times,' she'd say. 'We have to make sure they come out right.' Well, I guess that meant I couldn't be involved in their up brining. About a year ago, it got so bad, that I just left. Just took off and left. I quit my job, and moved out here to the coast."

"And how has that affected you?" questioned Kathlene.

Jack just shook his head. "It's the same all over. I haven't been able to get a job, at least, not a real job. I'm just not qualified. Every employer wants someone who's bipolar. Someone who's 'deeper,' or 'thinks differently.' They don't want someone who thinks normally."

Before Jack could continue, Kathlene held up a hand and stopped him. She took in the entire group with her smile, encompassing all the faces and stares. "Well, I think that we all know how Jack feels. I know it may seem hard, living in this world. We can't help who we are. The world has evolved around us, and, in a way, beyond us. There's nothing any of us can do to change that. We just have to accept the fact that we're not like everyone else. That we're just normal. And normal is good enough."

For the first time, Jack's heart jumped. He'd been told, countless times by countless people, that he was a relic, a fossil of a lost age, where being normal was just that-normal. A dinosaur of a time when having some mental affliction was actually considered a stigmata, not a sign of humanity's next evolutionary step. Jack felt at home.

Kathlene stood up. "Now, Jack has been very brave in coming here and telling us his story. I think he deserves a group hug."

The others stood up, some moving faster than others, and enclosed Jack with their arms and bodies. He couldn't breathe, he couldn't move, but for some odd reason, he didn't mind.

Jack had found himself with other relics, other dinosaurs. And now, Jack did not feel alone.

TARGET PRACTICE

Kirby Wright

My big brother Ben was still waiting to hear from the University of Hawaii the week before our high school graduation. We were both seniors because he'd been held back. Ben's grades were poor but rumor had it that UH never turned away Punahou grads. Still, there was that element of doubt. I knew the pressure was getting to him because he worked out like a madman, usually when my father was at the firm. Ben always lifted weights barefoot.

"I thought you were supposed to lift every other day?" I asked while he curled forty pound hand weights out on the lanai.

He studied the biceps flexing under his skin. "Not if you wanna get big, Jeff."

"How big do you wanna be?"

"As big as a Dallas Cowboy."

Ben slept on a bed without sheets, pillow, or pad. "They just get dirty," he would say. The wall beside the bed was stained with strands of dried mucus.

There was no rug covering the asbestos tiles in his room. He'd tacked up a poster of a rifle-toting skeleton sitting on an American flag; the flag was spread over a chair of bones. There was a goat's head on the wall above his desk. Ben had shot the goat point blank on Moloka'i with my father's .3006 from World War II. He'd wounded three goats that day, but two managed to crawl into an impassable gully. "Caught 'em completely by surprise," he'd said, "musta bled to death in that gully." Because Ben had used the rifle without permission, my father took it to work and gave it to a partner who collected wartime memorabilia.

The only books on Ben's bookcase were a manual on isometrics and an autographed copy of Pumping Iron. His textbooks for Physics, French, and Geometry were thrown in the far corner of his room—their spines were cracked and their covers inked with graffiti. He had bottles of Sun In and Lady Clairol's Honey Blonde on the bottom shelf of his bookcase. On the top shelf was a trophy of a gold soldier aiming a gold rifle. Ben had won it before flunking out of ROTC. He'd taken close-ups from different angles and sent glossies to all my mother's relatives in Boston.

The high point of Ben's last semester in high school was buying a shotgun on sale at Honsport Gun & Tackle. The deal included ten boxes of double lot shells. He started shooting skeet at Koko Head Crater, a volcano that had been converted into a rifle range. He spent less and less time bodysurfing at Makapu'u Beach and more and more time at the range. He claimed he could hit two clay pigeons with a single pass.

"Can I go sometime?" I asked while he rammed a cleaning rod down the barrel.

"No tenderfoots."

"Come on."

Ben pulled out the rod—he examined the swatch of white cloth attached to its tip. Then he worked the pump action and ejected a shell. "Do what you do best."

"What's that?"

He puckered up. "Kissing the General's ass."

* * *

Ben was in a sour mood the week after the prom, mainly because I'd gone and he hadn't. One evening, while my mother was out shopping at Ala Moana, Ben took the transistor radio out of the kitchen and plugged it into an outlet on the lanai. His bench was on the cement and he pressed one hundred pounds over and over. Tina Turner sang "Proud Mary" as winged termites circled the ceiling's recessed lights. I found an old Ping-Pong paddle and swung at the termites.

The night was hot and humid and I could see my father through the glass doors watching TV. After knocking the wings off a few termites, I put the paddle on the cement and sat on the ottoman. My father had covered it with sheets of plastic because he said the oil from Ben's body was staining the fabric.

Ben grunted as he did his reps. He wore a Dallas Cowboys tank top and white sweat pants. His blond hair was down to his shoulders and I could see the roots. His hair length violated the dress code but administrators were going easy on seniors. Some of the guys had even grown mustaches and beards. Ben moved the bar up and down and finally rested it on the arms of the bench. He sat up and grimaced.

"Something wrong?" I asked.

Ben did windmills with his arms. "Stupid UH turned me down."

"No."

"Wanna see the letter?"

I leaned back and the plastic under me crinkled. "I'm sorry."

"I'll bet."

"You can still go to KCC."

Ben stopped doing windmills. "High school with ashtrays."

"Go one semester, then transfer."

"Easy for you to say."

My father opened the sliding screen door. "Turn that racket down!"

"Thought you loved Tina Turner?" Ben asked.

"You heard me, Ben."

Ben nodded at me and I got up and turned it down.

My father walked out holding his martini in a water glass. He was a thin-lipped man with a ruddy complexion. He wore leather slippers, a V-neck undershirt, and gray pants. There was a black mole the size of a quarter below his collarbone. He pulled off his bifocals as Ben added more weight to the bar.

"Now, Ben," he said, "no lifting weights out here."

"Why not?"

"Because you'll drop 'em and bust my cement."

"I won't drop 'em."

"Bullshit," my father said. "Now do as I say."

Ben saluted. "Aye, aye, General Gill."

My father returned to the house. I could hear him digging for ice.

"Someday," Ben said, "that kanak's going to get his. Let's move my bench out."

I helped Ben carry his bench and weights out to the lawn. We set the bench up next to the stump of what had been a fifty-foot breadfruit tree. My father had hired Tongans to cut the tree down a week earlier because he was sick of Samoans coming by asking for fruit. The night sky seemed naked without the leaves covering it.

"Can't hear the music," Ben said.

I turned the radio up and Ben did curls with hand weights. When he finished, he dropped the weights on the grass and returned to the bench. He put on two hundred pounds and squirmed under the bar. He studied the weight until Santana started singing "Black Magic Woman."

Ben locked his hands around the bar. "I love this song," he said. "Crank it, Jeff!"

I turned it up and he benched the weight like it was made of foam.

"Way to go!" I said.

Ben rested the bar on the bench and pressed again.

My father whipped open the screen door and shuffled out. His slippers slapped against the cement floor of the lanai. "Now, Ben," he said, "no throwing weights on my grass."

Ben rested the bar on the arms of the bench. "Big deal."

"You're destroying my roots. Wanna re-sod this whole god damn backyard?"

"You never know when to quit, do you?"

My father pushed the bridge of his glasses back with his thumb and straightened his back.

"You heard me, Ben."

"Yeah, yeah, yeah."

My father shuffled back and slammed the screen door.

"Let's move to my room," Ben said.

"You got it."

We carried the bench and weights into the house. I scraped the end of the bar against the redwood wall.

Ben ran his had over the gouge. "Terrible kids."

We set up the bench in the middle of his room and I went back for the transistor. I handed him the radio and he stood barefoot in his doorway.

"See ya, Jeff," he said.

"Want me to spot you?"

He shook his head and shut the door. I heard him lock it and turn the radio on. I started washing dishes. My mother had baked a roasting chicken earlier that night and, after my father told her it tasted like rubber, she left the table and sped off in her Barracuda to go shopping. I could hear music from Ben's room as I scrubbed the burned rice sticking to the bottom of the pot.

My father entered the kitchen with his martini. "Didn't I tell that guy to turn it down?"

"Yeah," I said, "but that was outside."

"Same rules inside and out," he said. He walked back to the dining room and gazed up at the clock. "That bastard's deliberately defying me." He put his martini on the table and proceeded down the hall.

I put the pot down and trailed after him.

My father pounded on Ben's door. "Ben!" he said. "Open this god damn door! Do you hear me?" He pounded while the DJ talked about the big Blowout Sale at Ala Moana. "I know you hear me, Ben! This is my house!"

I could hear weights clinking and grunting behind the door. There was a framed picture on the wall of my father in his helmet and Major's uniform. He stood on the shore of Tarawa Atoll while amtracs struggled over the reef. He held his glasses in one hand and a rifle in the other. His eyes were small and calculating.

"If you can't live by my rules," my father said, "move the Hell out!"

A commercial for Lippy's Used Cars blared.

"So loud he can't hear," my father told me. "Go around to his window and have him turn it down."

"He won't listen to me."

"You heard me, Jeffrey."

"Quit bugging him."

"Want me to pay for the University of Colorado?"

I nodded.

"Then you'd better damn well do as I say."

I walked out the back door. I slipped by my parents' sheets drying on the clothesline and squeezed past the lemon trees on the side of the house. I looked in through the louvered windows of Ben's room—he sat on his bed with his back to the wall. It was the same bed my father had him lie naked on when he'd beaten him as a boy. Ben's arms looked huge sticking out of his tank top. The shotgun rested on his lap. He was loading red shells into the side of the gun.

The bench supported a load of weights. There was so much weight on the bar that it bowed in the middle. The radio was next to the trophy on the bookcase and Mick Jagger sang "Gimmee Shelter."

"Ben," I said.

He kept loading.

I cupped my hands. "Hey, Ben!"

He jammed a shell into the gun and didn't look up.

"The General says, 'Turn it down!' "

Ben got up and placed the gun on the bed.

He turned the volume down and walked over to the louvers.

"You're his li'l yes man."

"Am not."

"You're spying for the General."

"He just wants quiet."

Ben plucked hand weights off his desk. "Know what he really wants?"

"What?"

"To kill the part of me that's still me." He curled the weights and his biceps bulged.

"It's only the radio."

"Don't you see?" Ben asked. "It's not your life, it's his."

"I'm doing what I want."

He smirked. "Run off to college, Jeff. Become a lawyer, you li'l kiss ass."

"You're such a dunce."

He stopped curling. "At least I'm not hard-up."

"What?"

"Didn't you take a slant eye to the prom?"

"You punk," I said.

He held the weights in front of him and began a rowing motion.

"At least I had the balls to go," I said.

He dropped the weights on the asbestos tiles and I heard one of the tiles crack. Sweat rolled down his cheeks. "Rather not go than be hard-up like you. Mummy's pissed, you know."

"I'm glad I'm going to Colorado."

"I'm glad too," he replied. "Now if the General asks, tell him I'll be waiting with Fred."

"Who's Fred?"

Ben turned the volume back up. He plucked his shotgun off the bed and smiled.

* * *

I found my father pacing back and forth in the dining room. His hands were locked behind his back and he glared at the floor. It was the way he got before all his big cases. The music drifting down the hall sounded tinny. My father looked at his Timex, then up at the clock. He was grinding ice the way a horse grinds barley.

"Well?" he asked. "D'you tell 'im?"

"Yeah."

"That son of a bitch." My father walked into the kitchen. He opened a drawer and pulled out an ice pick. "I'll fix his wagon."

I followed him down the hall. The transistor was turned so high that the music was distorting. My father inserted the tip of the ice pick in the lock on Ben's doorknob. The music quit.

"I wouldn't do that," I said.

My father turned the handle of the pick and the lock popped. I heard the pump action on Ben's side of the door.

"Did you hear that?" I asked as I eased my way down the hall.

My father scowled. "Hear what?"

"Fred."

"Who the Hell's Fred?"

"Ben's shotgun," I said.

"Where'd he get a shotgun?"

"On sale at Honsport," I said. "It came with ten boxes of shells."

My father grabbed the knob with his free hand. "He's bluffing."

"It's up to you."

He studied the door.

No sound came from Ben's room.

My father took his hand off the knob. He backed away and shuffled down the hall with the ice pick. I followed him to the living room, where he switched on the television. He placed the pick on the end table and hunkered down on the couch.

I returned to Ben's door and did our special "shave-and-a-haircut" knock, the one we'd exchanged as small kids on the wall dividing our rooms; it had been our way of acknowledging a shared pain after beatings and telling each other we'd survived another round. Ben didn't respond to my knock so I tried again. I could hear weights clinking.

"What?" he asked through the door.

I could hear weights clinking. "Can I come in?"

"No hard-ups."

"Come on. I'll tell you all about the General."

The radio came back on. The DJ talked about a rock concert coming to Diamond Head Crater.

I knocked again. "Please?"

Ben turned up the volume and the door shook in its frame. "Cisco Kid" blew through the house.

I put my hand on the wall and it vibrated. My father's picture, the one taken on Tarawa Atoll, was above my hand. The eyes under the helmet were cold and they peered into the future.

MISS LAVINIA'S PORTRAIT

Laura Mae Oldham-Brownell

The masterful hands of the artist, Jean-Luc Devereaux, pause momentarily as he contemplates the few remaining brushstrokes necessary to complete Miss Lavinia Brighton's portrait. He cast his dark, knowing eyes upon her form. Then, with great care, he surveys every aspect of her pose; critically comparing this vision against his nearly completed work. Jean-Lucs' mind keenly focuses on each subtle detail, scrutinizing the likeness he has been creating over the past several weeks. Finally, in an instant of profound clarity, he knows instinctively where his artists' bristles must once again anoint the canvas, to lend precision of highlight and shadow thus completing his endeavor. This being accomplished, Jean-Luc examines the painting, and cautiously smiles to himself. He is pleased with the portrait, but he requires the approval of his subject, before he will truly know his labors have been well spent.

Miss Brighton, aware this is tentatively the final session between herself and Monsieur Devereaux speaks softly as she inquires as to when the painting will be available to view. The portrait had been commissioned month's earlier through written correspondence involving Jean- Lucs' agent, Monsieur Jacques Le Blanc of Versailles, France, and Mrs. Dorothy Holcomb, Lavinia's widowed aunt, and legal guardian.

Lavinia, having graduated in the spring of 1874 from the Wilhelmina Bostwick Finishing School For Young Ladies, was thrilled at the prospect of traveling abroad upon the suggestion of her aunt. Mrs. Holcomb planned the European excursion not only to celebrate Lavinia's successful completion of study in the ways of polite society, but also to arrange an introduction between her niece, and the reclusive artist. The portrait, no longer a secret hidden from Lavinia, is nearing completion and about to be unveiled.

Lavinia sits poised, thinking about her good fortune; receiving such a generous gift from her aunt was completely unexpected. She knew her aunt as a devout patron of the arts, but never anticipated such an extravagance being afforded her. She soon decided not to question the circumstances any further, and to thank her aunt properly at her next opportunity.

Lavinia rose from the blue-velvet settee she'd patiently been positioned on these many weeks. She timidly crept toward the artists' easel, limbs trembling, breath faint and shallow, her palms moist with perspiration, impatiently hoping to garner a glimpse. Hesitant to intrude, she anxiously waits for an invitation from Jean-Luc to gaze upon the painting. Instead, he turns the easel toward her, and as she scans the canvas, her cheeks flush with crimson, her pulse quickens, and her mind is awestruck by the vivid composition of colors before her. Lavinia looks upon the mirror image, and smiles. Every detail, from her dark auburn tresses, to the intensity of her deep, emerald-green eyes, and the soft burgundy folds of her velveteen gown, Jean-Luc, has skillfully captured. Her portrait is a masterpiece, a timeless treasure and keepsake as far as Lavinia is concerned.

ALONE AND LOST

LeRoy Doran

AT SIX MONTHS OLD

The first night that I was lost and alone in the woods it was cold and scary. It was time for me to eat and I was hungry. The hungrier I got the colder I got. Then came the dark and now I had a problem. Where would I sleep, for the snow was deep, the ground frozen, and it was getting colder?

Remembering the warm place where I had always slept I started to bark, but no one came to find me. Then I knew I was in for a long, cold night and I still had found no place to sleep. But now I had to find a place and in a hurry.

I looked and finally found an old tree that had fallen and under it was a place with no snow. I curled up in a tight ball, and shivering, I fell asleep.

The next morning I was awful cold so I started to run. The more I ran the more lost I became and I still had nothing to eat. The more I ran the more I knew I was in for another long, cold night.

This went on for over a week and I was cold, skinny, and sick. I may not have lived through another cold night and I was about to give up. Then I came upon this man who was sitting on an old log about to eat his lunch. I went quietly and lay down beside him trying to get warm. He looked down and said, "Come, little dog. I will give you a warm place and something to eat."

He took me to his truck where the sun was shinning in the window and it was warm. He covered me with his extra shirt and said, "Here, little dog, have part of my peanut butter sandwich, I don't mind." Now that sandwich was real good.

1

He then went looking to see if he could find where I came from, but no one had seen me before. He took me home with him. Now I have a nice home, plenty to eat, and a nice, warm place to sleep. There now is a deep friendship between him and me.

He named me Gypsy because I was looking for a home and care. I am very content, for now I have plenty of both and real friends.

2

MY NEW HOME

I am now settled in my new home. But when I first came to my new home all I did was eat, sleep, and lay by the heat. It seemed I just could not get warm.

After three days I warmed up and started to find new places in the house. Then I started to run from one end of the house to the other just to show my new friend that I was well again. After about six trips I'd jump up in his chair and look at him as if to say, "See how fast I can run?" Now that I have a place to live I feel like running again. I do not like for him to go off and leave me home alone.

Every Sunday he and his wife, my other friend, go to church and leaves me home all alone. I tried to chew myself out one time to follow them but that didn't work out very good. I get kind of upset and I worry, wondering if they will come back. When I hear their car coming down the street I get all excited because I can tell their car from a lot of others.

My friend is old and retired but his wife still works and I can tell her car from the other cars. I stand on the back of my chair and watch out the window waiting for her to come in. Then I meet her at the door. And again, I am content, for my family is all at home for the night. Then they make supper and I get a few bites. I really like it when they share with me. This is what true friends are all about. Thank you, my friends, for sharing your home with me.

3

BEWARE! GYPSY IS ON GUARD

I wanted to be his seeing-eye dog but no one would let me bring him into a store and such places. They said that I was too small to be a seeing-eye dog, so I decided to become his guard dog. When someone comes to the door I am so glad to see them I forget to guard my friend.

I really do a good job when we are at home alone. I go ahead of him every place he goes to keep the Goober Grabbers at bay. We have never seen any Goober Grabbers so I must do a good job. I hope if we ever see any they are little ones for I really am kind of small.

Now those Goober Grabbers, they are real tough dudes. But I can handle them. I am good at my job especially if there are none of them Goober Grabbers around. They tell me the closets are full of them, but with me around they don't dare come out.

I do have a bark that makes me sound six foot tall. I use it every time he is out and I am in or when he is in and I am out. How can you expect me to do my job when there is a door in between us? For I must protect my friend.

I do have one problem I do not like cats. In our neighborhood there are a lot of cats. When one comes close to the house I am ready to fight. But my friend says. "Oh, leave that cat alone, you would lose the fight anyway." They make the hair stand up along my back and I sure would like to chase the cats. I'm glad my friends don't have a cat.

I love to chase anything that will run. I used to chase a squirrel that my friend was feeding. Then I found out that a squirrel could run up a tree and I could not. I said to myself, "Oh, what a waste of time."

4

Now a rabbit is another story for they can really run. When they hide I sniff them out just to get them to run. Now chasing rabbits is a lot of fun. Once, when I was chasing a rabbit I crossed a main highway and it was really scary. That was no fun. So all of you children please listen to me, never cross a busy highway when you are alone.

I do like to travel even though I spend most of the time asleep. When we stay at a motel I don't like those elevators for the crazy floors moves up and down and that is no fun. The first time I rode in one my friend had to drag me onto it so we could go to the second floor. Well, the next morning when we were leaving he had to carry me back on. I sure don't like those moving floors.

The trip was a lot of fun. We went to North Carolina and visited a war ship, the USS NORTH CAROLINA, but they would not let me go aboard. I had to stay in the car but it was early in the day so it didn't get too hot. I am sorry I didn't get to go on that great big ship.

5

GYPSY AND THUNDERSTORMS

I told you the one thing I didn't like was cats. I didn't want you to know that I am afraid of thunderstorms. When I first came to my new home and a thunderstorm came up I would run and hide under the bed, but then I found I would be alone. My new friends didn't crawl under the bed. I found that when I jump up into his chair with him and get down between him and the arm of the chair I do feel safe. When he sits in a straight chair I hide by his feet and stick my head out between his legs. I do shiver and shake but I feel like he is protecting me. He says, "It's ok, Gypsy, you are safe." Then he reaches down and rubs my head and ears.

At night when the news and weather is over on TV my friend takes off his glasses and house slippers then I know it is time for bed. I run into the bedroom and sit by his side of the bed where I always sleep. He always snaps on my leash so I won't bark at cats at night. He then reaches down and rubs my head and ears and says, "You are a good little dog, Gypsy, now it is time to go to sleep." I sure like for him to rub my head and ears because it makes me feel like he really cares for me.

When he works at the computer I am always right there beside his chair. That is where he started calling me his guard dog. He and I are home alone a lot and he always talks to me. He says things like, “Are you going with me or, come on, Gypsy, we have computer work to do.” He makes it a real nice place to live and makes me feel that I am really needed.

THE JUST DREAMING PHASE

Lori D. Laird

I know there has to be other women like me. Someone that feels like they live in a dream world. Meaning that you're whole life feels like it's all a dream. Whether it's a good dream or a bad dream. But is life nothing but a dream? Or is it real?

Do we all feel things the same? Take love for instance. Do we all believe that we have to have a love that fills us to brimming? Or do we settle for what we can find?

Do we just give up on love? Because we can't find that "true" love? Or do we keep living for it until we find it? Everyone can't feel the same, can they? If so, then am I just a nut case with a couple screws loose?

We dream of the perfect life. Where we have 4 kids. A house on a farm. A new car/truck in the driveway. I would prefer for it to be a dually work truck. That way I can feed the horses and the cattle. But then again I'm just a country girl at heart. I'm sure that city people feel different.

We all dream of the perfect man/woman. One who would love us even if we were butt ass ugly. Because to him/her it's the inside that counts. One that would love us unconditional. And wouldn't ever bitch if we spent to much money on something. Or bitch because we bought something that we really didn't need. Or you just forgot to pick up the dry cleaning.

I know I dream about that type of stuff all the time. But in reality, I'm a married woman. Who isn't "in love" with her husband. I do have two kids. But they are a handful in itself. And I don't even remember what a new car feels like. But I wouldn't give anything for my truck.

I pay the bills. He works all the time. I take care of the kids and the house. But he wants to gripe if he doesn't get sex once a week. Or he doesn't have tea made. What is this? This my dear friends is life. Whether we want to live it or not.

So I've taken up a passed time of writing little erotic stories. It fills my daytime hours. And sometimes my nighttime hours too. It gives me a sense of purpose. And it let me let my imagination soar. Where ever I want to go with it. My mind takes me there. That's what makes life worth living. And it let's me unwind at the end of the day.

The just dreaming phases of our live. That's what makes life bearable. That's all friends. Atleast that is what I believe. And that is what I'm going to try to write about this time. The just dreaming phase of my live. I'm going to tell you what I dream about.

My dream always starts out in the same place. I'm with a man that loves me for me. Not what I look like. Not for what I can do for him. Not for just sexual release. Just me being me. And I love him for the same things.

And that's why it's a dream. Because men nowadays have atleast one thing they want in a woman. Whether it's large breast. A great mouth. A great pair of legs. No one loves people anymore for just who they are.

Well I should say that no one loves me like that anymore. But as usual I'm getting sidetracked. Sorry and please forgive me.

The man of my dream is warm and tender. Who just wants for us to be together. It wouldn't matter to him if I was old and wrinkly. He would still love me. And he prays for the days where we are old. That way we can sit on our front porch and watch our grandchildren at play.

The man of my dreams is a wonderful lover. He's always thinking about my needs first. If one of us doesn't feel like just sex. Then we will pleasure each other. Or if it's sex we do want. Then it's the kind we want together.

It's not just him. It's what we both want. It's a mutual understanding. And if one of us doesn't feel like it. Then there is always tomorrow night. There isn't any of the "If you love me you will do this one thing for me."

The man of my dreams is totally complete with me. He doesn't need anyone else. He's happy with the life we have. He doesn't look for something new. Or something to take his time away from me. It's us and only us and the kids.

I think I dream too much. I don't think that there is anyone out there that is what I want. So I guess I'm just like all the men out there. I'm looking for just one type of man.

But it's not based on looks. I don't think looks makes a person. You can be God's gift to women/men. And still be a pain in the ass. Or you can be the ugliest person in the world. But we all have feelings.

That is what most people need to remember. We aren't just shells walking around. Everyone has feelings. Whether they show them or not. They may just not be able to show them. Or they protect themselves by not showing them.

I'm not saying that beauty doesn't count. Yes, you have to be attracted to the person. But why can't we take a look on the inside every once in a while. It's the heart that counts. It's the way a person makes you feel that counts. Beauty is going to fade. But the love you have for someone isn't.

In an age where beauty counts. They are still people out there that aren't our ideal mate. But if we don't give them a try. Then we may be losing the best thing that has ever entered our lives.

I love to please my partner. In just about any way, shape, or form. If I haven't tried it before. Then I will try it, if it makes him happy. If I'm comfortable enough with him. And what he wants to do.

I love to make love. I also love to screw when we're both in the mood for it. I love just about anything sexual. I'm not dead. I'm just stuck with someone who I can't totally lose myself with. There's always this one certain something that doesn't let me go. It's like there is a brick wall up between us. And I can't, or won't, knock it down.

In my dream I'm in a bed of roses. I'm being worshiped, just as much as he is. Our souls are linked together. It's hard to tell where one of us begins. And where the other ends. It's magical. It's beautiful. It's plain and simple true love.

It's the hearts linking together. It's knowing what you both want or need before the other can do it. It's the dream that is so hard to believe that it's real. It's being in love. And getting loved in return.

It's the knowing what he/she is going to say before they say it. It's the soul searching look that you get when they look at you. The love is just right there in the eyes. And they don't care who sees it. They just want everyone to know that they love. And they want people to know they are loved back.

It's the pain of parting when they leave in the mornings. It's the smile you get on your face when they come home at the end of the day. It's the first kiss of the morning. And the last kiss at night. It's the cuddling before falling asleep in his arms. It's the cuddling and wrapping your arms around her, before you fall asleep.

It's the first stroke when you make love. It's the first kiss when passion is rising. It's the first mouthful of his member. It's the first lick of her sweetspot. It's the sweetness of juices when they get mixed together. It's knowing that you fit with someone. Totally and complete fit with them. That is the just dreaming phase of life. The reality is screwing someone because they've griped about it long enough. It's the "Ok, just get it over with", saying when you really don't feel like it. It's the "I have a headache tonight." That's reality.

But in my dream world. It's sweet and beautiful. It's full of passion and fire. It's full of "This feels so right." In my dream world the kids are perfect. They don't give you any trouble. There's no fighting. There's no hollering and screaming. There's no division between child and parent.

Why can't we escape to this dream world more often? Why can't this be reality? Why can't all the bad stuff just be a nightmare that you get to wake up from? Why? Because no one is perfect in this world. And no one is going to find the perfect person for them. Because that person doesn't exist. The one that does, is the one you are with.

Do we settle for being in love? Or do we just settle for what we can get? Do we just get comfortable in life? And change scares the piss out of us. Is there too much at stake to change? How high is the price of love? And who would really pay that price? Just how far do people go for love? If it came down to it. Would you really die for love? Or would you just let love die?

These are questions I ask myself every day. And I still haven't figured out the answers. I thought I met my ideal perfect match. He wound up breaking my heart. And almost destroying my world. I almost gave up my life for my true love. But most importantly, I almost lost myself. Instead of just letting it go, like I should have. I almost took it to the extreme.

Am I the only one that has ever felt this way? Does everyone just want to end it sometime in their life? Do you want the pain to just fucking stop? Or do you realize before it's too late what is important to you? Is someone really that important to kill yourself over? Is that someone more important then watching your children grow?

Was I wrong? Is it too late to get him back? Would it be different then before? Or would it still be broken promises? Would he give up his life for me? Would he be my prince and rescue me? What if I really don't need rescuing? What if I just need to feel love in my heart? What if I just need to feel again, period?

I guess all of life is full of what if's. But this I do know. I love my children. I can't wait until they are grown. To have a life of their own. To know that I raised two wonderful little boys. Who are now men with families of their own. That is reality. And that is what bets the just dreaming phase any day. That is unconditional love. It's the only true love out there for me. And that is my life. My children are my life and my reality.

The just dreaming phase will pass. But my children will always be here. They are the only constant things in my life. Love may come and go. But they won't. They will just grow. They will be my mark on this world.

What would your's be? Do you feel the same way I do? What is different between your life and mine? What would be something that you changed in your life? Think about it. Then live life to the fullest. Or atleast the fullest you let it be. It's all in our hands. We made our own destiny in life.

I AM THE STORY I TELL MYSELF I AM

Mary Barr

A single note rises, then falls like a raindrop at my feet, shattering into a thousand tiny rainbows. I think there must be an angel caged in the cell next to mine. If I could play the instrument of my voice as miraculously, would I be closer to God? It seems my destiny is to be an ordinary raven, even here, where birds are forbidden to fly.

My reverie is broken by the jangling of keys and slamming of gates. A prison guard bellows, "Get your a— out here crackhead!" I rise, as do the over forty other women who have shared this cell with me over the past three days. None of us is certain to whom she refers. It is not me, not this time.

I sink back to the floor that has become so cold I could ice skate on it. I seek out the largest woman (the fat ones give off the most body heat), and huddle close to her. In here we have no prejudice or pride. Out there we took each other's money and drugs, in here we give each other warmth and comfort.

A harsh voice shouts, "Barr!" It is my turn. I enter the shower room and strip quickly. I immediately squat and cough while bouncing up and down. I want to please the guards. I have been here before and I know the rules well. I am shoved into an icy shower and sprayed with horrid smelling lotion to 'de-louse' me. I wonder why they bother when they don't wash our clothes. I am pushed soaking wet into another freezing cell. I dry off as best as I can with my filthy pants.

Just as sleep comes to steal me from this misery, another voice intrudes, this one much kinder than I am used to. "Ladies, my name is Mr. Smith. A few years ago I was in a worse position than you, and look at me now. I have a fine job, fine clothes, and I'm fine lookin' too. If you want what I've got, you've got to do what I did to get it. I pledge my support to anyone willing to make a change."

I step out of my cell not even flinching when the gate clangs shut behind me. As we are walking to the dormitory where I will be housed I hear shouting and stomping. I am amazed when we arrive and I see that it is military marching and cadence.

"My God Mr. Smith," I exclaim, "you didn't tell me I was joining the army!" "There's a lot more to it than this Mary," he says.

A woman detaches herself from a marching group and comes towards me. "Hi, I'm Lori, the unit captain. In this program it's mandatory that we attend school. We have five minutes to line up so let's go."

We march down the bleak hallways to school shouting an army cadence. I suppress an urge to giggle, especially since the women in general population are watching us with interest. Unlike the adolescent population housed in jail, adults do not get to go to school. It took a lot of work to allow our special program into the computer class. Most of the women in general population spend their days bored and frustrated, sometimes fighting, and getting high. Yes, there are drugs in jail.

After two hours we march back to our dorm where a social worker greets us. She is the only social worker for over two thousand women so we are fortunate to have her tonight. She suggests that we go into residential treatment when we leave, but I can't see myself doing that after being locked up for a year. We meet with her in a group to discuss our issues, which run the gamut from being abused, to being illiterate. This is one time when I am glad there are only 100 beds available for treatment; I may get a chance to ask her a question.

A lady I don't know starts the group. "I'm lucky they let me back in here." she says through tears. "They told me not to go home, but I missed my kids so much. When I got there they just wanted to go out with friends, and my daughter hid her purse from me when she thought I wasn't looking. I didn't want her to see me crying so I went to a friend's house. Just like when I got busted, she was gettin' high, I was upset so I got high right along with her. This time I am going to take the cotton out of my ears and stick it in my mouth."

God works in mysterious ways. Though our stories are not the same I feel the same way. I have not seen my children or their father for two years. I do not want to make the same mistakes as this woman. I am no longer afraid to die, I am afraid of living my life the way I was. I decide to go to residential treatment when I am released and try to convince my peers to do the same.

The day of my release has come and I am sent off with hugs. I await the volunteer who will drive me from jail to the program and I laugh aloud when I see that it is Mr. Smith. There is a certain symmetry to arriving at yet another program with Mr. Smith, and I pray I will be as successful in this one.

A single note rises then falls like a raindrop at my feet, shattering into a thousand tiny rainbows. I step up to the cell and say, "Honey, you sing like an angel. A few years ago I was in a worse position than you, and look at me now. Would you like to hear more?" The angel looks at me and smiles.

THE MAGICAL PUBLISHING PEN

Mike Strictzer

One day — inasmuch as what we would consider one day — the Devil went on vacation to Las Vegas. The Devil wanders the earth from time to time; it says so in the Book of Job. The body that the Devil chose for this particular jaunt was tall: six-foot-two, with black hair, and an overall handsome appearance. His eyes were solid orbs of blackness. This was, perhaps, most disturbing. When a human encountered his eyes, they instantly became entranced, but upon turning away, they forgot all. His voice was almost as sinister as he was. It was a low voice that had a metallic edge to it like a DJ's, but it was a very charismatic and melodic voice and sounded like a southern drawl without the accent.

The Devil enjoyed Vegas. His favorite things to do were: shoot craps at Casino Royale, ride the go-carts out by U.S. 95, enjoy a lap dance at Crazy Horse Too strip club, and eat the seafood buffet at the Rio. The Devil did eat red meat, but he was on vacation, so why not lighten it up a little? After the buffet, the Devil normally went up to the Voodoo Lounge.

Peter Salinski worked in the entertainment industry in town. He was six-foot-one and had long, wavy brown hair and blue, seafarer's eyes — clear and calm, but tainted, wise to the storm. His girlfriend's nickname for him was the second cumming. He was in danger of losing his job for unprofessional and unethical business practices, but continued to gamble his paycheck every tenth of the month, after paying his creditors slightly less than the minimum of what he owed them. If he won at the tables, which did happen, he would go to Crazy Horse Too and blow his cash. His mortgage was perpetually eighty-nine days late and he owed ten-K on a title loan for his BMW. He always had several bad checks out and the district attorney had sent him a letter Friday saying he was prosecuting Pete for bouncing a check he had written to buy Girl Scout cookies (the ones with chocolate swirls). Pete's web of lies was so complex that even he often got lost inside of it, and at those times, he would start stuttering. Then, after payday, or if he had won at the tables, he would stop stuttering for a few days.

Pete drove his newly washed, burgundy BMW into Crazy Horse Too's parking lot. It is not a wide parking lot and its best to go down half a block and park in any adjacent lot; that is, so long as you're planning on picking up your car before morning on the next work day. Or, you can just pull behind the building by driving in the driveway at the opposite end of the building from the main entrance. Sure, you could just valet it, but there are just a few options for you.

Pete walked into the strip club and strolled right up behind two women with thongs on. It was early Sunday morning, before the sun had come up, so there was no cover charge. He went into the main room and took a seat in one of the large sofa chairs. A waitress soon came over. She wore a short, tight, leopard-skin outfit showing plenty of cleavage.

"What will you have, Sweetie?" She asked. Locals, living in Las Vegas, are very polite.

"Can you do a cash advance on my Amex card?"

"Sure, so long as it works," she said with a wry smile.

"Then bring me a beer first and then go and get the money."

"How much do you want?" She said, dropping her smile.

"Five-hundred."

"Okay," she said and walked off.

Pete looked over at the chair right next to him and noticed that a tall man with black hair was sitting next to him, holding himself very reserved. Pete was slightly taken aback because he had not remembered him being there when he had sat down. But he reminded himself how dark the place was and smiled at the gentleman, who did not say anything. Pete began to fidget and decided to break the silence. He looked over at the stranger and said, "How you doing?"

"Very well," the man's voice had an icy edge to it that made Pete's nerves crawl under his skin.

"You from around here?" Pete asked uncomfortably, trying to get the stranger to lighten up.

"No. Not too far away, though."

"L.A.?"

"Not L.A."

"Is this a game of twenty questions?"

"This is not a game. I am from hell. In fact, I rule hell. I am -- the Devil," he said, spreading his hands apart, which had been touching, finger tip to finger tip.

"Oh, well, why didn't you just say so? I live here, in Las Vegas. My name is Pete. We're practically neighbors."

"Well, I guess that's true."

"How long you've been in Vegas?"

"Only a matter of days; I'm staying at the Hard Rock Hotel and Casino."

"Oh, sure, I got thrown out of there once."

"That's too bad. What were you doing?" the Devil asked and the pointed eyebrow closest to Pete shot up fast, without the head so much as even being slightly disturbed.

"Drinking and trying to pick up women."

"Seems perfectly natural to me."

"I guess there is a certain level of drunkenness—"

"—A curious concept, mediating sin; I can't imagine. But what's your story?"

"My story? Oh, I'm a born storyteller. My grandmother always said so."

"That's very nice," the Devil said and then continued, "Let's hear one."

"Hear a story?"

"Sure. Why don't we make it a game and use your soul as collateral? Just like in Chaucer, the best story gets paid by the others."

Pete laughed out loud for a moment and raised his head up. Then he looked back down at the Devil and said, "All right. But what do you pay me with?"

"You win this magical publishing pen," the Devil said and reached into his coat pocket and produced a thick, solid gold, fountain pen. He held it up, a short distance from his face and they both stared at it. The dim lighting reflected the soft, pure allure of gold that moves the hearts of men.

"Nice," Pete said and then, "I have no doubt that's real gold. But where's the ink well; does it come with one?

"It is magic. Do you understand magic?"

"What good is a pen? And what do I do with a pen, anyway, write a story?"

"Of course; this pen will guarantee that you will become published."

"So you're a publisher? Listen, Mr. Devil, maybe you haven't been around here recently, but we use computers now, not pens. And writers do not even write stories anymore. You could say writers are more concerned with writing than storytelling these days. And movie deals," Pete explained as the Devil listened, scheming about something unknown and unrelated.

The Devil looked a little sullen for a second. He regained his composure and said, "What a shame. Alestair Crowley told me only the other day that in Paris—"

"—Look," Pete interrupted the Devil, "Big S — tell you what I'm gonna do —

I'll play your game for the pen anyway. Maybe I'll figure out some use for it."

The Devil picked up a little and said, "I'll go first, then."

"Fire away," Pete replied. The cocktail waitress came over and Pete signed the receipt to get his advance and took his beer. She nodded at him, as if to say she would return with his cash in a few minutes, but he ignored her. He took a long sip from his Bud Light, leaned back, and cradled it on his round belly.

"A very long time ago, there were two brothers who were to inherit a kingdom from their father, the king. The kingdom was to be split in two parts. While one prince would get the seacoast, with all its trade and abundance, the other prince was to receive the ripe farmlands of the inland valleys that lay in the mountain ranges, with their mountain routes that lead to bordering countries. Those mountain caravan routes provided an invaluable source of trade as well, since the bordering countries on the other side of the mountain ranges were particularly wealthy. It was there the Elysian Fields lie, on the other side of the mountains.

"The king was a just and lawful man, perhaps like some kings in — in — in — the Bible," the Devil was interrupted as a very voluptuous dancer, whose body was nearly completely exposed, sat down on his lap, and started rubbing him down.

"Hey Cutie, you want a dance?" she asked.

The Devil literally pushed her off of his lap. "Not right now, Aphrodite, I'm a little busy. But I'll get to you later," he said.

"Suit yourself, but you'll be sorry," she said.

The Devil mocked her with a sheepish grin and then returned to his story.

"When it came time to bequeath the lands to his two sons, the king called them to the side of his death bed. Both sons were very anxious. The king slowly said, 'Tartarus and Erebus, it is time for you to inherit my kingdom. Tartarus; you shall take the lower half of the kingdom, Erebus; the mountains and their lush valleys. Tartarus, I know how much you love the sea and the caves that line its cliff faces and how you used to get lost in those caves in your small boat as a boy. And Erebus, how you would forever wander on your journeys through the mountains trails to find "the other side" — the Elysian Fields — and how you never were able to. Ah, if you had only asked me.

"The problem was what to do with my castle. It rests here, right in between your two kingdoms. So, after much thought, I devised a solution. You will war against one another until one of you is victorious. And to that victor goes the spoils; for he shall be the retainer of this great castle, and thus have the upper hand on his brother.

From the looks of the expression on your faces, I can see that my decision has surprised you. Well, lawfulness is very important, my children, and since neither of you will die in this battle, what's all the consternation for? Regardless, this is my law and you will carry it out. Now, go to your separate countries, gather your armies and do battle. And let me die in peace!'

"The sons left their father's presence, after saying their final goodbyes. As the weeks and months passed, each son gathered large armies numbering tens-of-thousands. Tartarus, in particular, had a vast army, since most of the kingdom's population lived in the large, seacoast cities. His army outnumbered his bother's by nearly two-to-one. But the men of Erebus' army were more lithe and sinewy, had a higher endurance, and greater constitution than his brother's people, given their mountain altitude lifestyle. Still, Erebus had inherited his fathers mind, and immediately recognizing his disadvantage, set about creating all manner of new war weapons. In time, his army boasted a company armed with newly invented long-rifles, and, it was rumored, a secret weapon.

"Finally, the sons sent out messenger's to their rival's headquarters to say they were ready for battle. Of course, each brother tortured, and then subsequently disemboweled, alive, the messengers, because, by now, they were both very irritated with their sibling. After a few more messengers, a place and time for pitched battle was set: the wide flatlands surrounding the king's castle itself, where the high mountains level off into the plains, which then went down to the sea. It was also agreed that the castle would be off limits at all costs.

"The armies met, gathering over several days, and then commenced to fight spectacular battles. Ah, war — it is perhaps the only worthy human accomplishment. At war, humans are at your best, and it is there where you rise to my level; it is at war where you are almost godlike," the Devil said, and waxed nostalgic a second in silence.

The waitress came to Pete's side and handed him his cash, but the Devil was not distracted by her, and continued to stare at the ceiling, lost in his own world. Pete quickly stuffed his money into his wallet and leaned back again.

The Devil returned to his story, "Nearly every battle took many weeks, and the war covered the greater part of a year. The brothers would direct their armies to advance and withdrawal, retreat or get routed. At times, with Erebus' precision weapons well placed and hunkered down, it seemed the war might not end until every single soldier fighting in Tartarus' army had been felled.

"But regrettably, though admirably, Tartartus, the brilliant tactician, was forever sending out magnificent orders to his captains, who would launch the age-old hammer and pincer move, or perhaps dart forward in a sudden, Pickets-like charge, and take the field once more, sending their adversaries running in terror. The wrath of Tartarus was most destructive. Certainly, there were no prisoners. Erebus' army would then regroup in the mountains, nursing their wounds. And within days, begin again to slowly advance, pushing the enemy back, yet again.

"Blood was everywhere, and so many dead littered the battlefield, bodies came to be used as blockades. One of the greatest single battles came to be known as 'The Battle of the Smoldering Corpses.' Erebus won that one with nothing other than his secret weapon. It was so impressive of him to wait until the very last moment to use it, and he is to be commended for having done so. What was the secret weapon, you ask? Ah ha! Biological warfare! Yes! Hahahahahaha!"

By now, a small group of strippers had gathered in the seats around the Devil and Pete, and at this point in the Devil's story, the assembled strippers breathed in a chorus of gasps. A crowd of almost ten strippers were sitting in the surrounding sofa chairs. Occasionally, one from the group would have to leave, to go dance on stage. But she would dance only on the side of the stage closest to the storytellers, and spin around her pole a lot, straining her ear to listen, as she danced monotonously.

The Devil continued, "Erebus had taken the wild asphodel plant, so beautiful and abundant, growing around the castle before the Great War, and its pallid and strange, ghostly flowers, and had removed their spores and made them into a gluey substance that he launched from his catapults at Tartarus' screaming hordes of charging, hopeless masses. The genius Erebus had concocted his biological bombs into a chemical by adding other substances, such that, when they landed on top of the lost souls, they would explode and the tiny poison spores would fly up into the air, reaching an altitude of one hundred meters, and then dissipate across the sky, encompassing the entire field of battle. Then the beautiful death slowly and surely settled down upon the enemy. Indeed, initially, what seemed to simply be some muffled explosions, did not stir the huge army of Tartarus. But then, the poor, lost men literally stopped their fighting to look up at the sky, which by now had become a dull orange color, in a kind of pathetic wonderment.

"At this precise moment, Erebus' army ran away from the field of battle. Then the spores descended on the unwary, stunned soldiers. Unfortunately, the spores put out the burning corpses that the battle was named for. But Tartarus' army had been laid in waste. They died a most horrendous death, chocking on their own vomit, just like Jimmy Hendrix. It was a truly glorious day! The insanity of warfare is so truly awesome!"

The Devil paused a moment and looked around at the strippers. He surveyed the scene, judging them for their reactions, to see how good his story was so far. Then he continued, "The king, all the while, had been mysteriously recovering, and was able to watch the battle every day from behind his vast walled castle in safety.

After observing the last battle transpire, the king went inside for several days, mindful of the spores.

"Indeed, the Battle of the Burning Corpses was a watershed in the war. Thereafter, Tartarus's army never regained a foothold and the rough and ready warriors of Erebus' army were able to hunt down and tear apart the remaining deserters. Finally, Erebus reached his brother and his warriors forced him to the ground, where, withdrawing his broadsword, he beheaded his brother without so much as a prayer. The decapitated head rolled a few feet in the mud and Erebus spat on it, cursing his brother's soul to eternal damnation.

"Erebus and his ragged, yet veteran, army went to the front gates of the castle, but it was locked. Erebus expected the guard to quickly open it. The king had another plan, however, and signaled his guard to raise the portcullis and lower the drawbridge. Then the king's small, but precision guard of highly trained assassins burst forth and slew Erebus's now relatively small-numbered army. Erebus himself was brought before his father, who, as his son, showed no mercy, and drove a hot rod of rebar iron into his heart, twisting it several times to the right and left, while simultaneously thrusting, before his screaming son's face.

"Both brothers now dead, the land was in ruin. The king was once again king, he having made his sickness a fain. No one was left to challenge him and he ruled for several more years before he finally died.

"Isn't that a beautiful story? Your turn, Sir," the Devil said and the strippers sitting next to the Devil and Pete were struck with a kind of awe, unable to speak or move for several minutes, their mouths agape.

Pete also felt as if his stomach had become knotted up and for a second thought that the story was true and the "king" was sitting in a throne adjacent to him right now. But he dismissed the thought and said, "Whew, that was some story, Mr. Devil. Not sure if I can top it, but I'll give it a try. Here goes," Pete said and took a sip of beer and began.

"It all started when Ozzy Ozborne and his band visited my grandmother's house in L.A. He was there with his guitar player — Tony something — and the rest of the band. This also happened some time ago. My grandmother has this really nice Japanese garden behind her house. First, there's a large backyard, and then her garden that went on for a long while, and then there was the garage. The garage is big. I'm sure it could fit four cars with no problem. But you had to go through the alley to get to the garage and it was kind of an inconvenience and everyone always complained about how difficult it was to get to my grandmother's garage whenever they came to visit her.

"My grandmother had been something big in the music industry. Back then; I never really understood what her job was; all I knew, it was big, because every artist imaginable came to visit my grandmother at some time or other: Mick and Keith, Bono, John and Paul; even Peter Frampton. Sometimes, if the visitors were important like Peter Frampton, my grandmother would go to the basement and break out her stash and sit with her guests on her back porch smoking. I always lingered in my grandmother's Japanese garden for hours, even after it got dark, and I came to recognize the strange sent and the ensuing, strange conversations.

"In the garden, there were many tiny windmills that turned around, with each miniature blade piercing the water, submerging, deep into the water, and then coming back out damp. Tiny water droplets would fall from the blade, as it still rotated, for at least another one third of the wheel's continuous rotation. Flat areas lay with neatly raked sand, which the gardener had only finished raking that very morning. Flat limestone and feldspar rocks lined the edges of the pools of water in neat piles. The water was clear in the pools and streams and algae grew in them where shade was. Moss grew on the dark side of the small, Japanese Bushido mini-trees, too. I would literally get lost in my grandmother's Japanese garden for many hours.

"And the bridge, I almost forgot; the bridge is where it all started. There was a walkway through my grandmother's garden that ran from the garage to the backyard. About halfway through the garden, a bridge crossed over a small river.

"So, the time that Ozzy and his band came to visit my grandmother, they were all carrying their instrumentation for some reason — usually no one brought their instruments to my grandmother's house, but this time they did. I didn't know if they were going to conduct a jam session.

"The drummer was a kind of big guy and he was carrying his drums behind Ozzy. And behind the drummer was the guitar player, Tony, then the bass player, and last, the manager. He was short and had almost no hair on his head. But the manager had a big mouth that he was always running.

"Ozzy had gotten across the bridge and from there you were in the back yard. My grandmother and I were standing in the back yard to greet them. Just as Ozzy got across the walk bridge, he stopped and hollered at my grandmother, he kind of talks funny, 'Heya, der Miss-y- me-ma. Are ya bloody all right?'

"Everyone calls my grandmother me-ma. She was from Tallahassee, Florida, so she naturally had a very thick, southern accent. Between Ozzy and my grandmother, I don't think anyone else would have been able to understand much of anything resembling English.

"My grandmother called back across the backyard, 'Hey der, youins bigens-time-rockin-ana-rolling, rockin, rock star! Comon bover her and sit aside me-ma!'

"I will bes a comin ov na!' Ozzy shouted back, but behind him, the drummer had not looked up, since he had been schlepping his drums under both of his arms, and he ran right into Ozzy. Two of his big drums fell onto the walkway. One drum rolled a few feet and went plop! into the small river. Then, the guitar player ran right into the drum player, and he must have been a clumsy man, because he smashed right through the bridge railing and fell in the small river. The bass player stopped in time. Then, the manager came running up and started screaming about the damage to the drums. I thought for sure Ozzy would think the whole thing was pretty funny, but he didn't. Instead, he got very upset at his guitar player Tony for breaking my grandmother's bridge. He was cursing at his guitar player, who just lay in the small river, smiling.

"They spent the weekend, but before he left, Ozzy gave my grandmother a big check. She went to Australia for three months and when she returned, across the Pacific, it was with on big yacht, which is still parked in the docks, down in L.A. Then I understood that my grandmother was not one to be trifled with in the profession of music.

"About a year passed, and one summer my family and I were visiting my grandmother. One of our activities was playing croquet in her backyard. We were making our way through the course. Normally, the game would usually digress into this quasi-political discussion and I never cared for that. That was would be about the time I would go to my grandmother's garden.

"And then I found it; the magical guitar pick. It had been lying at the bottom of the small stream, a few feet from the bridge, under one of the rocks jutting out. So I reached in the water, under the rock, and grabbed it. I tore off through the back yard to tell my grandmother.

"Grandma, I found the guitar's player's guitar pick from Ozzy's band!' I told her.

"'Weehell, whohoo, well'ya looken at dat?

Does you be nowing hat that is?' She asked me.

"'No, grandma,' I answered.

"'It'sen a magical guitar pick! You can make a wishan it'all comeen truens,' she said.

"I was very excited and went back to the garden, clutching the guitar pick between my thumbs and index fingers, out in front of me. I intently studied the guitar pick's cat-shit yellow color and its sparkles.

"I went back to the bridge and meditated on my discovery. I was not sure what to do. If it was actually magical, and if I could indeed make a wish, what would I wish for? What if I wished for something too greedy and God punished me? Then what? I did not want to spoil my one magical wish, however. Finally, I said to the guitar pick I was squeezing, 'I'm just going to let you go.'

"I put it back where I found it, back in the stream, right underneath the same rock. And wouldn't you know, this year when I went back to look for it, the magical guitar pick had disappeared. That's it, that's my story,"

Pete said and took a long drink from his beer, finishing it. There was a long pause of silence.

The Devil seemed to want to hear more. The strippers also had the same astonished look on their faces that they had after the Devil had finished his story, but they seemed amused.

"I do not think you have won here," the Devil finally said.

"What? My story was ten times better than yours," Pete said emphatically.

"What is the point of your story, other than you lost a guitar pick? Besides, didn't you steal the idea of your guitar pick from my pen?"

"So what if I did? I think that the only way to decide the winner is to ask the girls."

The Sunday morning strippers had been very quiet as Pete and the Devil had told their stories. Pete knew all the girls, however, he having paid each of for many, many lap dances. "Fine," the Devil said and asked the dancers, "how many of you liked my story better?"

No one raised their arms up, except for the one dancer who had tried unsuccessfully to dance for the Devil. She raised her arm very slowly into the air. The Devil looked over at Pete, who couldn't resist, "and how many of you girls liked my story better?"

All the rest of the girls raised their hands up high and cheered loudly. Peter Salinski left with his gold pen. He drove from the back of the building with a big smile on his face, right into the rising sun. He went straight to a pawn shop on Las Vegas Boulevard (right next to the Say I Do Drive-Thru), and sold it for four-hundred dollars. But he returned to Crazy Horse and spent it on: three dances in the VIP room, two lap dances, a couple of beers, and the remainder he used to fill up his car with gas and get a chili dog.

TEARS
Moataz H. Emam

Patrick did not immediately accept his father's death. It was the first time in his eight years of age that he came in close contact with the concept of mortality. The fact that he saw it happen with his own eyes didn't seem to register. He was standing on his house's lawn, staring at the pulsating red lights of the police car that parked at their curb. Behind it, paramedics were collecting his father's remains. Their white suits were smeared all over with

(ketchup, it looks just like ketchup!)

blood; his father's blood. Still further back, in the center of the street itself, his street, the huge truck stood, looming like a prehistoric animal. The sun was setting behind it. The truck seemed hazy. The driver was standing next to it, talking to the cops, waving his arms frantically.

A woman

(I want my mom)

was standing next to Patrick, bending over him, trying to pull him away from the scene. She was saying something in a

(please, I want my mom)

soothing voice. Patrick didn't hear her. He continued to stare at his father's covered remains as they carried them into the ambulance. Inside him somewhere, his mind was realizing that his father was

(ketchup)

dead. Consciously, he had no clear thoughts. He just stood there, watching the scene as it started to blend in his vision. Slowly, everything seemed to change to a group of mixed colors, a surrealist's masterpiece of confusion. The droning sound of the unknown woman

(please)

was still there. She was the one who carried him off when his legs finally gave way and he swooned over. Patrick woke up at the sounds of whispering. He opened his eyes. Standing next to the bed were two unidentifiable shadows. Patrick blinked several times. The first shadow was familiar, it was the woman that stood next to him and

(where is she?)

spoke soothingly in his ear. A neighbor! She is a neighbor. Mrs. something. The other shadow was of a man he didn't know. For some reason he reminded him of his

(notmyfatherhedoesn'tremindmeofmyfather)

uncle Fred. They looked at him and noticed that he was awake. The woman, Mrs. Something, bent on him and stroked his hair

(?)

gently. He closed his eyes but didn't sleep. In his mind's eye, he saw the truck coming up the street. His father was waving at him. There was the deafening sound of a tire exploding. His father started to cross the street. The truck swerved as its driver lost control. His father was crossing the street. The truck skidded uncontrollably towards his father. Patrick's eyes bulged reflexively. The truck hit his father

(thump)

dead center. The body that Patrick identified as his father took off into the air immediately. It flew high up like a kite. His arms and feet waved about him unnaturally. The body landed

(crack)

on top of the truck, it bounced and fell

(bonk)

back to the street. the truck skidded a bit more before coming to a final stop right in the middle of the street. Patrick's mouth was open, his eyes round. He stood there, staring at his father's body. He wasn't aware of people gathering and the sound of a woman down the street screaming hysterically, he wasn't even aware that he was drooling all over his new T-shirt which his father bought him last week. He just stared blankly at the scene, his mind in shambles, trying hopelessly to interpret this as not happening, as real as a movie on T.V.

Patrick opened his eyes again. In the quiet shadows of this unknown bedroom, he could see another shape coming in and joining Mrs. Something and Uncle Fred's look-alike. It must be Mr. Something coming home from work and wondering who the kid in his bed was. The shape was out of focus, it spoke to Uncle Fred's look-alike and then moved towards the bed. The shape came into focus, but it still took Patrick a few moments to recognize it. The figure reached out for Patrick. He moved from his bed and threw himself into his mother's arms, letting himself go. They were both sobbing into each other's embrace. Uncle Fred's look-alike smiled uneasily and remarked to Mrs. Something that Patrick was going to be all right, now that the tears have finally come.

IN THE OLDEN DAYS

Mona Dash

In the olden days, they had a word for women like me. A word or phrase to explain just what I was. It would be used instead of my actual name, it would be used to describe me to the new visitor in the village, it would be used to call me, and gradually it would make its home on me. Become me. It would not take very long of course, these names stick on quickly enough.

There were many languages in the country and depending on which part of the country I lived, I would have a different name. 'Baanjh', 'kulanghini,' 'bandhyaa', 'alakhyini' being some of them. And in those days, in my motherland, they would have punished me as well. For the sins, they would say, I must have committed in my last life, to be punished this way by God. Since God had punished me, they had a right to as well. So they would offer sympathy and comfort to my husband, they would suggest gently he find someone else, for I had not been able to do what a woman was sent out on earth to do. It was my karma, who knew what I had done in my past Life to suffer this state? He was justified in connecting his life to someone with a better fate.

So one day, in those olden days, my husband would receive blessings from his elders and would be permitted to venture forward to a new, happier Life. While my husband's wedding would take place, I would be cooking as usual, over the coal fire in the small smoky kitchen. I would prepare the meal for the bride and bridegroom when they came home. Well out of the scene though, I would not see the new bride as she stepped in, for it was an auspicious moment and the sinner that I was, I might pass on my curse to her.

Of course, I would get some sympathy. But it would be the sympathy one gives the hanged man who had killed some small children brutally , not the sympathy one had for the disabled ; this would be the sympathy which the righteous feel for the damned - 'after all, he has got his just desserts'

They would say it was such a waste, these round wide hips which could so easily bear and push a child , the large breasts which looked fertile, which could have fed hungry babies with rich milk, it was all such a waste. What a sinner I was to have received these gifts, yet hide that I would not carry children. That even if I did, I would lose them at 8 months, before they could take learn to live on this earth.

They would blame me, saying it was my fault. That I had not been as careful as I should have. I should not have gone to Sarala's house two doors down that Sunday afternoon when it was quite cloudy outside, a clear sign that it was inauspicious for pregnant women. Or perhaps it was the 'samosa' I had on a Monday, forgetting that it had onions and breaking the 'sarthik' diet I should be following .

It would go up to my parents, they had given me a little too much of freedom. 'Her grandfather adopted too many of those white customs he learnt from the 'Sahibs' , in his tenure as mantri'. 'She used to wear dresses , till she got married. I had seen one of her photographs wearing shoes and socks and a dress only upto her knees, smiling trying to look like those white memsahibs.' 'But White customs don't work on Brown skins', someone would say and they would agree, nodding wisely. 'They educated her till the Std 8th, married her at 16, some years too late! No wonder the girl never understood the importance of keeping home, keeping her children.'

The old 'peesi', living here ever since her husband died, would rant 'I knew something was wrong with the family, with her, but does anyone listen to me in this house?'

The neighbors would come, the relatives would pour in to greet the new wife, resplendent in her red bridal finery. At her throat she would be wearing the heavy gold necklace, which had been handed to me when I was married; it would flow down to her breast, a huge round pendant with shapes of swans filigreed, her ears would be heavy with similar motifs, the swans dancing delicately as she moved softly in the house, the slight rhythm of her anklets on the floor.

On their way out, they would come in to meet me as well. In the little corner room , barer than all the others, with only a hard bed in the corner, they would see me and say –' These things happen. You must accept your fate . Be grateful that they still give you this roof over your head , a place to stay. Where else would you go , a woman like you, too old for anything ?' I would be perhaps 30, but I would see in front of me, this long lonely life, like the poor widow next door. Predictable like the Indian summer.

Some would wink slyly and say, ' Don't give up. Call him here when you can, God may be kind to you. And if you bear a son, you will be whole again.'

What would I have said to them? That I had suffered the loss, lay crying for that heap of blood and tissues which passed out of me, in the shape of a misshapen baby, not breathing, when I took those pains of labour, knowing at the end of it , there would be no loud baby cry . For the child had stopped breathing, stopped moving in my womb. The doctors could not say why, but they said I would have to go through an induced childbirth , and must try to push out as hard and well as I could, the dried remains of my womb. I went through my depression, my sorrows, but I survived, I lived. Or at least I tried.

The mirror on the wall reflected me, those long winding stretch marks on my stomach, spanning the area from below the waist to down on my hips, silvery marks on brown skin, which would always live on me. In the olden days, they would perhaps laugh at this barren woman carrying the signs of fertility.

They would not see, how when the doctor said I might never have another child again, I walked away in sadness and also relief, relief for I had no more duties to a marriage, to society. I did wish he could have been there, soft baby arms snuggling up to me, pulling my hair as his fingers would learn to grasp, but I did not, as they thought I must, yearn to care for another being every moment of my waking and sleeping time. I had a lot more to love, a lot to live for - a quiet read, laughter in my favorite movie, cycle up on the hills in shaded woods, new friends, new places to explore. I had lost a part of me, but I did not feel 'less me' for doing so, I didn't think I was any less a woman.

They would not see why I did not want to fade away, calling my Life a useless existence. Hence they would do it for me, remind me every moment of how I had nothing to stand on, nothing to live for. The traps they would have kept me in were endless. Sometimes, when the winter evenings drew up, and I would have to switch on the lights in the house at 4 p.m. these thoughts would attack me . I would almost forget that this was not the days of long ago, that I did not live in a small village in the state of Orissa in India. I was here in my warm, Laura Ashley decorated home in Surrey. In the corner drawer beside my bed, I even had a little red book to prove to the world that I could live here always, my Indian passport had long been given away.

This was 2003, present days and this was England. Modern Britain. Surely, here I was safe.

Glossary

Baanjh: barren (in Hindi)

Kulanghini: a disgrace, unfortunate

Baandhya : barren (in Oriya)

Alyakhini: ill fated, unlucky.

Sahibs: term used to describe the English rulers in India

Mantri: Minister

Peesi: father's sister.

Sarthik: vegetarian diet excluding onions and garlic as well

DRIFTING AWAY
Nancy Latshaw

I sit in the window looking out over the plains while looking back in time. I try to think of what all has happened to me in my life and yet I have to dig deep to find anything. The things that have passed seem tragic and lonely to me. Where does my life seem to think it is going? My thoughts are very unsure of the things to come. I think that sometimes in my life I feel very selfish and hurt by the things of other people with their lives. I know that people want to hold onto the past, but sometimes it is wrong and need a push to the future to lead their lives.

I have looked back into my life and for the most part of it I have pushed it in the back of my mind to be forgotten until something tragic happens to me in my life and then all the memories come back. I try so hard to not feel guilty about certain things but then I stop and remind myself that things are only what you make them. Only you can make them harder on yourself or make them easy. God has given us a gift and that is free choice with passion and love.

I have learned to take the heartache and push it away cause sometimes I feel like I get too much. I feel like all I want to do is just cry. Then I take the pain and sing it away. I drift off to think about all the happy times I had with each person within my life, which brings a smile to my face. Happiness is so great in a person's life. I know it is in my life. Make sure you go back and look at what makes you so happy and smile.

FRAGMENTS OF LOVE

Pat Phillips West

This is the most ill-fated love story I have ever known. I shake my head, reread the paragraph in Joy's diary . . .

While I was in the last few months of college, I met Ivan. I hesitate to put him down in words. He was the happiest and the deepest misery in my life. That was from age twenty-one to twenty-four. I had my first nervous breakdown that June because of him.

I never loved or wanted anything as much as I wanted Ivan Garcia . . .

When Joy ran late for a date, I would chat with Ivan, so I came to know him well. I remember their love affair - or, rather, her love, his affair. Perhaps Ivan embodied everything she had ever wanted in a man. I know the fact that he was the son of a diplomat attracted her. And that his Russian, Guatemalan heritage intrigued her. Along with his international sophistication and flair.

One of the times that Ivan and I chatted, he told me how intrigued he was with intermittent reinforcement, a topic discussed in his psychology class. The glint in his eye when he talked concerned me. Later I would come to recognize that glint as the first clue.

The cedar chest contains Joy's picture albums. I take out the red one. I know that the entire first page is filled with Ivan Garcia. The one picture of him in the doorway of our apartment captures my interest. I forget if he was coming or going at the time. Joy changed with each passage, he always looked the same.

In the photograph, Ivan stands a tall young man with thick, dark dollops of hair. Deep penetrating eyes stare back at me. When I look at his full, Latin lips, I remember not only his voice, but his tone. I remember how Ivan spoke low and made you lean into him to hear what he said.

Even after thirty-seven years, I still see the strong self confidence. Perhaps that captured Joy, drew her to him. I know that she always gravitated to strength. The aura of his charm shines through the photograph. Or do I sense it? For he possessed a charismatic charm generally only developed by men many years his senior. I don't see the passion, yet Joy talked about it. Perhaps Ivan didn't possess it. Perhaps instead Joy found her passion through him.

I remember the way he pursued her with great intensity. Joy had never been pursued before. I know that she never doubted anything he said, thought any word just "a line."

Ivan's interest in psychology continued. I discovered that he possessed a fascination with manipulation and power. He reminded me of my cat, Henry. I used to watch Henry play with the mice before he consumed them. I saw how my sweet cat turned into an animal I did not recognize. The cat used his paws and size to master the mouse. But Ivan had more tools in his tool box: lines that sounded smooth; not a hint of rehearsal, stature and swagger, and like my cat, a love of the game.

Perhaps he touched a layer in Joy that no other man reached before or since. I know that only for Ivan did Joy demolish every wall she'd ever built. I know that she trusted with total faith, held back no reserve. Perhaps Joy immersed herself in Ivan determined to fill empty voids from her childhood. I know that he filled a need.

About to close the album, I notice another picture. In the photograph, Joy stands back to the camera, her arms around Ivan. He leans down to her, his head nestles between her face and up stretched arm. I see his arms wrap around her. One hand clenches at the back of her dress. The other tucks under her hair to cradle her neck. Joy's right arm reaches up and around the back of Ivan's head. Her fingers spread through his thick, dark hair. I took this picture, but I never saw before. Now I know I captured more than a simple embrace.

Joy and I lived together at the time, thus I witnessed the meteoric rise of her emotions. I also witnessed the depth of her misery. That is, as well as it was possible to know anyone else's anguish. I know when Ivan terminated their relationship, Joy shattered. I remember how, even though shattered, Joy challenged. "But Ivan you said that you loved me. Did you not mean it? Was that a lie?" I remember how he replied, "I meant it when I said it."

I continue to read her pain . . .

After Ivan, I began drinking and having violent fits of hatred and anger. It wasn't so important who I went to bed with after that. It has never been so very important since. I worked hard, I drank hard. And when I became really emotionally upset about Ivan or about the past, I would take off to the mountains, Chaney Trail and sleep in the car.

There's nothing worse than to wake up to rumpled clothes, swollen eyes and a bad hangover with bright sunshine on your face.

I recall her period of violent anger. I remember the night I pleaded with her not to drive, asked her not to leave our apartment. She left. Later that night Joy attempted to drive her car off the cliff on Chaney Trail. She failed.

I knew her as well as it was possible to know anybody. And yet, I knew nothing at all. Only Joy knew how her insides felt when her need stood empty again. Only Joy dealt with the reconstruction of the walls. I know they went back up, with stronger mortar. Only Joy knew what Ivan brought and what he took away.

Today when I sit and reflect over the three years Ivan danced in and out of Joy's life, I know he was part of her destiny.

Every time Ivan waltzed back in to her life, she opened the door. Even though she had spent the time he'd been absent declaring, "never again." Ivan swooped her into his arms, dipped her backward, greeted her with a long, lingering kiss hello. I heard her sigh. I knew that sigh carried her protests to the rafters where they faded and floated away.

I know the details of when he came, how long he stayed, when he left, how she raged. Certainly I neither soared to her ecstasy nor plunged to her despair. I know nothing of how she survived it all. I know only fragments.

FLY ME AWAY, BILL

Peter Eric Williams

It was mid-flight, on a Boeing 747, somewhere over the Altantic... Over came the announcement: "I'm sorry, folks, but things are not looking good. The plane's instruments have failed. Say your prayers folks".

"Hostess", I said. "Take me to the captain. I have a laptop."

"But, sir", she said. "I don't see how that will help."

"It's loaded with Microsoft Flight Simulator. It can plug straight in and we can fly the plane."

"Quick. There's no time to lose", she said.

I grabbed my laptop under my arm and we made our way quickly to the cockpit. The plane was in a slow descent. Lindy the flight attendant said, "this man can help. He's got a laptop with Flight Simulator."

"We can plug it in. If the auxiliary port on the plane is still OK." I was already booting up the pc.

"OK. All I've got to do is double click on this icon to start the program. Here plug this into the console," I said.

"Great, it's auto-detected the plane. Now I've got to try to straighten her up."

"I'll use the cursor keys. Cursor rights. No cursor down. No cursor right and down. Damn it's no good. I need a joystick. Quick give me the mic for the plane's pa system." I grabbed the microphone and flicked the switch for the plane's public address system. "Does someone, anyone, have a joystick for a pc??"

I ran out of the cockpit. "You keep trying", I said to the captain. I spotted a kid in aisle three. He was playing Doom. "Quick, kid, give me that joystick!"

"No way. This is level 15."

"Give me that." and I SLAPPED him.

"Owww"

"Just pause the damn game." Stupid kid.

I ripped the joystick out of his computer and raced back to the cockpit.

I plugged it into the laptop.

"OK, captain, I can take it from here."

I pulled back on the computer joystick and the plane started to respond. I was working. I G-forces were incredible, but the plane was starting to level off. A couple of minutes and it was looking good. I just had to move the stick slightly to the right to level the wings. Great. Look good.

So there we were, flying along OK.

"Now to press 'A' for Auto Pilot," I said. It worked and in the corner of the screen it says "AUTO PILOT"

Then suddenly a seagull flies into engine number one. It bursts into flames. And at the same time Windows gets an "exception error!" A "blue screen of death" on the computer. It's just a messy screen of columns of hex codes and messages. "Quick. Reboot. Reboot," I say, as the plane starts to descend again. This time with the engine on fire. "We're going to die!!! DAMN YOU, Bill Gates!!!" I yell. The laptop reboots remarkable quickly and I restart Flight Simulator. The plane is still in a slow, uncontrolled descent, with the engine on fire. "Quick. Press control P for the parachutes". I press control P. The screen says, "Sorry, the Microsoft Flight Simulator Parachute Add-On is not installed. Please contact the Microsoft Helpline on 1800-MICROSOFT" I dial the number. I am pleasantly surprised that my call is answered quickly. I am talking to Tara, a Microsoft help consultant. She sounds nice. I quickly tell her the situation. After a minute she understands.

"What version of Flight Simulator are you using?" she asks. I tell her. "2000?" she says. "You really should consider upgrading to Flight Simulator 2002, sir. Would you like me to email you the upgrade price?"

"Oh yes. You say engine number one is on fire, sir," she says. "A seagull you say? I'm sorry sir, but I'm going to have to put you on hold for a moment, while I talk to my supervisor. OK? Please hold, sir..."

Music is playing on my mobile phone. Do do do, du do doo-doo, du doo-doo... and on the hold music plays...

SUICIDAL DREAMS

Paul Steven

HK Patterson thanked the waitress who brought him over his third cup of coffee. He stared hard at the empty chair opposite him; someone was late, very late. Spooning six large helpings of sugar into his coffee, he hung the spoon tantalisingly over the sugar bowl considering for a second or two to add another when, suddenly, the cąfé door opened. HK swivelled around to see who had just entered, no one he knew. Another twenty minutes crept past before he finally decided that she was not going to show and left the café.

Aimlessly he walked the streets, feeling like a stranger in his own city. He watched the lively crowds go about their Friday night ritual. Couples walked hand in hand or wrapped around each other would knowingly stare at him as if he had a sign around his neck saying-Stood Up: Again!

How had he let it happen? Time after time he had been hurt. God, he knew he was no oil painting, that the opposite sex might even find him peculiar looking, but he wished just once that someone would peel back his repulsive outer layers and find an incredibly caring person caged within. It was this harrowing thought that HK faced everyday, that no one would ever look. He thought this one would have been different. He had thought wrong.

Climbing the concrete steps, salted tears streamed down HK's face. He knew he was a loser, a sad depressive loner. Thirty-two years old with not a friend in-sight. Those who had taunted him throughout his life were right; he was a joke, the butt of a thousand jokes. It was time to finish the pain. Pulling himself over the metal railing of the footbridge, he looked down as the screaming lumps of metal passed below. Their cries of obliteration hollered up to HK, mocking him to jump. And so he did.

The traffic stopped screaming, the wind felt cold as it rushed over his face, it was as if he was flying. The driver saw him at the last second, the same way a mouse notices a declining hawk: too late. The windscreen exploded, showering the passengers of the car. It swerved into the inside lane and channelled into an oncoming vehicle. Metallic tombs entwined together as they hurtled towards the side of the motorway. Brakes howled behind them as frantic drivers fought to stop their chariots. Scattered debris littered the lanes of the motorway. Those that had managed to stop climbed from their cars and rushed to help. Traumatic cries came from one car, quietness emitted from the other. Minutes later the first sounds of the emergency vehicles filled the air.

"Tch, What a mess," said the voice, "Someone will have to clear that up y'know."

"I never expected people to die, only myself"

"That is some handy work though, quite impressive for a first effort." The voice said.

"What do you mean first effort?"

"Oh you'll see," said the voice," Try going for the white car next time, should take more of them out, if you do that."

"Are you serious, I mean I'm dead right! And anyway who are you?

"Just a friend." Said the voice.

"Friend! What kind of friend tells me to aim for a different vehicle to get a higher score."

"The only friend you have," said the voice," See you soon."

HK Patterson bolted upright in his chair, just as the café door swung open. He swivelled round to see who had entered, no one he knew. Someone was late, very late. Another twenty minutes he would give them and then, well then they could go to Hell for all he cared.

ALONE

Rachel Caris Thompson

The darkness was a colossal black hole eating up anything that came into its deathly reach and enveloping it into sheer horror. It was almost invincible except for its fear of the light and hatred for happiness.

Surrounding a small building the darkness tried to enter and failed. The light form a half moon watched it's progress, threatening the dark with it's unnatural light. Eerie patterns darted around a small cottage like a bizarre dance of the dead. The frosty night wind smashed against one of the cottage's gleaming windows, like a huge wave hitting a struggling boat. The cottage remained standing looking for help at the surrounding rolls and rolls of fields.

There weren't very many people who lived around the area, only a small run down farm, owned by a strange farmer who hated his neighbors. He lived the life of a hermit and never talked to anyone.

Danielle sat watching the television screen, she was alone in the comfort of her cramped living room. Her parents had gone to visit her older sister in Manchester, which was quite far away from her Devonshire home. They were driving back that evening after seeing her for the weekend. Danielle hadn't gone as she was revising for her GCSE's.

She hated being alone out there on the hillside where anything could happen to her, especially when the silvery moon was an evil glow in the sky and the wind blew like a wild monster's roar. That darkness trying to invade her home, trying to consume her. Into a world full of monsters and torment.

A sharp scratch at the window made Danielle's heart rate pound. She almost spun around at the noise. She sighed with relief as she discovered it was only spindly tree branches scraping the glass. She could feel her blood racing around her body over the small shock. A sharp noise from the television made Danielle's gaze return to its welcoming image.

A short while later her brown cat trotted into the room and rubbed its soft head against her. She stroked its smooth fur absent mindedly, happily the fluffy cat jumped upon her lap. It comforted her from the stormy night.

Danielle woke to hear the soft purring of her cat. The cat's purring stopped suddenly, with its eyes blazing like hot coals, it charged towards the old window. It arched its tail and the long hairs on it's back stood up, as if lightening had struck the creature, it then spat angrily.

Danielle ran towards the window, her heart beating rapidly again and her palms prickling with fear. She looked through the window and she thought she could see a dark figure stumbling through some bushes. "It's just my imagination." she told herself out loud, her voice was now a whispered croak.

As she was about take her place on the sofa again, Danielle heard a faint bang that got louder and louder. On trembling legs Danielle walked slowly out of her living room and closed the door quietly behind her. The miserable noise got louder and louder as she walked silently down her long winding hallway. Danielle reached the kitchen door and opened it slowly, she gasped in disbelief at what she saw. The back door was open and was swinging backwards and forwards. She rushed quickly towards the door and locked it, the sound echoed around the cottage. She had thought she'd locked it later the day. She slowly went back to the lounge, looking fearfully over her shoulder.

After a while Danielle phoned one of her friends to calm her nerves, perhaps Melissa would comfort her. She climbed slowly out of her clammy seat, her temples pumping wildly. She practically dragged herself towards the phone, every will in her body was telling her not to go to the phone, but she did. She was confused about this feeling and had to find out why.

She reached the phone, her hand shook as she picked the receiver up from it's place, on the brown table. She put it to her ear, she cried out in dismay and shook even more than she already was, the phone was dead.

A while later Danielle lay huddled in an arm chair, she kept telling herself that she was being stupid and should get a hold of herself, but she could not. Her heart seemed to miss a beat as she heard the sound of footsteps on the floorboards above. It started as a small creak working itself into a loud slap.

With horror she rushed to the sitting room door, she slammed it shut and threw a chair roughly against the shining doorknob. Sweat beaded her forehead as she sunk to the floor near the chair and desperately hoped the chair would save her. SCRATCH, SCRATCH. Danielle suddenly heard it at the door and her heart seemed to miss a beat. Slowly she got up, the cold scratching at the old door seemed to get louder at every shuddering moment. She could not help herself she had to open the door and discover what was behind it. She gently pushed the chair from under the doorknob and opened the door a crack.

As Danielle looked out she began to cry with laughter and relief at what she saw. There at the door stood the cat. Danielle realised that it must have been the cat on the floorboards. Danielle thought something moved from under the sofa, a high scream erupted from her lungs as she saw the shape of a man lunging from behind the sofa. It was the farmer from the old farm. A big carving knife glinted evilly in the light. Danielle stood stock still for a moment, she had to force her legs to run. She rushed out of the front door, it slammed behind her, she stumbled on the stones outside the cottage. Roots and branches scraped at her bare legs. The darkness evilly welcomed her, welcomed the man who pursued her.

***

Danielle's parents opened the front door, which creaked in protest. It was dark in the sitting room, so the mother turned the light on. She gasped at what she saw. A big knife glinted in the light. It was plunged deeply into the sofa. The seam was seeping a substance, and the blade of the knife was dark red.

THE BLUE PLASTIC BAG

Rani Drew

It was a victory for the environmental campaigners when they got the City Council to start a Re-cycling Collection Service. The scheme was launched with some aplomb. Plastic containers were delivered to each household, accompanied by an instructive letter about the need to re-cycle consumer waste. The aim was to raise the environmental consciousness in those who were not quite up to the 21st century concerns for the planet. A chart was enclosed, which laid out re-cyclable and non-re-cyclable materials clearly under separate categories. Plastic was distinctly outlawed, as it still defied a re-cycling technology to pulp it. The delivery of the containers created some excitement and activity among residents as they tried to arrange a spot for the container from where it could be conveniently collected. Everyone filled it with bottles, newspapers and squashed cans, and made sure none of the banned articles found their way in, and waited to see how the scheme was going to operate.

So, one fine autumn morning the collection service was launched and a lorry turned into our street. Those who were home came to the window to see whether it was the same as the weekly bin collection vehicle, or something new. To their surprise a brand new white lorry was making its way slowly up the street. It had three different colour-coded outlets on the right-hand side, and the staff was uniformed in matching design and colours – white outfits, three-colour stripes and a white dove carrying bags of re-cycling waste. For the street, it was a historic beginning of a 21st century project. No one was ready to miss it. Four in number, the collection men had a smart look and moved to and fro collecting the containers from the pavement, sorting the waste meticulously, depositing it in the appropriate outlets and then taking the containers back to the spot they were taken from. Their manner and mode were altogether different from the weekly rubbish-bin collectors. Bit by bit the whole length of the street was covered; the operation was smoothly conducted taking no more than half an hour; even the noise sounded mellifluous compared with the grating screechy sound of the weekly rubbish collection. And of course, there was no smell. The watching faces in the street windows did not disappear until the van turned round – the street being cul-de-sac – and this time whizzed passed the houses without stopping.

As the autumn advanced and the winter lurked in the air with its frosts, the weekly re-cycling collection lost its newness for the residents. The promised meticulousness was already fraying at the edges as the containers were dumped back by the collectors on the pavement any old how rather than positioned systematically as at the beginning. It meant the pedestrians had to pick their way round them carefully and cyclists, especially children who chose to use the pavement for extra safety as the street parking was now allowed on both sides, had to wheel their bicycles with caution. Parents warned the children returning from school in the afternoon to take greater care in going past the containers as they did not get removed until the evening when most people returned from work. Increasingly, the pavements were not left clean after the collection was made; bits of newspapers, advertising papers, juice cartons, coca cola and squashed tins were found scattered around and needed to be picked up by the householders. Any plastic material – bags, coverings etc – were firmly left out with an invisible reminder, 'You were told not to.' In fact, after the collection, the pavements were left looking like mini tips. And if the rain and the notorious winds of the region were up to their mischief, there was no telling how far some of these left articles would travel to make their impact.

As the cold settled in and the wintry north wind raged through the road, those who tended to consume stacks of newspapers every week tried to organise their waste by putting the paper in plastic bags. This provided a certain fortitude to the bundles in the face of winds that rushed past them at a hurricane speed, and prevented the street being strewn with newspapers. But this did not please the collectors, who in increasing displeasure at this innovation involving plastic, started to leave the bags in a discarded state, either screwed up in the container or just thrown on the pavement as a repeated statement, 'You have been told many times.'

It was on one such rainy and windy day that a blue plastic bag found out its outreach. The story of its trajectory goes like this. After a bag was emptied of its newspapers and magazines tightly stuffed in it, its blue plastic invoked a considerable irritation in the collectors. 'Why the f...they can't leave paper in the containers?' 'Teach them a lesson, mate; leave it out,' said his colleague, 'the only way they'll learn.' And so, the mate did what he was advised. The blue plastic bag was dumped next to the container and not put back in it. Next time, he muttered swearing, if the hint is not taken by the owners, he would pass up their container altogether.

The rain became torrential. The container filled up with water in no time, and the plastic bag got absolutely soaked and flattened out with no hope of serving as a filler-bag again. The downpour poured into it before making its way from the pavement to the drain below on the edge of the road. Soon the wind got up. It wasn't exactly a hurricane, but it was fierce. It swished around like a sword, ready to cut down whatever fell in its way. The patch of blue plastic glared at it as a challenge to its cutting edge. The wind went for the bag a few times, with the intention of picking it up, tossing it round and up and landing it somewhere. But when it came to tackling the plastic bag, the task wasn't as easy as it had looked. The bag had gone heavy with water, the plastic folds held bits of liquid in them, turning the bag into a small lake which wasn't easy to dislodge. The wind lifted itself high, took another swoop in the air like a bird of prey then dived down once again. This time it managed to pick up one corner of the bag, making the water run down one side of it. The lake was now almost half-emptied, but the bag still not empty enough for it to be totally at the whim of the wind. The wind was not pleased; in rage it lifted its current to a higher circle of air and took a mighty dive for the bag. As it hit the bag, to its surprise this time it turned neatly. Hurray! The wind whistled as it swept past it. The plastic bag, now light and dry, fluttered in delight. It was thrilled to sport with the wind. The wind was still circling and swooping when it saw that the bag was ready to take off. It swung down making merry round the bag and before it knew, the bag lifted itself into the flurry and started to float like a kite in the air. Suddenly the tree in front of the house across the road stopped it in its drunken flight. The blue bag was now firmly caught by its spiky branches high up. It waited to be disentangled by the wind but there was no sign of the wind anywhere. So it hung there a patch of blue plastic in a leafless tree.

Next day, it was sunny and still. A warm calm prevailed in the air. Not even the memory of the stormy weather remained in people's minds – except the sight of the blue plastic bag, glaringly visible from the street.

'Look, Mummy, a blue bag,' a child pointed to the tree on the way to school next morning. 'Dear, oh dear, look at that plastic in the tree,' said the old woman on the way to the pillarbox on the corner, to post her letter. 'What an ugly sight,' said another woman as she looked out of her window from across the road and saw the bag hanging in the tree. She vaguely remembered stacking newspapers in a blue plastic bag. Why the hell couldn't they stick it back in the bin? She was irritated by the bloody mindedness of the collectors and decided to lodge a complaint with the City Council about their tardy service.

After running the gauntlet of listening to message-machine for endless options on the diverse services offered by the Council, she finally got connected to the Environmental Cleansing Department number and heard a human voice. Exhausted by the convoluted journey to her destination, she got to the point right away.

'A plastic bag hanging on a tree is an environmental eyesore. Could the department get it down?'

A plastic bag in a tree?'

'Yes, between your servicemen and the north wind, we have a plastic bag stuck high up in a tree, and it will obviously stay there, unless taken down.'

'We see the point you are making, but unfortunately, any work to do with trees falls in the Spring Services category.

'When is that?'

'Not before April, I'm afraid.'

'It's November now. So, you mean to say the plastic bag will continue to wave from the tree until then?' Her exasperation was beginning to mount.

'I'm sorry but there's no other option. We work on seasonal rotas. I can make a note of this for our spring work on trees; and it can't be until next Spring, and there's a charge for the service.' There was no apology in the voice.

'I don't see why we should pay for the bloody mindedness of your staff. Why couldn't the collectors stick the plastic bag back in the bin, instead of leaving it on the pavement? It....'

She was interrupted. 'If I may remind you, madam, residents are expected not to put any plastic in the containers. A list of cycable and non-cycable contents was distinctly left in each container.'

'Does that mean any plastic left by mistake will be turned into litter by the environmental guardians?' It was worth giving them a piece of her mind, she decided. 'Let me tell you that the bag had a purpose. It was a caution against paper flying all over the road, in case of strong winds. Does that make sense to you?'

'Not really. We are thinking of bringing in a fine system against those owners of the containers who use plastic bags to bag their waste-material. That will be the only way to make sure people obey the strict environmental code. We cannot....'

She banged the phone down. She called the residents meeting, and spoke quite passionately about the need to put pressure on the Council to direct their collection-service to a more conscientious spirit, in case of any violation of the strict regulations. But there was not much response from anyone. Some mentioned Germany having even stricter regulations for the residents to put out waste materials in absolutely separated categories; others told stories of how in Norwegian countries the whole street could be left out if more than five households failed to comply with waste-collection regulations. There was a clear insinuation that she was to blame in the end.

From that day on the woman avoided the front-room window in the daytime – the sunniest spot in the house; and while going to work, she made sure she didn't look up across the road. Like a flag, the blue plastic bag will no doubt continue to fly through rain, cold or wind – and even the sun.

REAL
Rebecca

I was finally going home. After four years I was going to see the family I ran away from. I never would have left if I had known what awaited me in New York City. And the funniest thing was after all I'd been through; I'd never been so scared in my entire life. It was 1985, in the decade of teen angst, and I was unhappily living in Suburbia, New York. My parents and I fought everyday and it often got physical.

I can't even count how many times I had "accidentally" gotten a black eye or broken bone. Dad was an alcoholic, Mom was in denial, my sister was too young and me, I was the perfect target. I'd finally had enough and I knew just what to do. While everyone was asleep I packed a bag of clothes, stole my dad's wallet, and ran out of the house towards the train station. Before I knew it I was heading to the city. What would my parents say when they realize that I'm gone? Probably only, "Where's my wallet?" Suddenly amidst my thoughts the train whistled and slowed to a stop. I took a deep breath and stepped off the train to a new environment. Surprised couldn't even describe how I felt when I saw the subway. People in raggedy, moth eaten, dirty clothes lay all over the ground. Also, the smell made my stomach churn. I rushed out of there as fast as I could without tripping over someone. When I reached the outside I really wished I'd stayed in the station. People were everywhere and I had no idea where I was going. "Excuse me," I said as I tapped a person walking by on the shoulder, "Can you point me in the direction of a place I could stay? I'm visiting the city for the first time." The man stood tall, hovering over me. He was wearing a nice suit and seemed superior to the other people I had spotted.

My thoughts suddenly changed as he gave me a dirty look, "Go to hell!" he said and walked off. I traveled around for two hours before I found a halfway decent motel. A girl who looked barely older than me sat at the front desk popping her gum and chatting away on the phone. I cleared my throat and still she pretended that I wasn't there. Finally I snatched the phone from her hand and threw it down on the receiver. She shot me an angry look, "I don't know who you think you are..." I cut her off, not wanting to hear what she had to say. "I've had a really long night and I'd really just like to get a room." I paid and she tossed my key me, "Go straight through that hallway, your is the last room on the left." The place was tiny and hardly worth the $15 I had to pay. I knew that my money would never last like this. I pulled on my favorite pair of stone washed jeans and a flannel shirt and ran across the street to the grocery store I saw on my way. I didn't have much money and I needed to conserve so I bought sandwich fixings, cereal, milk, and plastic silverware. On my way back to the motel, my hands full of bags, I bumped into a girl who could have been a Madonna look-alike but younger. "Watch where you're going," the girl spoke harshly. But when she looked at me her tone suddenly changed and she quickly apologized, "Oh man, look, I'm real sorry. I didn't mean..." "It's okay," I interrupted, "I should be more careful. I'm just not used to all these people." "Really? Where are you from?" "Suburbia." "Wow, that's cool. I've never heard of the place myself but its got to be better than here. So what brings you to this dump?" "Well, it's a long story but basically I ran away, and here I am." Cool beans!" She paused sounding sad, "I guess you should probably get your things inside." "Yeah, I should. Why don't you come inside? I could sure use some company." "Okay." We walked into the motel and talked for hours, finding conversation easily. I told her about my money running low and she said she had an idea. "See I make money real easy, a good $300 a day." "Well what exactly do you do?" "I'm a prostitute." When she said that my face turned so pale I could feel it.

I couldn't imagine selling my body on the street just to have a place to stay and food in my belly. But before I knew it that was exactly what I was doing. I sat outside in a pink miniskirt and a black ripped up shirt with big, beaded necklaces and high heels. My hair was long and piled on top of my head with big, curled-under bangs. I think I spent more money on hairspray that I did on food. Heidi, who was the girl who I had met outside the motel, had really helped me. She introduced me to so many cool people including her boyfriend, Frank. We would hang out all the time and not really doing much but smoking pot and drinking. I was also making quite a bit more money than I was used to and it was a long awaited thrill. Frank was really cool. He was defiantly someone I would have never met if I hadn't ran away and in a way I was glad I did. He was about average height with turquoise colored hair and he dresses in the oddest way. Frank and Heidi were on the streets for the same reason that she was; they couldn't take home life anymore and came to the Big Apple. I was getting bored with things though, and Frank introduced me to the greatest thing in the entire world, Heroin. I never saw the world so beautiful until I shot up for the first time. For once in my life I thanked God for being alive. Coming down was awful! I slit up my wrists so bad one time that I had to go to the emergency room.

Now I always make sure that I have enough money for more later. Some people would be so quick to judge me for the things I do, but the simple fact is I'm just trying to survive this superficial and unhappy world. I never thought anything I did could hurt me. In my eyes, I was invincible. I found out that I was wrong at one of

Frank and Heidi's parties. They lived in an abandoned warehouse that they decked out. Basically it was just a drug and party house. I got there around 8pm and already the place was packed. "Tania! God, I thought you'd never show up!" Heidi yelled over the music. She handed me a beer. "Drink up!" I wasn't a fan of alcohol because it tasted so foul, but I also loved the feeling of being drunk. It made me the person I always wanted to be, confident and outgoing. After a couple more beers and a few shots I finally got the nerve to walk over to the hot guy I'd been eyeing all night. "Hi," he said smiling sly. We talked for a while and everything was going well, but then out of nowhere he started to become pushy. "Ya know it's really loud down here. Why don't we go upstairs and get to know each other a little better?" "No, I'm fine down here." He grabbed my arm, squeezing it hard, "Here you are leading me on..." "Leading you on? How am I leading you on? We were just talking!" "Look at the way you're dressed!" I tried to pull free from his grasp and scratched his arm. He slapped me across the face and I fell to the floor. The room was spinning and all I could see was Frank walk over and punch him in the face. Then the room went black. I woke up and I didn't know where I was or what had happened. Then I saw Frank on a chair next to me. I was in his room, on his bed. "You passed out so I took you up here. You've been out for almost an hour." I stared at him blankly. I still couldn't remember what happened. "James hit you. You don't remember?" "No, I don't. But thanks to you I'm okay," I said flirtatiously. I don't know why I did this. I just needed someone in my life and he was the one. He leaned close to me and we kissed.

I was sure it was wrong because Heidi was my friend, but it just felt so right. Before I knew it we were having sex. If it was so wrong then why was it so good? At that moment I felt like I had connected with someone like never before. Afterwards, while Frank was taking a shower, I got dressed and left without saying a word. I sat in my motel room for two days all alone. I didn't shower or change clothes, and I barely ate. Early in the morning on the third day I was watching infomercials when I heard a knock at the door. "Come in," I yelled, too lazy to get out of bed. Frank walked in the room. He looked worried, but I didn't care. "Get out of bed!" he said irritably, "This is no big deal! You're blowing it way out of proportion!" I ignored him. He sat down next to me on the bed and it reminded me of that night. I moved away from him. "Look, I'm sorry, but you can't be mad at me. You had just as much to do with this as me." "I'm not mad at you, I'm mad at the situation." I sat up, "I just don't know what to do. This sucks!" "I know it does, but I brought something to make it all better."

He smiled as he pulled out a little baggie filled at the bottom with white powder. "It's crack-cocaine. I guess this is some new stuff. I thought it'd cheer you up." I only did that stuff four or five times and before I knew it I couldn't stand to be without it. That was definitely more addictive than even heroin. I was also getting really sick. I was pale and thin and my whole body ached. I was so tired all the time that I barely got up for work. At night I'd wake up freezing cold, but my whole body would be soaked in sweat. Frank and Heidi came to visit me almost every day, bringing me all the dope I could snort up my pretty little nose. Money was running short and before I knew it I had no more money to keep the motel room. I was forced to move in with Heidi and Frank. I know you're probably thinking, well they're my friends so why wouldn't it be cool to live with them. I felt that I was burdening them. Here they were, working their butts off and I just lay around the place. Finally, Heidi dragged me out of bed and took me to see a doctor. He said it could be that I was pregnant and the drugs were hurting the baby, so he ran some tests and told me to come back in a week. The week went by slowly. I was feeling a bit better, out of bed once in awhile, and actually holding down food. Soon enough the time came to see Dr. Oden. I wasn't as scared as I'd been before because I looked and felt pretty good. "Tania, the doctor can see you now," the nurse said, and I walked into the room. A chill suddenly ran up my spine like ice. Right then I knew something was wrong.

"Tania," the doctor spoke calmly, "I ran all the tests possible and some even twice and I have your diagnosis." I looked at him waiting for him to tell me but he just stared at the floor. "Tell me doc., it can't be that bad." "Yes darling, but I'm afraid it is," he paused like he was collecting his thoughts, and then he continued, "You have AIDS, and advanced stage of HIV." I almost passed out right there. I'd heard about AIDS before. I heard mostly of people suffering and dying. "We don't know that much about this but we do know that it's deadly... and incurable. Most people with this disease die within the first 6months to year of diagnosis." I didn't say anything; I just did the only thing I knew to do. I stood up and walked out. I could hear the doctor calling me to come back, but I just kept on walking. I pulled out a quarter and dialed the vaguely familiar number on the payphone outside the hospital.

A woman answered, she sounded old and worn out. "Mom," I said, "It's me, Tania." She started crying. I told her some of the things going on and she cried even harder. She said she would send money Western Union and I could come home. I was finally going back home! I walked around all night and then caught the train in the morning. I didn't even say goodbye to Frank and Heidi or pick up my things. Home was better than it ever was. I found out that dad killed himself. I wasn't sure if I was actually bothered too much by that though. I was getting worse but I'd also never been happier. Mom brought a glass of water to my bed and gave me a kiss goodnight. She told me that she missed me very much and she loved me. I felt some sort of closure. I was finally at peace. Then I closed my eyes for the very last time.

BUBBLES AND SEEDS
Rebecca Chen

I'm gazing out the cafe's window, at the gigantic neon sun melting directly over an invisible horizontal stripe in the sky. Now watch this glass of chilled 7-Up. No really, just look, I paid three bucks for this. It's so cold its sweating onto the brown counter, a perfect watery circle. I squish my lemon slice into the fizzing soda, along with two pale seeds. Savior-bubbles rush to gather around the poor victim of a seed, lift it up to the sweet surface and inevitably vanish with an unheard pop as the seed plunges back down to the very bottom. Repeat. Such martyrdom for the seed happens over and over again, except for of course, the other seed—the fat one. Too heavy with shame or guilt or anger to even feel the hope of being saved. Those damn bubbles, Ruth would say, *think they're too good for me? Okay, they probably are, but you, oh slender one, you just wait til the soda goes flat...you'll be exactly where I am, then what? Huh?* Well maybe she would replace the word bubbles with the other b- word, and so on, but that's exactly how she feels. She reminds me of it every night over the phone. I motion for another slice of Mom's Freshly Baked Apple Pie (my last slice was still frozen in the middle) to-go, since it's a quarter past seven and she's been calling my apartment non-stop for fifteen minutes. I push open my door and musky air sneak-attacks my nostrils as I pick up the nearest phone.

Yeah, sorry I'm late.

Yes, I know you call the same time every night, for the past four hundred-something nights.

No, I can't guess, what happened?

Then I begin listening. And I begin thinking why I hadn't picked up the cordless phone instead. How I don't even know what musky truly smells like, but the word just sounds right, so close to mucky. Ruth's ranting on about three pink dresses, her perfect sister Angie, and mandatory whorish make-up.

Whorish make-up reminds me of girls reminds me of dates reminds me of the calendar. My calendar, yes; this is definitely the highlight of the day. It's sad but the feeling I get when I let myself X out twenty days just to catch up to the present one is satisfying. Oops, I unintentionally forgot to cross them out each night. There goes three weeks of this crap life—flew by without me even noticing, it was so nice. Ruth cuts me off with the words "no man" and "my fat ass."

Fat ass reminds me of marshmallows reminds me of boy scouts remin—wait a minute, if today's November 12th, tomorrow's Angie's wedding. Not that it has much to do with me, except it must be what Ruth is bubbling and moaning about. I ask where did she say the wedding banquet was going to be again, feigning interest. I don't bother listening to her answer; instead I stretch the beige phone cord completely straight and plop into my vinyl beanbag chair and shut my eyes.

Ruth's in front of me. Her medium height, brown hair, medium skin tone, brown eyes, and medium weight are all there, but not counting for much. She's standing there, cheery yellow balloon tied to her wrist, all content like the balloon is. Like the balloon has to be. Then tall and mocha brown-haired Angie skips down the aisle in her poofy white wedding dress, lips lip-sticked, hazel eyes eye-lined and curves somehow still curving through the big dress. The balloon suddenly pops without a sound and its shattered pieces morph into glass bit by bit as both sisters grab some. Rubbery glass flies back and forth across the bridge of my nose until all is still again. I look to my left and watch as the last sliver of glass embeds itself into Ruth's stomach, thhhuk. A bloated lemon seed is what she's become, and to my right is a skinny one sporting a veil. Before another thought, I'm run over by hundreds of bubbles, each with either an unruly handle-bar moustache, sideburns that meet at the chin, bleeding gum line, tacky fake pearls, bushy unibrow, unsightly bulky eyeglasses, rancid food speckled beard, or a pierced lip...everything Ruth has ever found wrong with her family.

What's wrong with my family?

My eyes open and Ruth's screaming into the phone that's two feet away.

I've slipped out of my vinyl chair and it's almost 9. I get up and hurry to the phone.

Hey don't worry, I can work everything out, I tell her.

I had a vision, enlightenment.

Trust me.

I will settle your whole little world by tomorrow night.

I promise this and ask again where the banquet is going to be. She warns me not to burst her bubble. I know I won't. Just her sister's.

A day later, I'm sitting in some Chinese restaurant watching slides of when Angie and her new hubby were babies. Ruth's lacey pink sleeve is scratching me through my dress shirt, but as long as she's happy having a date, a man, it's not so bad. Though the blue eye-shadow is, even a guy has to say, pretty bad. The MC is throwing up tired fake laughs and I'm fingering a little pocketknife from my boy scout days, which was the best I could do, through the pink napkin on my lap. I've already decided to kill Angie's biggest bubble—the one who's always there for her when she's down, constantly making her feel better about herself, and never taking any credit for it: Ruth. She's always there for Angie to bring down with her, constantly making her look superior, and never aware of it. I know this because in my revelation I saw the medium brown dreariness in the very first savior-bubble that ran me over to rescue that brittle seed of Angie.

Who would've thought you could be a bubble and a seed in the same glass?

The MC finally takes a seat and everyone focuses on the platter of fried duck coming on. I might as well do it now. Why let Ruth embarrass herself in her last hour by having to give a loving toast in a few moments?

I snatch a party favor, take a long, hard lungful of the pot-potpourri stench nested in the miniature ceramic swan, flick out my blade and stab. And stab and stab and stab, you know, just to make sure.

See, jealousy problems solved, gone. Angie's half of the soda has gone flat just like yours has been. Ruth thanks me through the thick muck of blood.

Blood reminds me of warmth reminds me of home reminds me of, well, my not going back there. Real bubbles do pop and vanish at the surface and besides, my seed is already dead and rescued.

An extra whiff of potpourri and my blade finds its way towards myself. I'm my own bubble.

ANIMATING THE MANNEQUINS
Rebecca Holder

He stood in front of the rows of glassy blank faces, cleared his throat, ran his hand through gelled blond hair and began. His arms waving at points – expressing and emphasising the words, the mannequins dressed in designer clothes staring. "Fact!" He declared, with a flick of a lightly tanned hand, "Is a lot stranger than fiction!"

One or two painted eyebrows slowly rose.

"And I, will prove this to you!"

So he continued, highlighting a true tale about an Italian lady who gave birth to sixty-three children in twenty-seven separate pregnancies, then one about three passenger ferries on different occasions sinking, the sole survivor being a man, each one different, but each bearing the same name.

"So!!" He yelled, making the mannequins jump in surprise, "Isn't the story of Jesus an example of this?!"

At that moment, glassy stares slipped over, they had heard enough about Jesus, a few shrugged that 'they guess' stranger things had happened. The young man, suddenly noticing that he was losing them, raised his voice even further – his arms flapping. "And! If Jesus was born today, what would he get?!"

"...?" Commented the rows of shop window dolls, now that the interesting stories were obviously over, sinking into a stupor. One track-suited creature raised an arm, slowly, lazily. "A TV crew!! Reality TV!!" It barked.

The assembled nodded at each other and started to mutter about 'Big Brother' while the man looked on in vain as this new deity consumed their thoughts. Another arm was raised and, now desperate, the blond man smiled hopefully at the perfectly painted features peering up at him.

"I don't think so. If a woman believed she was going to give birth to the son of God now there would not be a TV crew... or even the best doctors," her high soft voice rang clearly through the hall now, the plastic heads absorbing all, "She would be sent to some sort of home, and the baby put up for adoption. There may be already another Jesus with a foster family, badly behaved and on some kind-of drug for thinking God talks to him. In fact, I think its been done... if there was a God, and now God has given up... nothing can get through to us now, well, nothing like that anyway."

Another blank-stared doll nodded. "Yeah, if he was on TV like, it'd be boring, creepy religious people don't make good viewing. Especially without explosions... war... guns... you know?"

The assembled mannequins blinked in unison at the man, whose eyes were wide and had taken two steps back from the podium. His carefully crafted notes, done out of love, lay scattered all over the shining wooden floor. Smirking, the moulded creatures tilted their heads to one side, their almost identical haircuts in the fashion of the time. Only varying from girl to boy, moulding perfectly with their perfect heads.

Then, in rows, stood up and slowly walked out of the hall to their lessons.

THE GREAT SARS MASK GIVEAWAY

Robert M. Wilson

"What's with the mask, Lone Ranger?" asks a smiling passenger in the waiting room of the Miami International Air Terminal.

"SARS," mumbles the masked passenger. He is wearing a white surgical mask that covers his mouth and nose.

"SARS? You mean Severe Acute Respiratory Syndrome?"

The masked passenger indulgently nods yes.

"But I thought that was only in China."

"This is an international airport. There are many Oriental travelers like myself. Look, there's another one over there!"

The first passenger looks over at an elderly Fu Manchu type who just happens to be coughing.

"You wouldn't have an extra mask, would you?"

"As a matter of fact I do. I'm taking a shipment to my sister in Ohio, who is a nurse."

The masked passenger gives a mask to the man, who quickly puts it on. Within seconds, other waiting passengers come over and receive masks. Before long, three-fourths of the waiting room is masked. It looks like a hospital operating room.

The word spreads out into the hall and more passengers rush to get their masks, which Mr. Mojo soon runs out of. The terminal is now made up of haves and have-nots. Masks, that is. The travelers without masks start to panic. They begin shouting, even screaming. Passengers run to the airline counters to cancel their reservations, then stream out of the terminal. Some are even knocked down. Airport police, with their own SARS masks, try to control the craziness but are overwhelmed. Before long, a local TV News reporter shows up and is directed to the Lone Ranger.

"Excuse me, sir, may I ask you some questions?"

"Sure."

"What's your name?"

"Mojo."

"Mojo? What kind of name is that?"

"You don't like my name? What's your name, turkey? Mr. Turkey?"

"I'm sorry. I just meant that your name seems unusual."

"Yeah, well, where I come from it's very common. General Mojo and his army defeated the Japanese pirates in 1352."

"Where is your home, Mr. Mojo?"

"It's a little island off the south coast of China called "Tu zi bu chi wo bian cao."

"That's a long name."

"You're right. On most maps it is labeled "Oolong" after the exclamations of a female missionary who came to the island in 1765 and spread her love among the male islanders, who are traditionally well-endowed. It has something to do with the tea we drink. Would you like me to show you?"

"Uh, no, that's alright, Mr. Mojo. Have a good flight."

"Thanks. I don't think it will be very crowded. I love riding these silver birds."

"Hi ho, Silver, away!"

GOD HAS HEARD THY PRAYERS

Santosh Kumar

William Robbins felt very lonely living in a posh locality of Bombay, where due to compulsion of earning fast buck, the poor widows offer themselves to persons who have money. Especially charming widows living in slums are an easy prey. Here in India widow is regarded a curse, an evil spirit enough to mar one's future prospects. Time was when the scriptures ordained for her a macabre status of 'Sati' (Funeral pyre wherein a widow was forced to burn herself to death). In spite of legislation, hatred for the widow survives, and a widow's remarriage is rare. Even if she remarries, the Indian society won't accept her. Mere sight of a widow is an ill omen for a newborn child. This is vulgar superstition, but remains a brutal fact of Indian society.

Robbins found it impossible to abide by such taboos & despicable traditions. Why can't a widow remarry? Why no equal human rights for her? Legally yes, but the society recognizes it not. He met Rama whose husband was massacred in bloodbath unleashed by Hindu-Muslim riots after the demolition of Ayodhya mosque. She was so beautiful. Hardly twenty. Her relatives, thirsty of her blood, abused her: 'She is a witch, that's why she ate (lost) her husband. Don't touch or see her. Her very shadow will defile us'. Strange Hindoostan (India) in the new millennium. Sleeping giant!

In spite of widowhood, Rama pined for love, not power or money. She never aspired to become another Sonia Gandhi. No political ambition. Her humble ambition was a second marriage with the man who won't discard her after using, who won't burn her to death, as dowry deaths are common in India. 'Apartheid of gender' is shamelessly practiced. Final funeral rites must be performed by the son, or the departed soul would miss salvation.

Rama's sensuous body reminded Robbins of a rainbow in the heavens, a cool harbinger of rains. He remembered the celestial hours passed with her, touching her pink, smooth legs, rosy lips and eyes wild. He used to get lost in fantasying her: 'Oh my love, hear me, deadly beauty! Oh, oh, I'm dying without you.' To Rama, he seemed the right person, the ideal man, 'a suitable boy'. He was serious about philosophy, culture, human rights, gender discrimination. No alcoholism, no fundamentalism in him. He was Christian? So what? She argued. Here was a chance for her revival, a golden opportunity for stability in her life. Widows in India don't think of remarriage; they flee in terror, horror of social ostracism, but Robbins was earnest, uncoupled by complexes.

Their marriage was solemnized in the church. Catastrophe struck as the happy couple was assaulted by the Hindu fundamentalists. 'Ethnic cleansing by a Christian!' The pundits (the highest in caste hierarchy) roared," Christian marrying Hindu widow! Goddess Kali* would take revenge." Both Rama and Robbins argued before Bajpayee, the most respected pundit, there's nothing wrong in inter-community marriage. Besides, the wave of globalization should destroy old customs which are of no use. Robbins added: ' India became slave for numberless centuries because of casteism. The pundits humiliated and enslaved the lower castes, so these castes supported the invaders...'

'You dare destroy our heritage, culture, traditions!' cried a furious Bajpayee, inspired by Brahmanic pride, nurtured in his sub-conscious by the scriptures that divided human society into four rigid categories and castes. *

Meanwhile, Rama smelt wickedness in Bajpayee's starving lustful eyes concentrating on her full ripe breasts. All his sermonizing vanished by her two zeroes of swollen flesh! He condemned the marriage only to keep his sublime image intact. The moral guardian of other castes stooped before Rama's unravished limbs, and he exclaimed:' Only once, let me touch you, your nipples. O Beauty, I won't defame, but help you in stabilizing happy marriage with Robbins. Only once, let me kiss you.'

Rama was shocked by the natural man exposed in the venerable pundit. 'I'm Dalit. Lowest caste. Your caste highest. You truly like me, my...?' The Brahmin held her, and didn't leave her until he kissed her most passionately.

Rama pondered-was she betraying William? But, how'd he know this? This emboldened her with her passions afire. She kissed him, was swayed by the ecstasy. She thought: 'Am I going too far?' The fact was that Rama was in quest of an epiphany, the highest intensity, the highest joy, through the medium of love.

'Salvation'. Yes, this was the 'Mantra', motto ordained by Baba 'Sanyasi' (ascetic) preaching the gospel of Love to thousands of his disciples in USA, Europe and India. Baba looked giant among men, formidably tall in ochre robes preaching near holy Ganga, now polluted, in Rishikesh. Rama was determined to seek 'Gyan' (Knowledge) from him.

Baba talked about 'Vipasana' therapy which emphasizes watching of one's breath as it comes and goes. The hardened terrorists may be purged of the evil inside by this cathartic experience.

Rama found Baba unconvincing. Here was the archetypal female intent on seducing the ascetic. Her logic was simple: one may forget sex by austerity or penance, yet it would always return. She bluntly told Baba that no man is unreliable as far as sex is concerned. Baba looked at her. Her warmest spot preyed upon him. Piqued by the call of the flesh, he meditated through Ajapajapa technique (which stimulates 'somarasa'-nectar- collected n 'Sahasrar Cakra'-upper head). Yet, sexual passion as involuntary as respiration seemed to conquer him. He thought," I find it difficult to meditate Instead I imagine these fingers oiling tall Rama's big-sized bulging breasts. Fool I'm to mediate not on tip of the nose or tongue. Instead I'm thinking of this woman's thighs exposed by my wild fancy." Rama's steamy sighs, open legs, thighs and breasts partly visible stared at his thirsty lips and starved eyes. Yes, he recognized 'the forbidden fruit', twelve impurities mentioned by Manu-menstruation, semen, blood etc. made him tremble and sneered at him.

Baba was preaching in Rishikesh to about two hundred disciples, "Satan the Devil can't tempt you if you practise Yoga." Of all his followers, Rama was prettiest. She was in Baba's 'Ashram' to find 'Shantih' (Peace). Baba advised her, "Concentrate on belly (Hara in Japanese) below the navel, the seat of Yoga 'chakras.' Meditate on Tan Tien (Chinese) and Tanden. Power is here, below the navel. Inhale and then exhale into your navel. The life force 'Pran', 'Ki Chi' and 'Ruah' is the basis of health and vitality. Let your 'Pran' (breathing) flow freely. No obstruction in the flow of energy is allowed. Obstruction results in disease of the body."

"And when you're aware of this, what will you do?" Rama asked.

"Concentrate on OM, imperishable syllable. OM is the Universe. Past, present, future-all this is OM. You may concentrate on the Cross, Virgin Mary, Christ," explained Baba.

One day Baba found Rama doing Yoga in her room. He was unnoticed by her. He was amazed at her celestial body. He began to shiver experiencing breathless ecstasy, the suspension of corporeal breath. The furnace of her sensual power burnt him alive. What a terrible beauty! He was devastated by the radiant beauty. Baba realized that he had fallen in love with her. In spite of ceaseless meditations and chanting of holy scriptures, Rama's beauty seemed to end his delusion that he had conquered the temptations of the flesh. Looking up he could see Cupid laughing at him. Baba felt Rama shouting his name 'Baba, I love you.' He was torn between flesh and spirit. He decided to intensify his meditations and Yoga more and more.

Baba wrote in his diary:' I must conquer passion of lust for Rama by worshiping image of God and surrender of my individual self to His lotus-feet. Even stones or bricks could be divine, if their sanctity is maintained. God can easily assume form for the sake of His sincere devotee. A person's determination can create God. But Voltaire warns me that most men die of their remedies, not of their diseases. What should I do to forget Rama?'

Meanwhile, Rama was getting dissatisfied with her life, the momentary pleasures provided by sex. She heard the word of Lord inside her innermost being. The angels of God seemed to speak to her, Go and Preach the gospel in the villages of India. The Spirit said unto her: 'I have chosen you. Hear me.' There appeared to her angels in the flame of fire. 'Receive the lively oracles. Thus, you may feel the Holy Ghost. Remember, the flesh will perish with thee.' She reflected that she should avoid meeting sex-hungry men; this is not right in the sight of God. She was trembling with spiritual passion and said,' Lord, what will thou command me to do?' And the Lord said unto her, Arise, and have faith, pity, charity, and I shall tell thee what thou must do.

For several days, she neither did eat nor drink, but she increased the more in strength. Baba was afraid that her physical charm would disturb his meditation, yet he felt greater sexual passion towards her. Rama kneeled down, and prayed. And she opened her eyes, and when she saw Baba, she sat up. Baba wanted to kiss her passionately. And when he touched her, he was turned into a hideous viper. Rama heard in a vision the voice of an angel: 'God has heard thy prayers.'

- Brahman, Kshatriya, Vaish and Shudra were born of God's mouth, arms, thighs and legs respectively. Brahmanic tradition asserts caste superiority, complicated rituals and patriarchal bias (Rig-Veda: X, 90).
- Kali: Literally means black. She is Goddess of death, consort of Shiva. Worshipped as a supreme deity. The Puranas (Hindu encyclopedias) reveal that Kali was created by God to destroy Buffalo Demon, an invincible devil.

LONGING FOR LATTE

Sara M. Al Shami

It was like any ordinary coffee table we sat on, in any ordinary cafe, like any ordinary two people, but not any ordinary conversation… it was ordinary but not 'any'… it only engrossed the two of us… individualized. I ordered a latte. He ordered an espresso. He was eyeing everything except my eyes. He swept a nonchalant glance at me, then looked at the crowded tables around us, and said, "I like your necklace, is it new?" I nod my head. I had this necklace since ages, and it was my favorite.

I take a puff at my cigarette and it fills my mouth with a stinging taste. I take a sip at my latte hoping the bad taste will wash away. I look at him and ask cheerfully, "So what made you wake me in the middle of night for a cup of coffee?"

"Ah, I don't know…I thought I'd talk with you for a while."

I laugh,

"Well that makes me feel important."

I say, misunderstanding the essence of his words. He looks at me with his beautiful eyes and I see a fidgety shimmer. His fingertips do a jittery dance on the red tablecloth. I move closer, worry muffling me. I wrap my steady fingers on his sweaty hands and ask,

"What is the matter?"

He looks at me and avoids my searching gaze. His head falls in his palms and cries out,

"I don't know, really, I... ah…"

I draw back, and say,

"Well it can't be that bad can it? We can work it out, we always did."

But he looks at me and I know it is beyond 'working it out'. He takes a long sip at his espresso, and miraculously, as if it granted him the courage, he says,

"I think we should take a break."

"Break, you mean like a vacation?" I ask understanding, but not wanting to understand. But he crushes away that bleak moment of self-miscomprehension and says,

"Well, actually no, I was referring to us… I need a break from us."

I draw further back, back into myself. I sit there statue-like. I reach out for my Marlboro and take out a cigarette. I light it and it burns. I want to react outwardly, instead I react inwardly… in the head, and say,

"So you really think we should take a break?"

He nods his head and says, "It would be good for us." You mean good for you. There is no 'us' in this self-arranged decision.

"You don't feel good with this relationship?"

"Nah, I just feel crowded with the commitment and all."

I look at him questioningly. "What commitment?" I ask.

"You know, being together, loyal and faithful and all. I owe it to you when I am with you."

I look around me at the other tables. It is my turn to avoid his eyes. "Ok." I spell out this small word to the red tablecloth with so much difficulty and he nods his head. He tries to make conversation with me, but I am unable to reply back... I am no longer in the realm of the 'whispering pair'… I go back to the realm of silence that I secure tightly with a smile and converse with myself. He is drinking too much condensed espresso, condensed, unintended cruelty…I need more of my latte. I hold the cup to my quivering lips and take a gulp of the diluted coffee…it might dilute the slap of insult he aimed at my heart.

This arrangement called 'us'…I was never was used to it but I tuned myself to his frequency… 96.3, 96.2, 96.1, zero, the frequency of passion where waves mix and submerge creating a muddle in the mind and a longing in the heart. I used to work so hard, adjusting, monitoring myself to this new cast I wanted so much yet despised its unpleasantness. I was never born in a couple… only one body per womb... one body per coffin. But I made space for him, squeezed to the edge for his sake.

"You're a strong person. I envy you for your poise." His words come aiming at me. So it is person now…gender disappears. I look at him and draw a prideful smile on my pale face. I reach out for my mug and it slips from my hands by mistake…blunder caused by confusion. "Shit! I am so clumsy." I utter these words and kneel down to gather the broken pieces…I see my latte on the floor and moan. I needed that diluted coffee…milk…whiteness. Anami kneels down with me, but I say,

"No need, I can pick up the pieces." With privacy. "Just go call someone to wipe the coffee away." He goes, and I squat there on the floor sweeping the pieces trying to adjust them into place…to retrieve my heart. The waiter comes and wipes the latte with a mop. Just a quick 'swish' with his trained hands and weapon, the mop, and the mess is gone. Along with hope.

I walk back home and involuntary head to the cemetery, instead. When I do reach home, I realize that my mascarra sagged and created two black circles around my eyes. I look like a cat. "Well," I think, "that is good... a cat has seven souls."

Two months later.

I enter the café for a drink of coffee...it is cold outside and I need something to warm me up. The waiter, Josh, comes up and asks, "Usual order, Cass?" Then he takes a good look at me and adds, "Someone looks good today, any secrets for such radiance?" I look at him and say, "Ah no secrets josh, just waterproof mascarra."

He smiles and then says, "Good, I will try that... your normal order?"

"Nopes, I will take espresso please."

THE DREAM

Sherri Emily Avery

There is this woman, a very lonely and sad woman, but she was so very beautiful. No one ever knew why this woman was always so sad.... People in town knew that the woman had been hurt, for she was a very private woman, not very sociable, and you could tell she had many wounds.

She went through life always wondering what really happened to her father, he died in prison a long time ago, and never knew the truth of his death. He incarcerated most of her life and his life for a crime he didn't commit. He suffered many, many years there. And he died there, a young age of 46. She was lied to about his death, the prison said it was a heart attack and died at the hospital, the ambulance staff and hospital said he was dead on arrival, the autopsy doctor said it was a hanging and then changed the story... When she called the hospital to inquire about her father they transferred her to the police department, they would not tell her anything, they wouldn't even let a family member identify the body because they said that he was awarded to the state. So no one ever found out the truth of her fathers death and this ate at her for many years.

Then one night she had a dream.....

She is in front of this window in a old attic in a beautiful two story house, a house she had never been to before. She looks out a window in this attic to see the ocean and waves forming into hands calling to her as she hears a sweet melody, a jewelry box melody, like the sound of the same jewelry box melody that her father gave to her when she was very little and still to this day has this jewelry box. Not knowing where the music is coming from, she looks behind her only to see a woman's black dress (old fashioned) and a mans suit dancing together, with no one in it, they were dancing in air, floating, she is bewildered, but not afraid, she looks out back towards the window, the waves still calling her name. The music then stops, and she turns around again to see a old man in the suit but the black dress still empty, still dancing. She walks up to the old man, he had gray hair and his built was stocky, not that tall.

She asks him, 'where is my grandmother', he says 'in heaven', she then asks, 'where is my grandfather', he says ' in heaven', and then she asks him, 'where is my father?' and he says ' in hell!' She gets scared but she does not believe him and asks him to take her to him, she didn't care where her father was, she just wanted to see him.

So she follows this old man down a flight a steps, they end up in this most beautiful kitchen, everything in it was pure white, she's never seen such white in her life, it was so bright.... He steps over to a counter that looks like a bar, he is standing on one side and she is standing on the other side of it, she then says to the old man again, 'please take me to my father, I don't care where he is, please take me to him.'

So this old man looks at her in her eyes, he had the most ebony eyes she had ever seen, there was no pupil, just pure black eyes. As she was looking into his eyes she went into this trance, like she was going into this mans eyes, she then calasped, and then all she could see was pure red, like swaying red, almost like a slow moving river, it was a red she had never seen, nothing in her lifetime....She felt as if she was going down, deeper and deeper, then all of a sudden she heard someone calling her name from a distance... Sherri, Sherri... you don't have to go there Sherri, come back Sherri... You can see your father, but you don't have to go there to see him, it's a lie Sherri, come back....She awoke or came out of the trance and when she did, the old man was gone and there in front of her was this beautiful woman with long straight black hair smiling at her and she whispered, 'You don't have to go there Sherri to see your father'... The lady then looked down another flight of stairs and at the end of the stairway was a door with a small window and in the window she saw her father.... She started running down the stairs as fast as she could, but seeming like it was taking forever to get to the door, she just kept running and running, and finally she came to the door and her father ran away, ran off.... She started chasing him... (Outside of the house there was a pier on the right side of the house, with the ocean about, on the left side of the house was a slow moving stream with mountains and beautiful forest)

He ran up to the pier and she was chasing him, and while she was chasing him on the pier she noticed two other small children running with her calling out, 'Daddy please stop, daddy please stop running'.... she also noticed below her the ocean floor for there were large cracks on the pier, the ocean was moving rapidly.

Her father finally came to the end of the pier and jumped off into the yard, ran across the yard and then stopped near the river and as she jumped off the pier she noticed that the two other children were gone, but didn't really acknowledge it, she also ran across the yard, and as she began to get closer to her father, the woman with the beautiful black hair appeared in front of her, just smiling, and she then turned to look at her father, as well as she...

They were about 5 feet from each other, she couldn't get any closer, he was wearing blue-jeans and a black t-shirt, sleeves rolled up, white socks and black penny loafer shoes they use to wear in the sixties, he was very handsome and seemed young, probably a time when she last remembered seeing him, which was when she was 12 years old. She then said to her father, 'I Love you daddy and I miss you so very much.' He finally said to her, 'I Love you too Sherri, I always have, never a day went by that I didn't love you'...

He then bent down on his knee, one elbow resting on the knee, he looked down with a sad face and then looked up at his daughter, and said ' I was murdered Sherri'... and then she woke up...she got her answer....

Author's Comment:

Inspired by true life incidents and a real dream.

ISLAND OF LIFE

(From chapter fourteen of the comedy/romance, *Island Of Life*)

Stephen R. Foster

Peter's last footnotes of prayer would always end with: "I'm the last one in the world to have love; will I ever be worthy?" His faith became quite strong, and he was soon believing deeply within his own heart in that special someone looking back his way over the ocean; a lonely lady who longed only for him. An angel he could grow old with, who would never go away. Someone who would never let him ponder these feelings of lonely pain again. A woman who would bring out all the good things hidden deep inside his body and soul, just waiting and wanting to be found and released. A friend who would stay and comfort him when he wasn't well, and needed her healing. Someone who held the final piece of puzzle that made him whole. One with understanding, who would forgive his stupid mistakes in life and not be ashamed of him, even when the rest of the world has turned it's back.

A lady whose heart he would be more than happy to overfill, and she fill his to running over with that greatest of all things in life, that wonderfully blessed gift from God, known as "Love." Peter questioned in his heart if he would ever find a girl with those qualities, if she could even exist, and with her, find his peace of mind from the lonely madness. Often times, he would walk to his nearest neighbor's house up the beach wanting to meet a certain young lady named Susan, but he could never find the courage to go right up to the door. The loneliness that had dominated Peter's life, had by then introduced insecurity into his life also, and he didn't believe he could bear rejection again without losing what was left of his sanity. Although walking away many times, he couldn't seem to shake her lovely vision from his head; nor did he want to.

"So fairly featured and pleasing to mine eyes," he would ponder. "I would willingly give anything just for her to notice and keep company with me; if even only for a little while," he lusted with deep, unending passion. He had first seen her at a school gathering in the park, and she turned his head immediately; but then again, she turned the heads of all the boys in school. Peter liked her from first glance, but she acted as though he wasn't even alive; not to his surprise.

"You're just fooling yourself mister," he told the mirror in his room later that night. "You're not very handsome, not real smart, clumsy as a three legged mule, and you don't play football. Face up man, you'd have better odds at hitting the lottery than holding the hand of a beautiful girl like her." Even though his confidence was at an all time low, he decided with determination, "Nothing ventured is ever gained. After all," he figured, "all she could do is say no." He just hoped she didn't make him look like a jerk doing it. After a week of waiting for her to show herself outside the house, Susan finally came out for a swim. Then after building up his courage to a proper height, Peter made his smoothest move and approached her. "Hello Susan, my name is Peter. I wanted to.....," but Susan cut him off quick. "I know who you are; you're the boy down the beach. Get away from me.....psycho dweeb."

She had put him back in the box just that fast. "Girls are good at that," he was learning. Dropping his head, he turned and walked away. He now officially considered himself an amoebae. Susan no more than gave him a glance after that day, until something happened on the beach one morning; something very strange. It was warm that particular day. The sun was hiding just a few minutes below the horizon, giving the sky its morning glory. Peter had lain down on the beach to watch the waves coming in after a swim. Feeling relaxed, he counted them as they came and soon he slept. He began dreaming a most vivid dream while lying there; something that moved him. Susan and he were somewhere walking, and as with dreams sometimes, he couldn't make out where, although it seemed familiar. They had stopped, and were standing holding each other, when she tenderly kissed him and whispered, "I love you Peter." Oddly, she didn't say it in a sense one would speak it to someone else, she told him with singing, as if her words were song.

When she told him that in the dream, Peter became enlightened; as though he were floating in joy, as though joy could be a warm, physical liquid that surrounded someone. Such a pleasing feeling he felt, even though only a dream. Suddenly, as though lightning had struck next to him, he woke from a sharp pain down in his groin area. Jumping to his feet, he started thrashing around like a Zulu warrior preparing for war. Then he stopped, looked down, and saw the horror from the dark depths of the sea. Yes, there it hung, on the end of his happy manhood that was sticking out the bottom of his trunks; a big fiddler crab. It's claw vise-gripped tightly as it dangled there down below. Peter somehow noticed it was heavier than it looked, as it wiggled around and he stretched. "This is a touchy and painful predicament," he thought "and one that needs some extremely delicate handling." Reaching down with both hands, Peter very gently began to pry its claw apart, and while doing this timid operation, started a casual conversation with his little friend.

"Well, well, look what we have here. You're a big one aren't you, Mister Fiddler? Just out for a little squeeze this morning? What's the matter, nobody to play with? Now don't you get too excited, I'm going to slowly pull you off. You'd better not give me too hard a time either; just come off nice and easy for me. We wouldn't want to bruise anything down there, now would we? How would you like to be dipped in some warm garlic and butter my little friend? I think I'll take you home and warm you up with a good butter bath.

Doesn't that sound fun? Some warm butter to slide around in sounds like fun, now doesn't it, you tasty little morsel. After all, you like nibbling on me, so why don't I enjoy a piece or two of you? I hope there's no baby crabs with you down there hiding in the jungle, they'd be hard to pull out you know. Here, let me take hold of you. That a boy. Don't squeeze too tight now, it's already circumcised and we don't want to take too much off the top; now do we, you little pecker pincher? Easy now, easy, you're almost there."

"YOU ARE REALLY SICK!" a voice behind him called out. "You shouldn't do that on the beach. There are bathrooms you know...pervert."

Peter spun around to find himself eye to eye with Susan, the girl of his dreams, and slipped into a state of mind unknown to psychology. After cupping his hands around his genitals, he tried explaining, but the bottom depth of embarrassment had taken away his thinking and tied his tongue.

"But......you don't under......I was trying to ....it pinched.....I wasn't playing with......AAAAAHHHHHHHHHH!! he screamed at the sky. Susan quickly glanced down at his hands and saw the creature there, wiggling around just below them. Her eyes bulged with horror, just before she pointed and started screaming at the dangling vice-grip.

"OH MY GOD! WHAT IS THAT?!!...IT'S...IT'S ALIVE!!!"

Peter wanted to die and be buried in the sand with his little friend. Seeking to hide his embarrassment, he started hopping across the beach toward the ocean with his shorts down around his ankles; all the while the little fiddler was flip-flopping around and hanging on for dear life while putting a hurt on his manhood. With each bounce, he experienced a new form of pain down below as the creature's sharp claw was unmerciful and not letting go of its newfound friend. Finally finding sanctuary, he made it to the water and dove in. Thoughts of staying down forever and living in a giant clamshell entertained him, but finally feeling the need to breathe, he bobbed up where his eyes were just above the water line. He shifted left, then right, to see if she was still about.

"She must have fallen down and hurt herself," immediately went through his mind. "Poor thing," he thought, because she was lying in the sand with tears in her eyes and holding her sides. She kept repeating, "The fiddler.....The fiddler. 'HAHARAHAHA!"

Now Peter didn't know for sure, but it looked like she peed her shorts. After she regained control of her ribs, Susan asked him to come out of the water, but

Peter completely refused and politely asked her to leave, replying, "No, I think I'd like to die alone now, thank you very much." Giving up, she walked back down the beach; stopping for a look back and a giggle every now and again at his bobbing head. After she'd left, Peter pulled himself from the water, wounded, but still hanging in there. Down the beach he went with head hung low; to the seclusion of his dark room where he could wait, he figured, on a meteor to hit the house. He had emotionally snapped, and decided, "I'm going to the mountains in Italy to be a Monk." Feeling very restless that night over the ordeal, Peter had a bad dream. Thousands of crabs were picking at him; laughing, and nibbling his manhood until he was nothing but a big bone in the sand. He woke up screaming in a cold sweat at the horror, and checked to make sure everything was still there.

"That's the most horrible thing I've ever dreamed," he whispered. "What a way to go."

Little did he know that this particular dream would come back later to haunt him, and sooner than he knew.

THE HEARTS HIDDEN POEM
(From *Island Of Life*)

"I ponder my hand in yours, even if only for a moment and the moment is fleeting. My feelings for you are deep; my love for you as abounding as life. I desire you, and want for your touch. Just as the oceans waves yearn to bathe the beach with their unending constancy of caress, I will adorn you with affection, until you sparkle as brightly as Christmas tree icicles against the evening fireplace firelight. My mind will stay eternally open and know only wisdom and laughter for you; my fingertips will covet only the tender touch of yours....forevermore. I want to learn your life, with understanding, while comforting you, with the tenderness of my life. Given the chance, I will show you the hidden man within me, and his yearning for complete giving. Let me unlock your heart with the key of friendship, so that I may fill it with kindness and come to enjoy you fully, with you also coming to enjoy me. Let me know loves giving, and gift my ever lonely life with your beautiful company. Forever drawn with feelings of love for you, my heart will always find its way home to yours; for just as sure and steadily as the great river finds its undaunted way to the wanting and awaiting sea, my need for you shall never waver. Welcome me I pray, as the firmament of heaven welcomes the rains cooling kiss. Let us want life's joining; just as the sea yearns for the clouds coming and welcomes it home with blending waves of wanton. Strengthen my soul with your faith of love, and belief in its glory. I bequeath my heart unto you, so that you may see the honesty within and know my earnest devotion. May we explore loves deepest miracles and discover its greatest joys, until the stars twinkle their last goodnight for us, and ever so quietly, sparkle our hearts to sleep. Then after we have explored each the other fully and find that love stirs no more within us, we shall not simply fade from passion, nay, we will tenderly touch lips, and simply .... begin love again."

A RAINY DAY
Sudheesh V Nair

I opened the door, wiping my wet shoes in the carpet, and just as if waiting for me to reach home, the rain and the wind started to grow stronger. It's been a long while since I saw a rain so strong with wind accompanying it. I opened the shades completely and positioned myself in front of the window on the floor with a cup of hot water in my hand.

The same wind that gently invokes the branches and leaves to dance is now shaking the trees to their very roots. This struggle, this constant uncertain struggle, is a beautiful part of life for them. But how could they keep their spirits up when posed against such mammoth tasks of dealing with uncertainty for every moment of every day and night?

Everyday I wake up with a thousand tiny little uncertainties in my mind. I don't know if I should shave before taking a shower or after. I like to do it after my shower when my skin is moist but then I will have to wait until the bathroom mirror fog vanishes. I don't like to wipe it away, which results in marks on the mirror. Going to work, I don't know if I should take the freeway or not. I am equally unsure if I need to heed the ringing cell phone while I am trying to change the CD in my car. I would feel terrible if it is a call from someone I would love to hear from—more than likely it will be from my work, which I could attend in person within 10 minutes or so. Should I wait for the light to turn red or may be take a chance and try to get past the light at this junction? Maybe I have a control over these things, or maybe I don't—do I? How could I even think of controlling something that is not even defined. When was the last time a traffic light waited for a car to cross before turning red?

The rain is now pouring down. The tree just lost another branch. Whoa!

It fell right in front of me, landing in my balcony with a loud crash. I can't see any leaves clinging to the branch. Lucky them; they have already fallen beneath the tree I guess. One of the trees is getting smarter, I think; it very cleverly now handles the strong, cruel wind. It is now going with it instead of resisting it. The last time it tried resisting the tree lost a lot of leaves and branches in that one-sided battle. Not this time. I am happy for her.

The rain and wind stopped. A small bird came out and began fussing nearby—

looking as busy and serious as making a life or death decision in her life. They know better. They know it is not good to get drenched in rain unless it is absolutely necessary. So the rain must have stopped. I cannot clearly determine the weather with the trees dripping their last raindrops from their leaves. But it must have stopped as the birds, surely, know better.

I can see the change in mood of these trees around me. Yesterday they were playful indulging in the sunlight and light breeze. This morning they were a little worried, and then when the wind started. They looked as if they were scared out of their age-indicating rings—I felt their helplessness. But later they turned angry and then lost that feeling too, briefly. For some time I think I detected a strong sense of dedication to win the battle for survival. Now, when it is all over, I thought I would see elation, but on second thought, seeing all these leaves and broken branches, I was expecting to see grim pride. But to my surprise, I think I sense of calmness. I wonder how could they remain this calm after such an exhilarating experience. I don't think I made a mistake in reading their expressions. The drooping leaves and the indifference with which they are dropping the water down is a sure giveaway.

Maybe, they are tired and think that everything is over. No, it can't be that because they know better than to be that foolish about this strong rain and wind. They know the battle is not over until their life ends. I can't seem to fathom this turn of events.

I think it was one of those small birds that told me the secret of their calmness. It seems they have finally figured out the trick. They have finally figured out a way to eliminate the element of surprise. They have learned to cope with the surging emotions of elation created from a baseless expression of hope and expectations. They no longer hope for the sun's rays to return. They don't expect the strong wind to have gone away for good. Nor do they expect the light breeze to return. They do not, at the least, expect the branches not to fall anymore, down to the ground.

They seem to have created a sense of certainty. They know for certain that events are going to be uncertain. That should make it easier. That sweeps all the old rules and theories away, making room for a new one. Not having to have one.

This is going to continue throughout the nights and days for the rest of the infinite time this universe is going to exist. Knowing the secret rules of success, even if this big tree looses the battle in the next round, I am sure the small tree next to it won't take as long in its' life to understand the new rule, that of not having to have one.

LOVE IS LIKE . . .
Thomas K. Hyland, Jr.

An addiction! A bad habit! In short, it sometimes SUCKS! Can we take a moment to examine these rather rabid statements?

First, consider the addiction part, okay? You meet someone, your heart skips a beat, then: eventually, you "get a little" and — "Wham, bam, thank you Ma'am" - you're HOOKED!

You want MORE, MORE, MORE! Will Shakespeare put it well, in Romeo and Juliet: ". . . parting is such sweet sweet sorrow." Yeah, it's sweet alright! You can't stand being without her (him). No matter how hard you use your mind and will power to avoid this "Love Bug,' once it's in your system, even methadone won't help! You just gotta' have it!

Somehow, I managed to get through sixty years of my life without being a "gambler." I probably never lost more than twenty bucks playing "penny-ante" poker, throughout all those years. Then my wife left me after thirty-four years of marriage, and I suffered withdrawal for well over a year. I needed a vacation. Get away from it all, right? So I spent a week in Vegas, and lost more money than I ever dreamed of! Now, don't get me wrong. I had fun! I lived "high, wide, and handsome." Six hundred dollars might be a mere pittance, or "drop in the bucket" to a real gambler, but it's three thousand percent more than that aforementioned twenty bucks! Like love, a bad habit had just begun. I missed that wonderful noise of the "clickety-clacking" of coins being spewed into my hopper.

A case in point, by the time that a year and a half had passed since our separation, the pangs of lost love drove me to seek something else to fill the empty void, whereupon I discovered a local "watering hole" with those little computerized machines which some used to call "one-armed bandits." You know, the ones with the prominent signs claiming "for Amusement Only." Well, like an innocent lovelorn teenager, I just had to "test the waters." So, over a six week period, I did pretty good — well, at first!

I was a little ahead, then a little behind (nice buns!), then just even! Then, a month ago, I received the Final Divorce papers! Whoops! Gotcha! Those doggoned machines called to me like the proverbial sirens of Jason and the Argonauts. "Feed me!" "Feed me!" "Feed me!" They whispered their sweet chants. Not unlike the hypnotizing stare of Medusa, they drew me toward the rocks, sat me on a barstool, and turned my feet to stone! In short, in the space of a mere two nights I lost three hundred and fifty more dollars! Bad habit? Yep, you got it!

Well, what's that got to do with Love? Even though I have dated other women, and even "scored" a couple of times, like the Championship Ravens, it was only Lust, not Love! I miss her voice, her smile, her tender caress, her warm presence just lying next to me — and like an addiction, or bad habit, it still hurts! The conscious mind knows that it is all over — "irreconcilable differences" was the legal term. But the heart will not accept the loss, the void, the irreparable damage, it wants MORE, MORE, MORE!

Love Is Like . . .

Oh, I failed to mention those other machines of addiction. You know, the little grey boxes that transmit X's and O's and 1's through the air, or wires, or cables, or satellites, throughout the known world — The Web, The Internet! These camouflaged sirens are even more deadly and perverse than the former ones. At one time, I had posted six different profiles on six different web-sites, advertising my masculinity, seeking LOVE! Hours upon hours, upon hours have been spent — wasted — searching for that new "Soul Mate." Gee, Mommy, another love addiction! Time squandered away: looking at pictures, reading profiles, agonizing over details, searching for a MATCH — drooling, exchanging emails, then phone calls. Results? Sure, I had about a dozen face-to-face encounters, real live dates! But, guess what? Ten out of twelve of these "ladies" who demanded honesty somehow used the subterfuge of posting OLD pictures! In reality, they actually looked like the "grandmothers" of those beautiful sweet THANGS on the "puter" screen!

Did I mention that Love SUCKS? My "Ex" and I had a very calm, nice, civil, amicable separation — no more arguments, disagreements, misunderstandings and very rare contact, if any! So, I have sent her very nice greeting cards, some with animation and beautiful music, as well as emails for various holidays and birthdays — all the while, secretly hoping for just a glimmer of a spark of an old romance. All for naught! I got short, cryptic responses back, like: "Thanks." or, "I already saw that one." or, "I really don't have space on my computer at work."

So, my friends, the addiction, the bad habit — LOVE — continues! Someone much wiser than I once said, "Man does not live by bread alone!" He was most certainly correct! Without love, nothing else matters! So, what have we learned? Get back on our bikes (or little tricycles, like the Dirty Old Man on Laugh-In) and just keep peddling along until that wonderful little life-sucking Love Bug bites us — again — and again — and yet again — ad infinitum!

Sure, it SUCKS! But what's a fella to do? "The game is afoot!" as Sherlock Holmes might say!

P.S.:

Look for the sequel, "Alas, Woe Is Me!" which was somehow mysteriously written twenty-eight days earlier than this! So, how on earth could it be a sequel? Just look how they screwed up the order of the Star Wars chronologies! Huh?

HOW HAS THE WORLD TREATED YOU?

Tom Dwyer

I stopped in the Plaza Hotel to find a phone that worked. I figured if there was any place in New York that a phone should work it would be at the Plaza. I found one directly off of the main lobby. It was a small, old fashion booth type situated in a dark mahogany corner. It even had a wooden seat to sit in while I made my call. The doorman watched me for a moment or two as I searched through my pockets for the correct change. He decided that I was fine and that I wouldn't cause a problem in his hotel. The reason for my call was to cancel a meeting I had with an agent who was interested in a book I had just completed. He was always interested in things I wrote...but has never signed me to anything. So, it really wasn't that big of a deal to cancel on him. I didn't feel like getting rejected today anyway. Which is how I ended up going to the bar in the Plaza after making my apologetic phone call.

It was that wonderful afternoon hour when most of the lunch crowd had now departed, leaving only the professional drinkers to hold court. Well-dressed drinkers drinking expensive scotches and fine wines, while they sat in one of the most beautiful rooms in New York – a small, cozy, deeply paneled room that spoke of money, and the joys it brought. I, on the other hand, made my living as a freelance writer. I figured I have a beer or two, imagine being rich for a an hour or so, and then hurry back to my small apartment in Jersey City.

There were about eight people in the room when I sat down at the bar. Two business men arguing about stocks, a very well dressed older women with two large suitcases tucked under her table as she worked on her martini, a group of loud TV producers discussing some project, and a woman with her back to me sitting at a far table facing a mirror. I ordered a beer, stared around the room some more, and wondered what I would do with the rest of my day. After finishing the beer I walked to the bathroom. After finishing my business I washed my hands and stared into the mirror. I saw a man in his mid-forties looking back at me. A man who somehow missed the success boat that all his other friends had somehow gotten on. As I was making my way back to the bar I noticed again the women sitting alone in the corner. As I passed her I heard her say, "How are you, Jimmy?"

I didn't have to turn to find out who was talking to me. The voice was as familiar to me as it had been twenty-five years ago when we were in college together. I turned to see Margo Keene, one of the true loves of my life smiling at me, motioning for me to join her. I grabbed my beer from the bar and sat down across from her. It's hard to know what to say to someone you haven't seen in twenty-five years. Especially someone you almost married. She was the same Margo, except she had aged some. She was still beautiful with those green eyes and black hair that was now peppered with gray.

"So how long has it been, Jimmy, twenty-five years?"

"Just about," I said back, starting to feel emotions I hadn't felt in a long time.

"So what brings you to the Plaza, Jimmy Abbott? Have you finally hit the big time?"

"Not yet," I said back to her..."but I keep trying."

She reached over and touched my hand. "You'll never change," She said. The feel of her skin took me back to 1970, when we were just kids trying to find our way in life. She rubbed my hand and said, "No ring, you never married?" I reached over and placed my hand on top of hers and said, "No, it just never happened. And you?" She removed her hand from mine and drank some wine, her full lips catching a few drops that tried to escape.

"Divorced, two children."

"Do you live in New York now?" I asked, not believing that we might have lived in the same city for the past twenty-five years.

"No, I live up near Woodstock. My ex is a businessman, real estate. We broke up three years ago".

There was something about all those years between then and now that made me feel just how fast life moved along. I looked at her face and could see the beautiful coed I had loved for two years, the smart woman who was going to be a lawyer and save the world, the person I almost married but never did. I called the waitress and ordered two more drinks. Margo studied me with an intensity of someone trying to figure out a great puzzle.

"So why are you in New York?" I asked her. Breaking her concentrated stare.

"I'm here to see my doctor for a check-up."

"What, they don't have doctors in Woodstock?"

"He's a specialist...cancer," She said, her eyes locking on mine.

"Cancer? But you look fine."

"I am now." She said, squeezing my hand.

Suddenly, the past years seemed to loose their innocence. In my mind, the two of us were still somehow in that state college, frozen in time, nothing but promise. But now, she sat in front of me, telling me about her cancer, and I sat in front of her, a man who never fulfilled that promise. I was beginning to see how time had its own plans for people. We sat and talked for a good two hours. We covered our lives up to that moment. There is something so wonderful about seeing a person you had once loved after a long period of time. It clarifies one's existence. "I'm staying here for the evening before going back home," She said. "Let's go up and have a drink for old times sake."

I paid the bartender, and held Margo's hand as we entered the elevator. It was like old times, nothing had really changed I told myself. Nothing, could break the ties between the two of us. I wanted to believe that as the elevator stopped on the seventh floor. As we entered the plush room, we heard music coming from down the hall. We stood there for a moment listening to the melody drift towards us. The lyrics asked, "What's new, how has the world treated you? Gee but it's great to see you again."

We poured ourselves drinks and stared out the window onto Central Park. The sun was just beginning to set. We stood together a good five minutes, not saying anything, just staring and thinking. Then we turned towards each other, as if on cue...and kissed. A warm, forgiven kiss that almost made me cry for some unknown reason. I touched her back, her arms, her face. She softly moved away and told me to wait. She disappeared into the bathroom, where she reappeared wearing a silk robe. The room was now dark. The last rays of sun moving across the ceiling. She came to me and kissed my face. Then, she opened her robe, showing me the place where her right breast had been. Showing me the jagged scar that ran across the right side of her chest like an angry river. Showing me, showing us...what life had done to her. I lowered my face to the purple scar and kissed it. I kissed her other breast. I could feel something release inside of Margo, like a vast breath escaping from her. We moved to the bed and held each other like kids just learning about love. Then, she moved her mouth close to my ear and said softly, (as to not rile the gods, as if telling me a secret that she wanted only me to know...) "I beat it, Jimmy, I beat it." Then she lowered her beautiful face to my chest as if looking for something...then kissed my right nipple.

MY DREAM OF MY CELTIC LOVER

Tony James Lawless

I dreamt of a lady, coming forth out of the ocean, when I was very young. She had red, wavy hair, brown or green eyes, a very lithe gait, as if the water parted for her as she came out to me, standing there on the beach.

She kissed me, bosom to chest and our arms wrapped around each others bodies. Nothing carnal from that dream, but I know it was there, someway, somehow. I remember that dream from when I was nine or ten years old. The gist of it never let me go.

Thirty-something and divorced, my heart longed for the companionship of another. Then, in words, in prose, I was able to evoke my best and then to touch my feelings. I welcomed her with this fervor and passion I had found.

She was like me, wanting to be Spartan in all she did. Wanting to give more than receive. The outdoors were our adult playground, if I may say it as such, and we did play. Canoeing to islands in my beautiful back bay, or settling on a beach ever so private, knowing love making would be sacred and undisturbed. We were beyond pornography with it and knew it. Every act or non-act was never taboo. Consenting adults, and privately so where love making was concerned.

This is not where our relationship dwelled, however. The real love making came from waking up early, watching my lady sleep in a little longer, and simply enjoying the sight. A gentle peck on the cheek would wake her. Sometimes, roles would be reversed.

Also, we made love by reading prose; both written by the greats and also what we could do ourselves, our passions ever emanating in what we read. And there was definitely feeling, no matter what we read or who was reading to whom. We'd take turns being at each others knee.

It was very special to us doing that every other evening or so. There was the walks outdoors. Walking around the block, along the seashore or through a state park. It mattered not, really, as long as we were together, her hand in mine.

We would discuss stories yet to write, stories and poems written and getting together on a piece of prose that would be our epic, concrete evidence forever that we would last.

Understanding, communication and admiration only grew stronger between us. It was beautiful. Wonderful. And if we needed time apart, even within the home, never a problem. She could read or go online or sleep and I would occupy myself with music, writing or television. Or sitting on the back porch, wide open, overlooking the Gulf of Mexico.

There was nothing this love could not do, in it's simplicity, in it's understanding, in it's pure love blessed from above.

My lady, I love you. Let's keep going from here.

And may every child know that dreams do come true.

Sometimes........

REST IN PEACE
Travis Black

#

Halloween used to be fun. Our parents would take us to the school gym, where we would have a costume parade, dunk for apples and get bags of treats. That was fine when we were seven or eight, but we were fourteen now and going to school for a Halloween party was for little kids. I wanted to do something different, something exciting, and something kinda scary. So I asked my two best friends, Bob and Denny, "What are you guys gonna do on Halloween?"

"Don't know," said Bob bouncing alongside of me over the oiled country road in the Alhambra, Illinois, school bus. "But I don't want to go to the school gym again!"

"Me neither. Got any ideas?" Denny chimed in as he turned around to look at us.

The silence dragged on while I watched the trees that bordered my dad's soybean field pass through the bus's smeary windows. Then it hit me. My parents were going to a farm implement show in St. Louis on Friday. Why not have Bob and Denny come over that night?

"Hey, what about this?" I whispered. "Why don't you and Bob get off at my stop Friday and come home with me? My parents are going to spend the night in St. Louis after Dad drops off his grain at the elevator. We'll watch old Frankenstein movies on video tape. How about it?" "Your parents are gonna let you stay alone?" Denny asked.

"Shhh! No, Mom asked me to see if I could stay with one of you. I'll tell her your mom said it was okay. That way my mom won't know, and we can do what we want. Come on, let's do it."

"Come on Sam, what's the big deal with scary movies?" Bob questioned, shaking his head at me. "Well, what about camping out behind my old barn," I suggested.

Denny leaned his head closer to us and whispered, "No way! Campout in the backyard? That's for sissies. I have a better idea."

"Oh, yeah! What?" I said.

Leaning closer, Denny softly whispered, "The abandoned cemetery.

It's scarier than a movie or a backyard campout any old time."

"Why are you boys whispering? Dennis, turn around. Samuel get your books together. We're almost at your stop," snapped Mrs. Conrad the school bus driver.

We smiled. Okay, we all mouthed. It was decided. Denny and Bob would tell their moms they were going to spend Halloween at my house, and I'd tell mom I was going to stay at Denny's house.

Somewhere in the back of my mind, I remembered something about spirits of the dead waking up and roaming the earth on Halloween, but right now, it was just a little nagging thought. The cemetery was a great place to campout.

#

Friday after school, Bob and Denny got off at my stop, and we began to gather what we needed for the campout from around the house. Bob got the tent, a tarp and a hammer to pound in tent stakes. Denny got the matches, snacks, wieners and a couple of blankets; and I got a hatchet, three two-liter bottles of soda, a lantern, and flashlights. After eating Hot Pockets and drinking soda, we were ready. As we entered the woods, which started just on the other side of my dad's soybean field, I dropped back to let Denny lead the way as he usually did when we played war. He stopped. "What's the matter?" he asked.

"Nothin'. I always follow you when we go into the woods."

"So? You afraid of the dark?" Denny said with a sneer.

"You're the biggest," I said.

"You're scared! Aw, little Sammy is scared of the dark woods," and Denny began to make fake crying sounds. "They're your woods. You lead the way."

"Hey, we don't have to campout in the cemetery tonight," Bob said.

"We can campout in Sam's back yard. It'll be a lot easier".

"What? Now you're afraid of the dark, too?" Denny responded.

"What a bunch of chickens! Bawk, bawk, bawk, bawk," and Denny started flapping his elbows and prancing around like a chicken.

Watching him hop around would have been funny – in the day, but not tonight. "I'm not scared," I said; and I stomped off into the lead.

I looked up as we went into the woods. Its dark leafy canopy almost blotted out the sky. While we'd been here many times in the day, we'd never been here at night, and it didn't look quite the same. A twisting path led up a hill through weeds and over a small marshy area full of sticky, shoe sucking mud. Our shoes squished through the wet ground and we splashed in pools of standing water from the creek that emptied into the area. The sound of our footsteps did little to penetrate the eerie silence. I felt a little worried, but I couldn't back out now. Besides, what could happen? The closely spaced trees blocked any view beyond the path that was so narrow I felt the thorny fingers of brush scratch against me and tug at my clothes. I pushed through patches of undergrowth, skirted large brush piles, and passed huge trees as I worked my way toward the cemetery. Our flashlights probed the dark shadows. I began to feel uneasy. Other than the noise we made, there wasn't another sound. I decided to break the silence by saying, "Boy, this is great! Just think about it. Frankenstein was assembled out of parts from dead bodies dug up in a cemetery. A lot of ghost stories take place in cemeteries."

"What'd ya got? Frankenstein on the brain or somethin?" Denny sarcastically responded.

"No, it's cool," I said. Where else would you want to be on Halloween?"

"Shut-up! You two are scaring me."

"Aw, little Bobby is scared. Bawk, bawk, bawk bawk," and I copied Denny's earlier behavior.

I was pushing through head-high, tangled brambles that were as thick and tough as brown steel wool with spikes. I couldn't see to the other side. The sudden cry of a bird caused me to jump, and a thorny branch hit me in the face. "Ow! Damn it!" But I was through it and in the cemetery. "We're here," I called back.

"It's about time. I thought you were lost," Denny snapped, stepping through the brambles.

"My dad thinks the brambles are the remnants of wild rose bushes planted by church members as a kind of fence. Isn't this great? What do you think?" Denny and Bob sort of grunted and began to look for a place to build a bonfire. Maybe they were feeling that this wasn't such a good idea after all.

The cemetery was a bunch of old weathered headstones, some covered with moss, others jutting up like jagged teeth through the ivy. It was spookier at night than in the day, and I wished we had stayed home and watched scary movies. For me, it was getting easy to imagine fearsome creatures lurking in the shadows of trees and vines. That little thought at the bottom of my mind about spirits waking on Halloween moved closer to the surface, but even if it became a conscious thought, I would have said, no way. That only happens in movies or horror stories, not in real life.

"Hey, look what I found!" Denny was standing in a sunken grave holding a skull! "They sure didn't bury bodies very deep in the old days." He put it on the headstone.

Bob and I gathered around to see. Then I began to toss it up in the air like a beach ball. "Hey! Don't do that, it's illegal," Bob said.

I sneered. "Lighten up, Bobby Wobby. This isn't a real cemetery anymore. The grave markers are from the 1850s! Hell, nobody remembers anyone buried here."

"Keep your voice down," Bob whispered. "Show some respect. It was a cemetery then, and people were buried here, it's still a cemetery. When someone dies, you don't dig 'em up and play with their bones. It's illegal or somethin'," and he grabbed the skull.

"I didn't dig it up. I found it, jerk," Denny retorted and snatched it.

"Bob, you're a pain. Hell! Nobody will care. We'll re-bury the skull and no one will know." I swiped the skull from Denny, stuck it on a long stick and jammed that into the ground. The back of my neck tingled and I turned around, but nothing was there. A cold draft of air from the collapsed grave made me look down and then for some reason at the skull. The eyes stared back at me. They were two black pools of energy. My blood chilled. "Come on, let's get a fire started. I'm getting cold."

We built a bonfire alongside the old grave to roast hot dogs and settled in to tell scary ghost stories to each other. "Sam, when did you find out about this place?" Denny asked.

"Shortly after my family bought the farm, my father discovered the cemetery and asked our neighbors about it. The Hayfield Parish Church was here and owned the cemetery in the early eighteen hundreds, but then abandoned it."

"Why?"

"Some of the old timers around here said hundreds of spirits rose from their graves one night and returned to their earthly homes. Others said that the cemetery was cursed. The only thing that the neighbors agreed on was that the parishioners burned the church and abandoned the cemetery in order to rid themselves of the spirits. The place hasn't been used in over a hundred years."

Denny snapped, "You're shitting me! What's the real story?" "I'm tellin' you guys the truth!" A cracking branch made me jump and turn around. Only the skull in the flickering light of the bonfire was there, but something moved in the underbrush and then stopped. Beads of sweat went down my back, and my palms were moist. Without revealing itself, whatever it was moved away. Probably a deer I thought, but I shivered a little with uneasy thoughts of the Hayfield Church burial ground spirits. The skull glared back at me.

Denny and Bob told ghost stories as our Halloween campout progressed. As they talked, a wind began to moan through the trees, and the dried oak leaves rattled overhead before falling to the ground. The temperature dropped, and it seemed to me to be at least ten degrees colder. I pulled the collar of my coat tighter around my neck. Denny was having a great time loudly laughing and telling ghost stories. The dark woods seemed to absorb his voice like a sponge, and when no one spoke, spooky silence surrounded the place. I could tell Bob was afraid. When he spoke, it was just above a whisper; and he sat all hunched up with a blanket over him. I was uptight, so I jammed a burnt hot-dog into my mouth. It kept my teeth from chattering.

Heavy mist gradually filled the air. Trees became hazy shadows. Wisps of vapor lazily climbed the gravestones. We pulled logs up to the fire to sit on. For a while, the fog crept out of the woods and seeped along the ground hiding everyone's feet in a smooth, white cloud only disturbed by our movement. After our stories, it was easy for me to imagine devils and witches hiding just beyond the fire light. For some reason the image of a black caldron with a bubbling brew came to my mind.

The fire cast a flickering light on the cemetery. Beyond its warm glow, darkness covered everything like a black cloth. It was a perfect night for Halloween, but thoughts about spirits rising from their graves now slithered like snakes silently through my thoughts. I stuck another hotdog into my mouth and looked at my watch.

Midnight, the witching hour.

I didn't like the campout. I wanted to go home, but I wasn't going to be the first one to say so. Nobody wanted to be the first to say it. From the way Bob looked, I could tell he was just waiting for an excuse to leave. He was almost white. Denny was looking at me telling us about how hard he had laughed during Scream Three when Bob squawked,

"Look!"

He pointed at the nearest gravestone. Denny shouted, "Whoa!

What's that?"

The three of us jumped up as blue-white transparent shapes slowly rose from its base and circled it. They raced to the treetops. The hair on my arms stood on end. Were these the same spirits that frightened the Hayfield parishioners over a hundred years ago? I kept reminding myself that the dead don't return. It was physically impossible. That was the theory anyway.

As if on cue, more spirits rose from other graves and joined the first group emitting an ever-increasing hiss that sounded like a hundred blowtorches. The graveyard was thick with them. They swarmed in mad gyrations like crazy moths caught in the bright light of the bonfire and swooped down almost to our heads in their wild flights. We flailed away at them without success. It was like batting at smoke. They formed a whirling ring around us and slowly contracted until were huddled tightly with the bonfire at our backs. From the darkness of the woods, came shrill crazy laughter. Something was out there! Something I didn't want to see.

The ground above each grave began to bulge and ripple as though something was just beneath the surface. The smell of rotten meat filled the air. Thousands of white maggots began to ooze out of the graves forming a wet quivering carpet. I couldn't help it; I wet my pants. Trapped! The fire was behind us, squirming maggots were in front, and swirling spirits were diving at our heads. Again, dreadful laughter came from the black woods. It rose in pitch and fell into wicked snarls that made me shiver.

"SSShit! Let's get out of here!" Bob stammered. I closed my eyes, plunged into the encircling spirits, and stepped on the squishy mess of maggots with my sneakers. Bob and Denny did the same. My scalp tightened and tingled as if lightning were to hit. My ears filled with a loud hum. We fought through the spirits, but bony hands erupted from the graves, and grabbed and tried to trip us. One skeletal hand caught my pants' leg and wouldn't let go while another blindly clawed for my free foot. I jerked my leg away, and the hand popped out of the ground still clinging to my pants cuff. I kicked at the other and broke it to pieces. I grabbed the lantern and ran, but I tripped over a sprouting bone and fell. The lantern flew out of my hand, hit the ground and shattered spreading fiery kerosene over the dry leaves. Maggots swarmed over me. They were on my face, in my mouth, my hair, crawling up my nose, and under my clothes. I got up, stomped, shook, and pulled them off as best I could. Suddenly the graveyard was on fire. The bacon like crackle of frying maggots filled the air. The stench was awful. We began running blindly into each other like bingo numbers in a rolling drum. We fell over gravestones. We tripped over bones.

Above all the noise, the high grating cackle of laughter boomed out of the black shadows.

Bobby grabbed his flashlight and ran in the direction of the path. We ran after him. A volcanic eruption from the bonfire sprayed out burning embers and sparks, which arched in the air like Fourth of July rockets and fell around us like rain. Dry leaves and needles exploded in flame, and a tall pine turned into a hissing white-hot torch. The fire raced and gobbled each clump of brush like a wild animal tearing at its kill. I ran as fast as I could. Off to the side, out of the corner of my eye I saw a floating dark shape, black as night and barely visible moving between the trees. I was scared shitless.

"Denny, we're being chased!" I yelled.

"Those smoky things?"

"No! Something big and black," and I pointed to where I'd last seen it.

He turned his head. "Nothing there. Run!" We ran back to the bramble barrier we had pushed our way through earlier that night. Bob skidded to a stop and Denny and I ran into him. In front of us, a black hooded shape appeared to block our escape. A chill wormed its way through me as Bob's flashlight illuminated the head. It was the skull. The two black pools of darkness that were its eyes held and swallowed me in their stare. The mouth slowly opened revealing black teeth and a red tongue that flicked back and forth like a snake. Its screeching laugh trailed off to delirious cackles as we came closer. I'd had it. I could be burned up like an over toasted marshmallow, or fight. I was getting out of there. Bob, Denny and I glanced at each other and began to yell. We charged forward into the black mass like battering rams. It was cold and dark inside. I couldn't see anything. My feet felt as heavy as lead. An invisible membrane tried to wrap me in a cocoon and pin my arms against my chest. I frantically pushed against it. I clawed at it as it tried to cover me. It was like black plastic wrap – slick, smooth, and tough. My efforts tore a hole in it. Frantically, I yanked at the edge. First, I forced my head through. Then I ripped it from my chest and pulled my legs out. I was free.

But where were Bob and Denny? I saw a clenched fist pop out of the black shape. Then another hand grabbed at the hole the fist had made. Both tore at what looked like a black shroud. Then Denny's head appeared. I grabbed a black edge and ripped it back. Denny wrenched himself free and Bobby was right behind him. We ran out through the briers. As I broke through the last of them, something snagged me by the shoulder. I looked back. The skull was holding me through the shroud. It glared at me with its empty eyes. They told me something. I knew what had to be done. I grabbed the skull and pulled it off the stick. I felt its pulsating energy. We never should have removed it from the grave. I looked around for Denny. Great! Just when I needed his strength, he wasn't there.

I faced the briers. The fire was a gigantic monster. It was hotter, stronger and larger as it continued to feed on new sources of fuel. The fierce blaze was drawing air toward it making its own draft and becoming uncontrollable, growing ever stronger like a storm. Flames ran through dry leaves, bushes roared like fiery furnaces, and trees became torches to heaven. The smell of smoke filled the air. I stepped back a few paces, ran toward the briers and threw the skull as far as I could over them back into the cemetery. I didn't wait to see where it landed before I turned and raced toward the marsh. There wasn't time to find firm footing. I slipped, slid and splashed in the cold water before I reached dry ground. Dripping and squishing with every step, I raced up the hill to the road. I ran right into Denny and Bob on the other side.

"Where were you?" they shouted. "Run," I shouted and took off. All kinds of thoughts were flashing through my mind. What were my parents going to do when they found out? Aw man, I mean, a fire in the woods! Lying to mom about what I was going to do tonight. Aw, shit!

"What happened to the fire?" Bob yelled after me.

Without turning I yelled, "It's behind you, dummy."

This time it was Denny. "No it isn't! How did you put it out?"

How did I put it out? What did he mean? I looked back over my shoulder. I could see Bob and Denny because of the flashlight, but that was the only light. There was no fire behind them. It was completely dark. I turned around and stared. I couldn't believe my eyes. The night air was peaceful and still without even a trace of smoke or a minor crackle or spark, as if the fire had never been.

The fire was out! I remembered the thought that had flashed through my mind when looking into the skull's empty eye sockets. It was part plea and part threat. I had known to return it to the cemetery or the worse nightmares of my life would be nothing compared to what I would have had to endure for the rest of my life. None of us would ever have had any peace unless that skull was returned.

#

Now, in the autumn when the air turns crisp, leaves shrivel and die, and the days become dark, it reminds me of that Halloween with my friends. I'll always remember that night when we woke the spirits and met the souls of the dead. It's something I never want do again. May they rest in peace.

THE GOLDEN BOOT

Verne Morse

Once upon a time there was a little girl named Ashes-Ella. She lived in a little house with her step-mother and her three daughters. They were known as Sister Little-Attila, Sister Big-Etta, and Sister Enormous-Ina. Their dear mother was named Gargantu-Anna. All in all they were a massive lot. Little Ashes-Ella was petite, polite, peculiar and with long flaxen hair. Sister Little-Attila was grim, grisly and gruesome. Sister Big-Etta was hefty, huge and horrendous. Sister Enormous-Ina was feeble, flabby and flaccid. Their mother, Gargantu-Anna was without description. The house they lived in was owned by the step-mother and it was left to her by her late husband, Hewas Scrawny, who died prematurely due to insufficient nutrition. This little domicile was located in the woods outside the forest that surrounded the Castle of the Prince of Ug. The Prince was a tall young handsome dude in search of a bride to fill his lonely life. She had to be beautiful, talented, amusing and most of all be of fleet foot.

This was the day of the Castle's Annual Grand Bawl. All the Clans of the surrounding country- side were planning to turn out. It was the event of the season and naturally the Scrawnys were primping and preening to make the scene.

Of course little Ashes Ella was not allowed to participate. She had to stay home and clean the ashes out of the fireplace, scrub the floors and polish the handle of the big front door. (The events that took place, if you had read the fairy tale, you'd know what happened up to the time of the striking of the midnight gong. This story will resume at that moment.)

The twelve o'clock gong was banging out the midnight serenade and the Prince of Ug was in hot pursuit of our leading lady. She dropped one of her golden boots on the balustrade and she took flight hoppin' and skippin' the best she could. It was a sight to describe, she was holding up her dress and exposed her fancy laced Levi panties. At the sight of those fetching undies the Prince could no longer contain himself. He tripped over her golden boot, banged his head on the banister and was knocked unconscious. As he lay there groaning in the muck, the Tower Clock finished clanging, Ashes-ella's horses turned to rats and the carriage receded to its original state, a melon of the casaba family. Boy, this was a night to behold.

The next day, the prince a bit groggy from the preceding nights' episode, mounted his trusty equine and was off in pursuit of this feisty little feline with the fancy, devastating Levi lingerie. He stopped at all the eligible bacheloret's houses to see if any of the damsels had feet small enough to fit into this golden brogan. At last, in his pursuit he came upon the House Of Scrawny. All three step-sisters were agog over the chance to rub elbows with the Prince of Ug. Ashes-Ella stood back watching the ceremony. She knew full well that only pain would result in this exercise in futility of trying to get those big fat feet into her meager footwear. Alas, the unhappy Prince gave up and mounted his sturdy stead and as he departed the horse bolted and the Prince dropped the golden boot.

Ashes-Ella ran out to retrieve it for him and when she bent over she exposed her fancy laced Levi panties. This time the prince bolted for he knew that at last he had found the maiden of his dreams. He scooped her up onto his horse and they rode off into the sunset with her beautiful flaxen hair billowing in the wind and of course they persevered happily ever after.

Amen!

SUPER PATRIOTS

Voyat Sergey

United by the common idea of setting free the country of certain interest, the fighters for financial monopoly are trying to expand their bad influence on the new land. It's a question of honor-to help people with spending their money or to help them in finding new place for their wealth and usage. It is hard to define clearly the difference between super patriots and prostitutes because both offer something for money. The ideology of building the healthy society is based on the opportunities to take control over the brains and interfere. If you are not sure what is really meant, be sure it concerns money. People are extremely weak as someone mentions money and power, and all their rosy dreams they used to have.

Wasting money is a wide-spread method to help some countries to avoid the danger of civilized life with all the forthcoming problems. To free someone from own development and progress is treated like a serious charity and support. And the government does the best to show how much they care about the people by means of enlarging the bank accounts of hard-working politicians. Their enthusiasm is so inspirational for others to follow the ideology. Super patriots are hiding their true intentions behind the noble political missions. Financially profitable operations they call a mission against evil. Super patriots kill in the name of peace, super patriots steal in the name of love to the native land, there's some special new brand democracy, when someone points a gun on your head, and you are to follow the new rules of democracy. We should take the full responsibility when we bring our children to this cruel world with no excuses, no chances to escape this life.

The truth must be the only one, and no additional comments needed. Nowadays it's just the object of commercial speculation. When everyone's lying in order to hear the truth, we are more likely to hear everything except the truth. It depends upon the price for it or upon the Interest of the story-teller. The methods are regularly changed but the goals remain the same. It's much easier to cover all the crimes against humanity with patriotic slogan and funny propaganda than to be punished for own mistakes. For publicity to get a delicious meal the super patriots cook a special souse. The society has to eat what they cook otherwise we all will be suffering from hunger.

Neighbors often irritate each other by the size of the bordering walls and the treasure in the someone's garden. Who is able to stand this? Who can stand someone's being naughty? Or may be someone neglecting the opinion of those powerful and extremely important? How far are they going to go to reach the final point of destination? Our mental abilities allow us to think out so many ways of taking everything we need without special permission. It's like a good-looking candy with the unknown ingredients inside: may sweet chocolate or may be some shit inside. You'll never know for sure until you try. as far as the social rank goes, many owners of respectful surnames behave in the same manner and getting more and more predictable. Those big daddies are always in love with themselves. That sort of love is not like the one we used to experience. It's quite different To justify that feeling of self-respect they should take care of own demands and hobbies. They very much care about their places on the hit list of greatest liars.

The same words sound so differently depending on who says and on the shoe size of the speaker. The biggest irony is that the more they speak about principals the more they violate them. There are so many amazing plans to use public opinion for own profit and satisfaction. Washing someone's dirty underwear may be more pleasant than we think. It depends on who washes and whose underwear. What do we really need? Be important, play games or attract attention?

AHMEDA
W. S. Mayo

Her name was Ahmeda, which meant "Beloved Daughter of God." Yet she was hardly the most godfearing of women. Rather, she was possessed of the light within which is more than most of us can say. I saw her speaking with the Dictator who bore a strong resemblance to Saddam Hussein of Iraq, what with his thick mustache and hanging eyebrows, despite the fact that he and everybody else in my dream spoke with a Spanish accent of the Castilian dialect. He leaned over the long oaken table scowling at the woman while she gave him his subjects' grievances. As the meeting wore on, the exchange became more heated with Ahmeda making new demands and the soldier threatening her every move. Finally, she raised her 5 foot 5 frame forward and calmly said to him, "You shall bear the blood of the people upon your shoulders." At this, the Dictator shouted, "You're dead!" With that, it was war.

The first battle was fought not with missiles and mortar but with spears and scimitars, as a shaman of Ahmeda's tribe had sent out a virus, disabling the country's computers. Without the machines to back them up, the Old Soldier's warriors would be reduced to the same arms as Ahmeda's. Even with that it was a rout. Swords flashed on the blinding sunlight of the hungry season and men, women, and children lay dying on the plain. Ahmeda herself was wounded in the battle with a spear in her side and the doctors doubted that she would survive the night, so great was the loss of blood. She moaned and murmured the name of another and it was only with the greatest courage that she moved her golden face into the light and said, "The time is ours."

She marked her recovery from that battle with a swim across the Ganges. It was with ceremony and the beating of countless drums that she lifted the robe from her shoulders and dove naked into the rapids, her frail but full body fighting the waves. Her long black hair wafted about her back as she navigated the waters, gulped mouthfuls of river and air alike, and finally emerged on the opposite shore. A great cry went out from the crowd as the woman flailed her arms, searched for her balance among the rocks, and then stood proud. "Ahmeda! Ahmeda!" they shouted in unison as their leader faced them, her head held high, water dripping off her hair and fulsome breasts. "Ahmeda!" It seemed it never would end.

After that, things appeared to go her way. She rode a pale horse on a hill, sending wave after wave of her ragtag troops into battle, their scimitars and swords flashing in the sun. Then she galloped down into the war zone giving vengeance to the man who had snubbed her in his palace. Necks were wrung, hearts were pierced, and heads lay rolling on the plain where the warriors sacrificed their lives for the girl with the sword. Other battles followed in mountains and canyons and once forgotten cities where it was said that ghosts guided their footsteps with swinging doors and fallen rooftops. The journey to the capital to face the Old Soldier cowering in his rooms was a mere formality. Ahmeda pushed him to his knees and beheaded him with a single stroke. That she was elected with the overwhelming support of those she had led into battle was not surprising either.

It was with despair, however, that I saw that with each passing year she became more like the Dictator she had replaced. She took on lovers from the slums of the kingdom (each one a barbarian), smoked hashish with the shamans, and held onto the trappings of power as the country she had saved fell into a shambles, left neglected by the love she had once felt for the people who populated its far corners. It was only a jealous warrior's knife to the heart that delivered the final blow.

Still, the legend lived on in ways that would have astounded even Old Ahmeda. A century after her death her country's church proclaimed her a saint. And a century or two after that she was a symbol in one of those cyclical revolutions that marked the world for women's liberation and love for those who would be free. Even today (so the dream told me upon awakening) space voyagers and seafarers alike wear the medallion with her likeness and will gladly tell you if you ask, "This is Ahmeda. She leads all who will follow."

THE HOUSE

Yvo Maron Jouvenaar

The house had looked out over the same valley for nearly three centuries. Halfway up the highest peak, standing in a large clearing in the pine forest, it commanded all the lower terrain. The fields, the densely overgrown foothills, the narrow creek that cut through the valley-floor; this was the world the house had always known. Much had changed in this world. When it was built, the house had shared the valley with a few homesteads, dotted along the course of the creek. The house had been proud then, the only stone structure in the valley. But as the house grew of age, the valley changed. Many houses were built and more men lived in them. A church steeple made of red bricks rose above what was now a town, criss-crossed by earthen roads and cartpaths. And still more men came. The house too, was filled with ever more life. Men were born, spent their lives in its spacious rooms and found their resting-place in the shadow of its peaked roof. Some men were good, others were not. But always the house looked on, the grime of many years silently accumulating. After three hundred years of watching the world of men replace the original life of the valley, the house was old. Its timbers were rotten to the core and broken windows had not been refitted for many years. It would not be long before it too went the way of the generations it had provided with comfort and shelter. The house did not mind; it was tired.

Then new men came to the valley. They were soldiers, but different from the countless soldiers the house had seen pass by. They had always been scared and anxious to go home. The new soldiers were different. They smiled evil smiles and stayed in the valley. And they took over the house. It was sorry to see the last descendent of its family go; he was a good man, but he could not stand up to the smiling soldiers. Soon more of the men came and they changed the house. Rotten wood was replaced by concrete beams, priceless paintings replaced the crumbling sideboards and mouldy paper on its walls. When it was finished, the house was larger and more luxurious than it had ever been. Many other things changed as well. Now, when men came to the house, they were excited or scared. And smoke always filled the horizon, smoke from fires burning in far-off places. A man had taken possession of the house, a special man. The house had seen many men come and go, some strong, some weak, but none like this one. His presence filled the house and lay like a blanket over the entire valley and beyond. The other men with the evil smiles feared him, and tried to please him. The house did not like this man. He was like the slow corruption that had spread through its timbers for two hundred years, living off the life and strength of others and leaving only decay. Where once the house had heard the laughter and tears of people living their lives, there was now something much darker. Fear lay around the house and filled its halls.

The house became old beyond its days, and corrupted by the atrocities the man and others committed within its walls. Others came from distant lands to pay respect to the man, their hearts filled with fear. And never did they find comfort in the house, whose hearth had once warmed the hands and faces of loving families. It no longer looked like a home; it no longer was a home. It had become terror to all that knew it. Then servants of the man dug up the roots of the house and poured more concrete into the gaping hole they left. The last foothold of the original house vanished forever, along with the bones of the man who had once built it.

For the first and the last time in the life of the house, it let out a sob that was heard in every room and in every basement; and a sickness spread throughout. Slowly something withered and died in the heart of the house. Behind its decorated walls, through its hardened concrete pillars first small fractures crept, then larger and larger cracks. None of the men noticed. Day after day the house crumbled, until only the outer walls and the roof remained untouched. Still, the men did not notice. Then, one day, many men came to worship the one who now lived in the house. With them came the smell of more fear, the fear of a faraway people about to be trampled by iron-shod boots and evil smiles. Their footsteps ringing through the halls sent a tangible shiver throughout the house, widening every crack.

Now suddenly, the dilapidation around them was revealed to the men, and they were afraid. But it was too late. With a sigh that was not quite soundless, the house collapsed. And of that place, that had seen the world pass by for many lives of man, nothing remained but rubble and silence. All the evil men were gone too, bringing many changes to the valley once again. But the house was no longer there to see it. All that remained was the clearing and the valley, as empty as they had been when the house was first built.

Human voices were no longer heard in the clearing. And for many, many years, it never rained on that spot and no plants grew. For such is the way of things and places that have seen too much.

AUTHOR INDEX

Adrian Cadar was born in 08.03.1978, Oradea, Romania. "I do only one thing when I write a story. I imagine. My fingers are just typing what's in my mind in that very moment. As a famous quotation says, I don't know if I have or not talent. What I know is that I have something to say. And sometime, maybe this is what talent is about..." Visit at www.poezii.go.ro

Alex Kachmar (b. November 1981) from MA, USA; immigrated to the United States from Ukraine; short stories published in *Coelecanth Magazine, Santa Fe Writers' Project Literary Journal,* and the *WritersNet Anthology.*

Alexxa Abi-Jaoude is from Ontario, Canada. "I am just completing my second year at the University of Western Ontario in the Bachelor Health Sciences program."

Andrew Longworth from NY, USA; born in Germany in 1969; raised in Germany and the USA; served as peacecorps volunteer in Morocco 2000-2002; currently adult education teacher in Brooklyn.

Angie Hulme was born in Lancashire, England; she moved to the US in 2000 to follow her heart; writing all forms of poetry and short stories for many years; published in *Voyages.* Visit at http://angie.funurl.com

Annalee Johnson is from IL, US. "I have been writing since… I could write coherent sentences."

Brian Vincent Wemyss is from Selangor Darul Ehsan, Malaysia; teaching English in a secondary school in the city of Kuala Lumpur, Malaysia.

Candice Maryanne Borg is from NSW, Australia.

Carl E.Vance: Born and residing in the state of West Virginia, USA. "My writing consists of things I'm familiar with. It's what I know."

Casey Ponciano is from TX, USA.

Cassandra Marie Carlson is from MN, USA.

Ceirion James Rees is from South Wales, UK. "I am a practicing Christian and try to reflect my faith in my writing as best I can."

Clyde Mcdade is from WA, USA. "My wife and I share a music ministry called Redeemed M.C. Music Ministries. The purpose of any songs, books, scripts, or short stories to share the Gospel of Jesus Christ in an educational and entertaining way." Visit at www.redeemedmc.com

Crystal Timbeross is from Texas, USA. "I wrote this story a few months ago, now my friend is going back out with him. I'm not exactly happy about it, but you don't always get your way."

Dallas Cathcart, 33 yrs old, from AB, Canada, writes for his own enjoyment.

Danielle Ackley-McPhail, author of the award-winning novel *Yesterday's Dreams*, lives and works in New York. She has published numerous poems and short stories in *Through a Glass Darkly* (Lite Circle Books), *Voyages* and *Taj Mahal Review* (Cyberwit.net), *Sabledrake Magazine* (Sabledrake.com), and writes a bi-weekly column entitle *If We'd Words Enough and Time* for fictionauts.com. To find out more about her and her work, visit www.sidhenadaire.com

Darius Gabriel Bugarin is from Nueva Ecija, Philippines; a published international poet under poetry.com; "Wellsprings" published by the American's Poet's Society, USA also appeared in *The Golden Wings, Voyages* and *Taj Mahal Review* (December 2002 & June 2003*);* "A Moment To Remember" published by the Pen Pushers Poets, USA; was included as one of the 33 Best Poets and Poems, and in an internationally released compact dics (CD) or cassette tapes *The Sound of Poetry* published by The International Library of Poetry, USA, in the year 2002.

David Ferrier is from Renfrewshire, Scotland.

David Tumusiime (b. 26 April 1980) is from Kampala, Uganda. "Totally besotted by Ugandan life. If there is another country I should like to visit, it is the Gogolian Russia or present day Russia in the spring."

Denise-Annette Langner-Urso (b. 1960) is from Berlin, Germany; 5 Children (3 of them attending JFK-School of Berlin/before that an International British School in Spain where their grandma lives); her husband born in Italy/Sicily owns his own catering-store; owner of a car-store for 10 years; writing since 1980; published a book for children; *Dagegenhalten*-published in May 2003 at Das Boot, Blätter für Lyrik der Gegenwart; *Mahnung* will be published in an anthology in Germany in autumn 2003; "Give Peace" published in *Voyages* (2003) India; *Collateral Damage* was chosen Best Poem in March. "I am writing for The African Courier which you can find: www.theafricancourier.de"

Denise Cassino is from CO, USA. After earning a B.A. degree in English at Northern Illinois University, she moved to Denver. Denise, a lover of the written word, began writing years ago.

Donald Edward Kidd is from Florida, USA; a pharmacist by trade; has written about 50 short stories, one novel, and about 100 poems.

Duncan Reeves is from North Yorkshire, England. "Writing is the greatest of my hobbies."

Dylan Skriloff is from NY, USA.

Erma Hernandez is from CA, USA.

Floriana Hall (b. 1927) Author, Poet, Lyricist from Ohio, USA; She writes, "I have two new books out besides SMALL CHANGE, the true story of my life as a child during the Great Depression. The new book, DADDY WAS A BAD BOY, and POET'S NOOK POTPOURRI. I am getting a reprint of THE SANDS OF RHYME. my inspirational poetry book, which is selling fast since the September 11 tragedy." The poet's two poems written on behalf of Peace are due to be presented to the city of New York. *Out of the Ordinary*, a collection of short stories by Floriana Hall, "is dedicated to all people who believe in God, His Angels and His Spirit which dwells in all of us."

Honor Alisha De'Mandoren: "Born in Tennessee, and bounced to practically every place between the Pacific and Atlantic, I am a modern-day gypsy."

Ian Stuart is from Yorkshire, United Kingdom.

Inessa Cutler (b. July 28,1973 Kiev, Ukraine): "One of the few women in the technology field, I graduated in 1995 with a degree in Information Systems from StonyBrook University. I am married and live with my husband in Massapequa, NY."

Irving Bronsky is from Herzlia, Israel. Visit at www.irving-itchy-bronsky

Jeanne Owens is from Virginia, USA.

JirQUEST is from C'wealth Crescent, Singapore.

John R. Guthrie practised family medicine in the Piedmont of South Carolina for many years. He now lives in the Metrowest area of Boston, Massachusetts, USA and is a writer and social activist.

Joseph Aprile from WA, USA has written many poems, chapbooks, short stories, novellas and novel-length fiction. "I owe my strong attraction to the poetic form to my involvement with the New York Poets Cooperative in the early seventies at that time under the benevolent direction of Barbara Holland. If there is an underlying theme in all of my work, I believe it originates from the desire to understand the human experience and what it means to be human."

Joy Bennett from NY, USA is the author of *Under a Quarter Moon.*

Julie Failla Earhart from MO, USA is an award-winning fiction and non-fiction author. Julie Failla Earhart has a bachelor's degree in journalistic and creative writing and a master of fine arts degree from the University of Missouri-St. Louis. In 2002, Julie's essay, "We will Never Forget," which deals with 9/11, won first place in the essay category in Amy Kritchen's Angels Without Wings Foundation's "Born-Again American Literary Competition and an Award of Merit from the Writer's Challege Literary Association. Also that year, she was co-host of WGNU's (920 AM) weekly radio show, The Writer's Hour; founded Write it Right!, her own company that specializes in teaching writing classes, conducting workshops and lectures on all aspects of the writing craft, and offers editorial services for writers of all levels; and has been selected to be on the faculty of the New York College for Advanced Studies' Etech Programs and an adjunct as St. Charles Community College. She has been a reviewer of fiction for the *St. Louis Post-Dispatch, The Charlotte Austin Review, Booksights* (in the UK), *Amazing Authors Showcase, and Word Museum* as well as written a plethora of newsletters and brochures. In 2000, she was a runner-up in Book magazine's "Don Quixote Essay Contest." She has published a short story that was included in Milliken Publishing Company's CD-ROM Knowledge Works. Her work has been also been published in *Well Versed* 2003 (in publication); *Voyages* 2003 (in publication); *Stirrings: A Literary Collection*; *Palimpsest; Gigantic; Watermark; Words and Dreams*, Part XII; *An Archer's Dream*; and *Steps Astray*. She has recently put together a collection of short stories, *Home Sweet Home & Other Dangerous Places* Before starting Write it Right, Julie taught feature writing at the University of Missouri-St. Louis. Currently, she is a freelance writer, teacher speaker, and editor working in the St. Louis area.

Kathryn Gabrielle is from PA, USA.

Kathryn Lynn Wilson was born in Provo Utah in 1982 to Richard and Debbie Wilson, the third child of six. She enjoys reading, writing poetry and fiction, and performing literary criticism.

Katy Picard from MI, USA writes short stories, poems, thoughts, etc.

Kenneth F. Pearson is from New York, USA. "I would like to thank all that have given me the inspiration to write, including those I write about."

Kenneth Ormsbee is from UT, USA. "Writing as Kenneth Moon, I attend Weber State University in Ogden, Utah... I work as technical support for a local company."

Kevin Patrick Necessary is the design editor for the Chillocothe Gazette in Chillocothe, Ohio. He is a trained journalist and columnist, and writes fiction on the side.

Kirby Wright was born and raised in Honolulu, Hawaii. He is a graduate of Punahou School in Honolulu and the University of California at San Diego. He received his MFA in Creative Writing from San Francisco State University. Kirby has been nominated for The 2003 Pushcart Prize and is a past recipient of the Anne Fields Poetry Prize, the Academy of American Poets Award, the Browning Society Award for Dramatic Monologue, and Arts Council Silicon Valley Fellowships in Poetry and The Novel. His memoir took First Place at the 2002 San Diego Book Awards.

Laura Mae Oldham-Brownell from Kansas, USA is a recent college graduate, wife and mother of three and grandmother to two wonderful boys, Trey and Isaiah.

LeRoy Doran is from MO, USA; published in *The Still Horizon* and *Voyages.*

Lori D. Laird is from Louisiana, USA. "I'm a mother of two wonderful boys. They are what makes my heart beat. They are what makes me take each breathe I take. To them I owe the world. They are what makes me ME!"

Mary Barr is from NJ, USA. Her insights on substance abuse and related health and justice system issues have been featured on national television, radio and in print media. Her articles on these topics are featured in various publications and in her upcoming book, "Criminal Treatment." She has been a featured speaker on Capitol Hill and in conferences and universities internationally. Since 1998 her self-empowerment series has been featured in jails and prisons, for which she is the only private citizen to receive the STEP Medal of Honor from NYC Corrections. What makes these accomplishments even more amazing is that Ms. Barr educated herself, overcoming homelessness, drug addiction and 45 incarcerations.

Mike Strictzer is from NV, USA. "I live and write in Las Vegas. I just finished my latest book. When I make it big, you'll likely still find me at the strip clubs...however, I am still grinding my axe on the stone with such intensity when I fall asleep, my forehead gets cut on the limestone wheel."

Moataz H. Emam: Egyptian born and raised, Mr. Moataz Emam, an engineer and physicist, lives now in the United States and studies for a Ph.D. in Theoretical Physics. He has been writing short stories since his teens. Most of his works are also posted on the world wide web.

Mona Dash is from Orpington, UK.

Nancy Latshaw is from Ohio, USA.

Pat Phillips West lives and writes in southern Nevada. She is the editor for *All Things Girl*, (www.allthingsgirl.com) Women In Business, section. Her work has appeared in: *Labyrinth: Poems and Prose, An Eye for an Eye Makes the Whole*

World Blind: Poets on 9/11, The Golden Wings, Taj Mahal Review, Voyages, Kota Press Poetry Anthology, Volume 3, FZQ Poetry, *Poetictricity, Kota Press, and All Things Girl, Book of Remembrance.*

Peter Eric Williams is from ACT, Australia.

Paul Steven is from Ayrshire, Scotland.

Rachel Caris Thompson is from Devon, England.

Rani Drew is from Cambridge, UK.

Rebecca is from WA, USA.

Rebecca Chen is from CA, USA.

Rebecca Holder is from Northamptonshire, UK.

Robert M. Wilson is from New Mexico, US; Community college math teacher born in China.

Dr. Santosh Kumar: (b. 1946) is from UP India; Head of the English Department in A.D. College, Allahabad; Ph.D. in English; several awards; poems published in many anthologies; awarded for writing an epic *The Fire and The Garden: An Exploration of Beauty* in three volumes; Chief Editor of five World Poetry Anthologies, and an international literary journal *Taj Mahal Review.*

Sara M. Al Shami was born on the 27th of August in Beirut, and then moved on to live in Jordan. "To me, writing has become the best friend..."

Sherri Emily Avery (b. 1966) Fall River, Massachusetts is Portuguese, English and French Canadian. She is the oldest of 9 children and of Catholic religion. She is related to George Harrison (Beatles), Elizabeth Cleghorn Gaskell (Famous English Writer), Lord Byron (Romantic English Poet). "I love God very much! I feel without Him I would not have the gift to write, He gave me this gift." Visit at: www.lovepoetrycafe.com, www.lovepoetscafe.net, www.lovepoetscafe.net/teens, www.geocities.com/musicianshope/index.html, www.geocities.com/loveecards1/index.html

Stephen R. Foster is from Ohio, USA; author of *Island Of Life*,-comedy/romance; upcoming novel, *Empty Dawn.* Visit at: www.authorsden.com/stephenrfoster

Sudheesh V Nair is from CA, USA.

Thomas K. Hyland, Jr. is from Maryland, USA. Rather than posting a long-winded BIO here, please go to: www.authorsden.com/tomhyland

Tom Dwyer from NJ, USA; freelance travel writer, published novelist, and songwriter.

Tony James Lawless (b. February 25, 1967) is from Florida, USA; loves passion, poetry, love itself and music.

Travis Black has written one unpublished novel and over a half dozen published short stories, one of which appeared in the June 2003 issue of the *Taj Mahal Review*. His short story 'Trick or Treat' was nominated as one of the best of the Web'99, and his 'Here Kitty, Kitty, Kitty' won a first place in a short story contest in '00. A former engineer, Mr. Black lives in Missouri, U.S.A.

Verne Morse is from CA, USA.

Voyat Sergey from Rivne, Ukraine has recently published his book "Quiet sins talk loud" available at Barnesandnoble.com, Amazon.com; published in different anthologies.

W. S. Mayo is from MD, USA.

Yvo Maron Jouvenaar is from Hague, Netherlands.